The Barn Find

DISCARDED BY
WELLES-TURNER MEMORIAL LIBRARY
GLASTONBURY, CT

The Barn Find

By

F. Mark Granato

All rights reserved

Names, characters and incidents depicted in this book are products of the author's imagination or are used fictitiously. Any resemblance to actual events, organizations, or persons, living or dead, is entirely coincidental and beyond the intent of the author or the publisher.

No part of this book may be reproduced or transmitted in any form or by any means, electronic or mechanical, including photocopying, recording, or by any information storage and retrieval system, without permission in writing from the author.

F. Mark Granato
fmgranato@aol.com
www.facebook.com at Author F. Mark Granato

Copyright © 2013 by F. Mark Granato

Published in the United States of America 2013

The Barn Find

A Novel by

F. Mark Granato

Also by F. Mark Granato

Titanic: The Final Voyage

Beneath His Wings:
The Plot to Murder Lindbergh

Of Winds and Rage

Finding David

To my wife,
always and forever my dream girl,
to our adventures past
and those to come.

One

~~~

April 22, 2000

I wish you could have seen the look that came over the old man's gaunt, wrinkled face the very instant he saw her. The way it actually changed. The pain that melted away. The endless years of loneliness that disappeared. The waiting that ended.

Or that I could find the words to paint a picture of the radiance that suddenly burst from my grandfather's sad, weary eyes, and the unmistakable flash of happiness that erased the shadow that had long darkened his stare.

And I wish you could have shared the moment of joy that so overwhelmed him that his hands trembled and his whole body shuddered. That you could have felt the shock of his elation as he stood there for a long moment, finally moving his fingers only to bring them slowly to his lips, covering his mouth as if any sound or even taking a breath might scare away the vision that he saw before him.

You had to see it to believe it, but then again you also had to know my grandfather to understand what he was thinking. Much later, when it was all over, I came to terms with my own feelings at that moment. Secretly, I was proud to know that of those people who saw his reaction, only I really had a sense of what was going on behind his eyes and how scrambled his
~~~

thoughts probably were at that instant. It made our pact of love and loyalty to each other real, much more than words.

But there was no great mystery to why his whole being and the disposition by which people judged him had changed instantly from eternally cranky to joyful.

It wasn't the warmth of the sunshine, or stepping out of the nursing home into a fresh breeze of spring air that he sucked into his lungs after days of lying on his bed in a stuffy room, alone and despondent. Nor was it the perfumed scent of crab apple blossoms that sprouted from the fully bloomed trees outside the meticulously maintained entranceway gardens of the nursing facility that was now his home. It wasn't even one of his "spells," when he suddenly remembered a deliciously happy moment that came back to him from the past out of nowhere, causing him to smile and laugh out loud for no reason that was apparent to others. No, it was something else entirely.

"Ceily…" I heard him whisper and instantly I understood the wheels that were clicking and whirring in his mind. Before I could say anything, his knees buckled and he began to sag to the concrete walk beneath him, overwhelmed both physically and emotionally. Molly, the nursing home aide who had become more his friend than caretaker, caught him even before I could take a step forward, placing a practiced arm around his waist to support the little man. He was a mere shadow of the man I knew as a little boy.

I glanced over at my father who stood in silence, motionless. He took a tentative, awkward step forward to help him, and was obviously relieved when Molly caught him. He frowned, squinting in puzzlement, bewildered once again by his father's behavior. Not unexpectedly, Sam Evans closed his eyes, finding it hard to watch the old man struggle.

Twenty feet away, parked at the curb near the front door of the nursing home, was my sister, Sheila, gently revving the engine of the car. The slight growl that spewed from the exhaust was something my grandfather had once described to me as a "symphony of metal parts in motion." I had almost expected him to close his eyes and just listen when he heard that music again today. But he showed no signs of even noticing the engine's smooth idle and seductive rumble or even the car for that matter. Poor Sheila was holding her breath in fright, afraid the whole surprise we had planned was quickly becoming a disaster. She thought it was the car that had caused my grandfather to falter.

The car.

The reason we were all gathered outside.

It was his beloved Mercedes Benz, a 1955 190sl, two-seat roadster, resplendent in its newly completed total restoration, literally sparkling in the early afternoon sun. Every square inch of her, every one of her thousands of parts, every bit of her distinct personality had been rebuilt, re-chromed, repainted, re-stitched and ultimately, reborn. All of it had been done for this little old man whom I loved so much in honor of his Seventieth birthday. Still he didn't say a word to suggest that he had noticed anything different about the car. He just repeated, "Ceily…" in a voice so quiet almost to be inaudible. Again, I alone caught it. I had heard him say her name and watched his mouth move to pronounce it so many times over the years that I didn't have to hear him speak it. I could read it on his lips.

A dead silence overtook our small group gathered outside the nursing home, none of us really knowing what to do next. Of all people, it was my dad, "The Judge" as my sister and I had come to call him, the person who struggled the most to respect the old man who finally broke the quiet. He figured his father was simply transfixed by the beauty of the Mercedes and had been rendered mute. He underestimated him.

"Pop," as we called my grandfather, had never been the life of a party or even one to carry on a good conversation with a stranger. But if he had something to say, something that was really eating at him, I'd never known him to be tongue-tied.

"Well, how do you like her, Dad?" my father asked my grandfather. "Isn't she just stunning?" he declared, beaming with pride. But there was an edge in his voice and I could tell from experience that my dad was already losing his patience with Pop's lack of response. It was typical of him, I thought to pout because it wasn't going exactly as he planned. True, he had worked hard on being more patient and understanding with his father over the last long and difficult years, but he still struggled. For my father, instinctive kindness was an uphill aspiration.

Trying a different tact, he walked over and opened the passenger door and motioned to my sister to pull the lever that released the engine bonnet. The Judge lifted the hood, revealing the rebuilt engine and mechanicals that looked more fit and polished than the day in 1955 that the hand-made car had rolled out of the factory in Stuttgart, Germany.

"She runs like new, Dad, maybe even better than new." He stared at the engine bay for a few moments, waiting for Pop to say something. There was only silence. Sam Evans exhaled loudly, then quickly recovered, plastering a smile on his face out of concern that his impatience was probably obvious. Again, I was the only one of us to catch it, perhaps because I secretly knew my father was grappling with so many conflicting emotions. "Impatience" was not the attitude he wanted to show his father today. Quite the contrary.

Never one to give up easily, he moved back to the passenger door. "Even the interior is brand-spanking new, Dad. Your own grandson fit the new leather seat covers himself. Can you imagine that? Why Sean wasn't even born when this car was built." He looked over at me. "Frankly, I didn't know he had it in him." I smiled at the backhanded compliment. Like I said, he tried.

The old man just stared at his son, pursing his lips as if to say something. Instead, he shook his head in silence, a queer look on his face, and said nothing. Then, as if irritated by the interruption, he turned his gaze back to the woman behind the steering wheel. Just as suddenly, his eyes lit up with joy once again. It wasn't a delayed reaction to what my father had said or the sight of the restored Mercedes roadster that Sheila sat in. It was not for the birthday gift we each had been working day and night on for the last twenty months in anticipation of his Seventieth birthday. No. The excitement that stirred him, the aura of happiness that glowed from him that even a blind man could have sensed, was prompted by something else entirely.

It was because of Sheila.

As I took in the scene, awed by the look of happiness and relief, the depth of which I had never seen in his eyes before, I knew the Alzheimer's disease had reared its ugly head with its worst symptom:

Dementia. In his confused state, what my grandfather's suddenly sparkling brown eyes saw behind the wheel of his prize-winning car was not my sister, nor was she his granddaughter. The woman was a ghost – his beloved wife Ceily – my grandmother who had passed nearly thirty years before in a tragedy that had not only broken his heart, but also ripped out his soul.

As Pop stared at her, his eyes lied to him to satisfy what his heart so desperately wanted. There she was, his Ceily, young and radiant and even more beautiful than he could remember, gripping the steering wheel of the car that had meant so much to each of them. Given the profound blow her death had been to him, it would seem the car was but an insignificant backdrop for the scene being played out. Nothing could have been farther from the truth.

The Mercedes that we had brought back to life, what to many people was just an antiquated, forty-five year old machine, had been worth more to my grandmother and grandfather than any other thing in their lives together, with the exception of their only child, my father. The 2,500 pounds of steel and iron, leather and rubber that had been superbly shaped by German craftsman into a masterpiece of Teutonic engineering, was a magnificent touring car that had been a tangible symbol of their love for each other. It came to represent the romance of their relationship, which they cherished and would not let die from the moment they fell in love.

It was this car – once a rusted out hulk that they had purchased early in their marriage – that had allowed them to play out dreams that dwarfed their meager resources. It let their imaginations turn long simple drives along the New England coast into tours through the quaint villages of Normandy and along the shores of southern France, and had turned countless riverside restaurants into Parisian Cafes, transformed the Main Street of Essex into their own Avenue des Champs-Élysées and brought the Swiss Alps to them in the foothills of Litchfield. Their hours together in this car became the set of their own private but very romantic movie in which they were the stars that actually were very much in love. There was nothing make believe about their passion for each other.

All this I had learned from years of sitting with my grandfather, the two of us alone, in a barn behind our family home in Willington, Connecticut, watching his once stunning Mercedes slowly rust away, just as his own life was. In all the years we talked, he never once shooed me away from him, no matter how poorly he felt or how badly his heart ached. Sometimes he sat in silence, me at his side, just remembering. As the years passed, we became closer in that quiet, and eventually, in those precious moments when he found the strength of mind and heart, he shared with me memories of his time with Ceily, their dreams and even the story and the agony of losing her.

Now, his hallucination of seeing "Ceily" and the Mercedes together again, after a quite shattering absence that his dementia would not allow him to understand, was possibly more than Pop's weakened heart could take. I had not anticipated the enormous emotional response he was experienceing, nor had I fully understood the depth of his physical decline until this moment. My heart sank with sadness.

Even my sister Sheila, a gorgeous, green-eyed, red headed lass who literally could have been my grandmother's clone, hadn't caught on. That is, not until my typically crusty, grumpy old grandfather, a man who had been more of a father to me than my own, did something so unpredictable, so elegant, that he even fooled Molly, his most trusted nurse and friend who was still holding him up. Or so we thought.

Pop turned and looked at Molly with a calmly reassuring smile on his lips while he graciously removed her hand from his waist. He had found his legs again. Then, without averting his eyes from Sheila, he walked several steps into the garden bed lining the sidewalk into the nursing home, reached down as spryly as a man who was years younger and plucked a single linen white lily in full bloom. There wasn't a sign of the old man who just a moment before had to be supported as he was led outside.

He turned to me. "It's Sunday, Sean?" he asked. It wasn't, but I played along.

"Yes it is, Pop," I said. "It's Sunday, your favorite day of the week." I took hold of his elbow and walked him toward the car. There was lightness to his gait that had nothing to do with his diminished weight.

"Sunday is the day you take your ride with Grandma," I said.

He smiled again and walked with me, hesitating momentarily to dampen his fingers across his tongue, then dragged them through his thin hair to smooth it down. He wanted to look his best. Then, just as he reached the door held open by my father, he stopped and touched his son's arm. Pop shook his head, scowling, and looked my father square in the eye. The war between them would never end, I thought.

"Of course I like her, ya damned fool. She's your mother for cryin' out loud," he chastised my father whose jaw dropped an inch. My dad turned and looked at me in total confusion and mouthed the words, "My mother?" He was just catching on to what was going on in Pop's head.

"Now tell me," my grandfather demanded of his son while turning his gaze back to Sheila. "Have you ever seen a more beautiful woman?" He asked the question in a tone that suggested a strong conviction that he had raised the village idiot.

My father was speechless and I could see the red crawling up the back of his neck as his frustration and disappointment built. This was just not how he wanted it to go between them. Not today. Unwittingly, my grandfather defused the tension.

"But thanks for washing the car for me, Sam," Pop concluded, atypically showing his son a token of gratitude. He carefully examined the new hand-dyed and stitched German leather adorning the passenger seat and ran a hand along the supple boot covering the new Hartz cloth convertible top. "And I'll be damned. I hadn't noticed that the seats were in need of reupholstering. Very nicely done, Sean, very nicely done. I hope your mother and I run into a car show on our drive. Maybe we'll stop by and pick up another trophy."

My father's eyes softened. He was relieved that Pop was starting to come around. But his father certainly hadn't reacted to the car the way he expected.

"Want me to drive, honey?" Pop asked Sheila. Before she could answer, he leaned forward.

"Here, Ceily, this is for you." He handed her the lily and kissed the back of her hand as she took it from him. He lingered over the touch of her skin and the smell of her perfume.

"Chanel No. 9, as always," he said, his eyes sparkling with mischief. "I could close my eyes and know if you were in the room just by your perfume." He didn't know that Chanel had ceased production of its legendary No. 9 fragrance years before.

Sheila looked at me, panicking, still not used to Grandfather's confusion that she was his wife and not his granddaughter after years of such delusions. I winked at her. Her eyes were wet as he kissed her hand again before releasing it.

"Nah, Pop, Grandma wants to drive today," I said, coming to Sheila's rescue. "She deserves a turn every now and then," I said. "Right, Grandma?" I smiled at Sheila. "And remember. Mom is back at the house preparing Pop's birthday dinner so don't be long."

Pop hesitated for a moment, contemplating the odd request that Ceily drive. He always drove. That's the way his Ceily preferred it. I could tell he was struggling to process the idea, then suddenly let it go.

"Well, alright, Ceily, but the old girl's looking pretty good. You be careful, promise?" he replied. "I think the clutch is a little low. Have to adjust it one of these days but it just keeps slipping my mind." Then he went silent and stared at her. It was the look of a young man hopelessly in love with his girl.

"I'm so glad it's Sunday, dear, you've been so busy lately and I feel like I haven't seen you for so long," he said. Without warning, tears welled up in Sheila's eyes. "So very long."

At the very edge of his mind, a sad memory teetered. I could see him struggling to place it. Just then, a single drop escaped Sheila's efforts to retain her composure drawing Pops attention back to the present.

He leaned over and grabbed her hand and kissed it again. "Why, what's the matter, honey? I'm not angry, I just miss you," he smiled. "Now let's go enjoy this lovely day in this magnificent car."

Sheila wiped the tear from her cheek and smiled.

"Ceily?" he said.

"Yes, sweetie," Sheila said, now back in control and into the game.

"Did I forget to tell you how beautiful you look today?" he asked with touching sincerity.

Sheila clutched at the loveliness of her grandfather's words and swallowed hard before answering.

"Why, indeed you have, Mr. John Evans," she replied, pointing her nose in the air as if offended.

Pop leaned over close to his granddaughter and kissed her on the cheek.

"Well, Mrs. Ceily Evans, let's just say that one more time I get to hold the hand of the prettiest girl at the party." He smiled. I heard my father clear his throat. He was choking on a memory too. I doubted that it was pleasant.

"Drive on, my lovely, and remember, easy on the clutch," Pop ordered.

My father, Molly and I stood in stunned silence as the pale yellow car, gleaming with its new German Glazurit laquer paint job that had been wet sanded, buffed, waxed and glazed to a mirror finish worthy of any Concours d'Elegance, pulled slowly away from the curb. My grandfather waved absentmindedly to us as they drove away, not even turning to look back. I was surprised he remembered we were there.

He only had eyes for his Ceily and I imagined that memories were flooding his brain as he sat next to her. Some would get through and make sense to him as his waning intellectual clarity faded. Others would get lost in a jumble of emotion and confusion and would never surface again.

I hoped for his sake that at least for the next hour or so, his fading life would luxuriate in the peace and happiness that the company of the only true love of his life – even if only in his imagination – could provide.

He deserved at least a final taste of happiness after a life that had deprived him more often than blessed him. That's how I felt. My dad, on the other hand was still wrestling with his feelings for the old man. For a long, long time, The Judge had believed that his father deserved all the misery he had experienced in his life. But his anger had softened in recent years and he had finally come to understand that it was time to forgive his father for a mistake that had cost our family dearly.

What I always found so sad was knowing that none of us had lost what Pop did on that fateful day so long ago when my grandmother died. Not one of us had felt a greater loss or regret. My grandfather had not had the peace of a single moment without sadness since the day his wife had passed. The light in his eyes died the very moment she did, never to be rekindled.

Worst of all, for every day of the rest of his life he carried with him the knowledge that his Ceily might still be at his side but for an instant of confusion, for simply making an impossible choice. But when the person he loved more than life itself had needed him most, he had unwittingly abandoned her.

From one perspective, the Alzheimer's disease had been merciful. Until the dementia took control of his mind, not a night passed that his dreams did not awaken him to the reality that she had died alone in the freezing waters of an icy river, slipping from his desperate grasp as she dipped beneath the surface.

The image of shock and terror in her wide eyes as she sank below him never left his consciousness. Nor did the love and sadness they silently spoke to him as she disappeared forever.

My father and I watched in silence as the pale yellow Mercedes drove out of sight.

Two

~~~

May 1988

"Why are you hiding up there, Sean?"

The sound of his deep voice startled me. I'd been caught.

I poked my head out from behind a an old wooden crate high up in the loft and stared down at my grandfather, not knowing what to expect. I'd been discovered in the act of spying on him.

He had his back to me as he said the words, not even bothering to look up. Somehow he just knew I was there and was obviously tired of making believe that he wasn't aware of my presence in the old horse barn that stood just yards behind our rambling family house in the small village of Willington, just east of Hartford, Connecticut.

I'd been sneaking into the barn for weeks, watching him as he sat on an old, three-legged milk stool each afternoon after finishing his chores. Alone, he would sit for hours every day in complete silence, moving only occasionally to reach into his jacket pocket and sip from a pint of cheap Irish whiskey as he stared at the old dust covered Mercedes stored inside. I was only ten years old and didn't understand why he spent so much time alone, staring at the car, or why he didn't laugh and play with me anymore since my grandmother had disappeared.

"She's in heaven now, Sean," my mother explained to me one day when I asked when Grandma was
~~~

coming home. "It's a very happy place where good people like your grandmother go after their life here is over. Why I'll bet she's looking down on you right now, making sure you're a happy boy." And then she went back to her ironing.

I didn't understand. Heaven? I wanted to ask more questions, but didn't know where to start. Anyway, it could wait. What I did know was that my grandfather was not a happy man. And I needed to know why right away.

The dilapidated barn was nearly a century old, its weathered planks barely holding back the elements. Anything stored inside enjoyed a bare minimum of protection from the weather and small critters that nested inside. Uncovered metal, in particular, simply rusted more slowly than if left outside directly exposed to rain and snow, the leaky roof, dampness and earthen floor of the great old shed doing little to slow the process of corrosion.

The fate of the old car was predictable and grim. But my grandfather didn't seem to notice as the German machine slowly began to show the inevitable signs of deterioration. There had been a time when a speck of dust on the pale yellow Mercedes would have him dragging out the wash bucket and his special chamois cloths to bring back the old girl's sparkling good looks. Now it was hard to tell what color it was at all.

"I'm not hiding, Pops," I stammered, somewhat afraid he was angry with me.

"Then come down here and sit with me," he said. There was no anger in his voice. Only sadness. He wasn't a very big man, probably a shade under six feet but not more than a hundred and seventy pounds. But he was muscular for his age and looked like he was in better shape than my father who was shorter and had gotten sort of fat. I'd always thought of him as a really tough guy and knew that he'd been a soldier and had fought in a war. Knowing that made the sorrow in his voice even harder to bear and I worried that he wasn't quite as strong as I had thought.

I climbed down the ladder from the loft and went to him, stopping at his side. He smelled of whiskey and needed a shave and a bath. But I didn't care. I could almost hear his heart breaking inside and one look at his eyes gave me the answer I had been searching for.

He missed Grandma, missed her terribly. Being close to the car they had loved together – the same car in which I had watched them hold hands from my perch in the cubby that passed for a back seat when they took me along on their magical rides along the shore – either eased his pain or made it worse. I couldn't tell. But whatever the truth, he could not stay away from the barn and the little yellow car that sat motionless inside it. Spontaneously, I wrapped my arms around him and hugged his neck.

I was only a few years old when my grandmother died, old enough to remember her but not to really know her. Still, a part of me missed her and I wasn't sure where she had gone. But I missed my Pop even more. After all, he'd always been my best friend, and although I would not come to terms with it for many years to come, he was a better father to me than my own.

He didn't say anything as I hugged him, but reached up and placed his big hand on my back, giving me a pat. "It's alright, Sean," he said. "I'm glad you're here. But I hope you won't mind if I don't say much.

I've a lot of thoughts in my head to try and sort through. Sometimes, I just need to be quiet."

"Ok," I said, relieved he wasn't mad.

"Do you understand?" he asked me when I sat down in the dirt next to his stool.

I shook my head, no.

"Not really, Pop," I said, "but its OK if you want to be quiet and think about your car."

"Oh... it's not just the car I think about, Sean."

He looked down at me and smiled, then ran his fingers through my hair.

"My," he said. "Your hair is just the same color as your grandmother's. Fire engine red. You've got her freckles, too, lad. She'd be very proud of you, Sean, do you know that?"

I wrinkled my nose in curiosity, not at all sure why.

"Why would Grandma be proud of me, Pop?" I asked him.

"Just because she would, Sean."

He took the little bottle out of his jacket pocket, unscrewed the cap and took a sip without explanation. I didn't ask him to explain.

"Do you miss her?" I asked, looking up at his face. He winced. I regretted the words the instant they came off my lips. Even being so young, I knew the question had hurt him.

He didn't respond, but let out a huge sigh. "I...

He began to answer me but suddenly stopped, dropped his head and put a hand to his face. Quietly, he sobbed, but did not want me to see. I put my hand on his back and felt his shoulders rise and fall with anguish. Tears came to my eyes, too. I hadn't meant to make him sad.

"It's all right, Pop, I miss her too," I said, trying to make things right. "We can miss her together, OK?"

I climbed up into his lap and hugged him again when he didn't answer. He squeezed me tight, then whispered in my ear.

"Run along now, you little pip squeak, I'm sure your mother will be worrying about you."

He eased me off his lap and gently sent me on my way without another word. And there I left him, tears rolling down his cheeks as he went back to staring at the car. For some reason I suddenly thought of the "Tin Man" in the *Wizard of Oz* and worried that Pops might get rusty out here in the damp barn if he cried a lot. In a way, that's just what happened.

I walked slowly to the door, turning once to see if he was all right. He was still sitting on his stool in a slightly drunken fog, watching the Mercedes rot away while dreaming about the short time he and my grandmother had together.

It would take me many years of growing up and long conversations in the barn with Pop to learn that for many years after grandma died, he was oblivious to the rest of the world, caring for nothing or the company of no one, not even his son and daughter-in-law or my sister and me. He subsisted on pain, guilt, anguish and self-pity and sought neither relief nor freedom from the burden of heartbreak that now filled his every breath. He had lost the love of his life and her loss had cost him his life, too.

I closed the door of the barn quietly behind me and went back to the main house. Inside, my Dad was home from work and reading the newspaper, cursing about something he was reading. He didn't bother to look up when I came in and ignored me. I was used to that.

Silently, I went into the kitchen looking for my mom and found her leaning over the sink, peeling potatoes. Even with her back to me I could tell she was crying. She did that a lot now. I climbed the giant staircase to my bedroom on the second floor and closed the door. Lying on my bed, I squeezed my eyes tight and tried not to think about all the unhappiness around me, with one exception. I wondered if there was a way to make Pop happy again. It seemed everyone was mad at him for something he did, and it made no sense to me. I needed to know what it was that he had done.

And what did it have to do with Grandma?

Three

I didn't sleep very well. Between thinking about Pop and trying to shut out the noise of my parents arguing, I seemed to spend most of the night staring up at the ceiling, my mind racing with questions. Sheila, only seven-years-old, woke up several times crying and that took away whatever little peace the darkness cast over our weary home. I watched with building anxiety as the sun came up behind the barn that I could see from my bedroom window.

The next morning at breakfast, I went into the kitchen all washed and dressed for school. Mom was busy making breakfast and looked terribly tired. Dad had his head buried in the newspaper again, drinking his coffee in silence and generally ignoring everyone, including my sister who was fussing that she didn't like her breakfast. Pop was nowhere to be seen, but I knew that he was sitting outside on the back steps, drinking his coffee and staring at the barn as he did each and every morning. He'd been up for hours already splitting wood and tending to the chickens behind the barn.

"Good morning, Sean," Mom said to me, trying to hide her sadness. She couldn't. "Sit down and eat your oatmeal," she said, wiping her hands on her apron.

"No thanks, Mom, I'm going to be late for school," I replied and gave her a peck on the cheek. "C'mon, Sheila unless you want to walk to school alone again," I hollered to my little sister who was dawdling as usual.

The two of us went to Willington Elementary School, a walk of about a mile and a half. I was in the fifth grade and Sheila in the second. Actually I was in a rush so I could see Pop before I left.

I ran from the kitchen and down the hallway to the back steps where I found my grandfather right where I expected.

"Morning, Pop," I said, yawning. He grunted and looked up at me with bloodshot eyes, a steaming cup of black coffee warming his hands. I guessed he hadn't slept much either. That wasn't unusual. Some nights I'd find him at the kitchen table, drinking little glasses of whiskey out of a big bottle while the rest of the house slept. He'd always send me back off to bed telling me that he'd just had a bad dream and that the medicine in the bottle would help him sleep. I was beginning to understand that Pop had a lot of bad dreams.

"Off to school, are ya?" he finally said to me.

"Yup," I replied. "I'm just waiting for Sheila. Want to walk with us?"

He hesitated. "Well, just part of the way, Sean. My old legs don't like to take that many steps anymore," he said.

"You're not old, Pop, just out of practice, that's all," I said, not wanting to hear him talk about getting old. He hadn't yet turned sixty, but his all white hair and the stubble that always lined his face made him appear much older. He'd hurt his legs sometime ago long before I was born — how I didn't know; it seemed to be another of those secrets in our family — and his hunched over appearance made him seem even older. I knew his legs caused him a lot of pain, but he never spoke of it.

He slowly stood up from the steps, left his coffee cup on the stairs and began walking towards school with me just as Sheila ran out of the house. We each reached up and held one of his hands as we crossed the lawn to the front yard and made our way to the long gravel driveway that led to the main road. He squeezed our hands without looking at us.

"It's nice to walk with you, my little ones."

I looked up, waiting for him to say more.

"Your grandmother and I used to take long walks together, too," he finally added. "But actually, we liked to take the old yellow car out for rides a lot more."

"Where did you drive it?" I asked, intrigued. "It doesn't look like it could go very far."

"Oh, there you're mistaken, grandson, "he said with a gentle laugh. "You underestimate that old girl."

"What do you mean?"

He didn't hesitate.

"Why that car could take your grandmother and me to far away places like Paris and back in a single Sunday afternoon. Even to the south of France if we wanted to see the ocean."

I laughed out loud at the thought.

"Grampa…" I said, knowing he was exaggerating.

"I'm telling you the truth, grandson. Your darling grandmother and I would drive along the coast at Cap d'Antibes, or through the streets of St. Tropez and the hills of St. Paul de Vence… yes, all along the French Rivera. We would stop at cafes and boutiques, drink espressos and wine and…" His voice drifted off and he closed his eyes.

"That little car made some of our dreams come true, Sean…" he said. "At least in our young hearts."

I stared at him trying to absorb all of what he had said. I didn't know the places he was talking about or why they wanted to visit them. It all sounded so crazy. But Pop was smiling, and that didn't happen very often. I tucked away the thought that those memories made him happy.

"*Some* dreams, Pop? Did you have other dreams?" I asked innocently.

He looked at me and shook his head. His voice dropped almost to a whisper as he answered.

"Yes, Sean, we had other dreams…"

In my naiveté, I had no idea that I was taking my grandfather down an extremely painful path.

"Why don't you take the car out anymore, Pop? Will it start?" I asked, not knowing why he had parked it so haphazardly to begin with.

I heard a catch in his throat as the question settled into his mind.

He hesitated. "Well, it's been a long time since I tried to start her, Sean. I don't know if she will or not. But no matter, it makes no difference," he replied, shrugging his shoulders and kicking at the gravel in resignation. His mood had suddenly become very sad.

"What do you mean it doesn't matter, Pop?"

He stopped walking. "It means I don't ever want to start the car again, don't ever want to drive it again," he said. His voice was soft but intense.

"Why…?

"It was never meant to be driven alone, Sean."

"But, you and me…" He cut me off.

"I know, Sean, I know," he said putting a hand on my shoulder and squeezing it. "But it wouldn't be the same. Someday you'll understand." He shook his head and sighed deeply, as if letting out a great breath of sorrow. I saw that his eyes were wet.

He turned away from me, wiping his cheeks with the back of his hand.

"Right now you better get going to school or you'll be late," he said, half choking on the words. "You have a good day and I'll see you this afternoon."

Sheila grabbed his arm and squeezed it.

"Grandpa?" she said.

"Yes, Sheila, what is it sweetheart?"

"I hope the rest of your dreams come true," she said, with an innocence that broke his heart yet brought the slightest hint of a grin to his face. It took him a moment to gather himself.

"Thank you, my little darling, " he replied, his voice quivering. "Now get to school before you're late."

With that, he turned and walked slowly back to the barn, his head down, deep in thought. He didn't look back. We watched him until he disappeared around the back of the house and then listened as the barn door creaked open, then slammed shut.

All that day at school I thought of him, sitting on his milk stool, looking at his old Mercedes and thinking about Grandma. I wondered what was going through his mind as he stared at the car and wished I could be with him.

Just to hold his hand.

Four

I walked in the back door after school and immediately heard them fighting. My mom and dad and Pop were at it over something. Mom was crying and my father was cursing at my grandfather.

"You mind your own business, old man," he screamed at Pop as my mother held him back. "You've got enough of you own shame to hide, you coward." His fists were balled and I could tell he'd been drinking.

I hid near the front door and held onto the stair balusters. I hated coming home to the screaming and never knew when it would happen or why. Sheila was upstairs in her room, crying, neglected. It made me mad.

"I made a mistake," I heard Pop yell back at my father. "You're just a weakling, Sam, a coward who would trade his family for a whore. I'd give anything for a second chance, but you're too stupid to know that you're throwing yours away."

I wondered what a "whore" was when I heard Pop use the word. It was new to me.

"Stay away from her, you hear me?" Pop threatened my dad. "If I see you with her again, so help me…"

"So help you what, you drunken, useless old leach," my father hollered back. "What are you going to do about it? I've told you before, stay out of this. It's between Marnie and me — it's none of your damned business, old man."

My mother ran out of the kitchen. Tears were streaming from her eyes. Her face turned ashen when she saw me.

"Oh, Sean, I'm so sorry," she said, hugging me and kissing the top of my head. "I'm so sorry..."

"What's the matter, Mom?" I whimpered, afraid from all the anger. I was sure Pop and my dad were going to start fighting.

"It's complicated, Sean," she said, at a loss to explain to me why her family was falling apart. She wiped the tears from her eyes. "Come now, let's forget all this and go and see about Sheila, poor little thing. She needs a hug too."

My mother grabbed my hand and pulled me behind her up the stairs.

"Now get out of my house before I throw your worthless ass into the street, you hear me?" my dad screamed at Pop.

My grandfather stood his ground. He was itching for a fight, too.

"Your house?" grandfather said. "Why if it wasn't for my disability checks that put food on the table in this house, your family would go hungry, do you know that? For all your success and money you haven't given Marnie a dime in months to support this family. You unfaithful fool... All your money goes into booze and whores."

"How dare you judge me..." my father screamed at him. "Go think about your own sins."

"That I will, Sam, that I will," he said with resignation. "But know that for all your success, for all your highfalutin reputation as a lawyer, I know the truth. You'll be one of the mistakes I ponder."

My father slammed his fist down on the kitchen table. "Get out, before I take you out," he screamed at Pop, his drunken voice shaking with rage.

I was relieved to hear Pop's footsteps head for the back door. Then he stopped and turned back to my father.

"I have a lot of regrets in my life, son. God knows my failures and helps me remember them every moment of every day." He paused.

"Being your father is one of them."

With that, Pop pushed open the back door and slammed it as he left the house. A few minutes later I heard the door to the barn open and close. I thought of Pop back in his own world, safe with his three-legged milk stool, the old Mercedes and his memories.

From upstairs in Sheila's room, I heard my father wrench open a cabinet door and slam a bottle of whiskey down on the kitchen table. The sound of a glass being dropped on the table followed. In a little while, he'd calm down, then drag his drunken frame upstairs to bed where he'd fall dead asleep with his clothes on.

"Marnie, get your butt down here, we need to talk," he yelled up to her as she rocked a whimpering Sheila in her arms. Mom smiled at me and ignored him, as she always did when this happened.

"It's all right, Sean, it's all over," she said soothingly. "Why don't you go outside and sit with your grandfather for awhile. You know he loves to have you near him. And I'm sure he's very lonely right now."

I gave her a kiss on the cheek and hurried down the stairs. My father heard me and yelled for me to come into the kitchen. I ignored him, too.

I ran to the barn and went inside. Sure enough, Pop was where I expected him. But he wasn't looking at the car. His head was down, staring at the dirt floor and his shoulders were stooped with burden. The fingers of his two big hands were locked together in front of him and he absentmindedly rocked back and forth on the milk stool. He didn't even notice my presence. It had rained overnight. There was a strong damp smell in the barn and the odor of rotting wood.

"Pop?" I said to get his attention. He didn't respond.

"Pop, are you OK?" I tried again. I reached down and shook his shoulder. He looked up.

"Oh... Sean," he said gently, his anger already receding. "I didn't hear you come in, grandson." He stared at me, reading my face and instantly knew that I had heard at least some of what had happened inside the house.

"What's the matter, Pop? Why are mom and dad fighting all the time?" I asked him, staring at the dirt floor. It was more a plea for an explanation than a question.

He hung his head and shrugged his shoulders before answering.

"Ah, Sean, there are just some things in life..." he began, then stopped. He didn't know how to explain.

"What's a whore, Pop?" I asked.

He shook his head in shame.

"Forget about that, Sean, just forget about that," he answered. "It's a word I shouldn't have used and it's not important."

He looked at me for a long time, staring into my eyes. I was on the verge of crying, and bless him, he knew I needed some understanding of what was happening to my family.

"Sean," he finally said, "this is not an easy thing to explain. But I'll try."

I shook my head.

He wrapped an arm around me, drawing me close to him. "Do you know what love is?"

"Love?" I replied, surprised by the question. What did love have to do with anything?

"Yes, love."

I looked away, confused.

"Do you know what love is?" he repeated. "And I don't mean the kind of feelings that you have for your mom or dad or Sheila, or even me. I mean the kind of love a man feels for a woman."

He paused and looked into my puzzled eyes. "What I mean is… well… let me ask you a question. Is there a little girl at school that you feel is pretty special?"

"Pop, what does that have…"

"No, think for a minute, Sean," he demanded.

I hesitated a bit before responding as if I had to think about it. Actually, I knew exactly what he was talking about.

"Well, there is Mary Kay O'Shanley… " I finally said, rather embarrassed. "I think she's pretty…and everything." I hesitated, worried he might laugh. He didn't.

"Is that love?" I asked.

"Maybe," he said.

He looked up at the rafters, knowing I wasn't going to let go of it. He sighed before going on.

"Let me ask you… does your heart tingle a bit when you're near her? Do you think about her a lot during the day and want to be with her more than anyone else? Does it make you very happy to be with her?" he asked.

I shrugged my shoulders.

"Yah, I guess so."

"Well, then, that could be love, Sean."

I waited for him to finish, not sure what he was telling me.

"Unfortunately, when you love someone, and some of those feelings go away, it can hurt a lot inside. That happens sometimes when people are in love. It's not all that unusual for something to happen that makes their feelings change."

"You mean that my mom and dad aren't in love anymore, Pop?" I asked, trying to put the pieces together. I was doing my best to hold back my tears.

He hesitated again before answering.

"I guess…" He stopped, considering his next words carefully for my benefit.

"I guess I don't know the answer to that question right now, Sean. Love is a very complicated thing."

We were quiet then for a long time, each of us contemplating what we had just talked about.

I thought our conversation had ended for the day. They often just came to an awkward halt. Sometimes he had made a point. Sometimes he hadn't.

Then, suddenly, Pop let down his guard completely and told me about grandma.

"Did I ever tell you how I fell in love with your grandmother?" he asked.

"No, never…" I said, shocked that he had mentioned her. He never talked about grandma.

He fell silent, perhaps regretting that he had said it.

"Tell me, Pop…." Somehow, I had never thought of my grandmother and grandfather as being in love. They were always just Pop and Grandma.

He reached an arm around me and dragged me down into his lap, squeezing me tight before he began talking.

"It's funny how something that happened so long ago can still feel like yesterday," he said, quietly laughing to himself.

Long minutes went by as he thought about the story, my anticipation building with every second.

Finally he began.

"It was a long time ago, long before you were born, sport. It was at a time when I was an Air Force jet fighter pilot in a place called Korea where we were fighting a war."

My jaw must have dropped, because he chuckled.

"Yah, it's true, grandson, your grandfather was a jet fighter jock."

"Wow…" I said, truly awed.

"Don't be so easily impressed, youngster. It was a very hard time in my life and I'm lucky to be alive." He caught himself and I could tell that his thoughts were drifting away. "Although sometimes I don't feel so lucky."

"What?" I asked, confused.

He stared at the old car for a moment before turning back to me.

"Never mind. Let's just say that being a U.S. combat Air Force pilot in Korea was the worst experience of my life and the best thing that ever happened to me."

My eyes crossed at the contradiction.

"I don't understand."

"I don't imagine that makes much sense," he agreed. He thought for a minute.

"It was sort of like a really bad dream with a very happy ending, Sean. Can you imagine that?"

I thought about it. "Yah, I think so," I said, although the concept was still a bit vague.

Pop explained that he was just twenty-one years old when he graduated from college in January, 1951, a full semester early. The ink on his diploma, an engineering degree from the University of Connecticut probably wasn't even dry before he faced the probability of being drafted and sent to fight in Korea.

"I was always one who liked to decide my own fate rather than have someone else decide it for me," he said. "So, I enlisted."

"Enlisted?"

"I volunteered to join the military and to go fight," he said. "It wasn't what I wanted to do, but it was inevitable. And because I was volunteering, I could pick out what branch of the military I wanted to join. I had a college diploma in engineering so the Air Force offered to teach me how to fly and become a fighter pilot. That sounded pretty neat at the time.

"So within a few weeks of graduation from college, I found myself on a train headed for Chapel Hill, North Carolina for preflight training. Ninety days later I was commissioned a second lieutenant. That means I was an officer. After that there were months of classroom work on flight theory and aviation mechanics and military flying strategy before I ever climbed into the cockpit of an airplane. It was like being back in college."

I finally couldn't hold it back any longer. "Wow!" I said. "I never knew you were a pilot, Pop, or that you were in a war. How come you never talk about it?"

"Trust me, Sean, it sounds a lot more glamorous than it was. I was miserable the whole time."

He shook his head to explain.

"I'd had it with school… and I have a lot of bad memories of that time. I don't like to think about it, let alone talk about it," he told me. "People sometimes think that wearing a uniform is very romantic. They forget that along with the uniform comes a mission to go off to war. I didn't really want to fight, I'm not ashamed to admit it. War is blood and pain and sadness. There's nothing romantic about it."

He stopped for a minute, deep in thought. There was a desolate look in his eyes."

"Pop?" I said after waiting for him to start again. "Please tell me more, tell me about Grandma?"

He abruptly came back to me. "Oh… yes… I'm sorry, Sean. Sometimes I lose my train of thought."

"It's OK, Pop."

He hugged me again and a grin came to his face.

"But then I learned how to fly and it changed my whole life."

My mind went wild with imagining Pop flying through the sky.

"The very first time I took the controls of an airplane, I found that there was nothing more exhilarating than flying through a huge empty sky with no one for company but big fluffy clouds. It was amazing, Sean, like a dream."

"I'll say! Man, you must have been so cool, Pop." A whole new picture of my grandfather had suddenly bloomed in my imagination.

He went silent again and looked at me, the expression on his face turning deadly serious.

"It was glorious, Sean, it really was," he said. "But a real man never hesitates to admit when he's scared. And let me tell you, I didn't feel very – as you say, 'cool' – I was scared to death." He looked up at the rafters again.

"As exciting as it was, it was just as terrifying," he said again, almost in a whisper.

"The lucky guys washed out of basic flight training. The rest of us went to Pensacola – that's an air base in Florida – and we went from the little toy trainers they had me flying in Chapel Hill to the cockpit of real monsters."

"Monsters?"

"Yah, the Vought F4U Corsair. That was the first real war bird I ever flew."

"Holy cow! Like the model that you bought me, the one hanging from the ceiling in my room? The blue one with the bent wings?" I asked in amazement.

"Yah, the famous 'U-Bird' fighter that tore up the Japs in the South Pacific. That's the one."

He shook his head at the memory, lingering over it.

"A lot of Marine pilots became Aces flying those beasts, but a lot died trying, too. Shit, I saw three guys from my own squadron killed just learning to fly the bastard let alone become fighter pilots. I have to tell you, Sean, I was one frightened fella back then. Never knew if I'd make it another day."

I was mesmerized by his story. Pop had so many secrets. It seemed every time he moved his lips I found out something new about him. And they weren't little things. An Air Force combat jet fighter pilot?

"It only got worse," he added. "Because as lethal as the F4U was, it wasn't good enough for Korea. Our guys were getting murdered over there against the Korean jets.

"So from there I checked out in the North American Aviation F-86 Sabre jet, the first swept wing fighter the Air Force ever deployed. Learned how to fly it at Nellis Air Force Base in Nevada. I thought the Corsair was bad..." His voice dropped off.

"The casualty rate for new F-86 pilots was so high I don't think I ever saw the base flag not at half-staff. Lost a lot of good friends back then. Just young boys..."

Pop paused and rubbed his eyes, difficult memories dredged up from a time long ago.

"I was so scared, Sean... I was just a kid..."

He looked over at me and saw that my mouth was open in amazement.

"You bored yet?" he said, laughing quietly to himself. I shook my head.

He took a deep breath and let out a long sigh. I was too young to appreciate how difficult these memories must have been for him.

"The Sabre was a frightful airplane because it was so capable," he continued. "Damn thing could do over seven hundred miles per hour and turn on a dime. Problem was you were flying so fast that if you had to think about making a decision, it was already too late. You were in trouble. We had to learn to fly the airplane instinctively. The training was a bitch, but without it, I wouldn't be here. Because waiting for us in Korea was an airplane even better than the Sabre. It was called the

MiG-15. The Russians made it and it was every bit a match for the F-86."

My eyes were bugging out of my head. I still couldn't believe this was my grandfather.

"Next thing I know, I'm in Korea assigned to the 51st Fighter Wing Group at Suwon Air Base just outside of Seoul, Korea. It was like being on an alien planet for a boy from Connecticut. This was in the fall of 1951, probably the longest year of my life."

It suddenly struck me how scary it must have been for Pop to be away from home, alone.

"Were you homesick, Pop?"

"Homesick?" He smiled, but it was a sad sort of smile. "Not really… there wasn't much for me back home, Sean."

"Oh." Another new revelation.

"Didn't your mom and dad care about you?" I asked, shocked by his response. It struck me that I couldn't recall him ever mentioning either of them.

"The truth is no one back home cared much about me," he continued. "My mom was long dead and my old man hadn't spoken to me since the day I enrolled in college. He thought going to school was just a waste of time and money. Called me a big shot, a 'spoiled brat' the last time I saw him. That was the day I left for school. We never spoke again. Even now, I don't know if he's dead or alive."

He laughed out loud, but I still sensed a tinge of sadness in his voice. "You know the whole time I was in school, in Korea, in the hospital… I never got so much as a letter from him or anyone in my family."

He stopped and took the little bottle out of his jacket pocket, put it to his lips and took a long pull. "In the end, I guess being on my own made me a stronger man.

I got so used to being lonely that I forgot I was alone. It was good training for when I lost your grandmother…"

His words shocked me. Lost grandma? In my naiveté, I repeated what my mother had told me.

"She's just in heaven, in a happier place, Pop. Mom told me."

He slumped over on the stool, his head dropping below his shoulders.

"Is that what she told you…" he said. It came out of his mouth so quietly I almost couldn't make out his words. "I guess that would be true," he said with a sadness I could almost feel.

He became very quiet then and stopped talking. I didn't think he was going to tell me anymore. But I had so many questions now that needed answers. I tried to get him talking again.

"You said you were in the hospital – in Korea? You were wounded, Pop?"

Surprisingly, he laughed. "You know, I almost forgot how we began this conversation. I was going to tell you how I met your grandma and how I fell in love with her."

His eyes drifted off. I knew images of her were floating in his mind.

"Tell me… please, Pop…"

"Yah…" he said, slowly coming back to me.

He cleared his throat and began again.

"Well, within a few days of arriving in Korea, I was flying daily sorties, providing escort cover for bomber missions. I didn't see much action and frankly was a little bored, just counting the days until I could come home.

"But that all changed real fast…"

He drifted off again for a few seconds, then began anew.

"I think I was there about a month or so when one afternoon I found myself over the Yalu River – the border between Korea and China – heading back to base alone with a hydraulics problem. My controls were heavy and I wasn't sure I was going to be able to lock my landing gear in place when it came time to land. But I was taking my sweet time making it back to base when all of a sudden I got jumped by three MiG's coming at me at my five over an area they called 'MiG Alley.' I thought I was screwed when they came at me from above. They'd been hiding in some cloud cover. I flew right into their trap."

My jaw dropped again.

"When I saw them come at me at full speed, I pushed my own throttle to the firewall and tried to run for home, but the MiG's were faster than the Sabre," he said. "They were gaining on me fast and it finally occurred to me that my only chance was to go on the offensive."

"You took on three MiG's all by yourself?" I said, incredulously.

"Don't make me out to be a hero, Sean, I didn't have much choice. But I knew the Sabre had a pretty mean punch – four 20-millimeter cannons instead of machine guns that could fire twelve hundred rounds a minute. It had lethal firepower. So I knew I had a chance if I could outfox the bastards."

"What did you do, Pop? Were you an 'Ace?'" I asked, jumping the gun a bit in my excitement.

"No, I wasn't an 'Ace,' Sean... I was no hero. Hell, I was just a damned rookie."

"Sounds to me like you knew what you were doing," I said, bursting with pride for my grandfather.

"I was lucky, Sean. What I did was fool them," Pop continued. "I pulled back on the stick as hard as I could and pushed the nose of the Sabre straight up, heading for as much altitude as I could find – exactly what they didn't expect me to do. Then, at the apex of my climb, I rolled over into a steep dive and came down right behind the first MiG I saw – I completely surprised the pilot. To tell you the truth, I was just about as surprised myself. I was pulling so many G's, it's a wonder I didn't pass out at the controls."

He shook his head as if wondering how he'd gotten through it.

"I was about fifteen hundred feet away from the first MiG and wasted no time leaning on my cannons when I got him lined up in my sights. A burst of incendiary rounds went right up his tailpipe. It happened so fast I was shocked to see his airplane catch fire right in front of me. He wobbled a bit, smoke pouring out his ass end, then he dropped out of the sky like a rock, wing over wing, completely out of control. I saw him blow off his canopy, but I don't know if the pilot ever got out. I was too busy looking for the other bastards."

"Geez..." was all I could muster. I was completely in awe.

"Sure enough, before I could even think about my next move, I heard a loud rippling bang and felt a shudder. A few dozen rounds had hit my left wing and the fuselage, just missing my canopy. I felt a sting in my leg but didn't have time to worry about it. Another one of the mothers was right on my tail, trying to set up a kill in honor of his lost buddy. I had no intention of hanging around for my own funeral so I broke right and dove, pouring on the coal, trying to get out of his line of fire.

"But he was good. Didn't hesitate to follow me and he had blood in his eye. The bastard was glued to my tail and machine gun rounds were flying by me as I dove for the ground. I thought I was done for. Then I had an idea."

"Did you climb again?" I asked, imagining myself in his situation.

"No, I did what amounted to the exact opposite. I hit my speed breaks, which just about cut my air speed in half and sure enough, the MiG shot right over the top of me and fell into my cross hairs. I pulled back the trigger again and let him have it with a long burst that strafed right up into his cockpit. This time, the MiG exploded in a ball of fire. Two down. I couldn't believe my luck."

"I'll say…"

"Not so fast," he said, holding up a hand. "Unfortunately, I was so close when he blew up, debris from his airplane got sucked into the engine of my wounded Sabre, already leaking fuel from the hits I'd taken earlier.""

"Holy cow!" I said, unable to contain myself."

He laughed, breaking the tension.

"Now I was really in the soup," Pop continued, vividly reliving the moment. "My Sabre was trailing smoke, it was beginning to get cloudy in the cockpit and I was suddenly feeling a bit woozy. Luckily, the third MiG got cold feet and the North Korean high tailed it out of there. He didn't want to mess with the crazy American who'd just shot down two of his brothers. That made me feel pretty good for a second or two. But that was all the time I had. Just about then, I realized I had taken a round or some shrapnel in my left leg and I was bleeding badly. The whole left leg of my flight suit was red with blood."

"They shot you?" I said in horror at the thought.

"Yah, that's what happens when guys fire bullets at each other in jet fighters," he laughed and hugged me. "Relax pal, I don't want you to have nightmares tonight. I'm here, aren't I?"

My eyes were bugging out of my head at the thought of my grandfather all alone, wounded and bleeding in an airplane ready to crash. I had read stories about soldiers and pilots who'd gone through similar experiences – what kid hadn't – but that's just what they seemed like. Stories. This was real, and it was my grandfather.

"Why didn't you just eject, Pop?"

"Nah, I wasn't going to give those Korean bastards the satisfaction," he said, an evil grin crossing his face. "My balls were bigger than my brains. I got two of them, they weren't getting me. I was only about thirty kilometers from Suwon, so I radioed that I was coming in hot."

"Hot?"

"Hurt and on fire," he said, in a matter of fact tone. I was horrified.

"Suwon rolled their crash trucks and were ready for me, thank the Lord. When I tried to drop my landing gear, nothing happened. I had no hydraulics at all and the stick was really heavy. The only way I could fly her was with bursts of the throttle. I was sort of pushing her around, aiming her with the power from my engine.

"Since I couldn't drop the gear the only way in was on my belly. By that time, I was too low to eject and I had no intentions of dying bouncing on my ass off a runway.

"As I flew over the horizon, a friend of mine who saw me come in told me later that I looked about as heavy and fast as any fighter he'd ever seen attempt to make a landing, and was trailing smoke and streaming a thirty-foot ribbon of fire. I had almost no control of the airplane, but just as I made the edge of the runway and was about to hit the ground, I yanked back on the stick as hard as I could, pulled the nose up and got just enough lift to pancake my girl right on her belly on the tarmac.

"There were sparks flying for nearly a half mile before friction finally stopped the bloody thing. By this time, the fuselage was almost fully engulfed in flames and both legs of my flight suit were burning. I blew the canopy off just as two guys in fire suits reached in, released my harness and literally jerked me out of the cockpit and threw me on the ground. I hit the runway so hard it knocked the wind out of me and I broke a couple of ribs. But thank God for those fire guys. They started beating the flames out of my suit and then someone aimed a foam cannon at me and it was over. I was a pile of smoldering, bleeding wreckage spread out on the tarmac just like my Sabre, but by God, I was alive."

"Holy..." I caught myself before I used a swear word. Mom hated that and usually blamed Pop. He laughed.

"I remember laying on my back as I went into shock, looking up at that big, beautiful blue sky and taking in a huge breath of fresh air. Then everything went black."

He was spent. Between arguing with my father and reaching way back in his memories to share with me one of the most frightening stories I'd ever heard, Pop was done. He reached into his pocket and pulled out that little bottle again, draining it.

Then, surprisingly, he found new energy.

"Damn, I nearly forgot again, boy," he said. "About how I met your grandmother."

"You mean, it was in Korea?"

"Sure was," he smiled. "Your grandmother was a nurse in the Army, happened to be stationed in a MASH unit not far from Suwon."

"MASH?" I repeated.

"Mobile Army Surgical Hospital," he said. "That's where I was taken right after the crash. I had second and third degree burns all over my legs and feet and some on my face, two bullets in my left leg and thirteen chunks of metal shrapnel in my right. I was in pretty tough shape for awhile."

"That's where you met grandma?"

"They had me knocked me out with morphine while transporting me to the MASH unit so I was unconscious when they pulled me off the helicopter that took me there," he said. "I'd lost a lot of blood and my burns were very bad – you've never seen me in a bathing suit, have you, grandson?"

"No," I shuddered.

"Not a pretty picture."

We were quiet for a minute. Then he went on.

"I came to for a few moments before going into the operating room. When I opened my eyes, I had no idea where I was and very little memory of what had happened. Actually, I thought I had already died and gone to heaven."

He paused.

"You know why?"

"No..." I said. "Did you see an angel or something?"

"The closest thing to an angel, Sean," he answered, almost in a whisper. He closed his eyes and a great big grin came to his lips.

"When I opened my eyes, staring down at me was the most beautiful redhead I'd ever seen," he said, relishing the memory. "She had eyes so big and deep and green they looked like the ocean. It was your grandmother. The prettiest girl I'd ever seen."

He kept his eyes shut, lingering over the remembrance of her beauty.

I couldn't stop staring at him. His eyes were wet all of a sudden, and he cleared his throat trying to catch his breath. The memory was that powerful.

"She had a hold of my hand and was squeezing it, telling me in the most lovely, lilting voice that I had been wounded and was badly injured. They were going to have to operate immediately, she said, and asked me if I believed in God."

"They thought you were going to die?" I was shocked nearly beyond words.

"Actually, the thought hadn't occurred to me up until that point, but yah, it didn't look good. I told her I wasn't a church going man but I believed in God. She asked me if I wanted to see a priest and receive the Last Rites."

"You mean like in the movies, when someone is going to die the priest comes and prays and says stuff about your soul?" I asked.

"Exactly."

"Did you?"

"No."

"You said no?"

"What I told your grandma was that I was afraid, but if God could make anything as beautiful as her, I'd rather just hold her hand then get the Last Rites. I figured that was as close to God as I could get."

A tear rolled down his cheek. I hugged him.

"Did she stay?" I asked.

"Not only did she stay, but she held my hand and wiped my face with a cool, wet cloth. She made me feel at peace. If I had died at that moment, it would have been OK, Sean. Because I knew in my heart that I had met the woman that I would love for the rest of my life – whether that was going to be for a few more minutes or for many years."

Suddenly, I understood what love was. Mary Kay O'Shanley wasn't the one.

"A few minutes later, some orderlies came to take me to surgery and got ready to give me anesthesia. Before they put the mask over my face, I squeezed her hand one last time and thanked her for staying with me."

"What did she say, Pop?" My own eyes were wet with tears.

He didn't hesitate. "She said, 'It was my pleasure, you handsome fly boy. Make sure you come out of there so we can talk some more, OK hero?'"

He laughed. "I may be the only guy on the planet who ever faced life and death surgery with a grin on his face," he said.

"Then the words just came out."

"What?" I leaned forward to hear him. He was almost whispering.

"I said, 'If I do, will you marry me?'"

"You asked her to marry you? On the way to surgery?"

"Yup." He looked at me and smiled. "Pretty ballsy, hey kid?"

"What did she say?"

She laughed at me, then smiled. Jesus, she lit up the room. My God, she was just so beautiful."

"What did she say, Pop?" I demanded again. The suspense was killing me.

He laughed once more and wiped away the tear. "She said, 'Why that's the best offer I've had all day, fly boy. Remember, I'll be waiting for you when you come out, OK?"

"Promise? I said to her, trying not to beg, but it must have been obvious," Pop continued. "She nodded and flashed me that amazing smile again.

"Then she did the most amazing thing. She squeezed my hand one last time, then leaned down and kissed me on the lips. No just a peck, but a long sweet kiss. "

"That ought to last you for a while, John Evans," she said and winked at me, then turned and walked away.

"It was a one in a million deal, Sean, but your grandma fell in love with me just like I fell in love with her. Instantaneously. Just like in the movies, it was love at first sight."

He was still grinning.

"Then it dawned on me," he said.

"What?"

"I didn't know her name!"

"What did you do?"

"I yelled to her just as they were putting the mask over my face.

"'I don't even know your name,' I hollered to her."

A look came over Pop's face that is burned into my own memories to this day. It was a look so deep and surreal that I'll never forget it. Whenever I think of him, I can't help but see that expression on his face. Pure joy.

"'Cecilia,'" she said. "My name is Cecilia, but people call me Ceily," she yelled back to me, just as the lights went out."

He hung his head, his eyes closed.

"Ceily," he repeated. "My Ceily."

I had to ask him, even though big tears were running freely down his face.

"Was she there, Pop, when it was over?"

"Was she there?" he repeated, laughing at me.

He hesitated, struggling to answer me.

"Was she there? Hell, it was her kiss that woke me up in the recovery room," he grinned.

His face was wet with tears as he hugged me.

"Yes, Sean, she was there for me. When I needed her the most."

He sobbed as he hugged me and he choked out one last sentence.

"Why couldn't I have been there when she needed me?"

We held unto each other for a long time after that, until well after the shadows of the afternoon that poked through the barn boards had disappeared into the darkness of night.

Just like Pop's stay in Korea, the day had been the worst of my life.

And the best.

Five

I lay on my bed most of that night, the covers pulled up around my chin, thinking about all Pop had told me. His life has been so much different than I had imagined, and I knew now that I didn't know the whole story even yet. The upheaval in my family was deeply frightening and my talk with Pop about love had me convinced that my mom and dad no longer felt about each other the way Pop described the feelings he and grandma had shared. I was afraid, but not sure what I was afraid of. What happened when two people stopped loving each other? What did it mean to Sheila and me?

The answer came later in the night, just as I was finally dozing off. It must have been about three in the morning and I was brought out of my slumber by the creaking of the door to my bedroom slowly opening. The light from the hallway cast the face of the person pushing open the door into blackness, and I couldn't tell who it was. I made believe I was asleep as the figure came into my room and approached the foot of the bed and stopped.

I opened my eyes just enough to make out the face of my mother. A bit of moonlight shining in from my window revealed tears running down her face. Her hair was disheveled as if she had been running her hands through it. I sat up in bed.

"Mom, what's the matter?" I said, my heart hurting from her sadness. I was suddenly very afraid.

At any moment I expected my father to come in behind her and the yelling and screaming to start again.

Sobbing, she did her best to wipe the tears away from her face, then came and sat by me on the bed. She was silent except for her crying and I could tell that she was desperately trying to compose herself.

"It's all right, Sean, my beautiful little boy," she whispered. "I'm sorry I woke you."

"You didn't, mom, I wasn't really asleep."

"Oh…" she said, wiping the back of her hand across my cheek. "You have school tomorrow, you need to sleep."

"I'll be OK," I told her. "Why aren't you sleeping, Mom? It's very late…" I asked, but I already knew the answer.

"Do you know how much I love you?" she said to me, reaching out to hold me even as she spoke. I felt her warmth envelope me as she hugged me hard and didn't let go. I held unto her as tightly as I could, equally afraid to let her go.

"Sean…" she began, her voice cracking and barely legible through her sobs. "I have to go away for a little while…"

I jumped out from my under my covers at the shock of her words and grabbed her by the neck and held on. Somewhere inside my chest I felt a sharp pain and my stomach began to churn. I thought I was going to be sick.

"No, Mom…it will be ok…don't be sad," I begged her. "Sheila needs you to be here for her… so do I… I'll keep my room cleaner, I promise and I'll take out the trash and do my homework…" I would have promised her anything.

"Sean, my little darling..." she said, pushing me back to look into my eyes. "This is not your fault. You've done nothing wrong. Why...God could not have given me a greater joy in my life than to hold you as my son."

"Than why, Mom? Why are you leaving me? Are you just going out to the barn?" I asked, hoping she was just going to hide for a while.

"No, Sean," she whispered. "Your daddy and I just can't be together right now... I don't know how else to explain it. Sometimes it just happens between moms and dads...and I'm so sorry it happened to yours," she cried. "Maybe your dad can explain it better than I can... What's important right now is that there's peace in this house and that you don't come home from school again and hear us screaming at each other. You deserve better, do you understand?"

"No, I don't, Mom, I don't. Stay, please, please."

She held me tight for a long time and rubbed my back to calm me. I could feel the tears on her face mix with mine as I cried, wanting to believe this was all a bad dream.

Finally she pushed me back down on my bed. The image of pain on her face was instantly etched in my brain forever. She was ashen.

"Always know that I love you with all my heart, and no matter where you are, I'll be with you, Sean. I know you don't understand this – I'm not sure I do myself – but I love you enough to leave you now, just for a little while, until your dad and me make some sense of this."

"Does Pop know?" I asked through gritted teeth. I had a mind to get out of bed, go into my father's bedroom and strangle him in his sleep. I hated him at that moment. And I would hate him for many years to come. I made up my mind right then that I would never love him again. I almost kept that promise.

"Yes, Pop knows," she said, composing herself. "He'll take care of you, Sean, you know how much he loves you."

"But he's so sad, mommy, and you're so sad. Why is everyone so sad?" I searched her eyes for an answer. They were empty, just full of tears.

"Let me come with you, please? I'll go and get Sheila and carry her for you, OK? Please, Mom?"

"No, Sean. That isn't what Sheila needs right now. She needs her big brother to remind her how much you and I both love her – and that she'll never be alone." There was a look of pleading in her eyes now.

"Can I depend on you to do that for me? Please, my love?"

I took her hand in mine and squeezed it hoping she would change her mind. Finally I closed my eyes in despair and told her what she wanted to hear.

"Yes, Mom," I whispered through tears that wouldn't stop. "I'll take good care of Sheila. But only until you come back."

I waited for her response, but she was deathly quiet.

"You will come back, Mom, you will, promise me..."

She looked into my eyes and smiled, then pulled the covers back up around my neck. "I'm going to stay with my brother – Uncle Jerry – just for a few days, not much more, just until things calm down and we can act like a family again.

"But no matter how long I'm gone, I'll always be with you, Sean, don't ever forget that. I love you with all my heart."

She leaned down and kissed me on the cheeck and ran her fingers through my hair, lingering over my forehead. Then she stood up, turned, and walked out of my room, quietly closing the door behind her. I waited, expecting her to come bursting back inside to tell me it was all a mistake. But she didn't. Pretty soon, I heard the click of the front door closing. I jumped up and ran to my window.

There, outside in the backyard was a bright yellow taxicab, its motor running. A man got out of the car, took the small suitcase she was carrying and put it in the trunk. Then he opened the rear door for her and she got in. I banged on my bedroom window trying to get her attention, but she either didn't hear me or wouldn't look up at me. I never did know which. It didn't matter. The cab pulled away from the back door and circled out to the front of the house where it pulled onto the main road. I watched its tail lights until they disappeared into the darkness.

I wanted to kill my father, yet I didn't even know what he had done. Instead, I leapt up onto my desk chair and ripped the F4U Corsair model that Pop and I had built together from its string hanging from the ceiling. I threw open the door to my bedroom and ran down the hall to where I knew my father would be sleeping. The door was open, but the room was dark and he was not in his bed. A surge of fear went through me as I thought for an instant that Sheila and I were alone in the house. I ran down the stairs and into the sitting room. There sat my father, alone in the dark, staring into empty space.

I walked over to a small table lamp next to the couch and turned on the lamp. A dim light immediately cast an ugly glow throughout the room, making a bad scene even worse. But I needed that light to make sure.

To make sure that the plastic airplane model that I still clutched in my hand hit him square in the face when I threw it at him with all my might. It did, shattering into a thousand pieces. He didn't even flinch when it smashed into his face. He was like a corpse. At that moment, I wished he were.

I turned and went to run back upstairs. At the base of the stairs, waiting for me, was Pop. He grabbed me, whisked me off my feet and hugged me, then wordlessly carried me up the stairs and into my bedroom.

Downstairs, my father pleaded for me to come and sit with him. His words echoed up the walls and into my room. Pop tucked me into my bed, then walked over and kicked the door shut behind him with a vengeance before settling into bed beside me for the rest of the night. I think my dad got the message.

The next morning, and for every morning thereafter until he got sick, Pop made breakfast for Sheila and me while we waited for our mother to come home.

It was the longest wait of my life. But if anything, it made me appreciate how painful Pop's life was without grandma.

Who wasn't coming home, ever again.

Six

~~~

November 1992

"Read it again, Pop, please?" I begged him, sitting next to him in the barn. I had my own three legged milk stool now, which Pop had dug up from somewhere in the clutter that was gradually building up around the abandoned Mercedes. It was late fall and the drafty barn was getting colder with each successive day. Neither one of us noticed.

He sighed. It was long after dinner hour and he was tired. I was noticing that he didn't have quite the stamina I remembered. I had always thought of him as indestructible, especially after hearing about his experiences in Korea. I wasn't so sure anymore.

He looked at me, puzzled. He was holding Mom's letter.

"Read what, Sean?" he asked. He had just finished reading it to me a few minutes before.

"Stop kidding around, Pop. Read Mom's letter to me again."

He raised an eye and shook his head in confusion. Then he remembered.

"Oh, yes, of course, your mother's letter.

"One more time and you'll have it memorized, Sean," he answered me. "Why don't you like reading it yourself?"

"Well, I do, but it sounds so much more real when you read it, Pop."
~~~

It was a letter from my mother. She wrote to Sheila and me every week.

"And this letter is different, Pop, I can feel it," I said.

"What do you mean?" he asked, puzzled by my reaction.

"She's coming home, Pop, I know it. I can tell it in her words. Maybe she'll come home for Thanksgiving." I looked at him, hoping for a sign of agreement. He didn't respond.

"Do ya think so, Pop?"

I waited for him to smile and celebrate with me. He didn't.

"I don't know, grandson. Your mom and dad are still talking about a lot of things…"

"No!" I abruptly yelled at him, jumping up from my stool. I picked it up by one leg and threw it across the barn. This wasn't what I wanted to hear.

"You're wrong, Pop. No more talking! She has to come home! You're wrong!" I stormed out of the barn and went to my room. I must have cried for an hour. Pop didn't bother me, never came to my room. I guess he thought it best that I let it all out on my own. He simply didn't have a cure for what ailed me.

Thanksgiving came and went; Christmas, too. My father never mentioned her and mom's letters kept coming with a promise of "Soon, Sean, soon…"

I had stopped believing in Santa Claus and the Tooth Fairy long ago. But by age fourteen, I was ready to add "hope" to the list of things I had lost faith in. The only person left in my world that I trusted was Pop. He never made a promise he couldn't keep and he never lied to me. Never. But neither would he allow me to create delusions that he knew would ultimately disappoint and hurt me more.

On the other hand, my father had become a pariah. I didn't know him, had no awareness of anything to do with his life and didn't give a hoot if he lived or died. The day my mother left —and I still blamed him completely for my mother leaving Sheila and me — was the day he died in my eyes.

Pop was my lifeline. Somehow he kept my spirit alive. Sheila was still too young to understand what was happening, but plenty old enough to miss her mother.

Our time together in the barn had changed a lot since that last night when mom had left. For a long time after, I'd join Pop in the barn after school and we'd sit together for hours on end without uttering more than a few words, none of much consequence. We both carried heavy burdens. He longed for the woman he had loved and lost. I longed for a mother who had seemingly given me away. The love I felt for my aging grandfather hadn't changed. But although we grieved together, we did so for different reasons. He was sad and quiet, in fact becoming more reticent and isolated with each passing day. I was angry and becoming more so with each moment I lived in a broken home.

It was about six months after my mom had left. I was still struggling with how two people, a man and a woman who happened to be husband and wife and parents of two children could suddenly stop loving each other. So I asked Pop. He always seemed to know the answers to such questions.

"Why don't you ask your mother, Sean," he said.

"Huh?" I looked up at him for a clue as to what he meant. "You mean ask her the question in my next letter to her?"

"No, of course not," he replied. "She's probably making dinner... in the kitchen, right now... I mean..."

I shook my head. He was so confused. Mom in the kitchen?

"Pop, Mom's not here. You know that."

"Well, where the hell..." He stopped and looked directly at me, then ran his eyes around the inside of the barn as if trying to remember where he was. Then he stopped and turned to me.

"Ah geez, Sean... I guess I'm just getting old. I seemed to have forgotten for a moment that your mom's not here. Maybe I'm coming down with a cold or something. Haven't been feeling myself, lately."

He was quiet for a little while as if trying to get his bearings. "Have you seen the Mercedes keys, Sean? I looked around this morning, can't seem to find them."

"Uh, no Pop... but why would you want the keys?"

He stared at me again. But this time it was if he didn't know who I was. Then, just as abruptly as his weird behavior had begun, it stopped.

"Oh, just forget about that," he said, laughing out loud. "Sometimes I get the strangest ideas lately. Now what were you asking me?"

I hesitated, studying him to see if he was really all right. He seemed fine.

"Well, I was just wondering how a man and woman like my mom and dad who've been a husband and wife for so long could suddenly stop loving each other."

"Well, I mean...the answer..." The words wouldn't come to him. He looked at the old yellow car and thought about it for a while.

"The truth is... well the truth is..." He shook his head, unable to put his thought together.

"Son, it just happens. People think one thing, they get a little older, they start thinking other things."

"I don't understand," I said.

"Nor should you have to, grandson. But life's full of mysteries, ain't she?" he said in his stark way.

I continued to stare at him, waiting for him to make sense.

He tried again.

"It's like making a promise, Sean," he said. "First you swear to keep it forever. Then a little time and a little distance pass and the promise doesn't seem quite so important. So you don't think about it so much. And pretty soon, you break it. You really didn't mean too, but it just wasn't as important any more."

I looked up at him and shook my head.

"I still don't get it."

He shrugged his shoulders, out of answers.

"I mean, they got married, didn't they?" I asked. "According to Father Mulcahey at Sunday School when you get married you make vows to each other. Didn't my mom and dad make vows?"

He sighed and shook his head.

"Yes, they did Sean."

"But they broke them. They were just lies."

"I don't think they meant to break them, Sean. Life just got a little ahead of both of them," he said. "The vows weren't so important anymore."

"So the whole thing was just bullshit," I said, cursing openly in front of Pop for the first time.

"Sean..."

"It was just bullshit!"

My father walked into the barn at that exact moment.

"Nice mouth, Sean," he said sarcastically. "Is this what your loving grandfather spends his time teaching you?"

"Screw you," I said to his face without hesitation.

He looked like someone had kicked him. I could see red crawling up his neck, the anger in him about to explode.

"What did you say to me?"

"I said screw you!" repeating it with enthusiasm. "Do you want to hear it again?"

Pop buried his head in his hands and groaned. "And don't blame Pop for teaching me how to swear. That's the only thing you've been good at."

"Why you little shit," he bellowed and lunged at me, bent on tanning my hide. Pop didn't hesitate, and although he was more than twenty years older than my father he jumped up from his stool and pushed his son back a half dozen yards away from me. My dad stumbled backwards and fell to the dirt floor. Enraged, he got to his feet and charged at Pop. My grandfather pushed him back again, then stepped forward, grabbed him by the shoulders and threw him to the ground like a rag doll.

Pop stood over his son, lying in the dirt, his fists clenched in anger.

"Get up you coward!" he roared. My father stayed put.

"Come at him again, you weakling... I dare you," Pop said. "You lay a hand on my grandson and I'll take your head off, Sam," Pop said, now remarkably composed but obviously itching for a fight. It was so uncharacteristic of him. "C'mon Sam, let an old fighter pilot show you a few of the tricks he learned in basic training. Why you won't show what's left of your face in a courtroom for a month when I'm done with you. You hear me?"

My father stood up and backed away from him slowly. He looked genuinely frightened.

"C'mon, Sam," Pop repeated, egging my dad on. "Or go in the house and sober up. Now – before you have any more regrets and embarrass yourself in front of your son anymore. And be quiet, Sheila is napping."

My father took a step forward, his fists balled. But it was all for show. He thought better of it quickly.

Instead, he turned his anger towards me.

"Get in the house and go to your room, Sean," he demanded. "And I don't want you hanging around with this sick old bastard every day after school. You hear me? He's not a very good example…"

I laughed out loud at his hypocritical assessment. My laugh stopped him in mid sentence.

"You haven't heard the last of this, wise guy," he said to me, raging. "You're just like your mother. All mouth and no guts."

Blinded by anger that overwhelmed me, I pushed my grandfather aside and charged at my father. I was going to kill him once and for all.

"Take it back, you son of a bitch," I screamed at him. "You forced her to leave…"

Pop came up behind me and grabbed me around the waste, lifting me right off my feet. I was swinging at my father even as he held me.

"Calm down, Sean, calm down," Pop said to me as I flailed away.

"I learned long ago never to waste ammunition on a falling target," he said.

My father's nose was bleeding and he spotted a red stain on his expensive dress shirt. "Now look what you did, you little ingrate," he said to me. Then he turned and without another word walked out of the barn, slamming the door behind him.

Pop put me down and I stood staring at the door. I had finally told my father how I felt about him. My hands were trembling. I began to cry.

Pop wrapped his arms around me and held me close to him.

"It's all right, Sean," he said calmly, "let it out, let it all out."

When I calmed down, we went back to sitting on our stools, huddling close together to stay warm. I was trembling from the emotion of the confrontation and Pop's odd and uncharacteristic behavior. It was very late when we finally made our way back to the house. Pop tucked me into bed and then lay down beside me.

I snuggled under the crook of his arm and fell asleep, taking comfort in knowing he was there.

That night I dreamt about my mother again, remembering the touch of her hand against my face the night she left.

It was a dream I often had that always ended the same. Pop, Sheila and me would be on the front porch waiting for her as she walked up the cobblestone path to our front door, her small suitcase in hand. We were elated at the sight of her and the smile on her face as she came closer made my heart feel like it was going to burst. Then my father would come out of the house and join us on the porch, a scowl lining his face. My mother would stop dead in her tracks at the sight of him.

Then she would shake her head sadly, turn and walk back to the main road where the yellow cab that had taken her away was still waiting. She would get back in the taxi and wave to us as the car pulled away again.

My father would go into the house laughing, a sneering look of satisfaction on his face. Pop would pull Sheila and I close to him and hold us as we cried. He cried too because he couldn't grab hold of his daughter in law and drag her home where she belonged. Where she was needed.

Just like when grandma died, my mother was always just out of his reach. But for a few meager inches, happiness escaped us all.

Seven

Pop never lied to me. And several days later, when I asked him what made my father what he was, he told me. Without pulling a punch.

He came right out and told me that Sam Evans had a reputation for being just about the meanest, orneriest SOB ever known in Willington, and certainly, he was the most miserable human being most people had ever known. As Pop said it, I was ashamed to think of my own father that way, but I was equally ashamed to admit that he was my father.

In the same breath, he was a fine lawyer, Pop said, the kind of attorney people flocked to when they had a real mean score to settle or were in big trouble. He had the reputation of being a pit bull in the courtroom and rarely lost a case. Demand for his representation grew with his years as a member of the Bar.

His success made him a rich man, and the great house we grew up in was something he had bought very early in his career, banking on making Partner in the law firm in which he was employed before he turned thirty. It happened at twenty-nine. The house, an eight room brick Colonial was just short of being a legitimate mansion and the day he carried his young bride across the threshold was one of the happiest of her life. He and my mother, Marnie, who had grown up in Willington, had only been married a couple of years when he bought the house.

Pop told me that my dad had swept my mom off her feet within a matter of months of moving to Willington when he joined his law firm after passing the Connecticut Bar. He was impressed by how his son had seduced my mother – he'd behaved like a guy who'd been around and was full of confidence. My mother was impressed with what she considered my dad's worldly ways – even though he hadn't come from a town much bigger than hers. But four years under scholarship at Dartmouth and three years at Yale Law had indeed changed my father. He was a lot more street smart than Pop ever gave him credit for.

Still, Pop was uneasy about how fast things moved between Sam and Marnie and he worried about their future and the way in which it was beginning. It sure was a far cry from the way he and Ceily had begun life together. By comparison, while his son and fiancé shared candlelit dinners in fine restaurants and weekends in Boston and New York during their whirlwind courtship, Pop and Ceily had held hands in a MASH unit in Korea and connived their way into being together throughout his recovery while they were both still in the military. A celebration dinner for them was a pilfered can of spam with a tin of peaches and maybe a couple of cans of 3.2 "near beer," the only thing they could get in an Army hospital. But for two people who were so in love, it was a veritable feast, even without the candles.

Pop was immensely proud of his son back in those days, he told me. But he worried that life in the "Ivy Leagues" had perhaps inflated Sam's expectations and appetite for the fine and complicated things of life. Still, he saw nothing but love in the way Sam treated Marnie, and he was as excited about their marriage as Ceily was.

After the wedding, Sam neatly coerced Pop and my grandmother to sell their small Maine farm and to come and live with us in Willington. It was one of the reasons he had bought the big old house with the barn to begin with. He wanted his family close to him and couldn't wait for Marnie to give them their own children.

Within a year of moving into the house, I was conceived and Pop told me that my father was ecstatic when I was born. I found that hard to believe, but Pop swore it was true. He told me how my father would relish getting up at all hours of the early morning to feed me as an infant, so thankful for the precious, uninterrupted time he had alone with his son. More than once, Pop recalled, he'd come downstairs in the morning to find my Dad asleep, with me snuggled to his chest, in the big old easy chair in the living room that was his favorite place to relax. He said we both always wore smiles of contentment even in our sleep. When Sheila happened along three years later, the man thought God had truly blessed him and he wasn't afraid to admit it.

For the truth was that my father was a happy, positive and thankful man back in those early days, as good a son, husband and father as there could be. He was a mirror image of his own father, except vastly more educated. But as a man, he was living proof that the apple sometimes doesn't fall far from the tree. For the first ten years of their marriage, my mom and dad couldn't have been any happier.

But then, Sam Evans changed around the time his mother died.

Perhaps it was his work, Pop speculated, the constant demands, long hours and stress that began to sour him. Or the pressure for continued success and victories in the courtroom that continued to build his reputation. Maybe it was the weight of growing the firm that he would eventually lead. Whatever it was, his work kept him from home more and more as the hours in the office continued to increase. Eighty-hour workweeks were not uncommon. It got to the point that his time at home was limited to stopping by for clean clothes. He showered and shaved at the office and most nights ate dinner — if he ate dinner at all —at his desk. He slept on a couch in his office. His obsession for work became an addiction.

Pop said that when my mom confronted him or tried to reason with him, he would explode with anger. She pleaded that his young family needed him, and that she needed him too. She was lonely. Life without him had become desperately unfulfilling and she begged him to come back to them, to live a balanced life where family, work and play were all important. She implored him to examine his priorities and to see that he was throwing his life away and that their future as a family hung in the balance. But he had become a modern day Ebenezer Scrooge, a cold-hearted man who saw pleasure as a waste, and happiness a weakness.

My grandfather said he was so worried about Sam that he secretly went to see a doctor about him. The doctor, a psychiatrist, said that my dad demonstrated symptoms of psychotic hypomania because he was too full of energy and overly, almost obsessively productive in his work. Pop thought that he'd probably come around eventually, mature a bit once he realized how much his family needed him and straighten himself out.

But left to live as he did, Sam's behavior grew increasingly erratic. His mood swings became nearly intolerable, impulsive and angry and on those rare occasions when he did come home, those who once loved him hid from his view and his wrath however possible.

My mother began to act like a church mouse in his presence for fear of unleashing his anger. Privately, she shunned his touch and the little intimacy he was capable of. It was inevitable that he would seek comfort in other ways and places. Alcohol became a staple of his life and paying for the pleasure of a woman's company was the only way he could tolerate and satisfy his need for sex. So long as he paid for affection, he controlled it. There was no room in his life for anything he could not control, including the emotions of his wife and children and his once beloved father. The only person who might have been able to reach him, to remind him of the real priorities of his life, his mother, was gone.

That's what Pop told me. My father had given me no reason to believe that anything my grandfather had said was wrong essentially because he barely acknowledged my existence. It was only years later that I learned there was more to the story.

So, I came to my own conclusions at a fairly young age.

First, no doubt, Sam Evans was mean and proud of it. He wore the distinction with deranged honor.

But second, he was one of the two saddest men alive. His own father was the other. The difference between the two was that my father chose to live his life the way he did, lonely but all-powerful. Ironically, happiness was his for the taking.

On the other hand, my grandfather, the kind John Evans, lived a life of sadness that he had not chosen and that he could not change. Pop, too, had lived many years of happiness with his wife and family. But that was all gone now. Happiness was something he would never experience again – though he would gladly trade every last remaining second of his life for one more day with Ceily.

Eight

~~~

September 1995

The water was rising faster now. A few feet away, across the aisle in the dimming light, he could see a young woman struggling with an infant, trying to squeeze them out of the small opening in the wreckage that could mean their salvation. "I can reach her," he said quickly to Ceily, who was clutching his arm, terrified at the slightest creak and groan that came as the broken machine settled.

"No!", Ceily screamed, begging him. "Don't leave me, John, please don't leave me. We have to get out!"

"We'll be okay," he said to her reassuringly, his voice full of confidence. "It will only take me a moment to free her."

"No, don't..."Ceily screamed, even as her husband kicked off and dove into the frigid water towards the woman.

"John, no, don't... please don't leave me, I'm so afraid," she said feebly, her teeth chattering and her body shaking from cold and shock. She was paralyzed with terror and the freezing water robbed her of strength and hope...

"Pop?"

The voice awoke him from the nightmare that would never go away. He had fallen asleep, hunched over on his stool in the barn. Sean's voice brought him back to reality.

"Pop, you OK?" Sean said, gently rubbing his grandfather's shoulder. "I'm sorry, I didn't mean to wake you."

John Evans rubbed his eyes and dragged a calloused hand across the stubble of his beard.
~~~

"Of course I'm all right, dammit. I was just looking for the keys. Where are the keys?" He said to no one in particular.

He looked around the barn, anger on his face. "Where the hell am I…"

I shook his shoulder harder trying to get him focused.

"Pop, you're in the barn. You fell asleep and you were just having a dream. That's all," I said.

He ran his fingers through his long, unkempt hair and across the stubble of a weeks growth of beard. I don't think he'd had a bath in at least that long.

"Yah?" he asked, sheepishly, starting to come back around.

"Yah, Pop. Everything's OK."

"What time is it, son?"

"Almost six, Pop."

"Six? You're home late today," he said.

"Football practice, Pop. Remember – I'm on the varsity football team."

The old man stared at his grandson for a bit, trying to remember the conversation. He couldn't.

He was still sharp enough to fake it. "How'd it go? You a quarterback yet?" Pop joshed him.

"Nah, I'm a wide receiver, Pop," I said. "I like catching passes and I'm pretty fast. I wish you'd come to a game."

I'd grown a lot in the last year and now stood almost six feet tall. At 170 pounds, I wasn't about to take on many interior lineman, but I could hold my own in a defensive backfield. I was slowly reaching manhood – with the help of the man I admired the most. More than anything, I wanted him to come and see me play. But he always begged off, saying he and crowds didn't get along anymore. The truth was, he never saw anyone outside of me, Sheila and my father. He had become a complete hermit. The only other person he ever communicated with was my mother, in his eternal, secretive efforts to get her to come home for the sake of her children.

I wrote off his growingly odd behavior as "He's just getting old," hard as that was to admit. But somewhere deep inside, I knew there was something else wrong.

I turned and looked at the car. The pile of junk now covering the Mercedes was getting larger by the day. It was almost like he was trying to bury it.

"I thought you were going to clean some of that stuff off today, Pop? Remember, we were thinking about cleaning up the old girl, maybe try to start her?"

He looked puzzled again and a look of annoyance flashed in his eyes. It wasn't like him to lose his temper, but it seemed to be happening more and more often, sometimes for the slightest of reasons.

"I don't recall saying we would try and start her, Sean," he replied, irritation in his voice.

Now I was confused. "It doesn't matter."

I sat down on my stool next to his in silence. I almost said, "What do you mean, it doesn't matter. Of course it matters." But I didn't. It would only hurt his feelings and I could tell Pop was pretty low lately. We hadn't discussed much of any consequence in a long time and we hadn't heard from mom for a few weeks. I needed to hear more of Pop's stories and sustain my own faith, and at the same time, I think it did him good to talk about them.

"You know, Pop," I said, turning to him, "I never would have known how mom and dad fell in love and came to be together if it wasn't for you. But nothing beats the story of you and grandma. Tell me again, please?"

That distant look was in his eyes again. I found it troubling and wondered what he was thinking when he just gazed off into space. Thirty seconds went by before he answered me.

"Again? I already told you how I met Ceily?" he said, a little flustered for no obvious reason. "These days I seem to have a hard time remembering what I've said let alone what really happened and when."

He sighed. It was a deep sigh, the kind that echoed of disappointment and hurt.

"But I'll try."

He looked at me, a bit confused. "I told you about her waiting for me when I got out of surgery?"

"Yup. Grandma was waiting for you when you came out of the operating room in the MASH unit in Korea."

He shook his head.

"It's a bit cloudy now sometimes, exactly what happened. I don't remember a lot about those next few weeks. They were keeping me juiced up with morphine because of the pain of my wounds and burns. I think the next thing I recall with any clarity was waking up in a hospital in Okinawa. That's where they sent the badly wounded guys like me before shipping them home."

"You mean you didn't see grandma again in Korea?" I asked.

"Oh, no… I remember that she spent all of her off duty time with me, caring for me, reading to me and generally making me love her even more. I think the same thing was happening for her. The more time we spent together – in the worst of times and in the worst of places – the more deeply we fell in love…." He suddenly stopped and set his gaze upon the old Mercedes and for no particular reason said, "You know, I have to get that car cleaned up. Ceily would hate seeing it so dirty."

I didn't quite understand that his mind was beginning to play little tricks on him. Every now and then he had difficulty distinguishing the past from the present. He needed to see a doctor, but I didn't know that. I thought he was just looking backwards from time to time.

Just as suddenly, he was back in the present and continuing with his story.

"They hauled me off to Okinawa in the middle of the night aboard a Red Cross plane, and I didn't even get a chance to see or talk to Ceily. I think I threatened just about every doctor, nurse and orderly in the MASH that if I didn't see her I wasn't going on the plane. I'd be damned if I was going to lose the only girl in my life that I'd ever loved to a bunch of starched shirt bureaucrats," he said, and was actually getting worked up over the memory. "That didn't work. The SOB's just knocked me out again and threw me on the plane. I was afraid – Lord, I was terrified – that I'd never see her again.

"Well, I got to Okinawa and a couple of weeks went by without any word from Ceily. I was desperate and ready to go AWOL if I necessary to get back to Korea and find her," he said. Then he laughed at the foolishness of it all. "Problem was I was trapped in a bed, the lower half of my body completely bandaged." He shook his head in sadness. "At that moment in my life I couldn't have cared if I lived or died."

"I'm glad you didn't die, Pop." The very sound of his words sent shivers down my spine. Sometimes I felt like he was all I had – just the way I'm sure he thought about Ceily back then.

"One morning, I'm up early waiting for mail call, hoping and praying that I'd get a letter from her or some news. No such luck. I really didn't know what to do and my heart was breaking."

"It must have been awful, Pop. I mean, being so alone and wounded…"

"Ah, I didn't give a damn about the pain or any of that, Sean, I just wanted your grandmother! Hell, I'd finally found someone who meant something to me and she disappeared right before my eyes…"

He stopped again, abruptly, choking on his words. I didn't know what was happening but some memory had just sucker punched him. Tears poured from his eyes in an instant.

"I didn't mean to leave you, Ceily, I didn't… please come back, won't you? Forgive me?" he said aloud, forgetting I was even there.

He shuddered, and a giant sob heaved from his body. I reached around him and held him tight, just to let him know I was there. I had no idea what was happening to him or what he was thinking.

Minutes went by. They felt like hours. Then a strange glow came over his face and color filled his cheeks. His tears stopped as quickly as they began and a smile came to his face. Something that made him happy had just emerged from his memories. His behavior was downright eerie.

He started up again as if nothing had happened.

"So I'm waiting for mail call and I get nothing. Then I hear all this giggling and ruckus out in the hallway, a bunch of nurses laughing about something." He was telling the story now with joy in his voice.

"All of a sudden, one of the nurses came in, this nice brunette who'd been really great to me and had listened to me whine for weeks. She's got this big, wide grin on her face.

"I said, 'You're wearing that look that says its time to change my bandages.' It was a standing joke that the more agony she caused me the funnier it was. Sounds bizarre but it was a way we all fought the boredom and the pain.

"'Nope,' she says, deadly serious. 'I've got a special delivery package for you. Came in from Korea this morning.'"

I wished I had a camera at that very moment to capture the look on Pop's face.

"The nurse stepped aside, and twenty feet behind her was Ceily, a heavy, army fatigue duffel bag slung over her shoulder, pushing a lock of her glorious red hair from her eyes.

"'Sorry, soldier, I didn't have a chance to fix my hair and make up,'" she said to me, then ran across the room and wrapped herself around me in my hospital bed."

"How'd she get to Okinawa, Pop? Did grandma go AWOL?" I asked.

"No, by God, she arranged a transfer from her MASH unit just to join up with me. I don't know how she did it, but she managed it all right. I swear… to this day I can remember how my heart went flip flop when I saw her. Most beautiful sight I'd ever seen."

His eyes were wet again.

"We celebrated that night with all the nurses on duty stopping by, dropping off a couple cans of near beer for the two of us and the other wounded guys in my ward. Best party I've ever been to. But then again, I had my arm around the prettiest girl in the room. I never went anywhere with her again where that wasn't true."

"You really loved her, didn't you Pop?"

He didn't answer right away, his eyes drifting off to stare at the car.

"Sean… I had never loved a woman before… and I have never loved another since," he said solemnly. "I could never love another woman like I loved your grandmother. If a man is lucky, it happens to him once in a lifetime. Women call if finding your 'soul mate.' I see it a little differently. I always thought that your grandmother gave me a soul."

I thought about what he had said and was puzzled.

"She's gone now, Pop," I said.

He nodded slowly in resignation.

"Did she take your soul with her?"

He pondered that for a while.

"I'm afraid so, grandson," he said, hanging his head. "But it's the price I pay every day…for letting go of her hand."

He brought his right hand to his face and stared at it.

"God forgive me…

"For letting go of her hand."

With that he drifted off for good, and was unreachable. His thoughts were somewhere where I couldn't join him.

What had happened to my grandmother, why she had died, was the best-kept secret in our home. No one would talk to me about it.

Whatever had happened was so painful that it occupied my grandfather's every conscious moment. I wondered if he dreamed about it.

It wasn't long before I found the answer.

Nine

Late that night, the old man quietly got up from his bed, slipped on his robe and slippers and walked out to the barn. He had been dreaming, again, of that wonderful day more than thirty years before, when he and Ceily had made their precious find.

He sat on his familiar stool and listened for a moment, making sure no one had followed him. This was a moment he needed to relive alone, a time that so captured Ceily's spirit he could barely stand to recall it, let alone recount it.

He looked at the car, and in his mind the mountains of rubbish that were now piled on the old car, almost burying the sweet memories that her miles could tell, disappeared in his mind. He drifted back to that afternoon in the farmer's field in the summer of 1961.

It was a total rust bucket.

One look at it from fifty feet away and I wondered what we were thinking to have driven so far to see a frigging wreck. A basket case. I should have known better than to trust a magazine ad.

But I quickly discovered I was alone in my reaction. Ceily didn't quite see it the same way. In fact, she didn't see it my way at all.

"John," she said breathlessly. "This is the one. It's beautiful. Just look at her lines." She ran to get closer.

"What?" I said, dumbfounded by her reaction.

We had driven all the way to Millerton, a small village of less than seven hundred people in upstate New York from our coastal farm in Westbrook, Maine, a more than three hundred and fifty mile, five and a half hour drive in our old Ford pickup over bad roads. It was a long way to come dragging a trailer that we thought would be carrying a treasure on the way home. Was I ever wrong. Or so I thought.

Somewhere beneath the rust, dirt, hay and weeds covering the car, lying uncovered and all but abandoned on the edge of a line of Sycamore trees lining a crop field, was a classic 1955 Mercedes Benz 190sl. The farmer who owned it pointed to it from the back of his barn and said "There she is, just like I advertised," with a straight face. The ad had read "Some repairs may be necessary."

"She's a mighty purty shade of yellow, don't'cha think, son?" he added. I couldn't tell what color the car was. There was so much rust you would have thought it was brown.

Ceily was putting her back into getting the driver's side door open by the time I caught up with her, her excitement showing all over her face. She was ecstatic at the find.

"This is exactly the car I've dreamed of," she said, her voice an octave higher with exhilaration. "Can't you just see us taking her out for long drives and trips along the coast, John? Why I would positively feel like Grace Kelly in this car."

Ever since she'd seen the elegant Princess of Monaco driving Frank Sinatra around in the movie "High Society" a year before, Ceily had set her heart on owning one of the little two-seat luxury roadsters. It was a dream we hardly could afford with the cost of the German sports car at over four thousand dollars. That was a new pickup and a big chunk of the mortgage paid off.

But, she reasoned, if we were able to find a used one, an older model that needed "some" work, maybe we could pull it off.

They said Helen of Troy was so beautiful that her face had launched a thousand warships. Well, I didn't own a single rowboat, but the look on Ceily's face when she revealed her plan to me was all it took for me to sign up. And off we went searching for our mystical Mercedes, something that needed a "little" bit of work.

Now mind you, I was pretty good with my hands, and having earned an engineering degree had a fair understanding of how mechanical things worked. The thought of putting a few hours into fixing up some foreign jalopy didn't intimidate me. Until I saw her.

While Ceily squeezed her trim figure into the driver's seat of the Mercedes under the appreciative gaze of the farmer, I took a serious inventory of the car.

I found it hard to believe that an automobile with such potential value had been parked so haphazardly in an open field and turned into a hotel for mice, rabbits, snakes and whatever else crawled or slithered around the fields of Millerton. The farmer explained that for some reason, the car, which he had won in a card game with a hapless tourist some years before, had inexplicably become impossible to shift. Its four-speed transmission had all but locked up. With the demands to keep his forty-year-old John Deere tractor running of much greater consequence to him than fixing a mostly useless two-seat sports car, the choice of priorities was a no brainer. He just never got around to covering it, he explained.

The body (I had done my homework, researching the car as much as possible in the Westbrook Library) of this Teutonic engineering marvel employed a monocoque design – meaning it didn't have a separate frame at all like most American built autos of the time. The body and frame were all one piece. It was an interesting, if not genuine automotive design breakthrough, but the structural integrity of the body was that much more critical. This one was full of holes – and those were only the holes I could see. I could only imagine what the floors looked like.

There was virtually no paint left on the car, the sun and elements having sandblasted the finish right off the metal body and corroded the aluminum doors, trunk lid and bonnet, the front windscreen was cracked, the canvas convertible top nearly extinct and the copious chrome trim bits that at one time highlighted the sensuous curves of the car's sleek design were pitted and dulled – where they weren't rusted through or missing completely.

Fearfully, I opened the engine bonnet, the squawk of ungreased hinges fighting every inch of progress. One look at the motor, a small four-cylinder, aluminum block, dual carbureted, water cooled design told me she wouldn't turn over if I dropped a stick of dynamite down a cylinder. Only the Lord knew what was lurking inside the transmission.

The nose of the car was virtually gone, only the headlight buckets remaining to confirm there had been a nose on the car when it was born. Inside, the leather seats were ripped and torn, mouse nests littered every nook and cranny, the smell of urine and feces was overpowering and the wool carpeting had all but disappeared. It made great stuffing for animal nests.

Despite what I saw, the grin on Ceily's face spread from ear to ear. What she saw was romance, intrigue and adventure. What I saw was a victim of the black plague.

"Ceily," I begged, "you must be joking..."

"It will take some work, I know," she said without hesitation, a little bit of her smile fading at my cynicism.

"A little?" I said sarcastically.

She walked up to me slowly and gave me a kiss on the cheek. "Please?"

Three hundred dollars later, the car had been literally dragged on to the trailer by the farmer's John Deere and we were headed back home to Maine.

My own wicked Helen of Troy sat next to me in the front seat of the pickup and every couple of minutes would turn and look out the back window at our "prize."

I thought she had lost the plot. But when you love someone the way I loved Ceily, the craziness and impossibility of her dream only made me that much more determined to fulfill it.

We laughed at the insanity of it all the way home and argued about where we would take our first drive. I said down the street.

She looked me right in the eyes, and without blinking said she had somewhere a little more romantic in mind.

"Where?" I challenged her.

She smiled a smile I can still see today.

"If you use your imagination Mr. John Evans, you will find that Paris is just a little farther down the street from our house!"

"Oh," I laughed and memorized the flash of excitement on her face.

"Then it would seem the world is at our door, Mrs. Evans. All we have to do is get the bloody thing to run!"

Ten

Sam Evans pulled his black Jaguar Vanden Plas sedan into the backyard well after midnight and immediately noticed the lights in the barn had been left on. Again.

"Damn that old coot," he said aloud, exhausted from another eighteen-hour day and angry to the core. "I've told that son of a bitch to turn the lights off in that shack a million times."

He sat in the car for several minutes and fantasized about burning the barn down, with the old Mercedes in it, just to get back at his father.

"It would break his heart," he said to himself.

"Just like he broke mine."

He got out of the Jag and walked into the barn expecting it to be empty. His father was sitting on his stool staring at the car like he did for hours every day.

Sam Evans lost it.

"What are you doing, old man? Have you lost your mind? You know what time it is? Is Sean in here with you?" He barked at his father in rapid-fire succession.

John Evans slowly turned to see his son standing at the door, holding his suit jacket and a briefcase. Without acknowledging his presence, he turned back to what he was doing. The snub only infuriated Sam more.

"Answer me, damn you. I asked you, is Sean in here with you?"

"No."

"Where is he?"

"He's in bed were he ought to be," my grandfather replied.

"If you were a decent father, you might know where your son was in the middle of the night. Or if you hadn't driven his mother away, she might be taking care of him. As it is, I'm the only one who seems to care what he's up to."

The briefcase came flying through the air, aimed directly at John Evan's head. He dodged and it sailed by, bursting open against a wall and scattering the contents of legal papers and briefs all over the barn.

"Why you hypocrite!" Sam screamed. "Who are you to judge me? If it weren't for you, my mother might be here to take care of Sean and Sheila, did you ever think of that?"

"The old man sighed and looked up at the car.

He didn't answer right away, letting his son stew in his anger and pushing down his own grief. Tears were welling in his eyes

"You're too full of hatred to know that I never stop thinking about her, Sam. Not for one second of any day," my grandfather said. "You needn't waste the energy it takes to hate me just to remind me of why your mother is no longer with us, son.

"I never stop thinking about it, " he repeated while slowly raising his right hand up before his face. In the gloomy light of the dimly lit barn, his upraised arm cast a bizarre shadow across the room, exaggerating the size of his hand. He stared at it and wondered if cutting it off would make the pain – and the memory – go away. He knew the answer.

"Never."

Eleven

"So, we got married the next day in Okinawa, me tied to a bed and your grandmother barely unpacked from her transfer from the MASH unit," Pop told me a couple of days later. "We were a pretty odd couple, I'll tell you." He laughed out loud.

"And it was the daffiest wedding reception you ever saw. The guests were all doctors and nurses we hardly knew and guys in hospital beds or wheel chairs that were all recovering from some kind of combat calamity. It was different, and certainly not the kind of wedding a bride dreams of. But your grandmother couldn't have cared less. We were together, that's all that mattered."

I tried to imagine the scene. The vision that kept popping up in my head was something akin to that of a circus. But it made Pop happy when he told the story.

"It was the only way," he continued. "I was about to get shipped back stateside for continued treatment at a VFW Hospital in Brooklyn and your grandmother would have been stuck on assignment in Okinawa unless she became my wife. So, we got married. January of 1952."

He looked at me, my eyes glued to him as he told the story. He laughed softly.

"Best day of my whole life, Sean," he said. "Best day ever. I married my dream girl."

The sun was setting. It was late afternoon and there was an early fall chill in the air. Pop was tired. It didn't take much to wear him out any more. He reached into his pocket and took a little drink from the pint of whiskey he carried with him all the time. I noticed that he didn't drink as much anymore, though. It was almost as if talking about grandma made him forget about the whiskey.

"Tell me just a little more, Pop… please?"

He leaned down and tousled my hair.

"You're insatiable, you know that you damned teenager?" he laughed. But I think he was happy for the excuse to talk about grandma just a little longer.

"Well, your grandmother and I were shipped home a couple of weeks later. I spent two more months in the Brooklyn VA Hospital – a horrible place – but then got discharged from the Air force. Aside from some bad burn scars, a couple of bullet wounds that still ache when it rains and some bad dreams, I left that hospital and the Air Force in pretty good shape. And I had won the ultimate prize for my service as a combat pilot."

"You got a medal? A Purple Heart? A Bronze Star?" I demanded, all worked up at the thought of my grandfather festooned with medals from the bravery of his exploits.

He frowned.

"Yah, they gave me a couple of medals," he said, frowning with disappointed at my interpretation.

"It was your grandmother that was the grand prize. If not for being shot down over Korea and damned near burning and bleeding to death, she never would have become my wife. Hell, I'd do it all over again to win her love."

He wiped at his eyes and stared at the car. I was surprised to notice that he had cleared away some of the junk from the driver's door while I was at school. It might actually be possible to squeeze behind the steering wheel with a little effort.

"Then what did you do?"

"For cryin' out loud... what are you? My biographer? I'm not that interesting, Sean," he said, smiling.

"Yes you are Pop," I said and hugged him. "Yes you are."

He stopped the conversation and began rocking back and forth on his stool. Leaning over, he looked at each of the legs then stood up and examined the bottom of the seat.

"God dammit, Sean," he cursed.

"What?" I said in surprise.

"Did you switch stools on me? You know how I like my stool more than yours."

"I didn't touch the stools, Pop," I replied, shaking my head. "Will you stop acting so crazy and finish the story?"

"You sure about the stool? And you didn't take the keys to the Mercedes?"

"Why would I possibly want the keys to the Mercedes?"

"Well. Now that you have a girlfriend, I thought you might be sneaking her out for rides in the old car."

I thought he was kidding and laughed. "I don't have a girlfriend."

"Don't laugh, Sean, " he said, deadly serious. "That car meant a lot to grandma and me. I don't want you out racing around in her."

I held my tongue and didn't mention the fact that the car had four flat tires.

"Trust me, Pop. I haven't touched the car," I said. "Now, can you stop acting nuts and finish your story? Please?"

He sized me up for a minute, staring into my eyes to see if I was lying.

"Well, all right. Just don't touch the car is all."

I shook my head in agreement.

Finally he got back on track.

"If you must know, neither one of us had any family to speak of, so we decided to find a place to live out in the country. Someplace far away from war and Army hospitals and all the ugly things we had both seen over the last couple of years. We each took out a VA loan and bought a little farm in Westbrook, Maine, right near the coast."

"Were you…"

"Yes, Sean, we were very happy," he interrupted, reading my mind.

"Now I wasn't much of a farmer, nor was your grandmother. We grew some vegetables, but that's about it. I got a job in a small engineering firm working on roads and bridges and your grandma went to work with the local doctor as his assistant. It was perfect. We had everything we needed, and by God, we were in love."

"Is that when my father was born?"

Pop suddenly looked sad. "Yup, your dad joined us just before Christmas that same year. We were best buddies, your dad and I."

There was more to be said there but he didn't want to talk about it. The conversation ground to a halt while Pop went off somewhere else with his thoughts. He closed his eyes for a few minutes and I almost thought he was asleep. Then he just blurted it out.

"Next thing I knew, we bought it."

"It?" I asked, confused. "What did you buy, Pop?" I asked, not knowing where he was coming from.

"That thing over there," he said pointing to the car. "The whatchamacallit."

"The what?" I said, completely perplexed.

He got red in the face from the frustration of not being able to think of the word.

I looked at where he was stabbing at the air with his finger.

"You mean the car, Pop?"

He threw up his hands in utter exasperation.

"Yes, the stupid damned car," Pop replied. "Why the hell couldn't I think of that word," he asked himself.

"Well, anyway," he proceeded, as if nothing odd had happened, "it was the most moth eaten, rat infested, rusted out hunk of junk this side of the Mississippi. Your grandmother fell in love with it and talked me into buying it."

I looked at the car. It was in pretty sorry shape after having been parked in the same spot since 1982. I wondered how much worse it could have been thirty years ago.

"Why did you let her?" I said innocently. "Was she mad at you for some reason and you were trying to make her happy again?"

He laughed out loud at that.

"Well, I'll be. It didn't take you long to figure out how to get out of the doghouse, did it," he said, still chuckling. "You sure you don't have a girlfriend you haven't told me about?"

I looked down at the ground and pushed the dirt around with the toe of my sneaker. "Well…"

"Ha!" he laughed again. "Now all I've been telling you about love isn't such a mystery anymore, is it boy?"

I was embarrassed.

"Sometimes girls can be pretty confusing," I said, hoping to change the subject.

Pop picked up on my discomfort. He was old, but still smart enough to know that my hormones were probably going crazy about now.

I quickly changed the subject.

"Tell me about the car," Pop.

"I can't find the keys," he said. He had become fixated on finding the Mercedes ignition keys, almost to the point of obsession. No one had seen them in years.

"Forget about the keys, Pop, I'll help you find them."

"Promise?"

"Yah," I said to get it off his mind. "Did you really buy it because grandma wanted it?" I asked.

"Yes…trust me," he nodded his head vigorously. "That's the only reason. I just couldn't say no to that woman."

"Why did she want it?"

He hesitated, and as so often happened now, his eyes watered up. It took him a few minutes to answer. I waited patiently.

"Because she had dreams," he said. "And an imagination more vivid than any human being I've ever known."

He paused momentarily.

"And I bought it because I wanted to make her dreams come true."

There were times when the noise of the wind whispering through the cracks in the barn boards and the holes in the cedar roof, the rustling of the critters who lived in secret nests among the straw and junk piled high all over, and even the birds chirping atop the open rafters all suddenly stopped – replaced by dead silence.

This was one of those moments.

Twelve

"Shall we take her out for her first road test, co-pilot?" the old man dreamed.

""Why, Commander Evans, do you think she's ready?" Ceily said with unmistakable delight, acting the part of a spoiled debutante.

"I do believe so, Mrs. Evans. I'm not sure she's ready for that excursion to Paris yet, but around the block might be in order. You up for the challenge?"

"Try and stop me, fly boy," his beautiful wife growled, switching to her practiced vamp routine. She certainly made life interesting. "Do you know how long I've been waiting for this day? Sammy is safely tucked into his crib for his nap and the baby sitter arrived right on time. So what are we waiting for? "

The car was finished. The drive train rebuilt, the body once again as elegant as it's designers had originally envisioned, it's yellow paint and black leather coachwork reworked to perfection.

"She is beautiful, my love," said Ceily. "Even Grace Kelly would be pleased. Maybe even a bit jealous. You've done a remarkable job, my remarkable husband. You really are my hero."

"With a little help from my friend," he smiled and kissed her on the lips. Ceily had ruined her manicured nails on more than one thankless project since the day they had purchased the wreck from the New York State farmer who thought he'd stumbled on the two biggest suckers ever born. The last laugh was on him.

John Evans opened the passenger door of the yellow Mercedes 190sl roadster and invited her to take a seat with a grand flourish.

"Your chariot awaits, my Lady," he said, grinning like a schoolboy.

With his precious passenger safely buckled into the car, he jogged around to the driver's side and like a college boy, hopped over the closed door, forgetting the pain of stretching the hardened scar tissue on his legs. He grimaced.

Ceily was unsympathetic.

"That will teach you to act your age," she said, laughing.

"Qui, qui, Madame," he agreed.

"Ready?" he said, as he grasped the ignition key and turned to Ceily, waiting for her nod.

"Ready!" she shot back fearlessly, holding up two sets of crossed fingers.

He turned the key. Instantly the twin synchronized Solex carburetors roared to life and the elegant purr of the motor was almost symphonic to the former fighter pilot.

"Well, no flames, no explosions. Good start," he jested to a beaming Ceily.

Dropping the clutch, he gently shifted the classic Mercedes into first gear and slowly engaged the gear. Smoothly, without the slightest slippage, the car moved forward.

"Oh what the hell," he yelled with abandon and ripped through the remaining three gears, winding out each to near red line on the huge tachometer behind the steering wheel.

"Easy, cowboy, this isn't an F-86!" Ceily yelled over the roar as the car quickly picked up speed and was cruising at sixty miles per hour in a little over twelve seconds.

"Listen," he said to his wife.

"To what?"

"To the sound of no parts going crash, boom or ouch!" he laughed. "By jove, we've done it, Mrs. Evans."

At that precise moment, the car coughed and died. Evans sheepishly pulled the car over to the curb. His brow furled, he began checking off potential reasons for the abrupt end to their test drive.

He began with the analytical approach of a forensic engineer.

"It could be the coil, or maybe a blocked gas line, or – oh Jesus, maybe we busted the camshaft. That means we probably threw a rod, broke a piston, carved up the head and busted valves and springs…"

"Or maybe we ran out of gas,"Ceily said, tapping on the small gauge on the dashboard which read precisely zero pounds of pressure.

"No… it can't be," John Evans said, mortified.

The expression on her face turned deadly serious. "Well, I'm not a college educated engineer, a former Air Force combat jet fighter pilot with two confirmed kills, a winner of the Purple heart and the Bronze Star…but I've got a strong feeling this gas gauge might give us a strong clue as to the problem. And we won't have to sell the farm to fix it."

They both burst out laughing. He leaned over and wrapped his arms around his wife who kissed his cheek.

"Flip ya for who walks to the gas station for a little go-go juice?" she asked, choosing not to rub any more salt in the wound.

"Hell, I'll go," Evans said. "It's my fault. But I'm sorry to tell my Lady that we may not get to Paris tonight. She was running so well, I thought we'd give her a go."

"You are forgiven, my love. Just because you're stupid doesn't mean I don't love you." The brilliance of the smile on her face would have challenged a full moon.

He got out of the car and began walking as she waited in the car. No more than ten yards up the road, he turned and stopped.

"Grace, promise me you're not going to give my seat to Frank Sinatra if he comes by?"

She was silent.

He waited. Nothing.

"Well?"

"I'm thinking, I'm thinking," she teased.

"Oh yah?" he said, running back to the car. "Well, just for that, you're coming with me for this little five mile walk."

"Why?" she said, not so amused.

"Ha!" he said. "First, so no handsome stranger steals my girl while I'm gone."

She smirked. "And? Second?" she asked.

"Second, I get the chance to hold your hand on a nice long walk and show off the best looking girl in all of Westbrook."

Ceily beamed and stepped out of the car.

"I'm all yours, Mr. Evans," she said and took up his hand.

He pulled her fingers to his lips and lightly kissed each one.

"I don't have to worry about Frank Sinatra?" he asked.

"Just so long as I don't have to worry about Grace Kelly, old boy."

~~~

He awoke from the dream, desperately trying to hold unto the joy it had brought to him in his sleep. Despite his efforts, slowly the image of Ceily, the touch of her hand and the laughter in her voice dissolved into the reality that she was gone. And once again, he was left without her.

Quietly, he slipped out the back door and into the barn. He slowly approached the car, sitting as it had for more than the last decade. It occurred to him that it was gradually returning to the forlorn shape in which he
~~~

and Ceily had discovered it, but this time he was powerless to stop its demise.

Squeezing the rusted button on the door handle, he pulled opened the driver's side door and carefully, for fear of waking up more memories, slipped behind the steering wheel. It was the first time in thirteen years that he had entered the car. He grasped the wheel with his left hand and took hold of the gear shift with his right. Then, looking at the empty passenger seat, he gently rubbed his hand over the broken leather where his beloved wife had patiently sat for so many hours over so many miles and through so many fantasies. The emptiness of the seat and the roughness of its worn hide shocked him. He leaned forward and rested his head against the steering wheel, tears coming to his eyes before he could begin to process the emotions, which were tearing at his heart and causing stress it couldn't take.

"Ceily," he begged. "Forgive me. Please come back and hold my hand." Then he closed his eyes and prayed that God would come for him at that very moment.

God was only half listening that particular night. The old man slipped into unconsciousness.

Two hours later, a frantic Sean, who never left for school without a chat and a hug from his Pop, found his grandfather slumped over the steering wheel of the old Mercedes and screamed hysterically for his father to help. Sam Evans, for once in his life, put his own feelings aside and saw the look of terror in his son's eyes. He called 911 and embraced the boy until the ambulance arrived.

Then he actually called the office and said he wouldn't be in.

He needed to be with his family.

Thirteen

"Your father has had a moderately severe heart attack, Mr. Evans. It's hard to tell, but if I had to guess I would suggest that it was brought on by a combination of stress and depression. Is he being treated for either?"

"No," I responded without giving my father an opportunity to respond. He wouldn't have known the answer anyway. My throat was dry and my hands were clammy. I hated hospitals and the sterility of the environment. It made me so uptight. I wished we were home in the barn.

"Well," he continued, "the good news is that Mr. Evans will recover with rest and medication. I see no requirement for surgery of any type at this point. But if stress or depression are issues we should address those as well."

I was standing next to my father at Hartford Hospital, and the cardiologist who had treated Pop, Dr. Charles St. Pierre, was giving us his prognosis. A wave of relief flooded through my veins when he said the magic words, "He will recover." Sheila held unto my arm, quietly sobbing. I was having a hard time holding back the tears myself.

But the doctor wasn't finished.

"However, I have another concern that I think you should be aware of."

Ever the wise guy, my father couldn't keep his mouth shut.

"If you're about to tell us that he's suffering from being a terminal pain in the ass, we already know there's no pill to help." He laughed at his own joke. No one else seemed to enjoy it.

St. Pierre looked at him with barely concealed disdain. I didn't handle it as well.

"Shut up, Dad, this isn't the time or place," I said. The look on my face told him not to mess with me at that moment. I was eighteen and a foot taller than him. One more word out of his mouth at that moment and I would have put him in a bed in the hospital.

"Daddy, be quiet!" Sheila added, embarrassed but like me not surprised by his behavior.

"My concerns were first raised in conversations with Mr. Evans as we were treating him," the doctor said. "At times in our talk, he was very confused and disoriented, neither typical of post myocardial infarction events. However, he demonstrated acute dehydration and is malnourished…"

"Malnourished?" I said, shocked. "You mean he's not eating?"

"If he is, he is not eating regularly and is in a severely weakened state as a result of his poor diet alone," the doctor responded. "And I'm sure I don't have to tell you that his personal hygiene is not being tended to."

My father let loose.

"For Christ's sake, he's a grown man. He's not a child – we shouldn't have to worry about feeding him and making sure he's had his bath," he said sarcastically.

Without thinking, I reached over and grabbed my father by the throat and squeezed. His eyes began to bulge as he struggled to free himself. If Sheila and the doctor hadn't pulled me off him, I would have choked the son of a bitch to death with my bare hands.

Correctly surmising the family situation, Dr. St. Pierre motioned to a nearby security guard. The guard, who had witnessed the incident and had already taken a step forward approached quickly and grabbed me by the arm, ready to haul me away.

"No, you misunderstand my intention, officer," the doctor said. "I think it is in everyone's best interest if Attorney Evans is escorted somewhere where he might be able to take a 'time out.' By his behavior, I believe he is under duress and therefore incapable of behaving like an adult. "

My father flew into a rage.

"Why you..." he sputtered for words in his anger. "Why, I'll have your license, do you understand me?"

"Or," St. Pierre continued in a calm, professional manner, "I have the authority to have Attorney Evans placed under a 5150 psychiatric hold here at the hospital." He stared my father directly in the eyes. Not many people had the nerve to do that.

"This will place him in a maximum security isolation unit for anywhere from two to six weeks or until I am convinced he is no longer a danger to himself or others. No judge in the world will overrule my decision."

The guard smiled and released my arm. Grinning, he grabbed hold of my father.

"Mr. Evans, the choice is yours. But I do think you'll find the reception area very comfortable."

"You haven't heard the last of this," was all my father could muster. "I'll own you and this frigging hospital before this is over." St. Pierre ignored him.

"Interesting," the doctor commented as my father was led away. "A man of his intellect with such anger issues. And if I recall, when he first arrived here with you, he was a model of concern for you both. If I was a psychiatrist, he would be a fascinating study in contradictory emotions. Or as we might say in the Doctor's lounge, a 'head case.'" He quickly realized the inappropriateness of what he had said and apologized.

Sheila said it for me. "No need for apologies, Doctor. You don't know the half of it. Thank you for intervening."

"My pleasure. My best friend is an otolaryngologist, more commonly known as an ear, nose and throat specialist," he laughed quietly. "I would hate to have had to call him this late in the day to come and repair your father's crushed larynx." He looked at me and then at my hands.

"You play football, son?"

"Yes sir," I answered.

"Thought so. Strong hands. Now, perhaps we should get back to your grandfather."

"Please," I said.

"If you add up all of what I told you in regards to his symptoms and my own observations, I believe your grandfather is experiencing symptoms of mild dementia, and unfortunately, the early or moderate onset of Alzheimer's disease."

Sheila let out an audible gasp and covered her mouth with a hand. I felt my shoulders droop and dropped my head. I thought he was invincible.

"I'm sorry," St. Pierre said. "Of course, I may be wrong and the truth is there is no single test to diagnose Alzheimer's. It is a progressive disease, and if I am correct in my prognosis, it is impossible for me to tell you as we stand here to what degree the disease has progressed. It is my assumption that it is has advanced to somewhere in the moderate stage.

"Alzheimer's?" I challenged the doctor. "That's for old people. He's only sixty-five. And you should hear him tell a story."

"Sean? May I call you Sean?" he asked. I nodded.

"Neither age or any single set of behaviors are necessarily indicators of Alzheimer's disease," he said. "I've known people in their early fifties who have succumbed to the disease who weren't even capable of nodding their head to communicate when the disease finally took them. It can strike over a wide range of age and the symptoms can be radically different for each individual."

He paused, collecting his thoughts, and as it turned out, his own emotions.

"I do know how difficult this is to hear; I have some experience with the disease in my own family. My father died of it less than five years ago. It is a progressive disease, as I said, and it is ultimately fatal. But the rate at which it advances can be all over the place."

""Fatal?" Sheila repeated, shocked.

"I'm afraid so, my dear," he said, sighing deeply. "Alzheimer's is a brain disease that causes a slow decline in memory, thinking and reasoning skills. Ultimately, the brain deteriorates to the point where it no longer communicates with vital organs and functions of the body leading to death."

Sheila and I were silent for a moment. I held her hand.

"What's next?" I asked, dreading his words.

"Well first of all we have to get him physically well from the effects of the heart attack and then proceed with a battery of tests to determine the stage of progression of Alzheimer's. That will involve a whole host of tests and interviews involving his medical history and a complete physical examination to determine if there are other possible causes of the dementia. But we will also conduct mental status tests and brain imaging through a CAT scan – short for Computerized Axial Tomography, which is a long-winded way of saying it gives us three-dimensional images of the brain. We will also need to spend considerable time with the two of you, and your father if he is willing, to gather your observations of his behavior. We'll start all this tomorrow morning after he's had a good night's rest."

We nodded.

""Can we see him now, Doc?" I asked.

"Yes," he replied, "But be cautious. We do not want to upset him in any way at the moment. No stress, under any circumstances. My advice is to give him a kiss and a hug and be on your way, tell him you'll see him tomorrow. OK?"

Sheila and I made our way to the Intensive Care Unit of Hartford Hospital and walked quietly into Pop's room. He was lying in bed with his eyes closed and looked very comfortable considering all that had happened. He was hooked up to a lot of scary looking monitors and had intravenous tubes and a catheter. I touched his hand. He immediately opened his eyes.

"Hey, Sam, did you find the keys?" he asked me, mistaking me for his son.

I felt like I'd been punched. Tears welled up in my eyes. Sheila turned away.

"It's Sean, Pop, not Sam. You're a little dopier than usual because of the medicine the doctor is giving you. You're going to be all right, everything is going to be OK." I smiled at him, doing my best to act like everything was fine.

"I need to get home," he said. "Ceily will be so upset if she sees the car so dirty."

"Don't worry about it, Pop," I said. "Sheila and I will go home and wash it for you. Grandma will never know."

He smiled and fell asleep.

We left him after each giving him a peck on the cheek, then stopped in the reception area to pick up my father. He was strangely quiet. We drove home in absolute silence. He never asked what the doctor had said.

When we got home, I went out to the barn, switched on the lights and stood and stared at the car for the longest time. It meant to so much to him – and now to me. After a while, I made my way to our stools and sat down on mine, remembering how particular he was about whose was whose.

I heard a noise behind me. It was my father.

He didn't say anything but slowly made his way to where I was sitting. He went to sit on Pop's stool but I stopped him.

"No, don't you dare sit there," I said. I got up and grabbed an old wooden chair from some of the junk Pop had removed from the stuff covering the Mercedes and placed it on the other side of my stool.

"Sit here if you want. You don't deserve the stool."

To my amazement, he didn't argue, just followed orders. And there he sat with me for the next two hours in complete silence. When I finally got up to go inside and write to my mother about what had happened, he stayed behind, sitting in his chair.

As I walked back to the house it occurred to me that my father was finally where he deserved to be.

Alone.

Fourteen

~~~

November 1995

Pop spent the better part of the next two weeks in the hospital recovering from his heart attack and undergoing the extensive battery of tests prescribed by Dr. St. Pierre and a team of specialists in the treatment of Alzheimer's disease. To say that he was not a happy camper would be a gross understatement. He was miserable. It got worse.

From the hospital, he was transferred to a rehab facility, a place right in Willington where Sheila and I visited him every day. But he hated it. He missed the barn and his stool, and of course, the old Mercedes.

The diagnosis of Alzheimer's was on the money. Pop's affliction had advanced, as St. Pierre's instincts had initially told him, to a moderate level. Things would only get worse and he was going to need a lot of attention and care. Handholding and watching were probably more accurate descriptions. I asked Sheila whether we should tell him or not.

"What purpose would it serve?" Sheila asked. "He's already so depressed and confused, this might just give him motivation to wish himself to death. I say we keep it to ourselves." I agreed. We both told my father to keep his mouth shut. Again, strangely, he didn't argue.

Several weeks after Pop entered the rehab facility, my father disappeared late one Saturday morning under
~~~

the pretense of going into the office. He had never visited his father while he was in the hospital and had not indicated any intention of visiting him at the rehab center. But later that afternoon, Sheila and I drove over for our daily visit. As we were about to enter Pop's room, I heard a familiar voice. It was my Dad's. He was reading to my father. I stopped dead in my tracks, stunned.

"What the hell?" I said to Sheila in the hallway, losing any sense of decorum. "Where did that come from?"

"I don't know," she said, as perplexed as I was. "They've been at war since right after I was born. Maybe Daddy's going crazy too…"

"Hell. He's been nuts for years."

"Calm down, Sean," she begged me. "People change, miracles happen. Who knows? Let's just leave it alone and see what happens."

We left without disturbing them. Later that night, my father came home and went right into his library, which doubled as his office and closed the door. He never said a word to either of us. A half hour later he emerged from his cave, his eyes red-rimmed, the smell of scotch on his breath.

"Come in here you two, please," he said, atypically in a voice that was actually an invitation rather than a demand. It was not a room either of us was very familiar with. This was not the place you wanted to have a conversation with my Dad. This is where he practiced being the world's biggest jerk.

The walls were lined with elegantly handcrafted mahogany bookshelves, which were filled with legal tomes. His desk was an historical antique, said to have belonged to Calvin Coolidge when he was President of the United States. The floors were covered in fine oriental rugs and there was a fully stocked bar by a sitting area of expensive leather chairs. A mahogany table fit for the Boardroom of a Fortune Ten corporation was the centerpiece of the large room.

Many a deal had been done here, and many a lawyer had paid a price for taking on my father in this room. The place reeked of power, arrogance and anger. I hated it. The only time I had ever been invited inside was to be berated for my schoolwork or some other childhood crime that he could not tolerate.

Today there was an open bottle of scotch on his desk and an empty glass. His briefcase lay closed beside it. There were no court documents, briefs or legal papers in sight. He had not been working. I wondered what he'd been doing other than drinking.

Despite his tone, I walked in with a mindset of being ready to do whatever battle he had in mind. I despised him. It was that simple. Sheila followed me, but she was so different. She'd watched my mother tiptoe around him for years and that was the only way in which she knew how to deal with my father. Hide from him. If I wasn't there, I think she would have run to her room and locked the door. These last weeks without Pop around to act as her perceived blanket of protection had been hell on her. She was only fourteen and should have been at the mall picking out cool school clothes with Mom instead of having to deal with this shit. Which only pissed me off more.

That's why I had blood in my eye walking into his library. And why he damned near knocked me off my pins when he began to speak.

He sat behind his desk and was silent for several minutes before he began. I had the distinct impression he was preparing a sermon and was about to walk out. My patience was exhausted before he opened his mouth. Then he began, haltingly and unusually uncertain of himself.

"You know...I've faced enough juries in my lifetime to know— even before a verdict— whether I've won or lost a trial," he said, strangely subdued. "There's not a doubt in my mind that I lost my case with the both of you long before the closing argument I'm about to give."

My jaw must have dropped. Sheila just sucked in her breath wondering what was coming next. We were too stunned to say anything and unsure of where this was going.

My father suddenly stood and went to the great picture window that was essentially one whole side of his office and that he always kept completely draped. I had always thought the light, especially sunshine, had impeded his ability to be mean. I envisioned him a vampire, comfortable only in the darkness. Without warning, he pulled the huge drapes open to both sides, flooding the room with sunlight.

"Wow," he said, looking out over the hills that surrounded our home. I got the feeling he was just remembering them. He gazed for a moment, then returned to his chair.

"I've been a very successful lawyer for a long time now. I have a reputation most trial lawyers would kill for." He paused. "If only they knew."

I couldn't help myself.

"Knew what?" I purposely didn't call him "Dad." I couldn't yet give him the satisfaction that he could ever earn my respect again.

He didn't hesitate.

"If only they knew what I gave up to be what I am," he said. "And if only they knew how much I regret what I have become."

Sheila began to weep. It was like sitting in a confessional. I really didn't want to be there, I didn't want to hear his bullshit.

"It's interesting how one can suddenly experience an epiphany and never see it coming," he continued. "For instance, although you have shown me every possible sign of disrespect, Sean, I've never really seen it or heard it. In a sense, I just ignored it — which was the greatest disrespect I ever could have paid my only son."

He stopped and poured himself another three fingers of scotch. I don't think he was drinking to get drunk, rather to help him maintain his courage to say what he had to say. He took a long sip from the glass.

"The epiphany I experienced came a few weeks ago at the hospital, the night we brought your grandfather in after his heart attack. I don't have to tell you how horrible my behavior was, you saw it for yourself. The irony is I wasn't there for your grandfather, I frankly still don't give a damn if he lives or dies, but that's another story. I was there to support you because you care for him. As I am prone to do, in my anger I not only wasted the opportunity to show you how much I really care for both of you, I also drove the wedge between us in even deeper."

"Give me a break..." I began to interrupt him.

He held up a hand to stop me.

"Please, Sean, I know I'm asking a lot, but just let me finish," he pleaded.

I willed myself to calm down and nodded my head.

"Thank you... son."

I refused to acknowledge his sudden respect. It didn't stop him.

"So, let me get to the conclusion of the first element of my epiphany. And that is, quite simply, that I am not the success I have talked myself into believing. Actually, I am an abject failure as a husband and father. And, as you have often reminded me, Sean, an embarrassment."

I could have fallen out of my chair. Sheila was shocked beyond even tears.

"It wasn't your words that hurt, Sean, or even grabbing me by the throat," he continued. "Upon reflection, while sitting alone in the barn later that night, it came to me when I first began to understand what a miserable failure I was as a father.

"I saw it in your eyes, Sean, when you bored into mine, bent on killing me. I am a master at seeing the truth in one's eyes. I've spent a professional lifetime developing the skill. What I saw was pure hatred."

He took another drink.

"Since that moment, I have wished countless times that you had squeezed my throat just a little harder and put me out of my self-inflicted misery."

"Dad…" I began, some of my anger draining, "I…

"Sean, please let me finish. Just let me say what I need to say. I'm not expecting anything in return."

I sat quietly while he continued.

"Secondly, while sitting on that chair alone in the barn, it came to me like a lightening strike what I had deprived you of. I'm not talking about a father's love and care… "

"Oh, Daddy, no…" Sheila burst out crying.

"I mean, your Mother's."

He drained the glass and I swear I saw his eyes fill with tears.

"Seven years ago, I drove your mother to do something almost incomprehensible. I abused her so badly, humiliated her so cruelly that I made her leave the most precious thing in her life: her children. She left you rather than risk you growing up in the insanity and violence that I was breeding in this house.

"I did that..." He began to choke on his words.

"I did that to a woman... a woman who loved me unconditionally, who was guilty of only wanting to experience the joy of raising a family and living in an environment of love and peace and happiness.

"Like my mother," he added. It surprised me because he rarely spoke of grandma.

"I did that... out of anger." Tears rolled down his cheeks. He did nothing to hide them.

"I punished her for something she had nothing to do with, had no responsibility for and for which she did everything humanly possible to console me in my own pain. "

He closed his eyes and leaned back in his chair, trying to make the image go away.

"I punished her... because I could. I took pleasure in hurting her to make my own pain go away."

He shook his head in shame.

"So, the second part of my epiphany was recognizing that I also have grossly miscarried my responsibilities as a husband and as a man. I consciously broke my vows to my loving wife, not to mention that I broke her heart.

"Does that make me the biggest jerk who ever lived?" he asked, looking directly at me.

"That hardly covers it, I'm afraid. There isn't a word in the dictionary that adequately describes the depth of my failures and the ugliness and cruelty of my behavior."

He got up from his chair again and stared out the window.

"I had forgotten how beautiful the hills are, especially in the fall when the leaves turn color," he said. "I guess I've forgotten many things."

My head was spinning and I had a knot in my stomach. My father's confession was perhaps the most painful thing I had ever heard or experienced, yet it was still not completely cleansing.

"Seven years ago, I drove your mother to leave," he continued, still looking out the window. "Her voluntary departure allowed me to get a court order giving me full custody of you and a restraining order to prevent her from attempting to see you. I took full advantage of the fact that I was driving her towards a nervous breakdown. Since then, we have had countless conversations where I have repelled every one of her inexhaustible efforts to get me to open my eyes and see what I was doing and get the court to lift the restraining order. Every one… and there have been so many."

He turned back to us and walked to his desk, reaching for his briefcase. Same old, same old, I thought. Head back to the safety of the office, you bastard. I watched him open the briefcase and reach inside. To my surprise, he retrieved a plane ticket and itinerary.

"I don't expect either of you to say anything. Actually, I don't really expect this conversation to change much between us at all. But perhaps the action I am about to take will begin to repair some of the pain I have caused you."

Now what?

"I am leaving this minute to catch a flight to St. Louis where I am going to your Uncle's house to beg your mother to come home to you... and to me, on the slight chance she will have me again, on her unconditional terms. I will do anything to get her back, to make amends for the love that I have squandered."

He tucked the plane ticket into his suit jacket pocket and buttoned his coat.

"I have come to understand that when a man has been a fool as long as I have, there is only one way to make amends, and that is to reprioritize his life. I may be a fool, but I am not stupid.

"It may take the rest of my life, but I am going to do everything in my power to try to prove that my love for you, although I've hidden it extraordinarily well for a very long time, is real and also unconditional. I know I can only do that through my behavior.

"Finally, if your mother – who I have recently come to remember is truly the love of my life – is so forgiving as to come home to us, I am going to ask her to explain to you where my anger came from... and how it is that your grandfather, whom you love so dearly, and me have come to where we are today.

"I can only tell you that it took me weeks to find the courage to confront you the way I have in these last few minutes, but I could not explain to you my relationship with your grandfather in a lifetime.

"It is that painful and involves something I can never forgive him for. I realize that is the ultimate contradiction coming from someone asking for forgiveness, but it is the awful truth."

He was finished. He left his briefcase and cell phone on the desk. There would be no legal business conducted on this trip, only the business of life. I watched as he walked to the door of his office and stopped with his back to us.

He stood there for a long moment. I think he was crying. I know he wanted to face us, maybe even to embrace each of us after so many years. But he knew he had no right to expect anything from either of his children.

"I love you both," he said finally, and left.

Fifteen

In his dreams that night, John Evans drove the car through the narrow streets of Saint-Paul-de-Vence, Ceily gripping the leather armrest of the Mercedes's passenger door for support as he swung the nimble sports car around the next bend of a cobblestone road. The walled village, one of the oldest medieval towns on the French Riviera and home to renowned European artists and celebrities made the destination in the region of Provence-Alpes-Côte d'Azur one of the most romantic in all of France.

They laughed together as he hurled their beloved car through the village, their imaginations wildly conjuring up the sights and sounds of the south of France even as in reality they never left the quaint coastal roads along the Connecticut River near the mouth of Long Island Sound. The car was their ticket to the wonders of Europe that few could afford, especially on the meager pensions they drew in retirement. Perhaps someday, they reasoned, fortune would smile on them and allow them to taste together the places they could only dream of today. For now, and for many years leading up to this moment, the pale yellow 190sl was the magical sleigh in which they could escape their humdrum but happy existence with a long ride on a winding road and a light lunch at a roadside stand with a view of the river or the ocean.

Living with their son Sam and his wife in their large home in Willington had made life simpler, and they were grateful for their newfound freedom of retirement and the chores of life.

Today they were in in Essex, Connecticut, a wonderfully simple, eighteenth century fishing village that had become one the Connecticut coast's most sought after addresses.

They stopped at art galleries and antique shops along the way, almost always looking, rarely buying.

It was not a new game for them.

Together, even while raising Sam on their small farm in Maine, the yellow Mercedes and their imaginations had brought them to Paris and the top of the Eiffel Tower, where they gazed down upon the stunning Musée d'Orsay on the banks of the river Seine, and drove the length of the Avenue des Champs-Élysées from the Place de la Concorde to the Place Charles de Gaulle. They would park and stare at their magnificent Mercedes as they shared baguettes and jam and a glass of wine or an espresso at a sidewalk café. Sometimes they would people watch, reveling in the stares and comments that the beautiful car would spontaneously elicit from fascinated strangers. There was nowhere the car could not transport them in their dreams so long as they allowed themselves the luxury of letting their imaginations run wild.

They were deeply in love, as much after decades of marriage as they had been barely out of their teens. A great part of the success of their wedlock was their refusal to grow old or stale or to let the romance of their relationship leak away like an old boat whose seams gradually opened from neglect, only to founder when the seas grew rough.

There were good times on the farm in Maine and there were not so good times. But they were blessed with a son who was healthy, happy and adventurous, and a brilliant, eager student who excelled academically. Their jobs were satisfying if not lucrative, and they never gave a thought to seeking more in trade for the happiness of their lives. All they needed was each other and a loving family. The car was their one absolute luxury in life, but also their lifeline to staying in love.

Each weekend brought a new trip to some European fantasy. John and Ceily Evans looked forward to Sundays like children anticipated Christmas – with unbridled excitement and joy at the prospect of sharing another day and another fantasy together.

John Evans awoke from the mirage, trembling, lathered in sweat and found it hard to breath. After all, he had no hand to hold.

If only their dream had lasted.

Sixteen

Perhaps it was the image of my mother leaving in a yellow cab that awful night seven long years earlier that made me expect her to return in the same fashion. Unconsciously, I spent the next several days after my father's startling confession – and supposed new respect for family as a priority – on the lookout for a bright yellow taxicab pulling into our back yard. My father had been gone three days and neither Sheila nor I had heard a word from him or my mother. A part of me wanted to pick up the telephone and call her, but I had given up begging her to come home a long time ago.

The truth was, even if she did return with my father, it wasn't as if life was going to suddenly return to some sort of normalcy. It wasn't like we had been a happy family before she left. Our home had been full of anger, dishonesty and sadness. Not only that, my sister and I had essentially been orphaned on that night, and if it hadn't been for Pop, I'm not sure anyone would have really looked after us.

Sure, my father would have provided for us as he did, there always would have been food on the table and lights and hot water, but the only emotional and spiritual support we had received had come from my grandfather.

My father and I were already at extreme odds. The more I thought about it, my mother and I weren't much closer in our relationship, it just wasn't as angry. Seven years was a long time. My childhood was over and her only contribution as I grew up came in the form of a weekly letter. As well, the time for nurturing a loving relationship that was founded on loyalty, hugs and good night kisses had passed. It could never be recovered.

Except for Sheila, Pop was the only person in the world I really trusted —or loved, for that matter. The possibility of any semblance of happiness for our family depended heavily on him being a part of it.

Only he was slowly dying of Alzheimer's disease.

As for Pop, Sheila and I continued our daily visits. He was always excited to see us, like it was the highlight of his day. But I could tell that he was doing his best to hide his true feelings. The rehab joint was an awful place, especially for someone like Pop who cherished his privacy and the isolation of the barn and the company of the old yellow Mercedes.

There he could be alone with his thoughts and memories of Ceily.

Where he was now, he was no more than a number, parked in a wheelchair out in a long hallway full of other patients parked in wheelchairs waiting for their daily session of rehabilitation. It was a demeaning, uncaring environment where people like my grandfather quickly lost whatever was left of the spirit or joy for life they had arrived with. I had half a mind to wheel him out the door, help him into the car and take him home. Every day, I fought the urge to bust him out.

Sheila and I kept another secret from him. We didn't mention my father's conversation, figuring it was far too emotional for him to deal with right now and would only fire up memories that would best be left to rest quietly. I also had a selfish motivation. I wanted to know the truth about what had caused the dramatic and painful schism between my father and grandfather – and it was finally time for me to know what happened to my grandmother.

Whatever happened, I vowed that no one would hurt Pop anymore, no matter what crime or mistake he was guilty of.

I'd come to understand, during those many hours sitting with him in the old barn that losing his Ceily was a sentence worse than death for my grandfather. Actually, I think he would have willingly chosen death if not for his loyalty to Sheila and me.

I made another vow on my last visit with him. Pop was coming home for Thanksgiving if I had to kidnap him. I wasn't sure who else would be at the dinner table for turkey, and I didn't care – so long as it was Sheila, me and Pop.

Now that was a real family.

Seventeen

It was well after nightfall a week before Thanksgiving and I had just finished studying for an exam when I heard the wheels of a car crunching on the gravel driveway that led into our backyard. I went to my window wondering if it was the yellow taxi after all. It wasn't. It was actually a black limo. I watched in silence as my father stepped out first then extended a hand inside the back door and helped a woman out of the car. It was my mother.

Even from a distance, I could see that the years of isolation and loneliness had taken its toll on her. She was slightly heavier and her hair was beginning to grey. But it was her face that caught my attention.

It was sad.

I don't know what I was expecting. Maybe some wild display of emotion. Instead, she showed no joy at returning to the home she had abruptly left seven years earlier, nor any exuberance or even some suggestion of apprehension at seeing the two children she had left weeping in their beds. I kept watching as the driver removed her suitcases from the trunk, waiting to see if she would look up at my window. She didn't. In my anger, that told me a lot.

I dropped the shade on my window and turned away, walked to the door of my room and turned the lock. Whatever needed to be said would not be said tonight.

About twenty minutes later, there was a soft knock at my door.

"Sean?" I heard my mother call, quietly. I started to get up from the bed, then stopped. I realized that the person on the other side of the door was a stranger now, and there was little room in my life for people who had abandoned me. Finally, after all these years, I was angry with her. I laid back down and turned over, closing my eyes while I tried to shut out the sound of her voice, softly asking me to open the door, again and again. Finally, I heard a voice next to hers. It was my father's. I noticed right away that the edge was gone in his tone.

"I'm sure he's just asleep, Marnie," he comforted my mother. "Now don't go getting all upset."

I wondered if he knew how I felt about her. That it actually wasn't much different than how I felt about him. And I'm sure he had no questions about that.

I forced the image of them out of my mind even as I heard the sounds of a joyous reunion between Sheila and my mother somewhere down the hall. The two women were squealing and crying. I was glad for Sheila. She needed a woman's presence in her life. Pop and I were poor excuses for giving motherly advice to a fourteen-year-old girl.

I blocked out the words and the sounds of celebration and thought about Pop. Right now, he was alone in his room at the rehab, probably staring out the window, thinking of his Ceily, and longing for his barn and the Mercedes. I might be in the mix too, I thought. We were more than grandfather and grandson. He was my best friend. I was his.

Tomorrow, I thought, he was coming home.

Come hell or high water.

Eighteen

To say it was awkward would be kind. It was awful, perhaps the single worst moments of my life other than the night she left.

I walked into the kitchen, ready for school and she was standing there waiting with a big grin and holding a handkerchief to her chin. My mother. She was seven years older, still beautiful but no longer a young woman with dreams of the perfect family. I was seven years older too, but I was no longer a child. Now I was a man.

My father had succeeded in changing us both. Most profound however, was his success is changing how I felt about my mother. The tiny bit of little boy left in me still loved her. The man in me only respected her as the woman who gave birth to me.

We both stood motionless, facing off, one waiting for the other to make a move. Finally, it was she who ran to me and wrapped her arms around my neck. She kissed me on the neck and cheek. I clumsily wrapped my arms around her, the top of her head only reaching my chest.

"Sean, I've missed you so much. You're all grown up," she said through a veil of tears.

"Yah," I said, stumbling for words. "I was just a little boy when you left, mom…" I held her lightly, not knowing what else to do.

She stepped back and took my face in her hands. "And you're so handsome. The pictures Pop sent me didn't do you justice," she smiled.

"What pictures?" I asked, surprised.

"Oh, he sent so many… over the years… I was so lonely, Sean."

I couldn't bring myself to be kind, to tell her what she so desperately wanted to hear. That it was all right, that I forgave her, that I was glad she was home, at last. It struck me at that moment what it was like to be my father. Unforgiving and cruel, so callous. In a gentler sort of way, I was treating her just like he treated Pop.

It didn't matter. I couldn't bring myself to do it. I'd learned many lessons growing up under the gentle, caring hand of my grandfather. Most importantly was that love and loyalty had to be earned, and once earned, cherished. My parents had failed miserably at both – not only as husband and wife, but as mother and father.

I tried.

"I'm… I'm glad you're home, Mom, especially for Thanksgiving. We'll have the whole family together for the first time in a very long while," I said.

"But Pop," she said, "it won't be the same without Pop."

"Leave that to me," I said.

She looked at me, puzzled, but just shrugged her shoulders.

"I've made you breakfast," she said smiling and wiping her hands in her apron. "Pancakes, your favorite."

Her naiveté took me aback. I felt like I was looking into the face of June Cleaver.

"Mom, that was more than seven years ago," I said, my voice rising a notch in irritation. "These days I just grab a cup of coffee with Pop on the back stairs before heading off to school."

She looked hurt. I didn't care. But it was enough to start me up.

"This is not 1988, Mom, I'm not ten-years-old anymore." She wiped her hands on her apron again and looked around the kitchen, a stranger in her own home and to her only son.

I tried to change the subject.

"Dad leave for the office already?" I asked.

"No," she said, relieved to move on. "He's upstairs. He's not going in again today. He said he'd stay and help me settle in."

I opened my eyes in amazement.

"We *are* talking about my father here…" I asked in mock amazement, my tone dripping with sarcasm.

"Yes…" she said, a somewhat disbelieving look coming across her face. "He seems… well, he seems to be a changed man. I don't know what happened…"

I lost it. My tongue temporarily disconnected from my brain and I let her have it.

"You don't know what's happened?" I snapped back at her, incredulous.

"Do you think that it finally might have dawned on the genius with a law degree from Yale that he has single-handedly destroyed his family? That he's lost the respect of his children and they hate his guts? That his wife left him because of his cruelty and caused her in a moment of insanity to abandon her children?

"What's happened?" I went on, so enraged I couldn't stop.

"Do you suppose that perhaps he's come to realize that he is a psychotic, ugly excuse for a husband and father? And as a son, that his own father thinks he is the second coming of Satan?

"Is there something I left out that might have caused him to rethink his life, Mom?"

It was if I had punched her. She actually staggered back from my words they hit her so hard.

"It wasn't my fault, Sean," she cried. "I tried."

"Bullshit. You're not getting off the hook that easily, Mom." I was merciless. "It was because you were so weak and cared so little for your children that you left the door open for that bastard to use the court to keep you from us."

I still wasn't done.

"The truth is a bitch, Mom. Face it."

Then she surprised me. She stood her ground.

"Yes, Sean, the truth is a bitch," she replied, emphasizing my curse. "But sometimes the truth is either easier to swallow – or harder – depending on what you want to believe, when you know all the facts."

I laughed at her.

"You don't really know what you did to Sheila and me, do you, Mom?"

She hesitated a long while before responding, dreading the question she knew would eventually come from at least one of us.

"And you really don't understand that I don't care what the facts were, do you? "

Tears were streaming down her face now.

"You're no better than he is," I said.

I had completely lost my composure now. I didn't care what I said to hurt her. It was my turn to do the hurting.

"And understand this. I never asked to be born. In fact, I never had any say in the matter. You chose to have me – and then you chose to abandon me. Those are the facts, and no matter how you sugarcoat them, they'll always be the facts. And because of that, we'll never really be a family."

This was not the reception she was hoping for.

"But there may be one way the Evans' family myth can be salvaged," I added. "And that would be by someone laying out all the facts. Little things, Mom, like why does Dad hate his father so much? How is it that he can despise a man his children love unconditionally? How could that hate be so strong that it drove my mother to leave her children? " I screamed the last question and pounded my fist on the kitchen table. She flinched, startled at the rage that was spewing from me.

"And finally, dammit, when are one of you weaklings going to have the guts to tell Shelia and me what happened to grandma?"

I thought she was going to go into shock from the way I was talking to her.

"Don't you think we know that what ever Pop did, and however grandma died is the real reason we aren't a real family?"

She stood stock still, her mouth open, unable to answer.

"You and that mutant who passes himself off as your husband had better start thinking about the conversation you're going to have with Sheila and me very soon – understand me, Mom? Or trust me, you're not going to have to think about sneaking out in the middle of the night again.

"No. You're going to have to start thinking about living life with Sam Evans – alone. Because this time it's going to be Sheila, me and whatever is left of Pop who are going to leave you crying in *your* bed."

She sat down at the kitchen table, weeping.

"Forever, Mom. Not just for seven years.

"Forever."

I forced myself to stop then because I was so furious my chest actually hurt. I could feel a vein in my neck pulsing like it was going to explode. My father couldn't have orchestrated a better meltdown, and he had a lot more practice than I did. It was time to walk away before I did any more damage. I poured myself a cup of coffee then headed for the back stairs before I remembered with almost overwhelming sadness that Pop wasn't going to be there. If I ever needed him before…

It was the worst possible moment to see my father.

He was standing at the bottom of the stairs and had obviously heard the last part of my speech. He took one look at my face and decided not to say a word. It was a wise decision.

In my fury, I turned and threw the ceramic coffee mug the length of the hallway. It smashed into a million pieces against the kitchen wall. Black coffee dripped down and puddled on the floor.

"Have a nice day and welcome home to the sad excuse for a family you and your husband have created, Mom," I hollered as I kicked open the back door and walked out.

Nineteen

I waited for Sheila after school. I had a plan to spring Pop from the rehab center and needed her help.

She knew something was up when she saw me waiting by my car. I never skipped football practice so she knew it had to be important.

"Get in," I said, offering no clue as to what was up.

She didn't argue. I drove away, angrily, chirping my tires as I pulled out of the parking lot. It would probably earn me a detention. I didn't care.

"I heard what happened this morning," she said.

"Good news travels fast," I responded. "I'm sorry. She just said the wrong things. It lit my fuse."

"She may not recover. I've never seen her so upset," she said.

"Yah, well how often have you seen her?" I asked.

"Point," my sister answered.

"Look, I understand how you feel," Sheila said. "I faked being all happy last night when she got home. I was hoping I'd feel something different, but it was all bullshit. I'm just not the type to get angry. I take after Mom."

I pounded my fist on the steering wheel.

"Don't ever say that again, " I warned her.

"The only good those two will ever do for us is teach us how not to live life."

My anger frightened her. We drove in silence for a while.

"Where are we going?" she asked.

"To get Pop out of that hellhole," I said.

"They're releasing him?" she asked, not catching on.

"Not exactly," I said. "We are."

She looked at me strangely, waiting for a sign that I was kidding. I stared ahead at the road.

"You're serious."

"Yah."

"And how are we going to pull this caper off? He needs written authorization from a doctor to leave," she said.

"I'll explain when we get there."

It was only a couple of miles away. We didn't speak again until I pulled into the parking lot. Then Sheila spotted the Jaguar and pointed it out to me.

"What the hell?" I said. "He had to bring Mom to see Pop now?" I complained in disbelief.

"I don't know what they're doing but they're not inside. They're both sitting in the car," Sheila observed.

I parked and waited, pondering my next move. My father got out of the Jag and walked over to us.

He looked tired and strained. I suspected it hadn't been an easy morning for him with my mother.

"I had a feeling you two might show up here," he said calmly. "I think I know what you have in mind and I'd like you to think about it before you do something rash."

I shook my head. "I see. You'd rather we wait until you take charge and get Pop out of this rat cage," I said. "Bet you've considered the idea that if you leave him here long enough the Alzheimer's will just kill him and you won't have to deal with it."

"No." He put both hands on the roof and leaned against the car. "That's not it."

"Then get out of my way, Dad," I said, kicking open the door and knocking him away. "Let someone who cares about him fix the problem."

"Sean, don't!" Sheila yelled to me. "Don't make it worse. Please."

"Screw that," I said. "I'm not letting him rot away one more day.

"Now get out of my way, Dad," I said menacingly. My fists were balled.

"We need to talk, Sean. That's why I'm here," my father said.

"You've had years to talk, Dad and I've been all ears. Get out of my way —now!" I demanded.

To my surprise, he charged at me, putting his head right into my chest and knocking me back into the car. Then he grabbed my wrists and pinned me back.

He was out of breath from the stress and waited a minute to calm himself.

"You know, I understand your anger, I tried to make that clear," he said with uncharacteristic cool. "And I've swallowed your physical threats as just your teenage hormones completely out of whack because of what all this has put you through. But I refuse to be intimidated by my son just because he's bigger than I am. Whatever, however you feel about me doesn't matter right now. I'm your father and you will at least listen to me.

"Understand?" He pushed me harder against the side of the car to emphasize his point.

Sheila was still inside the car and she had begun to cry. It disarmed me.

"Talk about what?" I spit out, enraged. "Let me go, you joke."

He slowly released his grip.

"Mom said you have questions that need to be answered. I promised you if I was able to convince her to come back home to us, they would be answered.

"So before you do something dumb here, let's go back to the house and talk about the demise of the Evans family."

He looked me right in the eye. It wasn't a challenge, it was a plea.

"C'mon, Sean. Let's go talk," he said calmly.

It was one of the few times I can ever remember my father speaking to me in a tone of voice that suggested I was his son, and not a client.

Twenty

~~~

November 1981

Night after night his tortured mind replayed the irony. It had been such a happy moment. How could it have set in motion the nightmare that would end their lives together?

"You know what would be better than driving this old heap through the Litchfield Hills, imagining that we're driving through the Alps?" John Evans asked his wife as they were passing by the Hotchkiss School in Salisbury, Connecticut. They'd spent the Sunday in the old Mercedes, now restored to jewel-like quality. It ran like a Swiss watch and traversing the quaint, old villages and towns of the northwestern region of the state, from the rolling hills in the south to the more mountainous climbs farther west was no challenge for the capable touring car.

They were both exceedingly proud of the now classic Mercedes, which they had rescued from certain extinction over the last several years. John Evans had become an outstanding mechanic and his knowledge of the 190sl was extensive. There wasn't a nut or bolt he hadn't either turned, tightened or replaced in the few years they'd owned the car.

They'd stopped in Litchfield and shared cheese and chocolate over a glass of a local vineyard's delightful unoaked Chardonnay, imagining themselves looking out over the Alps separating France and Italy at the Mediterranean on a perfect fall day of sun and cool mountain air. The foliage was spectacular as they drove the winding roads and hills in the little roadster, the top down, a sweater and scarf their only protection against the wind and chill. He would always
~~~

remember the look on Ceily's face as they drove, sometimes for miles at a stretch without saying a word. Their comfort together was such that conversing wasn't always necessary. Instead, they held hands in between his smooth, precise shifts of the synchromesh transmission.

He had broken a period of silence with the question.

"No, Mr. Evans, what could possibly be better than sharing an afternoon together in the Alps, even if they are in Litchfield."

He smiled. He'd been thinking about this a long time, waiting for the precise moment to surprise her.

"I've been saving for a very special occasion, my love," he said, turning to look at the sudden sparkle in her eye.

"And that would be…" she asked, thoroughly reveling in the game.

"Well, in case you have forgotten, we were married in January of 1952."

She drew a hand over her scarf, tucking it more tightly around her neck, the afternoon air cooling more rapidly now. Devilishly, she threw her head back as if surprised by the news.

"My word, Mr. Evans… could it be that long ago?"

"Yes it is, Ceily, nearly thirty of the most wonderful years of my life."

"I take that as a cherished compliment, my love," she said demurely. "And I would completely agree."

The time was right.

"I think to celebrate such a momentous event, that we should stop imagining."

She opened her eyes wide. "Whatever do you mean? Why some of my most wonderful moments have been spent with you in this car, the wilder our imaginations, the better. They are precious memories."

"What I mean, Ceily, is that we should finally fulfill our dream and really travel to Europe."

She leapt from her seat and threw her arms around his neck, causing him to momentarily swerve into the oncoming lane as she kissed him on the cheek.

He laughed out loud at her reaction.

"I thought you might like the idea, but we may die before getting there if you don't stop strangling me behind the steering wheel, my dear!" he laughed.

"Do you mean it? I mean really go to Europe? To Paris? To St. Tropez and Nice and Positano and the Alps and…"

"I wasn't thinking of moving there, Ceily," he said smiling sheepishly. "Maybe just a well planned vacation for a week or two…"

"I don't care if it's for a day or a month," Ceily said, clapping her hands together in delight. "Just to go to Europe. Do you realize how long we've dreamed and…"

"Made believe we were there?" John Evans humbly finished her thought. "Ceily, I would have given you the world if I could have…"

She looked at him long and lovingly.

"But you have John, you have," she said. "I have everything… because I have you and Sam and Marnie and the kids. That's all I've ever needed… with a little romance thrown in for fun. This wonderful car that you made for us is just frosting on the cake."

Evans smiled the smile of a satisfied man as he downshifted into a long winding, uphill curve. The striking pale yellow Mercedes gripped the road and roared as he accelerated through the turn.

"I'm very pleased to hear that, Mrs. Evans," he grinned.

"Ever, ever, so pleased. I will make the arrangements right down to the chilled champagne waiting in our suite upon our arrival in Paris on the occasion of our Thirtieth Anniversary in January, 1982.

"I wonder how cold it is in Paris in January?" he asked absentmindedly."

"Don't worry, John," she said, a devilish look back in her eye. "I can think of ways to keeps us warm."

He reached for her hand and on they drove.

Twenty-One

Pop wasn't happy.

He kept checking his watch, wondering why neither of his grandchildren had come to visit today. It was so unlike them. And it was the only thing that kept him from going stir crazy.

He tried to stop an orderly who walked by, but the man ignored him sitting out in the hall in his wheelchair.

"Say, son, would you know the time?"

The orderly kept on walking.

"You're wearing a watch, old timer. You want me to blow your nose too?" he said sarcastically.

"Kiss my ass," Pop mumbled under his breath.

The orderly stopped dead in his tracks, then slowly backed up to where Pop was sitting. He leaned down into the old man's face.

"What did you say?" he asked, glaring at the elderly John Evans.

"Nothing. Beat it."

"I'll beat it all right, you old fart," the orderly said angrily. "Get out of the hall and get in your room. Now."

Pop went to stand up, never willing to back down to anyone. If he'd had his strength it might have been an even match even though he probably had forty years on the punk.

The orderly pushed him back down.

"Sit your old ass down, man and do as you're told," he threatened him. "In fact, I'll help you."

The orderly roughly grabbed the wheel chair and raced Pop back into his room. He let go of the chair at the doorway and kicked it hard so it smashed into the bed, nearly tossing him out of the wheelchair. Then he walked out, closing and locking the door behind him.

Pop sat there seething for about ten minutes. Then he made his decision.

He slowly got out of the chair and walked over to his ground floor window. It was the kind that rolled out vertically. He grabbed the crank and starting turning it. The window probably hadn't been opened in a dozen years, so moving it took some effort. He banged his body against it hard a couple of times and it opened a crack. Eventually, he got it open just far enough so that he could lift a leg over the windowsill and maneuver his body through the small space. It was only about a three-foot drop to the ground. He pushed off and fell into some bushes beneath the window. He landed softly on the plants.

Brushing himself off, Pop turned around to the window and stuck up his middle finger.

Then he looked around to get his bearings. The streetlights came on just then and the little bit of light helped him figure out that he was maybe eight to ten miles from where he lived. He figured he'd better stick to the shadows in case someone came looking for him. It hadn't dawned on him yet that the night air was cold.

"No turning back now," he thought as he began the long walk home to his barn, the old Mercedes and his memories of Ceily.

Twenty-Two

Sheila and I were silent as we followed the Jag home. I suspected there wasn't a lot of conversation in the car ahead of us either.

The lights were coming on in the houses we passed as the sun was setting earlier now with winter fast approaching. It was getting colder, too.

Without a word, I followed my mother and father inside when we pulled up to the house. Sheila took my hand, surprising me. The poor kid was a bundle of nerves, not quite knowing what to expect from this meeting of four-fifths of the Evans family. She jerked on my hand to get my attention and looked into my eyes. Without saying anything, I knew she was begging me to be patient and not make things any worse.

"I want to be a family again, Sean. Please?" she whispered.

"Yah," I replied, not completely able to keep my sarcasm in check. "A family. We just left our 'family' to spend another night in misery at that rehab place. This better be worth it."

My mother went around the house turning on the outside lights, a habit she had always had before leaving us. It was like she'd never left. My father suggested we all sit in the living room. But first he went into his study and poured himself three fingers of scotch. I watched through the French doors as he downed it in one swallow, then poured another.

"That will help," I said out loud.

"Forgive me," he said, slightly embarrassed. "You'll understand shortly." He was nervous. It was unlike him.

Sheila and I sat together on the sofa that looked into a great stone fireplace that was the centerpiece of the living room. It had always been one of our favorite places to sit during the winter and watch the roaring flames of a fire my father had built, or to listen to my mother tell us bedtime stories. Somehow, it had lost its warmth.

My mother, looking terribly pale, almost grey with stress, sighed deeply as she sat in a cushioned high back chair that used to be Pop's favorite. I almost asked her to sit somewhere else but remembered Sheila's request. I let it go.

My father didn't sit, but paced behind my mother, occasionally sipping at his drink. He was deep in thought and looked terribly pained – as if he was facing up to something he'd tried to bury a long time ago. I didn't know how right I was.

My mother began. It was odd that the woman I had considered a little mouse at one time and who had hurt Sheila and me beyond measure —was to be the person that would once and for all expose the mystery the Evans family had been hiding, at an epic price, for so many years.

She began. I closed my eyes. Sheila snuggled close to me on the couch.

"There was a time when we were a very happy family," she said, tears immediately welling up in her eyes. "That was a very long time ago. A very, very long time ago."

She paused, collecting her thoughts and held out her hand to my father for support. To my wonder, he came to her and held it, for a moment, even bringing it to his lips.

"To say that I am sorry for what your father and I have done to hurt you is not nearly sufficient," she said, a point she had to get off her chest. "It's a sin how we made you victims of something you had nothing to do with."

"Yah," I said impatiently. "We can talk about sins later, Mom. Let's get to it. While we're sitting here getting ready to hold hands and sing Kumbya, the only person who took care of Sheila and me while you guys were off finding yourself is sitting miserable and lonely in a hellhole being ignored and mistreated. I don't intend for that to go on one more night, do you understand? So if you've got something to say, say it. I've got plans."

Sheila jabbed me with her elbow. I was already loosing it.

"Sean..." my mother began. "I understand your anger..."

I didn't hesitate.

"No, you do not. You absolutely do not, Mom," I replied mercilessly. "Get on with it."

My father glared at me for just a moment, then the look on his face changed to understanding. I was beginning to think he was eating Paxil for lunch. I don't know what it was, but something really had changed in him.

"He's right, Marnie," he said softly.

"Please. Tell them."

I watched as she swallowed hard.

"Your grandmother and grandfather were married in January of 1952," she began.

"I know, in a hospital ward in Okinawa when Pop was recovering from his crash in Korea," I added.

My father raised his brow, surprised at my knowledge.

"You don't think we've been sitting in the barn playing checkers all these years, do you Dad?" I said, sarcastically.

He ignored it.

"Then you probably know that he and grandma moved to Maine when they got back to the States and bought a little farm." I nodded. Sheila looked at me. This was all news to her.

"They lived very simple lives, your grandparents. Sometimes I think they lived on love." Her voice trailed off as she finished her words, a touch of envy obvious, at least to me. Grandma and Pop represented what she had always wanted of her relationship with the idiot she married.

"That old Mercedes in the barn was about the only thing they ever splurged on, but it was their ticket to fantasies I can only be jealous of," she said, smiling. "They used that car to imagine themselves traveling the roads of Europe on romantic excursions… the stories they used to tell me were quite precious…"

I nodded again.

"The one thing they had always dreamed of was actually travelling to Europe, but of course it was something they could never afford. When your Dad talked them into coming here, to live with us in Willington, it gave them a little more financial freedom."

"So they went to Europe after all? Before she died?" Sheila blurted out. This was sounding like some kind of Harlequin novel love story to her.

"Not exactly, Sheila," my father interrupted.

My mother wiped tears away from her eyes with a handkerchief.

"When their Thirtieth Anniversary came upon them, Pop surprised grandma with plans to take a trip to Europe," she said, shaking her head at the memory. She sobbed. "They were going to go to Paris first, a lifelong dream of Ceily's."

I watched the expression on my father's face darken.

"I don't think I had ever seen her so happy," my mother continued. "It truly was a dream come true for her and she talked about it for weeks before they left. She couldn't stop thinking about it or planning all the things she and Pop were going to see." She paused, pain visible on her face. "And Pop was walking around here like a rooster, he was so proud that he could finally do this for your mom."

"Of course, I'd offered to give him the money a hundred times before," my father suddenly interjected. "But no, his god dammed pride wouldn't let him take money from me."

He drained what was left in his glass and walked into his library again to refill his glass, muttering as he walked. "None of this would have happened," he said. "My mother would still be here."

"What?" I yelled after him. "What does that mean?"

My mother said it first.

"Sam, just shut up. That's got nothing to do with what happened and the day you admit it is the day this family may have a chance to right itself." I'd never heard my mother raise her voice to my father before.

"Yah," came the response from the library. He rejoined us with a full glass in his hand. I noticed it was shaking in his hand.

"Pop was also so proud that he made all the arrangements himself. The only time he'd ever been overseas was when he was in Korea, so he didn't really have experience at travelling. He made some strange decisions about the route they would take to get to Paris."

"What do you mean by strange?" I asked.

"It means he was trying to save a buck and scheduled the most ass backwards route you could possibly take to get there," my father announced. His anger at something so trivial surprised me, but his judgmental tone had me on the edge of trying to strangle him again. Of all people, my mother interceded before I completely lost it.

"Sam," my mother said, calmly. "Either keep it together or I'm going upstairs to pack." She looked at Sheila and me. "And the kids are coming with me this time. Screw you and your court order.

"Understand?"

He took a long pull from his drink, then shook his head, yes.

She paused, glaring at him as if to emphasize how serious she was. He turned his back and walked to the oversize windows overlooking the front yard. He stared at a tree he and I had planted when I was just a little boy.

"The cost of a flight to Europe for people like your grandparents was astronomical," she said. "And your father is right, Pop refused any help from us. So he booked a flight out of Washington National Airport, if you can imagine, where they would catch a flight to Tampa International Airport, then fly to London and finally on to Paris. It was a long circuitous route. "

"But I shouldn't have used the word strange to describe his plan. That's not fair to your grandfather," she added. "He had an ulterior motive. He wanted the Mercedes, their pride and joy to be part of their real life adventure. So he planned to drive it to Washington National Airport in Arlington, Virginia."

She leaned forward and buried her head in her hands.

"It was a long drive, so Pop made arrangements to drive to Pennsylvania, then check into a hotel for the night before going on to Washington National the next day. They left here on January 12, 1982."

Abruptly, she sat upright, as if finding some inner strength at the memory that flashed before her eyes.

"I'll never forget kissing Ceily goodbye, and hugging your Pop before they left that morning. They were just so happy… it was indescribable."

"I offered him some money," my father said out of nowhere. "I begged him to take it. He hugged me and said 'Thanks, but no thanks,' said he had it covered. Then he told me how proud he was of me. Imagine that…" His voice drifted off.

"And then I kissed my mom goodbye… never dreaming it would be the last time I'd ever see her. Alive."

He stopped talking and took a long drink. He kept his back to us, but I knew he was crying.

"Do you have any idea what she meant to me? How important she was to me growing up? How much I loved her?"

I looked at my mother who dropped her eyes. Then I turned back to him.

"Yah, Dad, I think I can understand," I said as sarcastically as I could. He didn't respond, the consummate hypocrite.

My mother ignored him. But in the next minute, I think she aged ten years. The memory of what came next was that painful.

"They made Pennsylvania with no problem and called the next morning from the hotel, to say goodbye again. Pop said the Mercedes was a dream to drive, they even put the top down for a while – in January! They were leaving after breakfast to catch their flight at Washington National to Tampa and then going on to Heathrow in London. She mentioned that it was supposedly snowing heavily in Arlington, but she was going to Paris if she had to ski there…"

The next words caught in her throat and she could only manager a whisper.

"That was January 13, 1982."

Twenty-Three

~~~

January 13, 1982
Washington National Airport

"You think she'll be all right out there in that parking lot, Ceily?" Pop fretted over his beloved car as they waited in the terminal to board their flight.

"Relax, honey, she'll be perfectly fine, you have her covered and stuck away in the corner of that lot – why the worst that can happen is she'll get a bit buried by a snow plow. The car was fun, honey, but let's forget about her now and focus on all the fun we're going to have.

"We're going to Europe!" she shrieked and jumped up and put her two arms around her husband's neck, planting a big kiss on his lips.

He laughed

"Why you hussy, you," he chided her. "At least wait until we get to the hotel, will ya?"

She threw her head back and laughed out loud. With her long red hair pulled up in a bun for convenience for the long trip and her ocean green eyes shining with delight, John Evans thought he had never seen his wife look more beautiful. Or more happy. And that made *him* very happy.

He thought for a moment that this was possibly the third best moment in his life, the first being Ceily surprising him in Okinawa, the second, the birth of his son Sam. The blood, the burns, the pain and anguish of
~~~

Korea were but faded memories. John Evans had lived a good life. And it was all because of his Ceily.

For some reason, he looked outside. It was snowing something fierce. He watched as plows streamed up and down the runways frantically trying to keep them clear and open. It seemed to be a losing battle.

"I'll bet we're going to be delayed," he said. "It's really coming down out there."

"Just as long as they don't cancel the flight, that's all I care about, John. I don't mind waiting a few more minutes for something I've been waiting my whole life to do."

Officially, they knew, the Airport was closed but was expected to reopen at noon when the rate of snowfall was expected to slack off. It was almost noon now.

As he watched, Evans saw ground crews scurrying to spray a mixture of heated water and monopropylene glycoldeicing liquid onto dozens of aircraft lined up at gates all over the Airport. That was a sign to him that they were getting ready to reopen the runways, even though snow was still falling at a moderate pace. Inside the warm terminal, he couldn't feel the 24°F temperature that the ground crews were fighting in addition to the snow.

"I'm going to go check the flight board, honey, see if there's any indication of what's happening, "he said. Ceily nodded and went back to studying her tour guide of Paris. She was still struggling with how to see everything she wanted to in the cavernous Musée du Louvre, housing the most comprehensive collection of art masterpieces in the world.

Evans walked about sixty yards to the nearest arrivals and departures kiosk and noted that flights, with adjusted arrival and departure times were beginning to populate the board. No sign yet of their flight, however.

"Oh, well," he said quietly to himself. "We've waited this long..."

Twenty-Four

~~~

January 13, 1982
Washington National Airport

The Boeing 737-200 pulled to the gate after a routine landing at Washington National Airport at 1:45 p.m., or 13:45 hundred hours, from Miami despite the still blizzard-like conditions. The pilot, Larry Wheaton, thirty-four years old with more than 8,300 total flight hours shook his head in wonder.

"I don't know how the hell they kept those runways open, Roger, but I'll be damned. We're sittin' where we're supposed to be sittin'," he said to First Officer Roger Pettit, his co-pilot who was three years junior in age.

"Roger that, Larry, I would have sworn we'd be heading for Philadelphia or somewhere else right now. There's a hell of a lot of snow falling on us."

"I imagine we're going to be late getting out of here to Tampa," Wheaton said. "I'm going to stretch my legs and go check on the weather reports. She's still coming down pretty steady. Make sure you keep an eye on any ice buildup, ok?"

"Will do, Captain," Pettit replied.

As he walked out into the empty cabin, twenty-two year old Flight Attendant Kelly Duncan stepped out of the galley and offered the Captain fresh coffee. She liked Wheaton, a quiet, gentle kind of guy who didn't fluster easily. That's the way she liked the guys up
~~~

front. She had her hands full babysitting some of her passengers and didn't have much time to cater to the whims of the flight deck crew. But the tall brunette was a natural for handling all types of travelers, from the fearful little old ladies clutching rosary beads to the college kids who often had spent the last couple of hours in an Airport terminal bar before boarding. She was a self-proclaimed party girl herself. There weren't many passengers she couldn't handle.

"Nice landing, Captain," she said. "Didn't think we'd be seeing Washington today."

"I'm as surprised as you are, Kelly, but I suspect we're going to be parked for awhile."

Petit called out through the open cockpit door.

"Surprise, Captain, looks like they're going to try to turn us around quickly before things get worse. Air Traffic Control wants us out of here around 15:00 hours – about an hour and forty-five minutes behind schedule. Not bad. Not bad at all."

"Tower just called?" Wheaton asked.

"Yah. They think the snow will lighten up enough for them to keep the runways clear."

Wheaton turned to Duncan.

"You heard the man, Kelly. I suppose we'll start boarding around 14:30 if we're going to push back at 15:00," the Captain said. "Roger, make sure you stay on top of that deicing. I'm just going to take a walk into the terminal to see if I can get a broader look at what's going on outside." Kelly Duncan nodded and picked up the galley phone to check on the status of catering for her new passengers.

It was now 14:15 hours. Wheaton made his way to the nearest information kiosk to see if his flight had been posted. Sure enough, there it was, scheduled for departure at 15:00 hours, ninety minutes late, but better than being stuck at Washington National all night. He looked outside to see ground crews everywhere deicing aircraft and getting ready to step up the pace of departures again. Already, there was a long line of aircraft headed for Runway 36, the longest of National's three main strips. That made sense, he thought to himself. With the added weight of snow on the wings, even after deicing, any sane pilot would be looking for as long a roll out as possible before rotating the nose up off the tarmac and into the air. On takeoff, a departing aircraft would be flying over the 14th Street Bridges – a complex of five bridges across the Potomac River, connecting Arlington, Virginia, and Washington, D.C. – almost immediately after clearing the end of the runway. There wasn't a lot of room to spare.

"We'll be all right," Wheaton thought to himself with the confidence of a pilot with over 8,000 hours at the controls of dozens of different types of aircraft. "Just so long as those wings stay nice and clean."

He hurried back on board his airplane, even as the gate personnel were calling for passengers on the flight that boarding would start momentarily. When he got to the end of the boarding ramp, Larry Wheaton stopped for a minute and patted the Boeing 737-200 on the fuselage. It was a good airplane, one he was very comfortable flying. The B-737 was the workhorse of the industry, accounting for a large percentage of daily domestic flights occurring across the country and had an excellent safety record. But it had one strange behavioral quirk that suddenly came to his mind.

The B-737 was known to have an inherent "pitch up" characteristic when the leading edge on the wings was contaminated with even small amounts of snow or ice. The result was something pilots knew as wingtip stall, which resulted in a rapid upwards pitch of the aircraft's nose. As it climbed for altitude on takeoff, wake coming off the wings could press down on the tail section of the aircraft, forcing the airplane's nose to continue to rise higher. Eventually, the unstable aircraft's forward momentum would slow, resulting in the reduction of its air speed to the point that sustained flight was impossible. It only took a few seconds for the whole situation to become untenable, and because it typically occurred within moments after liftoff and only a few hundred feet off the ground, a crash was almost inevitable. There was just no time and no room to recover. It wasn't a situation he'd had a lot of experience with, in fact he had only made eight takeoffs in snow situations during his long career. But he knew enough to make sure the wings were completely deiced and to double-check the leading edge.

"Let's get to it," he said and made his way to the left hand seat in the cockpit.

Waiting for him in the right hand seat was First Officer Petitt, another well-liked member of the crew with almost 3,500 hours logged in commercial aircraft. He had also been a fighter jockey in the U. S. Air Force and piloted the supersonic F-15 swept wing fighter. Larry Wheaton enjoyed flying with the affable Petitt, who relished in regaling his crewmembers with stories of life in a combat-ready fighter unit.

"Rog, you check on that deicing?" Wheaton asked.

"They're spraying us as we speak, skipper."

"Good let's keep a close eye on that, OK? I suspect it's going to take us quite a while to work our way down the line for roll out on 36. We could be stuck out there and get some more ice build up. Let's make sure that when we pull back from the gate we're smooth as a baby's butt."

"Yes, sir," Petitt replied, all business in what he knew could be a dangerous situation. He was a bit nervous. For all his experience, he'd only taken off in snow twice during his career.

""Ok, let's get going on the preflight," Wheaton ordered, referring to the standard checklist of operating systems and functions that was required before takeoff. Banging noises coming from behind the open cockpit door told him catering had arrived. The passengers would begin boarding momentarily.

Suddenly echoing into the cockpit came the voice of a boarding agent inside the terminal.

"Good afternoon, ladies and gentleman, and on behalf of your flight crew today, please accept our apologies for the delay in this afternoon's flight to Tampa," the crisply uniformed agent announced in as pleasant a voice as he could muster. From personal experience, he knew there was nothing worse than hanging around an airport. And most of these Florida bound flights were loaded with children who became particularly antsy at the inactivity.

"In a moment we'll begin boarding by rows."

He paused, looking around to see if he had the attention of most of the ticket holders. There would be seventy-four passengers and five crewmembers on board today. He glanced out the window before continuing and the sight of the near blizzard conditions depressed him. *What I would do to be heading for Tampa*, he thought. He had to force himself to return his focus to his job.

"Once again, ladies and gentleman we are about to board our flight to Tampa today with continuing service to Fort Lauderdale.

"We hope you have a pleasant flight on Air Florida Flight 90."

Twenty-Five

He was about two miles from the rehab center when he began to feel the cold.

"Son of a bitch," John Evans said aloud, walking along the median strip along dark Route 74, right outside the center of town. Cars passed occasionally along the sparsely traveled road, and he would duck into the shadows when they went by, not sure if his absence had been discovered yet. He doubted it. Chances are the staff wouldn't even check on him until they brought breakfast, or whatever they called that undercooked or overcooked mess, in the morning.

He wondered why neither Sean nor Sheila had come to visit him today, and in his somewhat confused state began to wonder if he had done something wrong. He wracked his brain trying to remember their last conversation – was it yesterday? – but couldn't recall it.

"You know, Ceily, sometimes I get confused now," he said softly, talking to himself. "I'm not sure why. I really miss you, do you know that? I hope you're waiting for me. I'd hate to think you've gone and found some angel to replace me.

"And you know how sorry I am, don't you sweetheart?" He began to cry thinking about that awful afternoon in the river, and the mistake he had made.

"I don't know why I let you go, Ceily. I've had all these years to think about it and I still don't know why I let go of your hand. You know how much I loved you, don't you dear? And how much I wanted to show you the Eiffel Tower?"

He wiped tears from his eyes with the sleeve of his flannel shirt and tried to stop thinking about it. Sometimes it made sense to talk to Ceily, like now, when he was thinking clearly enough to remember that she was dead. But other times when he talked to her, he couldn't remember that she had died and thought she was just away somewhere and would be back at any moment.

He shuffled along the road now where it was easier to walk. There were no cars in sight. There was a diner up ahead and he thought about stopping in for a cup of coffee to warm up. He was getting mighty cold.

"You idiot," he suddenly remembered. "How are you going to pay for it? With your looks? See what I mean, Ceily? Sometimes I just don't think straight now."

He walked by the diner and looked longingly inside at the few patrons enjoying a late dinner. He and Ceily used to stop in there once in a while on the way home from a day trip in the Mercedes. They knew the owner. What was his name? He couldn't remember, but it was on the tip of his tongue. "Angelo? Angie?" He cursed at his sudden stupidity.

He looked all around at the corner. It was clear and there was no traffic. But for some reason, he lost his bearings.

John Evans, a man who'd survived the crushing blows of a father who didn't care about him, a near death experience in combat, the loss of the only woman he had ever loved and the hatred of his only son, had finally lost his way.

He didn't know which way to turn.

Twenty-Six

~~~

January 13, 1982
Washington National Airport

Petitt went through the checklist with deliberate precision, having gone through the exercise hundreds of times. He and Captain Larry Wheaton weren't wasting any time, fully expecting Ground Control to back "Palm 90" – the flight's call sign – back from the gate as soon as they were fully loaded. Deicing and refueling had already been completed, now it was just a matter of getting the passengers buckled in, the checklist completed and the engines spooled up.

"Yaw damper?" Petitt called out.

"On," replied Wheaton.

"Instrument and navigation transfer switches?"

"Normal," came the immediate reply.

"Autopilots?" Petit inquired.

""Disengaged," Wheaton responded after a quick check.

"Stabilizer trim cutout switches?"

"Normal."

"Engine anti-icing system?" Petitt asked.

"Uh… off," Wheaton replied making a mental note to go back and check on the protocol for that one.

"APU?"

"On."

"Flight controls?"

"Checked."
~~~

On and on it went for a full ten minutes. Finally First Officer Pettit informed the Captain that the checklist was complete and they were ready for flight.

"Inform Ground Control that Palm 90 is ready to rock and roll, First Officer. And you have the controls, Mr. Petitt."

"Thank you Captain," Petit responded, a knot forming in the pit of his stomach at the decision by the Captain to give takeoff control of the airplane to his co-pilot. It was not an unusual decision. Wheaton had handled the takeoff from Miami. The flight crew usually switched back and forth on each successive leg.

At 15:16 hours, Petitt adjusted the microphone of his headset and spoke into it.

"Ground control, Palm 90 would like to get in sequence, we're ready."

After a false affirmative and then a six-minute hold, Ground Control replied, "Okay, Palm 90, your push back is approved."

At 15:25, a ground service tug was standing by to push the aircraft back from the gate to the runway but immediately ran into trouble. A combination of snow, ice and deicing liquid prevented the tow, which was not equipped with tire chains, to gain enough traction to move the 102,300 pound aircraft back away from the gate. It wasn't until 15:35 that a properly equipped tug was put into position and Flight 90 was pushed back. Petitt immediately started both of the Pratt & Whitney JT8-D engines and the crew began their brief post-start checklist. At 15:38, Ground control instructed Petitt to maneuver his 737 into position behind a New York Air DC-9, which was taxiing toward Runway 36 to fall into position behind seven other aircraft awaiting takeoff.

Petitt and Wheaton both began worrying about snow and ice buildup on the wings as it had already been some time since the aircraft had been deiced. Briefly, they discussed pulling out of line and returning to a hanger for an additional deicing after concluding that as much as a half an inch of slushy precipitation had accumulated already on the wings of Palm 90.

"Tell you what Roger," Wheaton finally said. "Let's pull up closer to this DC-9. The heat from her engines is going to melt all this stuff off for us. Just tuck in a little closer there."

Within minutes, the heat from the DC-9's engines had cleared the windshield of Flight 90 of snow and ice, leading Petitt and Wheaton to believe that the same had occurred on the aircraft's fuselage and wings.

At 15:48, while still waiting in line for takeoff, Petitt noticed a discrepancy in the instrument power readings of the two engines on the Air Florida 737.

He pointed to the thrust indicator gauges. "See the difference in that engine and the right one?" he said to Wheaton, who replied, "Yes."

Petitt pondered it for a moment. "I don't know why that's different – unless it's hot air going into that right one, that must be it – from his exhaust. It was doing that when we first pulled in behind him." They gave it no more thought.

At 15:57, the New York Air DC-9 was given clearance for takeoff and almost immediately launched down the runway. The Captain and First Officer of Air Florida Flight 90, next in line, quickly went through their preflight checklist including verification of the takeoff engine pressure thrust ratio settings. They needed to reach 2.04 before they could go wheels up.

The Captain and First Office each looked out over the wings and saw a heavy build up of snow and ice.

It's all right," Wheaton thought to himself. It will all fly off when we get up to about eighty knots. She'll be clean before we have to rotate.

"Betcha the sun is shining in Tampa, Roger," he said whimsically.

Twenty-Seven

~~~

January 13, 1982
Aboard Air Florida Flight 90

John Evans thought their trip was off to a bad start. As he and Ceily boarded Air Florida Flight 90 and made their way down the long aisle of seats, three abreast on each side, he kept looking at his boarding pass and their seat assignments. He looked up. Sure enough he was right.

He turned to Ceily, following right behind him.

"Damn it, we're in the second to the last row of the airplane," he complained to her. "Almost right up against the rear bulkhead."

Ceily cocked an eye.

"So what, John? I don't care where we sit as long as we get to Tampa in time for our flight to London. It's only a ninety minute or so flight anyway," she smiled.

Evans chuckled. It was so like Ceily to see the good in anything. "Besides," she added, "we'll be that much closer to the bathrooms! Speaking of which..." She disappeared into one of the tiny rest rooms as he took a seat next to the window. It occurred to him that this was the first time he had been on an airplane since 1952, when the U.S. Air Force shipped him home from Okinawa. Funny, after his near miss in Korea, flying never appealed to him again.

Ceily returned quickly and took a seat next to her husband, beaming. She buckled her seatbelt and
~~~

reached for the airline's inflight magazine, quickly thumbing through it. Her excitement at finally travelling to Europe was hard to hide. She leaned over and gave John a kiss on the cheek.

"Happy Anniversary, my love," she said, true happiness sparkling in her eyes. "You could not have given me a more wonderful gift if you tried. I am so excited," she said, clasping her hands together, barely able to contain herself.

"And to thirty more years of happiness, Mrs. Evans," he grinned and held her. "I may be the luckiest man on earth, do you know that?"

"What a wonderful thing to say," she said, glowing. "We're going to have a fantastic time, John, I just know it."

The plane filled quickly and within minutes, another seventy-one adults and three infants had filling the plane to about three-quarters capacity. The flight carried a total of five crew.

Chief stewardess Kelly Duncan wasted no time in standing up and demonstrating the proper procedure for putting on seatbelts and pointing out emergency exits and the location of life vests. It was clear to John Evans that the flight crew was moving things along as quickly as possible to get airborne. Even as the thought came to his mind, he felt a bump and a jerk as the aircraft began backing away from the jetway.

Despite the window heaters, the brutal cold temperature outside caused Evans' view through the glass to be clouded. He wiped away the moisture with his hand and stared outside. It seemed like dozens of ground services people were all busy at the same time, loading aircraft with baggage, refueling and deicing airplanes that had all been delayed. Abruptly, he heard the familiar whine of jet engines spooling to life as the flight crew of Air Florida Flight 90 started them. Minutes later they were taxiing across the airfield.

"I imagine they'll be using the longest runway available with all this snow," he quietly mentioned to Ceily. The thought of icing problems had crossed the former pilot's mind once or twice since they had boarded the plane, but he figured in this day and age that deicing a commercial airliner was something people much smarter than him had figured out long ago.

A long while later, he felt the jet's engines being throttled up and knew that they were about to take off. He instinctively reached over to Ceily and took hold of her hand. "

"Off we go," he smiled. She grinned, but he could tell she was a bit nervous.

"Relax, Ceily. Piece of cake," he said reassuringly. "Why if a guy like me could learn to fly an airplane, anyone can. These guys are pros, believe me."

In the cockpit, Captain Wheaton heard the radio transmission from Ground Control. It was nearly 15:59 hours.

"Palm 90, taxi into position and hold on runway 36… and be ready for an immediate takeoff." As Petitt taxied into position, the tower gave clearance for takeoff and the First Officer acknowledged it. "Palm 90, cleared for takeoff." Less than thirty seconds later the tower came back on the air.

"Flight 90 do not delay departure since landing traffic is two and a half miles out for runway 36." At 15:59:46, Petitt responded, "OK." At that point, Air Florida Flight 90 had not been deiced for nearly fifty minutes. The captain of a plane that observed Palm 90 preparing for take off commented to his crew, "Look at the junk on that airplane." He would remember later that almost the entire length of the fuselage was covered in snow and ice.

Unaware, Captain Larry Wheaton immediately ordered Petitt to push his throttles to the level to achieve "V1", the point at which time the aircraft hit a speed where the pilot could still safely abort the takeoff, and V2, the speed at which the aircraft could safely lift off the ground. Outside, the 737's twin Pratt & Whitney jet engines, each capable of producing 14,500 pounds of thrust, roared as they spooled up to their predetermined power level.

"Holler if you need the windshield wipers, Roger," Wheaton offered as the aircraft began lumbering down the seven thousand-foot long runway.

Petitt held the nose steady in the center of the runway despite deep slush as the aircraft picked up speed. But something was wrong. He could feel it in his bones and glanced at his instruments. The Cockpit Voice Recorder later told the story.

> **15:59:51 Wheaton: "It's spooled. Real cold, real cold."**
> **15:59:58 Petitit: "God, look at that thing,"** he said, tapping on the EPR gauge. **"That don't seem right, does it? Uh, that's not right."**
> **16:00:09 Wheaton: "Yes it is, there's eighty."**
> **16:00:10 Petitt: "Naw, I don't think that's right. Ah, maybe it is."**
> **16:00:21 Wheaton: "Hundred and twenty."**
> **16:00:23 Petitt: "I don't know."**
> **16:00:31 Wheaton: "V1. Easy... now V2."**

Pettit felt a rising panic. He was sure they were getting faulty readings. The aircraft's instruments were telling them they were travelling much faster than they actually were. He could just feel it. By this time, the Air Florida 737 had rolled more than eight hundred meters, almost half a mile farther down the runway than was normal for takeoff. It was now or never.

Petitt made his choice.

He pulled back on the yoke. The nose of the airplane rose up towards the snow filled sky, quickly. Much *too* quickly. In the cabin, the rollout had been long – far too long, John Evans thought – and he squeezed Ceily's hand. She looked at him, worry in her eyes.

The runway surface was rough and Evans' instincts told him they weren't going to get off the ground. He held his breath waiting for the sound of engines being shut down and the harsh forward shift of weight as the pilot stomped on the brakes to abort the takeoff.

But neither occurred. He knew what was going to happen next. Turning, he looked at Ceily and put his arm around her, pulling her close. She saw the fear in his eyes.

"Get down, Ceily, put your head down between your legs," he ordered even as he pushed her forward. 'We're not going to make it," he told her. "We're going in." He did the same.

In the cockpit, fate had already made up its mind. Eight seconds after the Captain had yelled "V1" and two seconds after calling out "V2" the sound of the stick-shaker, a mechanical device that rapidly and noisily vibrated the control yoke of an aircraft, warned Petitt and Wheaton that Flight 90 was in imminent danger of stalling. The nose of the airplane was climbing at an alarming rate as they sought altitude.

16:00:45 Wheaton: "Forward, forward, easy. We only want five hundred feet!"

The tail of the airplane was sinking and the nose was continuing to rise too fast. They were losing air speed and becoming unstable.

16:00:48 Wheaton: "Come on forward... forward, just barely climb."

16:00:59 Wheaton: "Stalling, we're falling!"

16:01:00 Petitt: "This is it. Larry, We're going down, Larry..."

16:01:01 Wheaton: "I know it!"

Long seconds later, the Cockpit Voice Recorder stopped with the sound of crushing impact.

Twenty-Eight

"The phone rang about five o'clock that night. It was Bruce Johanssen, a good friend of your grandfather who liked to talk about old cars with him," my mother said. My father was still at the window, staring into space, his back turned to us.

We were sitting in the living room. My mother was struggling to tell us what she knew of the events of that afternoon. It was a long time ago. I was only four when it happened, Sheila was just an infant. I'd heard none of this from Pop. It was another of those incredibly well hidden Evans family secrets.

"Marnie?" Bruce asked when I answered. His voice was rather shaky. 'You'd better turn on the news,'" he said.

"Why?" I asked him, completely unaware of what was happening," my mother continued. "I remember saying, 'What's wrong, Bruce? What's wrong?'"

"'It's bad, Marnie, I think it's bad,' he told me. Then he asked if your father was here."

"I told him that he was and he said he'd be over in a few minutes. He was here not ten minutes later."

"I hung up the phone, jumped up and turned on the television," she went on. "I think it was CBS," she said in a tired voice. It was hard work to remember something so horrifying.

"They were broadcasting live from the Airport, from Washington National. Down by the river. The Potomac. In the background was the tail section of an airplane sticking out of the water. All we could see was the tail number, which meant nothing to us. There was so much confusion, the airport was only just becoming aware that a plane had crashed. The news cameras had just happened to be driving by when it happened. The news media knew about the disaster even before the airport controllers."

She started to cry and wiped her eyes as she finished her words. I watched my father take a long sip of his drink. Sheila was sobbing.

"Then Bruce arrived. The poor man was nearly in shock.

"He held my hand when I met him at the door. He told me that the television people had already announced that they thought it was Air Florida Flight 90."

I heard my father quietly sobbing, his back still to us.

"That was the flight grandma and grandpa were on."

Twenty-Nine

~~~

January 13, 1982
Aboard Air Florida Flight 90

Three-quarters of a mile from the end of runway 36, the 14th Street Bridge was jammed pack with cars and trucks snowbound from the daylong blizzard. Traffic was barely crawling across the I-395 Interstate Highway connecting Washington D.C. with Arlington, Virginia. Many offices in Washington had closed early for the day because of the weather conditions, making the traffic that much worse.

At 4:01 p.m., from a maximum altitude of no more than three hundred-fifty feet, motorists trapped on the bridge watched in disbelief as the Air Florida 737 shockingly appeared out of the snow filled skies, its nose clearing the bridge but its tail dropping upon vehicles unable to move in the traffic jam. The airplane sliced through six cars and a truck on the bridge, nearly dragging several of them into the Potomac River below, as it also tore out ninety-seven feet of the bridge's railing and forty-one feet of its retaining wall. Four motorists died instantly from the crushing blow of the falling airliner, their cars flattened by the blow. At least two were decapitated. Another four sustained serious injuries.

From there, the heavily damaged aircraft twisted to the left and plunged into the ice-covered, freezing Potomac River nose first. The wrecked plane hit the water between two of the three spans of the bridge,
~~~

between the I-395 northbound span known as the Rochambeau Bridge and the HOV high occupancy lanes of the north and southbound spans.

The impact with the bridge caused the aircraft to take a slightly nose down attitude before it hit the water. Consequently, the Air Florida flight plowed into the river and its three-inch thick ice blanket nose down and continued forward, the fuselage slicing through the ice before it stopped, shattering into at least four sections. The wings – which also doubled as fuel tanks in a "wet wing" design – were torn from the fuselage and immediately released a flood of jet aviation fuel into the water. In seconds, the aircraft sank and all but the tail section was left visible above the surface, like a gigantic, obscene, sheet metal tombstone painted in Air Florida's vivid blue and green paint scheme. The remains of the aircraft came to rest in twenty-five to thirty feet of water about one hundred-fifty feet from the south shoreline, packed with more than two feet of snow.

Inside, from the tip of the nose to the far end of the fuselage just forward of the tail section, the aircraft was completely devastated. The floor of the main fuselage sections was sheared off, tearing the mountings loose of almost every passenger seat. Of the seventy-six passengers and five crewmembers aboard, all but eight were killed instantly, either of head or chest trauma from the forward impact. Autopsies ultimately revealed that none had drowned on impact, but three subsequently. Wheaton and Petitt died instantly of massive head trauma and of the rest of the crew, only Kelly Duncan lived to tell the story. Somehow, she survived the impact and because she was seated and buckled in just behind the cockpit door as the airplane hit the water, she was able to swim to the surface when the entire forward cabin separated from the fuselage.

The only others aboard who had any chance of surviving were those strapped into the tail section of the 737, which was separated from the fuselage but still intact and floating.

John and Ceily Evans were among those passengers.

On impact, both had been knocked briefly unconscious from the impact of hitting their heads on the back of the seats in front of them. But John Evan's instructions an instant before the crash to lean forward with their heads tucked between their legs had saved them from instant death.

The icy cold water shocked them both back to consciousness, and Evans quickly shook off the blow and assessed their situation. The good news was they were alive. The bad news was they were trapped under a mountain of debris that had been pushed aft by the huge surge of water that entered the fuselage.

He reached for Ceily and shook her to clear her head.

"Ceily, we're OK, the airplane has crashed, but we're OK," he repeated in as calm a voice as he could muster considering the situation. "Just sit still while I get all this garbage off us – I can see light and the tail section is still floating."

Despite his reassuring words, Ceily became hysterical, frantically trying to release her seat belt and flailing away at parts of seats that had their exit partially blocked. She began screaming, making guttural noises like a wounded animal cornered and unable to defend itself.

"Ceily!" John Evans screamed at her. "Listen to me!" He took her face in his hands and held her tight.

"We're okay, and we're going to get out of here. Stay calm. Put your trust in me. I will get us out of this!"

She squeezed his hands holding her face and gradually calmed herself. She shook her head, yes. But terror filled her eyes.

Evans managed to release his seat belt and pushed a heavy section of the seat behind him that had come loose off of them. Then he put his shoulder into the seat in front of Ceily that was pinned against her legs. She was squirming, trying to get free but each time she moved to the right, she screamed out in pain. Evans suspected at least one of her legs was broken, how badly he couldn't know.

"Stay still Ceily," he said to her evenly, "I'll get your legs free." Several rows ahead, a movement caught his attention. It was a young mother, her eyes wild with fear, holding an infant no more than a few months old, struggling to squeeze out of a small gap between two smashed seats. If she could manage to get through the slight opening, she would be able to climb forward and swim to the floating tail section with her baby. Suddenly, she caught his eye.

"Please, mister, please, help me," she screamed to John Evans, reaching one of her hands towards him. In the other, she held an infant, not more than a few months old. "Please, I have my baby… I can't get out… just pull us through, please!" His heart broke at the sight. It would take a miracle for the young, slightly built girl to get out even without trying to hold on to her baby. She didn't stand a chance without his help. He scanned the area. There was no one else moving in the airplane. From what he could see, they were all dead.

But Evans was now free to move himself. He turned to Ceily, still trapped.

"I can reach her," he said quickly to his wife, who was clutching his arm, petrified at the slightest creak and groan that resonated inside the broken body of the airplane as it settled into the water. The water was slowly climbing higher.

"No!" Ceily screamed, begging him. "Don't leave me, John, please don't leave me. We have to get out!"

"We'll be OK," he said to her reassuringly, his voice full of confidence. "It will only take me a moment to free her."

"No, don't go..." Ceily screamed, even as her husband kicked off and dove into the frigid water towards the woman.

"John, no, don't... please don't leave me, I'm so afraid," she said feebly, her teeth chattering and her body shaking from cold and shock. She was paralyzed with fear and the freezing, 34-degree water was robbing her of strength and hope.

Evans reached the young woman in seconds and tugged on one of her arms, trying to pull her though the small opening between the seats. After thirty seconds he realized they were making no progress. He ducked under the rising water and tried to pry the seats farther apart, but with no results. He could not free her. He thought of the baby.

"Give me the child," he yelled to her. I'll come back for you. "With both hands free you might be able to squeeze through."

"No," she shrieked back at him in fear. "No, I can't let go of my baby. Please get us out of..."

As she pleaded with him the section of fuselage she had been sitting in suddenly lurched downward. Evans hadn't realized that it was hanging by a thread to the tail section. Without warning, it broke loose and began sinking rapidly with the woman and her child still trapped behind the broken seats. With his left hand he grabbed a seat back in the tail section to keep his footing, then reached across the widening gap for the woman's arm and held her, trying to pull back as the fuselage sank ever deeper. But he was unable to fight the weight of the descending mid section and despite his desperate effort to hang on, he gradually lost his grasp of her arm. She and her baby slipped from his hands and disappeared into the inky black waters of the Potomac.

"No," he screamed aloud at what he had just witnessed. "No, I'm sorry, " he said frantically reaching through the opening trying to locate her arm or clothes or anything to grab onto. There was nothing.

In utter defeat he swam back to Ceily but there was no time to mourn. To his horror, he realized that in his absence, the water had risen almost to her neck. The tail section was settling lower. He had to free her now.

"John," she said, her voice no more than a whimper as hypothermia was overwhelming her, "I think we have to get this done quickly."

"Ceily, oh, my Ceily, hang on, please," he yelled to her in a panic. He dove again and yanked on her legs, still wedged under the seat ahead of her. She screamed out in pain.

"Forget the pain, Ceily, please, it's the only way." He rammed his shoulder into the seat again trying to push it forward but succeeding only in dislocating his shoulder. Despite the blinding pain, he would not give up. Again and again he dove into the murky black water, trying desperately to pull her trapped legs free. He was nearly exhausted when he finally came up for the last time.

"John," Ceily said, "no more. Please, just stay with me," she begged him as the water was almost to her lips.

"No, Ceily, I won't give up. Keep your head above water!" He dove again and yanked at her legs so hard he heard her scream in agony even underwater. He felt her hand pulling at his hair to come back to the surface.

When his face broke through the fuel-fouled water, he saw that her mouth was already immersed and it was about to reach her nose. He frantically looked around for a section of hose or tubing and quickly saw an emergency oxygen mask hanging limply from the ceiling of the aircraft. Ripping a section of plastic tubing loose, he placed one end into Ceily's mouth and hung the other over the top of her seat, giving her a sort of snorkel. It would give him a few more minutes.

He looked around frantically for something to pry back the imprisoning seat, swimming into the galley in search of anything to use as a tool. All he could find was a small fire extinguisher and immediately dove beneath Ceily with it and banged it against the seat like a battering ram. But the seat would not budge.

The water was now a foot over her head and about to close in over the top of the tubing. She reached up and grabbed him by the face, pulling him to her beneath the water. He watched in disbelief as she spit out the tubing, looked lovingly into his eyes, then locked her lips to his. He thought for a moment she wanted him to give her air by mouth to mouth.

But what she wanted was to say goodbye.

She kissed him as long as her breath would hold out, gripping his face. Then abruptly, she let go, and with her last bit of life pushed him away and back to the surface. He gasped for breath as he broke water then immediately dove again, refusing to give in to the inevitable. He found her, but already she was still and lifeless. The look of terror in her wide eyes had been replaced by one of love, serenity, and sadness.

It was a look he would carry with him, in graphic detail, for the rest of his life. He screamed into the water, the excruciating pain of watching her die driving him to the edge of madness. He was overwhelmed with grief and dove again to try one last time to free her, praying that he could breath life back into her body. Suddenly, the fuselage seemed to slip forward and her legs were freed. Without warning a hand grabbed him by the collar of his jacket and pulled him to the surface. It was another survivor, precariously hanging on to a seat bracket screaming at him to leave the airplane or he would die. He fought the strong arm fighting to save his life. "Let me go, let me go, let me die! Please, please!" he screamed. "Ceily, don't go, come back…"

Above him, like so many years before, he heard the sound of an arriving helicopter that would bring him to safety. The downblast of the helo's whirling blades blew more toxic, fuel laden water into his lungs and he was near death from drowning and hypothermia by the time the rescue crew flew him to shore and he was rushed to a hospital.

He was incoherent as the ambulance raced to George Washington University Hospital. The freezing temperature of the water had taken it's toll far more than any of his other injuries. As doctors worked feverishly to clear his lungs of toxic fluids, he was suffering from severe hypothermia. His body temperature was in the mid-eighties and would not register on a conventional thermometer.

Despite his grave condition, John Evans, delirious from the nightmare of the crash and losing his beloved wife, screamed out to her over and over again. Doctors had to restrain him as they administered warm oxygen to raise his body temperature back to normal. Eventually, exhaustion and the morphine used to minimize the pain of his dislocated shoulder and dozens of deep bruises and lacerations caused him to lose consciousness, despite the relentless hallucinations of trying to rescue his wife.

In a dreamlike state, he relived the final moments of their lives together and the horror of watching her die.

"Ceily, Ceily, wait, I'll come and get you," he dreamed. *"I didn't mean to leave you, it was only for a minute.*

"Don't leave me now, Ceily... please... we have to see the Eiffel Tower... I promised you..."

Thirty

"We watched the television for the next hour and actually saw the helicopter pull your grandfather from the wreckage. We saw others rescued, but couldn't make out their features enough to know if one of them was Ceily."

She dabbed at the tears running down her cheeks.

"We prayed together. Bruce kept saying 'Don't give up hope, she may be all right. If John got out you can bet he pulled her with him. He'd never leave her behind.'"

I was dumbstruck. Pop had never talked about the crash, never even hinted at it to either Sheila or me. I thought I knew the rest of the story before mom told it. I was wrong.

"By six o'clock, the media was reporting John Evans as one of the survivors but it wasn't until almost an hour later that George Washington University Hospital called to confirm it. They told us he was in an intensive care unit but was stable. They said they couldn't give us any information on Ceily, that we would have to speak to the airline for that information. She was not at that hospital."

"The bastards at Air Florida told us their list of survivors was incomplete," my father said in a somber voice, still facing the window. "They knew, but they were trying to figure out how to put the best PR spin on the whole mess. We didn't know until three o'clock in the morning that she was even listed as missing."

He laughed sarcastically and threw back the rest of his third drink.

"Missing..." he said with bitterness. "Can you imagine having the sheer arrogance to list her as missing after she had been submerged in below freezing water for more than eleven hours?"

He sighed, deeply.

"My mother was dead, and they didn't have the balls to tell us. It wasn't until mid-morning the next day that the airline announced there were no other survivors."

My mother put her head back against the chair and closed her eyes.

"Your dad and I left immediately for Arlington, figuring it would be faster to drive than to fly. The hospital was telling us that Pop was stable, although still in intensive care. He was pretty banged up and still delirious."

"Grandma died in the crash, Mom?" Sheila asked, her voice wavering. She didn't believe it.

"Yes, darling."

"I don't even remember her, Mom…" she said. "But what an awful way to die."

I was completely puzzled now. My grandmother had died in a tragic airplane accident in 1982. Why were we just finding out about it nearly thirteen years later? Why was it a secret? And what did it have to do with my family coming apart?

"What happened?" I asked first. "What caused the accident?"

"You can research it to death on the internet, Sean," my father said, finally turning to face us. "It was a major event in U.S. aviation history because of all the errors in judgment and decision making that went into causing all those people to die. The National Transportation Safety Board instituted a lot of changes after the accident.

"But the bottom line was pilot error. The crew never turned on the engine anti-icing system, which caused sensors in the idling engines to freeze and give them false power readings. They should have made the decision to return to a hanger and had the aircraft de-iced again. They never should have gotten so close to the DC-9 in front of them. The heat of its engines did the exact opposite of what they expected. It caused ice and snow to build up on the leading edge of the wings, thereby causing the aircraft to 'pitch up' on take off. They thought their engines were producing a lot more power when they attempted takeoff. They should have aborted the take off."

He just stopped and shook his head. "I could go on for an hour. The list of mistakes they made is endless. Including the motorists on the bridge, seventy-nine people died directly because of pilot error." He paused.

"All but one of them, that is."

He came around to sit in an easy chair opposite my mother. The look on his face was one of rage so deep that it startled me. I didn't comprehend.

What he said next was so shocking that I quickly stopped thinking about his anger.

"I'd like to tell you that those foolish young pilots caused the death of every passenger on board that flight and the motorists on the bridge. But that would be a lie."

"What do you mean? I asked, my own hackles going up at this new unnecessary mystery.

"It wasn't the pilots, or the airline, or the control tower at the airport that caused your grandmother's death," he said. "They simply enabled her to die."

"Well, who was responsible for her death?" I yelled jumping to my feet.

Slowly and dramatically, like a lawyer with blood in his eye ready to convince a jury that a man was guilty and deserved the death penalty he stood and faced me. My mother slumped in the chair, her face buried in her hands. Sheila whimpered.

The top of my father's head only came up to my chin. But that didn't stop him from looking me square in the eye. Seconds ticked by and the vein in his neck bulged as he thought of the most succinct, damning words he could, just for the satisfaction. He was good at his job as his lips finally moved.

"Your beloved grandfather."

Thirty-One

John Evans finally stopped walking after another hour and hid in the shadows off Route 74. He was shivering now, but tried to shake it off. He sat down to think a bit.

"I should have known how cold you were in that damn water, Ceily. I hope you're warmer now. But most of all, I hope you forgive me."

He thought about it for a few more minutes then came to a conclusion.

"You were right to leave me, you know. I made a very bad decision. I never wanted to be a hero, not that day or even in Korea. I only wanted you. But I would have left me too for treating you so badly."

He shivered and wished he had remembered to bring his old cardigan with him. It was hanging in the closet at the rehab. He thought about going back and sneaking in to get it, but decided against it. They might catch him and then they'd probably lock him in for good.

The air was turning frigid and it was so quiet. He looked up at the stars and remembered flying his Sabre at night over the Yalu River in Korea many years before. There were no lights on the river and you lost touch with the earth flying at night. If you forgot about your instruments, there were times when it almost felt like you were part of space. That's where heaven was, he reckoned. Where he was sure Ceily was now.

"Are you waiting for me?" he said aloud while watching the stars. There was no answer.

"Well, I don't blame you, Ceily," he said, sadly. "After all the love you gave me, I let you down when you needed me most."

His eyes moistened. It was always a mystery to him that he could still cry over her. He should be all cried out by now, he thought. But then a question came to him. Does a person cry forever when it hurts so much, he wondered? He thought that perhaps they could.

"We never saw the Eiffel Tower, Ceily. I'm sorry for that, too," he apologized, and wiped away tears that escaped his eyes.

"And I have one more thing to tell you, honey. This time I really blew it."

He took a deep breath and sighed, not wanting to share more bad news with her.

"I've looked everywhere, but I seem to have lost the keys to the Mercedes."

He dropped his head in shame, his chin touching his chest.

"Jesus Christ. I can't find you, I can't find the keys, I'm freezing my ass off and I don't know how to get home."

He was still then, his eyes closed. The night was so quiet. Suddenly, in the blackness he could see her.

She was waiting for him and she had such a wonderful smile on her face, so unlike the last time he had seen her alive. Her long red hair was down around her shoulders the way he liked it and her eyes were still as green as the ocean.

And then she talked to him. It was so wonderful to hear her voice.

"John, my love, I'm not angry with you and I will wait for you forever," she said. "I'm just passing time now until you get to join me again. But now is not the time. You have to get up and walk, John, or you're going to freeze to death.

And we can't have that, because you're needed there. Sheila and Sean need you so much right now."

"Are you sure, Ceily?" he answered her in wonder. "Because I can come right now if you want. I'd like to come..."

"No, you mustn't, John. They need you for a little while longer and then we can be together again. All right? You must trust me, my love."

The apparition paused.

"Now get up, John, and walk. Please, for me."

He thought for a minute while gazing at her, memorizing every detail of her face again.

"Yes... just for you Ceily."

He got up from the brush in which he had hidden, wiped the dirt off his clothes and began walking again. He didn't know where he was going, but he was walking.

"That's good, John, just keep walking. Someone will be along soon and give you a ride home, I'm sure of it."

"You always knew what was best, Ceily. Sometimes I get really confused now.

"You promise to wait for me?"

"I promise."

"Okay. Can I ask another favor?"

"Of course."

"Will you come and talk to me sometimes, like now?"

"When I can, my love, when I can. But I'll always be watching you."

"Okay. Love you, Ceily."

"I love you too, John. I tried to tell you how much when I kissed you on the airplane. It was the only way I knew how."

He sobbed. "Thank you for telling me that."

"And John..."

"Yes Ceily?"

"I've seen the Eiffel Tower. It's no big deal. We had more fun in the car."

"Yah?"

"All I want is what I've always wanted. You."

"Can't I come now?" A shooting star flashed across the clear night sky.

"No. Now is not our time. Be there for Sheila and Sean. Promise me."

"I will, Ceily," he said as her image slowly dissolved before his eyes.

"I will."

Thirty-Two

~~~

January 14, 1982

When Sam and Marnie Evans arrived at George Washington University Hospital late the day after the crash, the scene outside the hospital was bedlam. It seemed every reporter in the country was there to try and get a story from one of the few survivors of the crash of Air Florida Flight 90. There were also representatives of the NTSB and even the FBI waiting to talk to the survivors. It took the exhausted Sam and Marnie nearly an hour just to get to Pop's room in the intensive care unit.

He was fully awake when they got to him, still buried under blankets and being fed warm oxygen to ward off the aftereffects of hypothermia. He also had a drain in his stomach and tubes into his lungs that were siphoning the residue of toxic aviation fuel from his system. His dislocated shoulder had been set and was resting in a sling. Despite the pain and discomfort, he refused any more morphine and was screaming for someone to tell him where Ceily was.

A nurse quickly took them aside and explained that the events of the last few minutes aboard the sinking aircraft and his rescue were lost to him, at least temporarily, and he was unaware that Ceily was dead. He had not yet been informed.

"Sam!" John cried with relief when his son and daughter-in-law entered his room. "Where the hell is
~~~

Ceily? Is she hurt? How bad is it? Why won't they tell me, Sam? I'm her husband for Christ's sake..."

Marnie went to him and wrapped her arms around his shoulders. Sam took in the situation and was bewildered. He needed time to think.

"Calm down, Dad, I'll try and find a doctor and ask, OK? Just calm down."

It was Sam's excuse to escape and compose himself. The sight of his father was shocking enough, but it was also obvious he was going to have to break the news to him. He was afraid he didn't have the strength. His mother's death had not yet completely sunk in, and the young lawyer was living in a fog. It was all so surreal. He felt faint and sat down in the hall until a nurse stopped to ask if he was all right. He introduced himself and the nurse went to find the doctor who was treating John Evans.

The doctor appeared within minutes, with his hand extended in condolence.

"Mr. Evans, I'm Dr. Bill Garnes," he introduced himself. He was a tall, almost gaunt man in his early forties, whose red rimmed eyes and stubbly growth of beard gave clear indication that it had been some time since he'd been off his feet. His eyes were filled with sadness. The young trauma doctor had seen things over the last twenty-four hours that he would remember for the rest of his life. At times he felt as if he would be overwhelmed with emotion by the crushed bodies that were wheeled into his emergency room since early last night. The worst were the dead mothers still clinging to the bodies of their children. Despite his intensive training, nothing could have prepared him for the onslaught of victims and he knew that it would continue for days as more and more bodies were recovered from the wreckage. For the moment, he shook off the nightmare.

"I've been treating your dad since they brought him in last night," he said to Sam. "Please accept my sincere regrets for the loss of your mother...

Sam swallowed hard at the words, which still seemed so impossible. "Yes, thank you Doctor... it hasn't quite sunk in... so sudden..."

"I understand," Garnes said. "I will give you something to help you sleep when we finish. The days ahead will be most difficult, I know."

Sam Evans composed himself.

"My father...?"

"He appears to be in no danger. From the welt on his forehead it appears that he took a tremendous blow to the head upon impact but seems not to have suffered a concussion. He must have protected himself someway...I'm not sure. He has been almost impossible to talk with, delirious, which of course is not unusual given the shock he has just experienced.

"We nearly lost him from hypothermia. His body temperature had dipped into the low eighty-degree range and frankly I don't know how his heart kept beating. In addition, he ingested large amounts of highly toxic aviation fuel and suffered a dislocated shoulder and various lacerations and bruises. The good news is he will make a fully recovery. At least physically."

"Yes, I understand," Sam replied. "He appears not to understand that my mother is dead..."

"Unfortunately, the blow to the head, and the severe crisis he endured in those final few moments during and after the crash have left him in a semi-amnesic state. He recalls that there was an accident, he just cannot remember what happened in the minutes that passed after the accident until arriving here."

"Why hasn't he been told?" Sam asked, desperate not to have to be the one to confront his father. He wasn't sure that he was emotionally strong enough himself to survive the loss of his mother. But for his father… my God, he thought, Ceily was his whole life. It was an entirely different level of grief – he would be inconsolable. It suddenly struck Sam that John Evans would never be the same. He ached for the man he loved so much.

"Frankly, his heart was so weakened by the hypothermia, we could not risk the shock of telling him that his wife was gone," Garnes said. "I believe we would have lost him."

There was an awkward silence. Garnes knew what had to be done.

"Unfortunately, I have much experience in this situation, Mr. Evans, and I will talk to your father, if that's what you desire," he offered in compassion. "It never get's easier, but it is part of my job."

Sam appeared to be looking in the Doctor's eyes but was actually staring right through him. He too knew what had to be done. He steeled himself.

"Thank you, Dr. Garnes, but I will tell my father. I owe him that."

"Perhaps we should sedate him first," Garnes offered. "I am under the impression that they were extremely close."

Sam choked on his words, and almost lost it.

"There are no words to describe the love affair my mother and father enjoyed for thirty years, Doctor. No words could do it justice. But I think we had better do this with him in a completely aware state. He is not the type of man that takes dancing around the truth very well."

"I'll be here if you need me, Mr. Evans."

"Sam, Doctor Garnes. Just call me Sam."

"Then call me Bill, Sam… come and see me when you have spoken to him."

"I will."

When he entered his father's room again, Marnie was still holding him, tears streaming down her face. She looked at Sam, wondering what to do. One look in her eyes and he knew that his dad still was unaware that he had lost his life's partner. He shook his head at Marnie.

"I'll take it from here, honey. Just stay close, OK?" he asked her. "I'm a little shaky myself."

Marnie let go of John and got up from the bed making room for Sam. He embraced his father and sat in a chair next to him.

"How are you feeling, Dad?" he asked.

His father just shrugged, exhausted and confused. He was beyond pain.

"You're a lucky man…" he began, then stopped abruptly, realizing what he was about to say. John Evans caught it.

"Where's your mother, Sam?" he asked, frantic. "They pulled her out right behind me… didn't they?"

His son looked back at him blankly, tears welling in Sam's eyes.

"No… " he said.

"No?" his father repeated. "How long did it take to get her out, to get her on the helicopter? What room is she in, Sam? Dammit, Sam, where…"

"She's gone, Dad."

It was if he had hit his father in the face with a hammer.

"What?" he whimpered, in real, physical pain. "What did you say?"

"We lost her, Dad, we lost Mom," he said, his voice breaking. He reached out for his father to support him but the elder man pushed him back.

"No... there's a mistake here Sam... you're a lawyer, go and see where they've taken her... she's just not here..."

Marnie burst into tears and turned away from the scene. Sam grabbed his father and wrapped his arms around him, squeezing with all his might.

"It's OK, Dad, she's not suffering. She died quickly. It wasn't your fault."

"Nooooo..." John Evans began to moan, like a wounded animal that knew it would die a slow, agonizing death.

"Ceily... go get her Sam, please..."

"She's gone, Dad...she's dead," Sam answered, tears streaming down his face.

His father went limp in his arms, the words of his beloved son finally sinking home.

"That's not possible, Sam... I was taking her to see the Eiffel Tower... we've been married thirty years, you remember?"

He began to tremble in Sam's arms, an uncontrollable shake. He needed to scream or hit something, anything to release the rage and agony that was building inside him.

"Marnie, go tell the nurse to find Bill Garnes. We need that sedative." Marnie quickly left the room.

"Bring me to her, Sam. I need to see her," John demanded.

Sam looked away, unable to look in his father's face as he said the words.

"I can't Dad, I can't."

"Why?"

His son could not get the words to come out.

"Why not, Sam? Why can't you bring me to her?"

"Because!" he finally blurted out.

His father looked at him, even more confused.

"Because they haven't recovered her body yet, Dad."

John Evans grimaced through his tears, his heart literally tearing from his chest with each word his son spoke.

"Mom's body is still in the river."

Thirty-Three

Sam and Marnie stayed in Arlington for the rest of the week while Pop was mending and recovery efforts continued off the banks of the Potomac. The news was full of the grim details of retrieving bodies from the wreckage and the awful impact Flight 90 experienced when it hit the thick ice.

If anything, the results of autopsies performed on passenger's bodies as they were recovered gave Sam some peace that his mother had probably died instantaneously when the plane crashed and had not suffered. Autopsies revealed that of the more than three-quarters of the passengers recovered thus far, only three had died of drowning. The rest had succumbed to instant blunt force trauma. One of the passengers who had drowned had actually made it to the surface but had died after the effects of hypothermia robbed him of his ability to stay afloat until he could be rescued. The other two were a young mother and her infant child. Unfortunately, there could be no closure yet for the Evans family. Ceily's body still remained beneath the icy waters of the Potomac, as yet unrecovered.

The fact that Evans had survived with as few injuries as he had was nothing short of a miracle. But given the choice, he would have forsaken his good fortune and died holding Ceily. Her death was the equivalent of a death sentence for him. The John Evans who had boarded Flight 90 no longer existed.

My grandfather's physical recovery was speedy. The same could hardly be said of his mental state. He went days without speaking, eating or sleeping. He sat in a chair by his bed next to a window and just stared, unmoving. It was if he was in a sort of vegetative state – going through the motions of being alive but showing virtually no indication of awareness. But Sam knew his father, knew the stories of his valor during the Korean War and the awful road to recovery he faced. He knew how strong his dad was. He would recover, he knew it.

What he didn't know was what was going on in his father's mind. What he was thinking, what he was sorting through. Pop had still not indicated any memory of the final moments before the crash and the awful minutes after.

Sam was sure of what his father was doing and he was right.

In his silence, John Evans was digging deeper and deeper into his badly bruised recollections to remember his final moments with Ceily.

No matter how painful they may be. He had to know if he was ever going to come to grips with the tragedy of losing her.

Worst of all though was the frighteningly persistent ache in his soul that something profound had happened in those last few minutes.

Something beyond the accident.

Something that involved him.

Something that had cost Ceily her life.

Thirty-Four

~~~

January 19, 1982

It wasn't until the sixth day of recovery operations that they discovered Ceily's body when they hauled up a huge section of the fuselage that had finally separated from the tail. She was still sitting in her seat, but her badly broken legs were free from the wreckage. Recovery personnel simply lifted her from her seat and brought her aboard a Coast Guard ship assisting in the recovery of passenger bodies.

Marnie had flown back to Connecticut to care for Sheila and Sean, and Sam was alone when he got the news. Despite the acute grief he felt and the cold, sterile post-mortem facility in which the task had to be performed, he met Bill Garnes to identify his mother's remains.

Bill gently and slowly pulled back a sheet to reveal her face. Although Sam had steeled himself for the experience, nothing could take away the shock of seeing her. Mercifully, the bitterly cold water and the relatively short period of time in which she had been submerged had slowed the effects of decomposition. Other than the hideous pallor of her skin, she was well preserved. Her appearance did little to relieve Sam's grief and he buried his face in his hands for a moment, trying desperately to remain composed. He forced himself to look at her, to take in the lovely features of the only woman other than Marnie he had ever loved.
~~~

Childhood memories of their time together flooded his mind, almost overwhelming him. Walking him to school. Letting him lick the spoon when she baked his favorite cake. Tucking him into bed and reading him a good night story. The two of them sneaking off for rides in the old yellow car when dad was busy with work.

The Doctor's official question actually came as a relief.

"Is this the body of your mother, Mrs. Cecilia Evans, Sam? Please indicate yes or no."

He didn't hesitate and shook his head yes.

"These are the remains of my mother, Mrs. Ceily Evans," he responded. "I have no doubt about it."

"Thank you," Garnes replied and went to pull the sheet over her face again.

"Wait," Sam asked. "Just give me a second with her."

Garnes and the attending orderly turned and stepped back from the gurney on which Ceily Evans lay to give her son time alone with his mother.

Sam lingered over her face and gently touched her cheeks. The coolness of her skin startled him, but it was still as smooth as he remembered. He bent over her and kissed her on the forehead, fighting the urge to scoop her body off the gurney and embrace her. Tears welled in his eyes at the hopelessness of it all. This was not what she had deserved for her Thirtieth Anniversary.

It was time to let go of her.

"Thank you gentlemen," he said as he turned and walked away.

Sam desperately wanted a drink, although he also oddly felt a sense of relief. Now that her body had been recovered, they would finally know for sure that his mother had died instantly in the crash. For himself, the thought that she had not suffered would help him heal from her loss. For his father, he hoped the facts would help break him out of his trance-like state. Somehow, he had to help him regain his life, even if it was without his beloved Ceily.

Considering the circumstances, the Virginia chief state's medical examiner rushed Ceily's autopsy results as a favor to Bill Garnes. Less than twenty-four hours after she had been pulled from the river, with the sallowness of her skin the only visible sign that she was gone, the cause of her death was identified with certainty.

It was two o'clock in the morning when Garnes entered John Evans room and woke Sam, asleep in a chair next to his father. The elder Evans appeared to be completely awake but showed no indication of awareness that the doctor had entered the room.

He shook Sam awake.

"Yah, Bill," he said, struggling to come out of the fog he was living in. He looked around in a panic for his father. "Is something wrong? Dad? Marnie?"

"No… Sam, no, I'm sorry to wake you. I just think we need to talk."

"Talk?"

"Yah… I just got a copy of the autopsy report." He took a deep breath.

Sam picked up on his hesitancy.

"Good… well, it was blunt force trauma, right?" Sam said, almost ashamed at how simply the words came out of his mouth. That was what he was prepared to hear.

"Not exactly, Sam," Garnes said, looking down at a sheath of medical documents in his hand.

"What do you mean, not exactly?"

"Her legs were broken, she submarined under the seat in front of her on impact. She might have been pinned in at some point, but her legs were free when they took her out of the water." He stopped. Sam shook his head, waiting for him to describe her other injuries. His legal training was kicking in and he was listening for the right words.

"There were no other injuries, Sam."

The lawyer looked at him incredulously.

"What? That's impossible? The other passengers suffered horrible…"

"I know. But that's not what happened to your mother," Garnes said. He thought for a moment of how bad it was to have to tell someone that a loved one had died in an accident. This was worse.

"Well, how did she die? Hypothermia? She didn't…"

Garnes knew he had to say it.

"She was the last victim to be autopsied. Unfortunately, she is the fourth we have found that died as a result of drowning."

Sam's jaw dropped.

"Her lungs were full of water… and fuel."

"There must be a mistake." This was impossible.

"I'm sorry, Sam, there's no mistake. She suffered no head trauma, other than a possible mild concussion and there were no upper or lower torso injuries. Nor were there any internal injuries.

"She simply drowned."

Sam focused on Garnes' face for several minutes but did not see him. There were scenario's going through his head faster than he could process. One was worse than any of them.

"You mean… she drowned after he got out?"

"Whoa, Sam..." Garnes pulled his head back sharply. "You're getting way ahead of yourself. I don't know what this means – other than the fact that the cause of death was drowning."

"Well...how did he get out? Was she still alive when he got to the tail..." Sam Evans' mind was raging with the worst thoughts imaginable.

"Eyewitness accounts said John Evans was pulled out of the wreckage, and resisted getting into the helicopter. He kept trying to dive back into the wreck," Bill Garnes countered.

Sam shook his head, unsatisfied with the answer.

"Can you tell how long she lived after the aircraft hit the water?" Sam probed. He was being a lawyer again.

"That's impossible to determine. You're father was in the airplane nearly thirty minutes before being pulled out. The aircraft hit the water at 4:01 p.m. There's no telling when or if she actually expired sometime during the next half hour or after that."

As impossible as it seemed, it appeared that John Evans, sitting within earshot of their conversation, was oblivious to it.

Sam turned to his father.

"He knows. He's the only one who knows."

The doctor shook his head in agreement.

"It may end up like that, Sam. He may be the only one who ever knows. Your father may take what happened in those few minutes to his grave."

"No, Bill... I can't accept that," Sam said in utter frustration. "Wake him up."

Garnes looked perplexed.

"I can't just wake him up, Sam. It's not quite that simple, I'm afraid, it's not as if he's just sleeping."

"Bill, please, I have to know what happened. Wake him up," Sam pleaded.

"There are things we can do to try to bring him out of this...but there are no guarantees," Garnes said hesitantly. "He may never recall what happened."

"He knows, trust me. My father is a tough bastard. I'm willing to bet you that he's reliving the whole bloody disaster right now."

Sam leaned down and took his father's face in his hands.

"Dad, look at me," he begged. "Look at me! You have to tell me what happened to Mom on the airplane. Now. Do you understand me?" He grabbed his unresponsive father by the shoulders and shook him.

Garnes jumped up and grabbed Sam before he went any further.

"Sit down, Sam, now!" Garnes ordered him. Pull yourself together. Whatever happened in the crash, happened. It's over. Your mother drowned in a tragic accident. There's no going back to fix it no matter what he tells you."

Sam Evans shook off Garnes' hold on him and stepped back, still staring at his father. The torment he felt inside was actually making him sick to his stomach. He bolted for the tiny bathroom in his father's room. The sound of wretching told the rest of the story.

When he emerged, Garnes had pulled a chair up in front of John Evans and was looking into his eyes with a small penlight. After several minutes, he pressed on the intercom connected to the nurse's station.

"Jackie," he called to the head nurse on duty, "please schedule Mr. Evans for an fMRI and an EEG, stat. Find him a slot immediately, I don't care who you have to bump by an hour. Let me know as soon as possible."

"Yes, Dr. Garnes, I'll get right on it. They're not real good about picking up phones at this…"

"Then take a walk to Imaging and make this happen," he said. "Understand?"

"Yup," the nurse said. Garnes could just imagine her rolling her eyes.

"In the meantime, please put a call into…" he hesitated for a moment and turned to Sam.

"Does your father have any history of seizures?"

"None that I'm aware of."

Garnes resumed talking to the nurse. "Jackie, put a call into Pharmacy and have them send up ten milligrams of Donepezil, immediately. Got that?"

"Donepezil? Why, isn't that used for the treatment of…"

He interrupted, in no mood to be second-guessed by a staff member.

"Yes, I know. Just do it. Tell them I want it right away. I'll be in Mr. Evans' room." He clicked off the intercom and turned to Sam.

"Man, you had better calm down," he warned Sam. "Losing it is not going to help a thing."

"Yah."

"You heard what I just did?"

"Of course, but it was all pig latin," Evans replied.

"I just ordered two tests for your father, both to rule out any head or brain injuries that may have been missed when we got him in here and that may be contributing to his current behavior," Garnes explained.

"I do a lot of personal injury work, so I know what an MRI is, but what is an 'fMRI?'"

"It stands for Functional Magnetic Resonance Imaging," Garnes responded. "An fMRI is very similar to the MRI procedure but looks for a change in magnetization between oxygen-rich and oxygen-poor blood. It has many uses, but for our purposes it will hopefully rule out for certain any head or brain injury that we may have missed."

Sam nodded. "And the EEG?"

"In simple terms, Electroencephalography records electrical activity in the brain. It's another test to determine the same thing," Garnes said, patiently. "I want to rule out the possibility that there are no psychogenic non-epileptic seizures at work here before we go much further."

"Psychogenic what?" Sam Evans asked, genuinely confused.

"I am relatively certain – and the tests will prove me right or wrong – that your father's amnesia and lack of cognition is not a functional memory disorder, but something we refer to as Organic or Psychogenic Amnesia Disorder. It can be caused by many things, but is defined by lack of injury to the brain, is impermanent and is often caused by severe emotional trauma.

""Something similar to what sometimes happens to assault or rape victims, I'm assuming," Sam guessed from his legal experience.

"Precisely."

"And the Donepezil? Am I saying that correctly? It's a drug?"

"Yes," Garnes replied. "I'm relying on my instincts that we are not dealing with a head or brain injury here. Donepezil is often used in the treatment of Alzheimer's Disease, but it has also proven to often relieve the symptoms of psychogenic-related amnesias. Donepezil could possibly help him to think and remember. In short, I'm hoping to jump-start his memory.

"Any danger?" Sam asked.

"Not at the dosage I'm going to begin with. If there's any reaction, we'll see it inside of a few days."

Sam sat down in his chair again, resigned to more waiting. But he was deeply troubled. The possibility that his mother had died alone – by drowning – in the freezing waters of the Potomac while her husband escaped sent shivers up his spine. It just wasn't possible that Pop had abandoned her. Yet the autopsy could imply that.

Sam turned and looked at his catatonic father, the most important man in his life. He was the only hero he'd ever had, and his admiration for him was second only to his love. Somehow, the thought of him abandoning his mother shattered all that.

Sam Evans was not a religious man, but as Garnes said goodnight and left the room, he began to pray that there was a plausible explanation for the way in which his mother had died.

And that his beloved father could erase the horrific scenario playing out in his son's mind.

Thirty-Five

~~~

January 23, 1982

As Garnes had predicted, neither the fMRI or EEG scans performed on John Evans had revealed any head or brain injuries. The catatonia he manifested was, as Garnes had also predicted, almost assuredly the result of the extreme emotional trauma he had experienced. What confused Sam was that his father was already suffering from psychogenic amnesia when he arrived at the hospital, but it wasn't until after he learned that Ceily had been killed that he lapsed into the stupor that was now nearly nine days long.

There had been some improvement in his behavior. Garnes felt the drug he had prescribed, Donepezil, was having an effect on his Hippocampus, a major component of the human brain located in the medial temporal lobe that played a significant role in short-term memory. Within forty-eight hours of administering the drug, John Evans began showing signs of recognition when people entered the room and he was moving his eyes. Gradually, his cognition was improving to the point that on the third day of taking the drug, he shook his head in response to Sam's question, "Are you thirsty, Dad?" It was a simple question that yielded signs of extraordinary progress.

By the next day, John Evans was beginning to speak again, actually asking for Marnie and his grandchildren.
~~~

Sam managed to get him to eat something and he seemed to sleep off and on. Bill Garnes had warned Sam not to push him too fast. Any shock to his emotional state at this point could set him back weeks or even cause permanent, if not catastrophic damage.

"Let him get stronger, Sam. As hard as it is to wait to get the answers you need, the more you are assured of getting them if he is physically and emotionally ready to purge whatever he may remember," Garnes cautioned him. "And even then, I would not attempt to interrogate him without the assistance of a trained psychologist. This is going to be a little more delicate than questioning a witness to a crime."

In the meantime, Sam preoccupied himself with making arrangements to have his mother's body transported back to Connecticut for a funeral. It had taken a solid week of arguing with the investigating authorities to get them to release the body.

"We have questions about your mother's death, Mr. Evans," Sam was told by a representative of the NTSB when he inquired about what was holding up the release of her body.

"What kind of questions, exactly?" the lawyer asked.

"Well, as you know," the investigator said, "the autopsy indicated that she was one of only four passengers who died of drowning while all others were killed by blunt force trauma. Frankly, we need to understand why to be able to complete our investigation."

Reverting to form, Sam pressed hard. He knew that holding his mother's body would not shed any additional light on the outcome of the investigation. Interviewing his father was a different matter entirely.

Rather than argue with the bureaucrats at the NTSB, he sought and won a court order with the assistance of a Washington, D.C. lawyer who did work for Sam's firm in Connecticut, granting release of the body into his custody.

The only stipulation the judge had was that when the time was appropriate and his father was physically and emotionally capable, Sam would produce John Evans for questioning by the NTSB.

"I assure you, your honor," he told the judge, "I have an equally vested interest in the questions the NTSB wishes to pursue with my father. But he is not at this time capable of handling the stress." He produced a letter from Bill Garnes attesting to John Evans' current medical condition.

Marnie made arrangements to have the body received by a funeral home in Willington. That night, Sam watched as his mother's casket was loaded onto an Air Florida flight to Connecticut. He could not shake the ugly thought that there should be two caskets being brought aboard — or none at all. Standing at a terminal window, he followed the Air Florida aircraft as it taxied to runway 36 and took off for the short flight to Connecticut. Unconsciously, he found himself holding his breath until the airplane cleared the wrecked 14th Street Bridge.

He couldn't bear the thought of going back to the hospital again that night, knowing he would not be able to talk to his father yet. Instead he took a taxi back to his hotel and headed straight for the bar. He sat at a small table in a dark corner until last call, speaking to no one, deep in thought.

The drunker he got, the darker his thoughts became.

* * *

Across town, in the darkness of his hospital room, that night John Evans came back to the light. Slowly, exhaustingly, as if swimming his way through thick, murky waters, he rose back to the surface of consciousness, breaking through the memories of the terrifying – and heart breaking – ordeal he had just experienced. His mind began to function again and his thoughts to clear. Although his eyes had been opened for days, now suddenly he was able to see.

For the first time in more than a week, he recognized that he was in a hospital and remembered the reason.

The crash.

The helicopter.

The chaos in the emergency room.

Little by little, bits and pieces began to fall into place. But they were the insignificant memories.

Like an explosion, his horrifying talk with Sam came hurtling back at him in vivid detail. Great chunks of information began to pelt him, to hurt him.

Ceily.

Shes's gone.

Her body is still in the river.

He shuddered at the memory of Sam's tears and his own shock.

And then, like a man standing at the base of a huge mountain, he felt an avalanche of reality begin to roll towards him, picking up speed with terrible quickness – so fast that he could not step out of its way. It hit him with a force greater than he thought he could withstand, rocking his fragile toehold on sanity. John Evans closed his eyes again and waited for the onslaught of guilt to sweep his mind into oblivion. But somehow, some way, he withstood the assault and the truth that was trying to bury him.

The truth had a face. It didn't have the features of cowardice or panic. No. It resembled a bad decision, an error in judgment, an impossible predicament there was no way to revisit.

The mistake could not be rectified.

The price to be paid for it was appallingly hideous.

And permanent.

He spent the rest of the night, eternal hours in darkness, praying to die so that he could join Ceily. He could not bear the thought of her all alone.

Where — God help him —he had left her.

* * *

Sam arrived at the hospital later than usual the next morning, hung over and miserable. But his wretched state of mind was short-lived. He was stunned to find his father up and pacing in his room. He couldn't believe the transformation. John Evans seemed lucid and aware, but was highly agitated. From years of courtroom experience, the lawyer knew what signs to look for when a man had something on his mind. He studied his father's face. All the signs were there.

"Dad!" Sam rushed to him and held him, wanting to believe that this man he had loved all his life could tell him what he needed to hear.

John was silent and accepting of his son's embrace but was unable to return it. Inside, the torture of the truth he had come to understand had turned him stone cold.

"I'm so relieved... I have to call Marnie... Sean has been asking for you..." Sam's emotions were tearing him in every direction.

"How are you feeling? Have you eaten? We must get you strong again, Dad. There are..."

He stopped, remembering what Bill Garnes had advised him. Pop picked up on it and finished his son's thought.

"Questions?" John Evans asked.

Sam hesitated. The moment was upon them. The truth was between them.

"Ceily?"

"They recovered her body several days ago." Sam watched his father's reaction, unsure if he should go on.

"Where?"

"Still in her seat. In a section of fuselage that separated from the tail section, which stayed afloat. The piece they lifted you off of."

"Was she pinned in?"

Sam thought he was going to be sick to his stomach. He forced himself to answer.

"Yes. Her legs were broken."

There was silence between them.

"But there were no other signs of injury." Again, he watched his father's reaction. There was none.

"Certainly nothing that would have killed her."

"I know," John Evans replied.

"How...?

He looked at his son. His eyes were hollow, empty as if whatever he had seen had burned the life out of them.

"I was there."

"Yes."

There was silence again. Sam broke it.

"The autopsy report..." John was startled by the word and gazed at his son. He was suddenly shaky and sat down heavily on his bed.

"The autopsies performed on every victim indicated the vast majority died of blunt force trauma. Only four drowned."

The elder Evans buried his head in his hands.

"One, a man who made his way to the surface but drowned after succumbing to hypothermia."

John Evans began to sob.

"A young woman in her late twenties and her infant son.

"And Mom. She drowned as well."

Silence.

"From all indications she was alive after the crash."

The room became uncomfortably silent, save for John Evans tears.

"You were sitting next to her, Dad. How did you escape... and she drowned?"

His father did not answer.

"What happened after the crash, Dad?"

He waited for an answer. Nothing.

"Tell me, Dad, please!" he screamed, finally losing his patience.

Sam tried to restrain himself. He took deep breaths and listened to his father crying.

"You know, don't you?" he said to him. "You remember, I know you do..."

John Evans clasped his hands together and began to rock on the edge of the bed. Tears were flowing freely down his cheeks.

"Ceily!" he cried out. "Forgive me, please... I didn't mean to leave you... I wasn't thinking.

"Please, come back... oh, Ceily... please..."

Sam had heard enough. He reached for the nurse's station call button.

"Yes?"

"Please page Dr. Garnes and have him come to Mr. Evans' room. As soon as possible." He didn't wait for a response.

"Oh, Dad..." Sam Evans said aloud in a voice teetering with confusion and despair.

"What did you do?"

Thirty-Six

~~~

January 27, 1982

It took Garnes two days to regain the progress he had made with John Evans, and he was not pleased about it. The situation came to a head in the hallway outside his patient's room, from which Sam Evans had been barred for the last forty-eight hours.

"Look, it's none of my business what kind of relationship you guys have going forward," Bill Garnes said to Sam, his finger pushed into the lawyer's chest and his voice strained with barely contained anger. "But so long as he's my patient, your father's well-being is my responsibility. I told you specifically how important it was to avoid interrogating your father until he had regained his strength both physically and emotionally. You chose to ignore my medical advice. Now it's no longer in the form of 'advice.' I'm giving it to you straight. I'm in charge and don't challenge me again, Sam. You got it?"

Before Sam Evans could respond, Garnes turned to a hospital administrator standing next to him who was accompanied by a staff lawyer and two security guards.

"You gentlemen just heard what I said to Mr. Evans. Under no circumstances is he to be allowed anywhere in this hospital or to visit with his father until I have given my permission for him to do so. If he chooses to challenge my authority by entering the building, have him arrested immediately. If he chooses to challenge
~~~

my decision in a courtroom – where it would seem his extraordinary lack of empathy has been finely honed – so be it. You will have my unconditional support in fighting any challenge he makes to my course of action."

He turned back to Sam, his anger unabated.

"Am I understood, gentlemen?"

Doctor William Garnes had never been clearer about his intentions at any time in his professional career, they all thought.

"Bill… Dr. Garnes…" Sam began to gently protest, "I do apologize and…"

"Save it, Sam. I'm not interested. You put my patient – your father – at risk. I won't have it. Now, officers if you will escort Mr. Evans from the building I can get on with my practice of treating people who are ill and desire and respect my professional opinion."

The guards looked to Sam, wondering where this was going to go. The lawyer meekly turned and walked to the nearby elevators without a word. One of the guards spoke into his radio. A few minutes later a response indicated that Evans had left the building.

Sam went back to his hotel room, chastened and embarrassed. But he was far from over his anger. He picked up the phone and called the NTSB's lead investigator on the Air Florida Flight 90 crash, Harold Steiner. Steiner had been dissecting catastrophic aviation incidents for more than thirty years and was extremely well regarded in his field.

"My father can explain the circumstances of my mother's death," he told the forensic expert. "Please contact Dr. Garnes to arrange for the deposition. It may take a few days."

"Has your father's condition improved, Mr. Evans?" Steiner inquired.

"Yes, but he is still recovering his strength, both physically and emotionally. However, I would not hesitate to push Dr. Garnes for a meeting at the earliest possible time. I want to put this matter to rest for the sake of my family," he lied.

"But let me make this clear," Evans added. "There is to be no questioning of my father in my absence. Do we have agreement on that?"

Steiner promised to let him know when the meeting had been arranged.

Sam Evans then flopped on the bed and placed another call.

"Room service, please," he said to the operator.

"Yes?"

"This is Mr. Evans. Please send up a bottle of Johnny Walker Black and a bucket of shaved ice."

"How many guests will you be entertaining, Mr. Evans?" the voice asked.

"Just send the scotch, the ice and one glass," he said and curtly hung up the phone.

While he was waiting, he made a final call to Marnie and quickly, almost tersely told her he'd be in Arlington a few more days. He offered no explanation and cut her off when she inquired about Pop's condition.

"Later," he said. "It's not important. In the meantime, let's hold off on the funeral arrangements until I can get back. I don't expect it to be more than a few more days."

"Of course," she said, somewhat concerned by the agitation in his voice.

"I must see her one last time," he said.

Marnie expected him say how important it was for him to tell his mother how much he loved and missed her and that he would always make sure Pop was cared for. Instead, her husband's words made her cringe with uneasiness.

"I have to tell her that the way in which she died is not going to remain a mystery. If it's the last thing I do, the truth will be heard."

Thirty-Seven

John Evans continued to walk aimlessly around the small town of Willington, his escape from the rehab center as yet undiscovered. He'd been wandering outside in the cold night air for more than three hours with the thermometer hovering just above forty degrees. He was shivering uncontrollably, despite his efforts to tough it out. He didn't know it, but at that same moment, his family was safe and warm, dissecting the worst time of his life.

"Where the hell am I?" he asked himself in frustration. Don't understand why I can't seem to get a bearing..."

He sat down on the side of the road again, the cold beginning to sap him of what little strength he had regained since the heart attack. He thought about turning back, but wasn't sure of which way to head, and besides, after chatting with Ceily, he was becoming comfortable with the notion of dying rather than being locked up in that hellhole again. Then he remembered that he'd made a promise to Ceily. Sheila and Sean needed him. He decided that he couldn't break another promise to his wife. After all, it was all she had asked of him in such a long time. Considering the terrible mistake he was guilty of, how could he deny her?

He forced himself to his feet and tried to focus on a plan. The old soldier was still sharp enough to know that he had to take shelter from the cold or he was probably done for and Ceily would give him hell if he arrived looking for her too soon. There was some bizarre irony, his brain told him. His wife giving him hell for meeting her in heaven. Then again, he was banking on the assumption that he had lived a good enough life to have the chance to be with her. Maybe he was headed in the other direction. Lord knows he had screwed up enough for the guy with the keys to the Pearly Gates to be on the fence about letting him in.

A sharp clarity suddenly washed over him, and he wondered what he had been thinking about. Heaven? Pearly Gates, talking to Ceily? Why, he'd left the rehab center because he was pissed off at the orderly. That's all it was. Get your head together, he told himself. This is nothing like having a dead stick over the Yalu with a bogey on your tail, right?

He heard the low rumble of a motor approaching behind him and stepped out of the shadows. A late model pickup truck emerged from the darkness and Pop waved him down. I gotta get warm he thought. The truck pulled over and the driver opened the passenger side window.

"What can I do for ya, buddy?" a man about half his age asked. "You look like you could use some warming up. Where you headed?" he asked.

Pop was slightly surprised at how friendly the driver was and had to think fast.

"Well, I was actually headed for the bus station in Hartford," he lied. "You know, down by the railroad station at Union Place?"

"Sure I do," the stranger said. "And it just so happens I'm heading into Hartford. Just about to jump on I-84. Give you a lift if you want bub, wouldn't mind the company at all."

Pop didn't hesitate to reach for the door and climbed in.

"Well friend, thank you very kindly," he said, taking a seat in the warm cabin. "Lord that feels good," he said. "I didn't realize it was going to get so cold tonight, would have dressed a little more warmly."

"I'll say. Probably going to dip below the forties before the night is over, maybe even down near freezing. But you'll be warm enough on the bus. Where did you say you were heading?" he asked my grandfather.

"Oh, uh... Arlington, going to Washington National Airport. Heading to Paris."

"Wow, that's some trip," the driver said. "Where are your bags?"

"Uh," Pop hesitated again, making up lies as fast as he could think.

"My wife is going to meet me there," he said, a little too quickly. It's our anniversary. She has all the bags."

"Oh," the stranger said, a little puzzled at such an odd answer. He began to wonder about who this older man was. He didn't know him from around town, or at least didn't recognize him. Or did he... He stole a glance at him every now and then, trying to place the face.

"Name's Charlie, Charlie Morton," the driver said.

"John Evans," my grandfather replied, not thinking anyone would recognize the name.

"John Evans?" Charlie repeated. "Why you're not related to Sam Evans, are you? They live in that big old place down off Route 74?"

Pop panicked, all the untruths catching up with his own inability to distinguish fantasy from reality.

"Why, no... uh, no... I mean..."

Morton was catching on that his elderly passenger might be a bit confused. He seemed harmless enough, but that wasn't what he was worried about. And the more he thought about it, the more convinced he was Sam Evan's father.

"Never mind there John, it's not important. Sure hope you have a good trip."

Pop had fallen back into a very confused state by this time.

"Yah, Ceily's been waiting a long time to go to Paris," Evans said.

That did it for Charlie Morton. He knew the story of Ceily Evans far too well. His own mother had been a friend of hers and he was aware of how she had died. He had her husband in his truck and the old timer wasn't thinking too clearly, that was for certain.

He thought for a moment about how to handle the situation.

"Hey John," he said, "you don't mind if I pull into the Sunoco for some gas, do you? And I could go for a cup of coffee. Bet you could , too."

"Oh, no, of course not... I'm sorry, I forgot your name," Pop said.

"Charlie, John, it's Charlie. How do you take your coffee, bud?" he asked. Pop just stared ahead and didn't answer.

They were silent for the couple of miles to the gas station, at the entrance ramp to I-84. He pulled his pickup to a pump and began refueling.

"Gonna get that coffee, John," he said. "Be right back. You stay right here, okay?"

Pop looked out the window, unresponsive.

Charlie Morton went inside and asked the teller if he could use the phone for a moment. He called information and asked for the number to the Evans' residence in Willington. A minute later, the phone rang at our house.

We were all sitting listening to my mother tell the story of my grandfather's tragedy and my father's war with him when the call came. We nearly let it go, the timing was so awkward. Sheila finally got up and answered it.

"Yes," she said, after listening for a moment. Her face quickly paled and she looked like she was going to cry.

"Yes, that's my grandfather," she said shakily into the telephone.

"He's where?"

Thirty-Eight

~~~

February 1, 1982

It hardly looked like a hospital room, with the exception of the star witness wearing a terry cloth bathrobe and slippers instead of a suit.

There were eleven people in John Evans' room that afternoon to hear what he had to say about the Air Florida Flight 90 accident, his own subsequent actions after the crash and the death of Ceily Evans. There were two others present to protect him from the stress of the ordeal.

Harold Steiner, chief investigator for the National Transportation Safety Board was there to lead the proceedings, and three members of his staff were also present. Two lawyers from Air Florida, counsel from Washington National Airport and a representative of the US Airline Pilots Association all sat nervously in chairs against a back wall, about as far way from my grandfather as possible. An NTSB stenographer was also in attendance to record every word spoken as was a technician to run a tape recorder of the interrogation. Bill Garnes stood quietly near my grandfather, who was connected to a heart monitor that was readily visible to the doctor and a staff nurse. And finally, there was my father.

No one in the room truly understood his motivation for being in attendance, whether it was as John Evans' son or as his lawyer. But there wasn't a man in the room
~~~

with the balls to challenge Sam Evans' presence or even inquire as to his status. The look on his face said one thing: stand back. His reputation preceded him both in his excellence as an attorney and for his abhorrent emotional behavior at the hospital since the crash.

My grandfather was tired but lucid. Bill Garnes had done a masterful job of bandaging his emotions after recognizing that he was not going to be able to get in the way of the freight train of the NTSB or Sam Evans for very long. But he was determined to pull the plug on the circus that was shaping up in front of his eyes at the first signs that John Evans was in distress.

Harold Steiner wasted no time in initiating the proceedings, first identifying the date and time of the meeting with John Evans and the name and association of every person present in the room. To his credit, before beginning his questioning, he stopped the official actions to first offer his condolences for his subject's great personal loss and to apologize for the urgency of their meeting.

"Mr. Evans, I cannot imagine your sorrow and I am deeply sorry for it. I have been doing forensic crash work for more than thirty years, and I must say that interrogating victims who have suffered as you have is the hardest and most distasteful part of my job that I have never grown accustomed to. I must also add that I do realize what a strain it is for you to have endure questioning so quickly after the accident and your loss. I can only hope that you will understand that it is a necessary part of the process of understanding what happened so that we may prevent it from happening again, and that garnering all facts as it relates to the crash of Air Florida Flight 90 is a crucial component of the process of imparting justice and or restitution to the victims and their families."

John Evans did not respond or show any indication of letting anyone off the hook. Secretly, that included himself.

"So, I hope you understand our reason for being here today," Steiner added, hoping for a blessing or even a nod from John Evans. He got neither.

Instead, he served Harold Steiner with a warning that if there was any expectation of him to rubber stamp some "cover you ass" scheme, he wasn't about to be a part of it.

"Mr. Steiner," he began. His voice was slightly more than a whisper, causing every head in the room to lean closer.

"I was a combat jet fighter pilot in Korea. Shot down two MiG's. Crashed landed. Suffered severe wounds and burns as a result. Damn near died. Spent months in recovery and rehabilitation."

You could have heard a pin drop in the hospital room. Not even the normal drone of activity in the hallways of a facility racing with activity served to lessen the impact of John Evans' words.

"I flew in the harshest conditions you can imagine." He paused. "No, I take it back," he said. "You can't imagine the conditions I flew in. Bitter cold, ice, snow… they were all facts of life of flying in Korea in the winter months. As a result, I knew when I could fly, and when I couldn't. When I had to adjust for weather conditions and when the weather was a non-factor. And I was only a twenty-one year old kid with a few hundred hours of flight time under my belt who had to take all of that into consideration and still worry about getting my ass shot off."

"Mr. Evans…I hardly…" Steiner attempted to interrupt my grandfather.

John wasn't about to be stopped.

"If you interrupt me again, Mr. Steiner, it will take a court order to get another word out of me, am I understood?" he warned the investigator.

If Sam Evans hadn't been so enraged and vengeance driven at that moment, he would have been very proud of his father. Instead, he sat back and appeared to be calmly listened, masking what he truly felt with a look of complete composure that would have worked in front of any jury.

Steiner was instantly quiet.

"As I was saying," John Evans continued, "I was only twenty-one years old with a few hundred hours of flight time. On the other hand, the crew of Air Florida Flight 90 had amassed more than eleven thousand flight hours, yet the two of them had only ten snow-involved take offs between them. That's point number one, for which, I might add, the NTSB can take partial blame for the lack of experience of the crew."

"Point number two is that the brain trust managing Washington National Airport obviously wasn't bright enough to recognize the inherent dangers of flying in blizzard like conditions and failed to close down its runways. I'm sure you'll agree the NTSB should have had something to say about the decision making process involved in keeping that major airport open under those conditions.

"Point number three is that neither the ATC or Ground Control had brains enough to see that they were fighting a losing battle, that it was just a matter of time before something went haywire and did nothing to stop the operation of the airfield. Again, let me add that your esteemed organization might have had a say in that decision making process as well.

"I can go on, Mr. Steiner, for I have arrived at many more conclusions that I am certain you have or will concur with before this investigation is closed, which should have your organization hanging its head in shame and embarrassment and perhaps attract the eyes of Congress.

"As to the vultures sitting against the back wall who, in the interest of profits and accountability are here to cover their backsides, let me just say this: I hope you and your employers forever rot in hell."

John Evans paused and took a sip of water from a glass he was holding. He looked around the room. There were only three people who weren't looking at their shoes or rubbing their eyes from the sting of what he had just said. Bill Garnes was smiling at John Evans' remarkable composure, his nurse had her mouth open in surprise, and his son Sam... well, his son was just staring at him as if his gaze could burn holes through his head. But Pop thought that was to be expected, considering what he knew and no one else did.

It was then that he took a deep breath and allowed the NTSB to proceed.

"And now Mr. Steiner, I am ready for this kangaroo court to begin its charade."

Steiner too reached for a glass of water, buying time to collect his thoughts. This was going to be no walk in the park, he thought.

"Yes. Thank you Mr. Evans for your thoughts and I believe it will be in the best interests of all here to leave it at that." It couldn't be heard, but one could sense the collective sigh of relief that Harold Steiner had elected not to defend the indefensible.

"Mr. Evans, may I begin by asking you your earliest recollections of Flight 90?"

My grandfather looked at him with disdain. Is that the best you can do, he thought?

"Boarding the 737 and trying to find our seats."

"Did you notice anything unusual about the aircraft at this time?" Steiner asked.

"Well, considering that I hadn't been on an airplane in thirty years, yes."

"And what was that?"

"That airplanes had gotten bigger and they squeezed large people into tiny seats. I had more room in my F-86 Sabre."

There was a sniggering in the room. Garnes had to muffle an outright laugh.

"Yes," said Steiner. "Thank you for that observation. What I meant, Mr. Evans is did you notice any activity that caused you any particular alarm?"

"I did notice that a crew of ground personnel was deicing the wings. That's not the most reassuring thing to see. I also was aware that the engines were not spooling and I wondered whether there had been some advance I was not familiar with to operate engine anti-icing sensors without having the engines running."

"You mean you thought the engines would have been running?" Steiner asked.

"Considering the conditions outside, I was somewhat surprised they were not," Evans responded. "I'll be quite interested to read your final findings on engine anti-icing."

Steiner looked puzzled. He was not aware that his witness had as much of a grasp of aviation technology and flight operations — although dated — as he did.

"Mr. Evans, your focus on engine anti-icing intrigues me. Why would you believe the issue so important?" Steiner asked.

"Well, it was quite obvious to me as we rolled out that the aircraft was struggling to reach V1 let alone V2 speed. I had quite a bit of time to watch aircraft taking off on that same runway earlier in the day. We were well beyond the mark where those other flights went wheels up when the pilot of Flight 90 rotated. If I had to guess, he was struggling with instrument readings that were telling him the airplane was going faster than it really was." He paused.

"I don't know," Evans continued. "I could just feel it. I knew we weren't going fast enough. I remember pushing Ceily forward at the last minute and telling her to put her head down because we were going in. I just knew we were. Next thing I know we're in the water."

Steiner was stunned at how close Evan's guess was to the actual cause of the accident. The NTSB had arrived at its conclusions days earlier but had not yet released its findings. The engine anti-icing sensors had frozen causing false instrument readings. Consequently, even though the pilots were second guessing the instruments based on "feel," they elected to go for it. The instruments were wrong, their instincts were right, their decision was catastrophic. The aircraft did not have enough power to make it safely over the bridge, especially with the additional weight of thousands of pounds of ice and had stalled. The rest was inevitable.

The NTSB investigator went pale at his explanation but chose not to respond. He moved on to Ceily's death.

"Mr. Evans, can you tell me what happened after the aircraft impacted the bridge?"

"Well, I'm a little fuzzy here, " he said. "I was leaning forward so I didn't see what was happening outside the window. I know we were very nose high because the tail – where Ceily and I were sitting – just sank. I think the tail hit the bridge or cars or maybe even the railing of the bridge… whatever… the impact caused the aircraft to veer to the left – I recall feeling G's in that direction and then we seemed to level off for a second or two before the nose slammed into the ice."

"'G's,' Mr. Evans?" Steiner queried him.

"C'mon, Steiner, what the hell is this, third grade? You know exactly what I'm saying. G forces, gravity pull. Christ, don't waste my time."

Garnes raised his eyes. It seemed short fuses ran in the family.

"Sorry," Steiner smiled. "Just have to be clear for the record."

"Yah. Was that clear enough for you?"

"Yes. Describe for me what you remember about the impact?"

Evans closed his eyes.

"We hit hard. I don't know how many pieces that Boeing broke in to but I suspect it was quite a few. Both of our seats were propelled forward. I hit my head hard, think I was out for a few seconds, Ceily too. But the water came in fast – that's how I know she broke up on impact. The seats behind us came over the top of us and I can remember struggling to push them off. They were completely ripped off the floor and loose so I was able to push them ahead of us. We were still in our seats, but the section of tail we were in was still floating."

"What happened next?"

"I got my belt undone and Ceily's and could see light behind us. I knew we could swim towards it and make it to the surface."

"Did you?"

My grandfather stopped dead and took a deep breath.

"Not immediately."

"What?" Steiner said, somewhat stunned by the response.

"Ceily's legs —at least one of them, I thought - were wedged under the seat in front of us. I couldn't move her immediately. She was trapped but I thought if I climbed over her I could free her. But then…"

There was dead silence in the room. Even the sound of the steno machine stopped. Every eye was on John Evans.

"When I looked down the length of the fuselage, there was no movement. Every chair had been torn from its mounts and it appeared everyone was dead from the impact. All except a young woman several rows in front of Ceily and I… she was holding a baby and screaming for help."

Sam Evans suddenly perked up. What was this?

My grandfather didn't immediately continue and Harold Steiner prodded him.

"Go on, Mr. Evans, please."

If looks could have killed, the daggers shooting from my grandfather's eyes would have sliced and diced Steiner to death.

"The woman was stuck in between two seats. There was a space but she couldn't squeeze through, especially with the baby in her arms. If she could have gotten through, she and her child probably would have survived."

He paused again and took a drink from his glass. Sam's eyes were riveted on him and he could feel them. His father's hands were shaking. Only Garnes picked up the tremor.

"I jumped out of my seat. I was completely free now and dove into the water, which was climbing higher where the girl was. I thought I could pull her and the baby free."

"Did you?"

"No, I was unable to pull her through, the seats were still partially bolted to the floor and I couldn't force the opening any wider."

"What did you do?" Steiner continued to probe.

"I kept diving, trying to pry them apart. At one point I told the woman to hand me the baby, that maybe she could squeeze through alone. But she wouldn't give up her child… I can't blame her. Then the floor gave way… I didn't realize it but that section of the fuselage was hanging to the tail section by a thread. All of a sudden it just dropped and the woman and the baby went straight down. I braced myself on a seat back in the tail and grabbed her arm but couldn't hold on. They sank and I lost sight of them."

The vision of the girl and her infant drowning so close to salvation left the room in silence again.

"That was quite heroic on your part, Mr. Evans," Steiner complimented my grandfather. "About how much time had elapsed since you first went to the girl?"

Evans stopped again and thought. A distant look came into his eyes. "Several minutes…at least," he hesitated.

Sam Evans stood up in the back of the room.

"And where was Mrs. Evans all this time?" he asked in a tone that shocked everyone in the room.

"Attorney Evans, please contain yourself," Steiner bellowed angrily. "I remind you this is not a deposition and you are only an invited guest here as a courtesy to your father. Now sit down. I am the only voice that will be heard here, do you understand?"

"Answer me, Dad," Sam Evans continued, completely ignoring the NTSB investigator.

"She was screaming for me to come back to her, she begged me not to leave her to begin with!" Pop blurted out, his conscience overpowering his only chance to keep the truth a secret between he and Ceily.

"Oh, my God…" Sam Evans said and sank back down into his chair.

"Mr. Evans, I am so sorry," Steiner said. He waited a moment, hoping that John could compose himself.

"Are you able to continue?" he asked.

"Yes." John Evans had spent sleepless nights wondering what he would say when the time came. As a boy, suffering through Sunday school, he'd been taught that the Bible said, "The truth will set you free." He was far from being a religious man, but at this moment, the Bible was all he had. It would take him many years to understand that neither the truth nor a lie would have made much difference. He would have lived with the torment of his mistake either way, forever.

"What did you do next, Mr. Evans?" Steiner asked.

"I shook off the woman's death and swam back to Ceily as fast as I could. It was at this time that I realized that the water in the tail section had risen much higher."

He shuddered at the vision of fear on Ceily's face as he returned to her and her recognition that time was short.

"I dove beneath her seat and tried to free her legs, but she was wedged way up under... I think they were broken because every time I pulled on her she screamed. I begged her to deal with the pain and to let me pull. It was our only chance..."

Living a nightmare can drive a man mad. Reliving one can make him want to tear out his eyes. John Evans would have traded his soul to be struck dead as the next words came out of his mouth.

"I couldn't budge her and the water was about to close over her face. I looked around for a piece of hose or tubing, anything to act as a snorkel. I ended up ripping one of the dangling oxygen masks off the aircraft ceiling and forcing it into her mouth. I was able to drape it up higher over the seat back. She could breath and it gave us more time.

"I needed a crowbar or something to pry back the seats. The nearest place to find any kind of tool was the aft galley so I swam back there and found a small fire extinguisher. I thought I might be able to jam it under the seat and leverage it forward enough to free her legs. I dove again and again and again..."

He stopped and put his hands over his face, praying silently that the vision of Ceily's face dipping below the water would disappear, but it would not. It remained as clear and vivid as the moment it happened, the terror in her eyes just as astonishingly horrific.

He hung his head, taking deep breaths, trying to calm himself. It needed to be said.

"I gave up on the fire extinguisher and dove again, now pulling on her legs as hard as I could despite her screams. I came to the surface again, caught my breath one more time and dove back down. This time she stopped me...."

John Evans finally sobbed. There probably wasn't a dry eye in the room.

"She ripped the tubing from her mouth and put her hands on the sides of my face. I thought at first she wanted me to breath into her mouth but it wasn't that at all. She looked deeply into my eyes and then pulled me closer to her and kissed me as hard as she could. She held my face and kissed me until she could hold her breath no longer..."

He still felt the kiss, the softness of her lips, her hands on his face holding him to her in an alien world.

"Then she pushed me away. I came to the surface then dove again... but she was gone. Her eyes were open but she wasn't breathing. I tried again to pull her out. I felt the aircraft settle just a bit and suddenly her legs came free. Before I could pull her out of the water, I remember somebody yanking me up by the back of my jacket collar...

"The first thing I recall after that was being here, in the emergency room, I think, and seeing Dr. Garnes."

Steiner wanted to press for more.

"Mr. Evans, was there..."

"That's all there is, god dammit! There ain't no more!" John Evans interrupted him loudly. "That's it, I'm done, get out of here, all of you."

Steiner sighed. He hated this job some times. He was about to end the proceedings when a voice called out.

"Mr. Steiner, if I may." It was Sam Evans from the back of the room.

"Let me summarize for you what my father just said."

Sam Evans turned and looked his father in the face, hatred in his eyes and venom on his tongue.

"Mr. Evans abandoned his wife, trapped as the aircraft was filling with water. It is entirely possible that he could have saved her had he attended to her situation instead of wasting precious time playing hero with some nameless passenger."

Sam Evans' voice was shaking with rage as the words spewed from his mouth.

"In short, he traded my mother's life for a stranger's."

Sam Evans closed his eyes as he considered the words he had just spoken and the terrible truth behind them. Then he turned and walked to the door, stopping only to speak with Bill Garnes.

"Dr. Garnes," he said. "Please call my wife when my father is ready to be released. She'll have someone pick him up and bring him back to Connecticut."

He looked back at his father one last time.

"Now if you'll excuse me, I must return home to bury my mother."

Thirty-Nine

My father took the telephone from Sheila and asked the caller to identify himself.

"I don't think we've met, Mr. Evans, but I'm Charlie Morton, I live here in Willington. My late mother Suzanne was a great friend of your mom's many years ago."

"Yah," Sam Evans replied curtly, in no mood for small talk. "I take it you're calling about my father?" he said.

Charlie was a little surprised by the tone in Evans' voice but let it slide.

"I was driving down Route 44 heading for Hartford when I passed this older guy on the side of the road, about a half hour ago. He looked pretty cold, hardly dressed for a night like this so I stopped, talked him into getting in the truck with me.

"He said he was heading for the bus station in Hartford, was going to meet his wife in Washington because they were going to Paris. That didn't make much sense to me and I realized he was kind of confused. When he told me his name I had a hunch he was your dad and thought I'd call and let you know he was with me. It ain't right the way he's dressed..."

"Uh, thanks – what did you say your name was?"

"Charlie Morton."

"Sorry. Yah, Charlie, I have no idea why my father is wandering around out in the street. He's been recovering from a heart attack and must have just walked out of the rehab center up the road. Is he all right? Where are you?"

"Yah, he's fine. Got him some coffee and turned up the heat in the truck. I'm at the Sunoco station at the entrance to I-84 West heading into Hartford. Should I bring him to the bus station? I don't mind, but…"

"No, please, no… I'll be there within fifteen minutes, tops. Thanks very much for your help." He hung up quickly.

"What the hell," he bellowed. "Marnie, would you call that damned rehab center and find out what's going on? I'm going to get my father."

Marnie cringed. "You can't drive after all you've had to drink, Sam. Sean will go."

Sam was about to snap at her but thought better of it. He didn't argue. "C'mon Sean, you drive," he said. "We'll both go. Sheila, why don't you go put on some coffee. Your grandfather will be staying here tonight, and at least until I can find out what happened with those idiots at the rehab center."

He didn't even bother to grab a coat, just threw me the keys to the Jaguar. "Let's go, Sean." My head was spinning.

We got in the car silently and I pulled the black Jag up onto the highway. I hadn't had time yet to digest all that I had learned in the last hour – essentially the secret that had torn my family to shreds. I had questions. Dozens of them. He beat me to the punch.

"Maybe now you understand…"

"No," I interrupted him, "I don't. I only know what happened to grandma and why Pop lives in a state of constant sadness and guilt."

My father didn't respond as I turned on to Route 74, about five miles from the gas station.

"How did Pop get home from the hospital?" I asked.

"Your mother drove to Washington in a limo about a week later and picked him up. He came home here. As soon as the funeral was over, he went right out to that barn and he's been there ever since, staring at that German heap."

More silence as we ate up the road.

"So that's why you hate him so much?"

He sighed deeply, not wanting to have this conversation with me.

"Do you know that once upon a time, I was a happy man? Before he took my mother from me?" he said.

I couldn't help myself.

"Do you know that once upon a time, I was a happy boy? Before you drove my mother away from me?" I replied.

"Touché."

"But yet you expect me to forgive and forget just because now I'm supposed to understand what made you become so pathetic."

He sighed again. I could imagine it wasn't easy to hear your son call you pathetic.

"How's it feel?" I asked.

"How's what feel?"

"To be treated like shit by your son."

He didn't hesitate.

"I guess I can live with it – I recognize my son has never understood the reason for my anger." He sounded just like a lawyer. The guy could rationalize any behavior if it was in his best interest.

"You mean you can forgive me for making a mistake?" I said, closing in.

"Yes."

"That's interesting, Dad. You can forgive me for hating you because you think I've made a mistake."

"Yes," he said again, a bit wary this time, his eyes not leaving the road.

"But you can't forgive your own father for making a mistake."

"Have we missed the point that it was a mistake that cost my mother her life, and me my mother?" he asked angrily. "You're telling me I don't have a right to be angry that he was so intent on being a hero that he ended up killing my mother?"

I let him stew for a couple of minutes.

"You ought to think about something, Dad," I said.

"What's that?"

"There's not much difference between the two."

"I don't understand what you mean. The two of what?"

"What I mean is that by your definition there's not much difference between hate and death."

"How do you see that?" he asked genuinely puzzled.

"The answer is right in front of your eyes. Pop's mistake may have caused grandma's death. But your hatred has just about killed our family."

"Sean..."

"Just think about it. If you ever want to see your family reconnect, it's your hatred that has to disappear."

"And your grandfather gets a free pass in all this?"

"You still don't get it, Dad, do you?"

"I guess not."

"Grandpa screwed up. He made a mistake he's been paying for a long time. Have you ever thought what it must be like to know that your wife died because you were distracted trying to save a mother and her baby? Can you imagine what a nightmare that is for him?"

He didn't respond.

"On the other hand, you decided a long time ago that you were never going to forgive him for making that mistake, no matter what the situation. And in the process you've made us all pay a price for grandma's death with your hatred."

He stared out the window in silence.

"You're a great lawyer, Dad, but let me sum it up for you.

"Grandpa 'screwed up.'" But in my book, you're just a mean, miserable 'screw up.' You need me to explain the difference?"

I drove the last couple of miles in silence and pulled the Jag into the Sunoco. But there was time for one more thought.

"You know what, Dad? If grandma was the wonderful, kind, loving person you've always said she was – she'd be proud of her husband for doing what he did.

"And she'd think *you* were the ultimate loser for the way you treat him and what you've done to your family."

Again he didn't respond. I wondered if I was getting through to him. I parked the car and wandered over to the only pickup truck parked in front of the gas station's mini-mart. Sure enough, Pop was sitting inside. His head was against the passenger window glass and he was sleeping. A guy came out of the store wearing a John Deere hat and walked up to my father standing next to the Jag.

"Sam Evans?" he asked while sticking out his hand to greet my dad. "Charlie Morton." I could tell my father was sizing him up as he almost reluctantly shook Morton's hand. He'd already written him off as a country bumpkin, I thought. Always judging people.

But his years of charming jurors and judges had served him well. He could play just about any role. Before my eyes he became a "concerned son."

"Charlie, I can't thank you enough for stopping to pick up my father," he said, his voice dripping with false gratitude. "I didn't realize how cold it was out here. And he's been under the weather lately."

"Yah, it was odd how when he got in the truck he seemed to be clear headed and talking just fine. But the further we drove, the more confused he seemed to get. I think he was making up answers about as fast as I was asking questions," he laughed.

"I'm afraid my dad is beginning to show some signs of dementia," Sam Evans said. "We're going to have to keep a closer eye on him. But first I have to find out how the hell he got out of the rehab facility outside the center of town. He supposedly was being supervised." Even to a stranger, the words were awkward. I saw Morton's eyes squint when he heard "supervised." He didn't know my father. The words "cared for" never came to his mind.

"Well, nowadays it seems like you can't take anything for granted," Charlie said. "Though if he was my dad, I wouldn't turn my back on him for a minute." I saw my dad flinch. He turned to me for an escape route.

"This is my son, Sean, Charlie. Pop here is just about his best friend, I guess." He said it in such a way that I think he was almost a little sad. Or maybe jealous. Or both.

"Hey, Mr. Morton," I said, "nice to meet you, and thanks for taking care of my grandfather. He might have frozen to death out here tonight the way he's dressed. If you'll open the car, I'll help him out."

"Sure son," Charlie replied as he unlocked the doors to the pickup. I slowly opened the passenger door and Pop nearly fell out. He was dead weight against the door. The sudden movement woke him up. He looked at me, and an air of surprise crossed his wrinkled face. For a second, I didn't think he recognized me.

"Sean… oh, I'm glad you stopped by to see me after all. Is Sheila with you?" He had no idea where he was.

"No, Pop," I said.

"Well, let's go down to my room where we can have some privacy, I hate all these people listening to everything we talk about. Say, did you happen to find the keys to the Mercedes yet?"

"Not yet, Pop, but I'm still looking. We'll find them, I promise."

"Geez, I hope so. Your grandmother will tan my hide if I don't find them before Sunday. You know how she is about our Sunday drive." He laughed softly.

"I'm really tired today," he said out of the blue.

My father interrupted us and went straight to the point, as usual.

"Dad, how the hell did you get out of the rehab center and why did you leave? Who was watching you? How long have you been gone?"

He was peppering the old man with question after question, none of which he understood.

"Dad, he doesn't even know that he's not at the rehab joint. He's very confused," I whispered.

"Damn those people. Somebody's head is going to roll right into the unemployment office tomorrow by the time I'm done." I didn't doubt it for a minute. The "how" of the situation was a lot more important to my father than the "why."

I put Pop in the back seat of the Jaguar and buckled his seatbelt. Before we even pulled out of the gas station he was asleep again.

My father was beside himself.

"If he's going to start getting this confused we're going to have to put him in a convalescent home, or get him nursing or something," he said.

"Yah, the 'convalescent home' thing worked out real well," I said sarcastically.

"I have to talk with his doctors in the morning and see what they recommend," he said, ignoring me. "With your mom just coming home and Sheila in school, you're going off to college next year… we're going to have to find some place to park his tired old butt," he said without one ounce of compassion.

That was it. I pulled the car over to the side of the road, pulled the keys out of the ignition and told him to get out of the car.

"What?" he said, completely ignorant of how much he'd pissed me off.

"I said, get out of the car!"

He did, slowly, and met me in front of its blazing headlights. Before considering the consequences of what I was doing I launched a wild, right hand haymaker at his head that thankfully missed by a mile.

"Whoa!" he said, backing away from me. "What the hell did I say or do to deserve that?"

"You don't know do you, you heartless son of a bitch…"I screamed at him. I couldn't help it. I was so emotionally wound up I started to cry.

"Wait, Sean, calm down… what the hell… Jesus, I'm sorry," he said, for the first time in more years than I could remember.

"Damn you!" I screamed. "How can you be so cruel? What is wrong with you?"

"Sean… I can't…" he began.

"I'm leaving. Tonight," I hollered, choking back tears. "I can't be near you anymore, Dad. Do you understand?

"I don't want to be your son." I turned my back on him.

"Sean, please, I'm sorry. You have no idea how I feel…"

"That's the problem, Dad. I know just how you feel." I turned to face him again. I could see wetness glimmering in his eyes.

"I feel the same way about you as you do about Pop."

Forty

We arrived back at the house a little before eleven. My mother and Sheila came running out to greet Pop and see if he was all right. I had to shake him slightly to wake him up. In just the few minutes we'd been driving he had fallen into a deep sleep.

Mom took my father aside to tell him what she had learned from the rehab center. Sheila helped me with Pop. She reached inside the car and gave him a huge hug, which brought a tremendous grin to his face. I hadn't seen him light up like that in such a long time. Between the two of us we were able to guide him into the house and upstairs to his bedroom, foregoing the coffee Sheila had made. What Pop needed was a good night's rest after his adventure.

As we tucked him into bed, he reached up and grabbed a hand from each of us.

"I'm so glad you two finally came to see me today," he said, a genuine grin across his wrinkled face. "I didn't think you'd forget your old grandpa that quickly. But I'm tired now. Why don't you run along home and I'll see you tomorrow, okay? I'm going to catch a few winks, now."

I rubbed the back of his hand and said goodnight, relieved that he was no worse for whatever had caused him to escape from the rehab center. I couldn't wait to hear what my mom had learned. I went to turn out the lights and close the door, thinking Sheila was right behind me. She wasn't. Pop was still holding her hand.

I guess I hadn't been paying much attention to my little sister, whom I suddenly realized wasn't so little any more. In the dim light, with her long red hair and strikingly beautiful features that were so similar to my grandmother's, she almost looked like her ghost standing next to my grandfather. Eerily, the similarity wasn't lost on him, either.

Pop squeezed her hand and Sheila bent down to give him a kiss good night on the forehead. He closed his eyes at the touch of her lips, a glow of happiness on his face.

As she pulled her hand away from him, he held her a moment longer and opened his tired eyes again.

"It was so nice to talk with you tonight, Ceily, I've missed you so much," he said softly, looking directly at Sheila. "And I'm so happy you got to see the Eiffel Tower after all, even if you didn't think it was such a big deal. You know how much I love you – and Sean promised me he'd find the keys to the Mercedes, so don't worry about Sunday."

He brought Sheila's slender hand to his lips and gave it a gentle kiss.

"Good night now, Mrs. Evans."

He let go of her hand and closed his eyes again, this time to sleep. I'd never seen him at such peace.

I was too stunned to move. Sheila stood by his side a moment longer, then turned towards me. Tears were streaming down her cheeks and she held a trembling hand to her mouth to keep from crying aloud. I put my arm around her and helped her out to the hall, shutting off the lights and closing the door to Pop's room on the way out.

Sheila reached for me outside his room, badly in need of a hug. It was hard enough to have spent the night listening to the story of how Pop had lost Ceily to begin with, but for her beloved, confused and heartbroken grandfather to mistake her for his wife was more than she was able to bear. I held her tightly and she sobbed into my chest for long minutes.

"It's okay, Sheila," I tried to comfort her. "He's just very confused now, it's all part of the Alzheimer's."

She began to calm down and I wiped the tears from her cheeks.

"I'm guessing that something happened out there tonight," I said, "something that made him think of grandma, or maybe he imagined talking to her when he was all alone on the road. We'll never know. But he was feeling close to grandma just now, and you reminded him of her."

She shook her fourteen-year-old head in amazement.

"It's just so weird," she said. "He thought I was his wife, Sean..."

"Take it as a compliment, little sister. Grandma was a very beautiful woman, inside and out," I said. "So are you."

She smiled and looked up into my face. I'd never noticed that her eyes were just like grandma's too – such a deep green color you'd sweat her pupils were little puddles of the ocean. She was an Irish lass if there ever was one and I reminded myself that I was going to have to start acting the role of big brother at school. Any day now, there'd be guys knocking on our door looking for her attention. I wasn't real happy at the thought.

Up until that moment, I'd had every intention of going to my room, stuffing my backpack with some clothes and walking out on Mr. and Mrs. Sam Evans for good. The conversation with my father on the way to and from the gas station to pick up Pop had convinced me that I would never have a normal relationship with him – in fact, I really disliked him, just short of hate. I swore I'd never use the "H" word again after all it done to my family.

But now seeing Sheila alone with my grandfather, I recognized that if I left, all the burden of caring for him – I mean "caring" for him, not "supervising" him – would fall on her young shoulders. And although I didn't know for sure, I figured there would be more nights like this in store for Pop, more long episodes of delirium and confusion, and more hours of anguish over the death of his wife. And in the process, I'd be treating her no better than the parents who had abandoned her so long ago. I made up my mind right then that from that night on, it was going to be Sheila and I who provided Pop with the love and care he needed until he breathed his last.

"C'mon," I said to change the subject. "Let's go find out what the hell happened at the rehab center. I gotta know how he pulled it off and who 'The Judge' is going to hang in the morning."

"The 'Judge?'" she asked, confused.

"Yah, the guy we call 'Dad' who believes he has the right to pass judgment on other people."

"The Judge," she repeated, listening to the sound of it. "How fittingly disrespectful. I love it!"

"Just let me check on Pop, real quickly," I said.

I carefully turned the doorknob to his room and cracked it open just a hair. The old man that Sheila and I loved so much was sound asleep, a look on his face that suggested he'd had a night to remember.

"Pleasant dreams, Pop," I whispered.

"And say hi to grandma for Sheila and me, OK?"
I closed the door.

Forty-One

The orderly who had mistreated Pop didn't have a prayer against my dad's wrath, and the rehab center was counting its blessings that no harm had come to the old man.

"The Judge" would have shredded the place if he'd had his way, just for the sheer enjoyment of watching people squirm. It was my mother who demanded – yes, demanded – that he drop the whole thing.

"We have to live in this community, Sam," she said, "and there are some folks who really do depend on that place, bad as it is. Leave it alone." Amazingly, he backed right down. Sometimes I wasn't sure who this woman was who had come back to live with us again. She sure wasn't the little mouse who'd left us years before. And it was clear that part of the negotiation involved in her coming home involved a change in the rules.

The next morning, Pop came down for breakfast as if nothing had happened, clean shaven and wearing fresh clothes. It was as if he'd never been in the hospital or the rehab. He never mentioned his adventure and I'd swear he had no memory of it. The old man sat down next to his granddaughter at the kitchen table as he always did and said, "Good morning, Sunshine. Did you sleep well last night, Sheila?" There wasn't a hint of the confusion over her identity that had caused my sister so much distress the night before.

After breakfast, he took his coffee and sat on the back step for a while, then marched over to the barn. I peeked in on him about a half hour later and he was where I expected him to be: sitting on his stool gazing at the old Mercedes. There wasn't a doubt in my mind about whom he was thinking of.

Surprisingly, my father did not object to Sheila and I accompanying him to a conference with Pop's doctors to determine the best course of care for him as his Alzheimer's progressed. Marnie promised to watch him closely while we were gone.

My father didn't mention it, but I guessed that he was relieved I hadn't left. It would have been nice if he could have said something, but that would have been more than his ego could handle. That's the way it was always going to be with us. But I wondered if I'd reached him at all last night.

Talking with Pop's doctors was important, because after what had happened, it was obvious that he was going to be a handful as his Alzheimer's worsened. I wasn't about to miss the conversation.

When the meeting began in Dr. St. Pierre's office later that morning, my father surprised me again when he outright dismissed the immediate recommendation by the cardiologist who'd been treating Pop that he be re-admitted to rehab.

There was no hesitation in his response. "When pigs can fly," Sam Evans told the doctor in his own direct manner. "I think my father has seen enough of that joint. If I had my way..."

He paused and looked over at me, blood in his eye. I shook my head. He dropped it with a sigh. For Sam Evans, It was a wasted opportunity to chew someone out.

"My first question is what changes should we expect to see in his behavior as this thing becomes a bigger issue," my father said to Dr. St. Pierre, who had been leading my grandfather's treatment since the heart attack and the discovery of the first signs of Alzheimer's.

"To be frank, Mr. Evans, that is an extremely difficult question to answer," St. Pierre began. "On any given day, your father's behavior might suggest that he is perfectly healthy and thinking clearly. But the next day, you may think he is a lunatic and not recognize him at all. The same goes for life from your dad's perspective. One minute things will be clear and organized in his mind, the next he may not remember how to tie his shoelaces and get angry in the process. You have already seen these contradictions in his behavior. It will only get worse as time goes on.

"That is perhaps the most insidious element of Alzheimer's disease. It is sneaky, deceiving and above all, dishonest. You never quite know when it is going to go into hiding or when it will rear up its ugly head and bite. That goes for the victim – as well as those who love him.

"But it is important to remember – always – that the disease is there. I don't mean to be cruel, but Alzheimer's is a death sentence. It will not suddenly disappear, reverse or cure itself. Consequently, you can't let your guard down," he concluded. "That's a lot to ask of anyone. It's almost a full time job."

He let that sink in before going on. I could see that my father was getting more anxious by the minute and Sheila's eyes were full of tears. This just wasn't fair.

"There are some specific types of behavior you can expect to see and their frequency to increase over time.

For example, you may find him asking the same question repeatedly within the same conversation. He may put his wallet or his clothes in the refrigerator. At times, he will be unable to recall a simple word for 'shoes' and then say in frustration, 'The things you wear on your feet.'

"You may find him suddenly becoming the life of the party rather than the uncommunicative person you live with for days on end. It's those kind of odd behaviors which will gradually get worse and worse."

St. Pierre looked at our gloomy faces and expressed his remorse.

"I wish I could give you better news or soften the reality for all of you. But it's better that you know the truth and understand what's coming than to face this blindly."

We all nodded in agreement.

"It's also important that you be aware that certain people will try to take advantage of him. His financial affairs should not be left unsupervised. It is not at all uncommon for a person with even early symptoms of Alzheimer's – and I emphasize that your grandfather's symptoms are far more advanced than that – to find it difficult to balance a checkbook or even to figure out the correct amount of money to pay for something. And there's always the scam artists who may attempt to convince him of some outlandish scheme. Such as, 'If you'll just give me $10,000, we can arrange for a perpetual candle at your wife's headstone in the cemetery.' "

My father nearly came out of his chair.

"Yah, that's an actual example," St. Pierre said. "The guy got away with it, too. You're going to have to learn to be diligent about assessing his judgment and decision making and always be on guard for people who would harm him in any number of ways."

"Jesus… how can people be so cruel," I asked aloud.

"I wish I knew the answer to that question," St. Pierre offered, "but I have learned not to be surprised at how low people will stoop to abuse and take advantage of those unable to defend themselves.

"Finally, it's very important that you watch his diet."

"But he has a great appetite," Sheila answered, full of hope. "I made him pancakes and sausage for breakfast this morning and he just about licked the plate."

"That may be an indication of the problem, Shelia," St. Pierre responded. "He may not have eaten in quite a while. Forgetting to eat, skipping meals entirely or eating the same foods at every meal are all typical behaviors. And with his weakened condition, good nutrition becomes vitally important to his..." He paused, hesitating to say the words to us.

"Longevity and quality of life," he finished. That hurt.

"Look, this isn't going to seem so hard at first, because you love him," St. Pierre continued. "But eventually, it's going to become a mind bender. "At some point, you're going to have to deal with severe mood swings, hallucinations and even wandering. The kind, gentle person you know now is going to become extremely aggressive, sure as I'm sitting here, and he'll probably be more than one of you can handle alone. And then one day, the final process will begin when his organs begin to shut down."

I dropped my head, knowing what was coming.

"That's when he will die."

Sheila buried her head in her hands and began to weep.

"I'm sorry to be so blunt with you," St. Pierre apologized again. "But those are the facts."

The silence in the room was awkward as the full realization of the curse that had descended on Pop settled on us. He'd won a lot of battles, even survived the loss of the love of his life and lived with the guilt that he might have prevented it. This was one war he wasn't even going to get a chance to fight.

"How long can he be with us, Doctor… I mean, how long will he be able to live at home without hospital care?" I asked.

My father shook his head.

"Sean, after what happened last night, it's possible he needs to be institutionalized now," my father said with atypical gentleness.

"No," Sheila barked in a tone of voice I'd never heard from her before. She was angry.

"There is no way he's going into one of those places now… not one minute before he has to."

He was back. The Judge disagreed with complete disregard for Sheila's feelings. My father's own emotions were so erratic you might almost think he was exhibiting early onset Alzheimer's himself. "The important thing is what's best…" he began to argue with her. St. Pierre put a stop to it.

"Forgive me for interrupting you, Mr. Evans, but Sheila is nearly correct."

"Nearly?" I said.

"Well, what I mean is that to place him in a hospital environment now, to take him out of the place in which he's most comfortable at this stage of his illness would be counter effective. I can guarantee you that he will lapse into much deeper depression than he already suffers from and it will contribute to an acceleration of his decline.

"To be blunt, taking him away from his grandchildren, his coffee on the back porch, his barn and car and his memories would kill him."

Sheila smiled with satisfaction at hearing what she needed to hear.

"However," St. Pierre continued, "there will be a point in the future – perhaps a couple of months or even a couple of years, it's impossible to tell – when it will be incumbent upon you to place him in a safe environment. There will come a time when he will become a danger to himself, and perhaps even to you."

My father was wringing his hands. It was obvious that he would rather have the problem go away right now. But after last night, after our conversation and my attempt to knock him on his ass and leave, I think he finally understood what was at stake. Pop was going to get a fair shake or the Evans' family children were going to make other living arrangements with our grandfather in tow. Mean as he was, this was my father's only chance to save his family. He was smart enough to know it. The question was, how bad did he want it?

"All right," Sam Evans relented. "So if he stays at home now, do we need nursing or any special care?"

"No, not at this point, Mr. Evans," St. Pierre replied. "What he needs is attention, patience and love. Based on the passion of your two children, I don't think that will be a problem."

Sheila beamed and wiped her cheeks dry. My father, the ultimate contradiction in terms, put his arm around her and kissed her on the cheek. I'd never figure the guy out.

"In the meantime, I would use your time to research some of the facilities available that you may consider when the time comes," St. Pierre concluded. Then he surprised us.

"For whatever it's worth to you, I plan on having a conversation with the State licensing board over the treatment your father received in the rehab facility in Willington," St. Pierre said, bringing a smile to my father's face. "And you can rest assured that facility will never again be recommended or utilized by this hospital."

As we left Hartford Hospital my father was quiet. With his crazy mood swings, that in itself wasn't unusual, but typically he would be frantic to get at his cell phone to talk with his office the second he could and just ignore us.

Shockingly, not today.

"You guys cool with school? I mean, they're not expecting you for the rest of the day?" he asked. We both nodded.

"Then let's get some lunch."

Lunch?

We piled into the Jag and my father drove through the south end of Hartford to Maple Giant Grinder on Adelaide Street.

"Your mom and I used to come here a lot when we were first going out together," he said, a smile unconsciously crossing his face. "You can't get a better or bigger grinder in the city - maybe the State. You're gonna love this." He waved to the owner — Ritchie Lavoie — an old friend.

"You're not going back into the office, Dad?" I asked. This just wasn't like him.

"Nah, it can wait."

Sheila and I exchanged glances and shrugged our shoulders. After the last twenty-four hours, nothing should have surprised us.

We sat down at a booth along one wall and looked over the menu. My dad flipped his open and closed it just as fast.

"Some things never change," he laughed. "A whole sausage with sauce and Provolone cheese for me. Toasted in the oven. Just like the old days with your mom." Then the smile slowly faded from his face.

"I've wasted a lot time with your mother, " he said. "I regret it a lot."

"Yah," I said, looking over the menu. I was not about to fall for his melancholy routine. I didn't trust him at all.

"Aren't you forgetting someone?" I asked without looking up.

The waiter who came and took our orders interrupted the conversation. She was sweet and I dropped it, not wanting to embarrass her. It was just as well, I figured. I doubted that Sam Evans would even know what I was talking about.

To my surprise, he answered me right away when she left.

"Sean… I heard you loud and clear last night," he said, looking me right in the eye. "I've been doing a lot of listening lately. That doesn't mean I can make everything right with you guys overnight." He shifted his eyes to Sheila and reached for her hand.

"I'm not talking about Sheila and me," I said. "We're just young enough and maybe stupid enough to forgive you for everything that's happened. You can't change the past. But you sure as hell can change the future, Dad."

"I guess I don't know how else to say it, Sean…"

I didn't let him finish. "I'm talking about your relationship with Pop."

By the look on his face, you would have thought that I'd hit him with that punch I wildly swung in the direction of his jaw last night. He leaned back in the booth and his whole demeanor changed.

"Some things aren't possible," he said. "What's done is done."

"Unacceptable," my little sister piped in, conviction in her voice.

He took a deep breath and blew it out slowly.

Our food came and sat untouched as the Judge digested the ultimatum his two children had just dropped in his lap. He wasn't used to being boxed in and didn't take kindly to it.

"Let me ask you a question, Sean," he said.

"Go for it," I answered.

"Do you love your sister?"

I looked at her. "Very, very much."

"Well, if a crazy man blew through that front door over there with a gun in his hand and he aimed it back and forth between Sheila and that nice waitress, who would you try to protect?"

I shook my head, refusing to play his game.

"You can twist anything to make it fit your rationale, Dad. Is that what a career in the courtroom taught you?"

His eyes sharpened and he leaned forward.

"No," he said.

"What it's taught me is that a man can be guilty as hell and walk free."

"And you think he's free, Daddy?" Sheila snapped, getting right in his face, just loud enough for the waitress and a couple of other patrons to turn in our direction.

"You think Pop doesn't carry the weight of the way grandma died in his heart and soul every second of his life? Are you stupid or just blinded by hate?"

It was like she had slapped him in the face. He looked at me.

"Back to hate, huh?"

"Seems to be a reoccurring theme, Dad. Are you getting the message?"

"You have to fix things with Pop, Daddy, you have too," Sheila said, tears in her eyes once again. For someone so young, she'd certainly had a lot to cry over in her brief lifetime.

I swear to you, after all that I had said, after Sheila pleaded with him, he just shook his head.

"No."

The color drained from his face. He knew he had to explain, but the man who could convince a jury that the earth was flat couldn't find the words.

To my amazement, his eyes filled with tears.

"I love my father," he said. "I know you don't believe that because I've hardly given you reason to."

The words were incredible to hear, even to see come off his lips. As long as I could remember, they had been at war.

"I love him… but I can't forgive him."

He choked up and it took him several minutes before he could continue.

"His mistake in judgment cost my mother her life. What it took from me was a woman I revered… a woman I loved with all my heart. And that's the problem. All of my heart."

There'd be plenty of leftovers for dinner tonight. Our food remained untouched. It was such a fragile moment for my family that his explanation could easily shatter the remains into a billion pieces. By comparison, only a few cracks were showing now.

"None of you knew or understood the relationship I had with my mother, what she meant to me — you couldn't. It was unique in its depth. She wasn't just my mother — she was my world."

"Don't you think we felt the same about our mom?" Sheila asked.

"No… what I did to drive Marnie away, to push your mother away from you is unconscionable. And, believe me or not, I won't ever forgive myself. But I did bring her back to you…you have a chance to love her again, to grow old with her. I didn't have that chance."

"You keep arguing that your hurt is greater than ours, Dad… how can you justify that?" I asked.

"Perhaps only in my mind, Sean, maybe you're right. But let me tell you a big difference."

He was silent for a moment, collecting his thoughts. Always the lawyer, he knew when a win or lose situation was staring him in the face.

"Pop will tell you that he was the happiest man on earth when he survived Korea and your grandmother agreed to marry him. And he'll tell you that having a son — me — made him feel blessed to be alive. That's how he remembers it.

"But you know what? It's not true. Unfortunately there's no one left to tell the truth — no one who can tell the real story except me, and I have no credibility with you. The only person you would have believed died on January 13, 1982.

"The same day I died."

Sheila leaned against my shoulder in our booth, a napkin pressed against her cheeks to blot the tears. I wondered if we should continue this somewhere more private, but there was no stopping him now. The truth was finally coming out. All of it.

"When my mother and father came home after he had recuperated enough from his wounds to be released from the hospital, they moved to the backwoods of Maine for a reason. You see, although he was physically healed from the horrors of Korea, he was an emotional basket case. Today, doctors would probably diagnose his condition then as PTSD. Post Traumatic Stress Disorder. It took him years to fully recover, and it was only with my mother's love and patience that he did. That's the reason they bought that old frigging car. It was all part of my mother's instinctive plan to heal him. She thought it would be good therapy for him to rebuild something, to breath new life into it, and a way for her to open up his imagination and get him to stop perseverating over the war."

Sam Evans took a deep breath, fighting to keep his nerve.

"When I was born in 1952, he was still very much an emotional train wreck. I know that from what my mother told me. I have no reason to doubt that he was elated to be a father, but his psychological problems kept him from being able to touch me, let alone hold me. He was afraid. My mother once told me that I terrified him."

"Why…I don't understand… why would grandma tell you something so awful?" I asked him, trying to be gentle.

"Because, as a young boy — I'm thinking I was maybe about five or six — he still had great difficulty in showing me his love. He was still struggling to regain his emotional strength. I point blank asked her why he didn't talk to me, why he never touched me, why we couldn't have a catch... why were weren't like other fathers and sons I saw..."

I wasn't sure he could go on. I had never seen my father so tenuous or fragile.

"She tried to explain to me how badly my father had been hurt in the war and how much he hurt inside. She said it made him 'special' —an interesting choice of words — and that showing love was extremely hard for him.

"Sometimes, he has trouble holding me, too, Sean," my mother reluctantly admitted. But she promised me that all would change if I didn't stop loving him. That she was working hard to help him get better. I can remember the conversation like it was yesterday.

"I don't think even she realized how little attention my father paid to me, she was so wrapped up in caring for him."

"Oh, God..." I said, not able to think of anything more profound. Talk about a new twist on the story.

"Eventually, because of my mother's persistence in bringing him back to life, he began to warm towards me. If you can believe it, we became best buddies. He ultimately became a fantastic father — and husband — whom I loved dearly. I was lost without him — without both of my parents — when I moved to Willington to be with your mom. That's why I dragged them out of that farm to be with us. Because I wanted them to stay in my life and to be a part of the family I imagined having some day."

He took a long drink from a glass of water. "I really need something a little stronger than this," he said. "But I guess this conversation is very, very overdue."

"Yah, Dad, you could say that," I replied and hugged Sheila.

"My mother became everything to me in his absence. It was like my father wasn't even there at times. She gave me love, made me laugh, hugged me when I was afraid. Not him. He just couldn't. She was all I had."

He looked up at us and said it. "My Mother was your Pop. Do you understand what I mean?"

"I think so," I said. Sheila nodded.

"During those early years, I didn't really have parents either. I had my mother. You had Pop. Each of them became the rock we leaned on for love and comfort and security. If you think about it, there's not a whole hell of a lot of difference between how we feel about each of them – and each other.

"Now I don't understand what you mean, Daddy," Sheila said.

He shook his head sadly.

"What I mean is you both hate me for what I am, for taking away your mom, for being so cruel to your grandfather. Maybe we can fix things so you don't hate me so much, but I know that you will always have the memories to deal with. I'm truly sorry for that."

He took another drink of water.

"Now all I ask you to do is look at it from my perspective. I hate what your grandfather did to my mother. He abandoned her when she desperately needed him. I know he had a noble reason, but that simply doesn't help me. He let her die. And I can never forgive him for taking her away from me. I can't bring her back the way I brought your mother home to you."

He paused long enough to call the waitress over and asked her to wrap our lunch. "Your mom is going to be worried sick if we don't get home soon. I need to learn to think about her feelings again. God, what an idiot I am."

Silence descended on the little booth we were crammed into. I listened to the sound of the traffic going by outside and wondered if all families had secrets. It would take something to top the whoppers the Evans family held, I thought.

"I told you both that I know I need to change in many ways. Words aren't worth much, I'll have to prove myself to you and to your mother," he continued. "I want my family back again… desperately."

He took another deep breath before going on.

"But when it comes to life between your grandfather and I, there is only so far I can go. I will force myself to treat him better, to be kinder to him, especially as he endures the difficult years he has ahead.

"But I can't love him again. It's not in me, nor will it ever be. What he took from me will always be in the way. That's something I can't change.

"However… I promise you… we can, and will, live in peace."

Sheila leaned across the table and kissed the Judge on the cheek. I just smiled. He was right, they were just words for the moment.

On the way out the door, he stopped and said one last thing.

"Forgot to tell you. Mom was going to take Pop out with her this afternoon to the supermarket to buy a turkey.

"We're planning a huge Thanksgiving celebration next Thursday.

"Together, the way real families do."

Forty-Two

~~~

April 1997

Eighteen months later, daily life for the Evans family was as close to normal as it could be – considering none of us could ever predict what world my grandfather would wake up in. Every day with him was a new experience for all of us.

There were those mornings when he couldn't understand what socks were. There were those when he got up early from a good nights sleep, stole into the kitchen and whipped up Eggs Benedict for us for breakfast and asked about the local elections.

On the good days, Sheila and I reveled in his clarity, enjoying our morning coffee with him on the back step before heading off to school. On the bad days, we helped to dress him, make him breakfast and get him confortable in an easy chair in the living room where my mother would sit with him for hours on end, typically reading to him until suddenly and inexplicably he would rejoin the world.

So there were good moments and bad, but nothing we couldn't handle, especially knowing the alternative. My father was always civil to Pop, never raised his voice and held a level of patience with his father I didn't think possible, knowing what he harbored against him.

Early on, my mother, Sheila and I agreed that the extra attention he was going to need was going to
~~~

require us to make some sacrifices if we wanted to keep him with us.

For Sheila, now a high school sophomore, that meant coming home right after classes most days and giving up some of her social life. I knew from experience that was a bigger deal than it seemed. But she never complained, and was always there to take Pop for a walk, drive him to the doctors or just give him a hug. For me, it meant enrolling as a day student at the nearby University of Connecticut for college instead of going away to school like I had hoped. My schedule allowed me to help out a lot with Pop, and especially to ensure he got plenty of time on his stool in the barn with his beloved Mercedes. My mother gave up her plans to open a small gift shop in town, preferring instead to become my grandfather's personal sort of family au pair, caring and cooking for him and seeing that all his affairs were kept in order, including Ceily's estate settlement. She was also his personal guard dog. God help the person who tried to take advantage of him. The pain of her exile had resulted in Marnie Evans becoming a very self-assured, much more realistic person, a change that served Pop well.

My father didn't contribute much more than whatever financial support Pop required, but on those occasional moments when we needed his help, he responded without complaint if not with love or compassion. He had gone after Air Florida with a vengeance that none of us could question, determined to break the airline's financial back if necessary to adequately compensate the families of victims of the crash. In the end, a small settlement was made to Ceily's estate, Air Florida by that time having declared bankruptcy largely because of the disastrous effect the accident had on its reputation. It didn't matter. No amount of money would have satisfied Sam Evans' taste for vengeance. It had been fifteen years since his mother had died, and quietly he still grieved for her like it had happened yesterday. His love and closeness to her would have made recovering from her untimely death under normal circumstances an agonizing process. But the manner in which she died made it virtually impossible.

Despite their years apart and his awful treatment of my mother, my parent's relationship steadily grew stronger until I believed they were actually in love again. The man who at one time found work as his only reason for existence, now surprised her occasionally with a romantic dinner out, coming home early from the office for a long walk together, or a glass of wine and a chat by the fireplace about anything but work. He stopped drinking almost entirely without prodding from any of us.

Sheila, much more quickly than I, welcomed my mother back into her life. I was delighted that they bonded almost immediately and that my mom had come home at such at such an important time for my little sister. My mother responded with all the love and motherly wisdom that had been missing in Sheila's life for so long. At sixteen, my sister had grown into quite a beauty and the telephone never stopped ringing at night. She was popular and attracted lots of attention from the opposite sex. I would have been a poor substitute as a mother.

Unfortunately I had to admit that I was much more like my father when it came to forgiveness, and it took me a lot longer to open up to her. The memory of her leaving me as a little boy, so many years before, just would not die. I didn't hate her for it – it wasn't like the blind anger my father felt towards Pop – but she had hurt me in a way I didn't think I could get over. We lived in a sort of perpetual dance around the pain, neither of us wanting to face the issue for fear of where it might lead. But slowly, trust began to build between us again, mostly because of the love and comfort I saw her give to Pop.

We certainly weren't a model family, and I doubted that short of some kind of miracle would we ever be. But nonetheless, we were finally a family pulling together to help one of our own.

In those hours we spent alone in the barn together, staring at the old car, Pop either sat in stone cold silence or would continue his stories of adventures with my grandmother in the yellow Mercedes. But now, they had become real. He no longer recognized that their adventures together had once been conjured up to satisfy their lust for adventure in Europe.

When he was clear-eyed and his mind wandered back to those wonderful memories of what had once been imagined journeys, his recall of details was almost mind-boggling. I could only guess that his knowledge of Europe's most romantic and scenic drives came from the world his wife force fed into his imagination while she worked so hard to jumpstart his brain again.

His stories were fascinating, and in his mind completely true. He would describe long drives in the Mercedes to Marseille in the south of France – and tell me how much he and Ceily had enjoyed the Escargot that night, cooked in butter with a splash of cognac at the restaurant Le Fouquet – as if he had been there the previous evening.

One afternoon, he spent more than two hours delighting in describing how he and grandma had driven the actual race route of the Monaco Grand Prix with the yellow Mercedes, screaming through the narrow course laid out in the city's streets.

"It was extraordinary, Sean, the car was so tight through the incredibly sharp corners, and the constant elevation changes and the long tunnel left us with our hearts in out throats," he laughed. "Ceily was screaming at me to slow down, but I was actually only doing the speed limit. But with all the gear changes and hard braking through the corners, the roaring exhaust through the tunnel, you would have thought we were doing over a hundred miles per hour.

"It was one of the most exhilarating things I've ever done," he said, "probably even more exciting than the first time I flew a fighter jet, if you can believe it. Your grandmother didn't talk to me for an hour afterwards, then we laughed about it at dinner that night at Le Café du Cirque on Chapiteau de Fontvieille.

"What a wonderful evening that was. She looked so beautiful," he said, his mind wandering off even as he said it.

Every word of the story was imagined. He no longer understood the difference between fantasy and reality.

What harm was there, I wondered. The memories, real or imagined, made him happy in his brief moments of clarity. But then I realized that I was only fooling myself, because he was no longer suffering from episodic dementia. He was no longer in touch with reality at all. For the most part, he was living in a dream-like state. That was very alarming.

We spent two more hours in the barn that afternoon, finally going into the house as the sun was setting when my mother called us in for dinner. In that entire time, he never said a word, never even moved from the stool to adjust his weight or position. He sat stone still just staring at the car. I couldn't imagine the scene playing out in his head, only that it involved my grandmother.

As he always did when we left the barn, Pop slowly stood up from his stool and walked over to the passenger seat of the Mercedes. He reached inside and touched the worn, black leather of the seat back, rubbing it with his fingers, which he then brought to his nose. It had taken me years to understand why he did it. And then one day it struck me.

He was searching for the perfumed scent of his Ceily.

Forty-Three

~~~

November 1997

The belligerence began without warning.

It started over small, inconsequential things, like arguments about wearing a sweater when he went outside. It quickly graduated to not wanting to eat or bathe.

We all knew it would eventually happen. As Dr. St. Pierre had predicted, Pop's behavior was following the course of someone who had been suffering from Alzheimer's disease for at least several years, and it had now reached a higher stage. But then suddenly, in November, three years after he had been diagnosed and just before the holidays, there was a marked change in his behavior.

I noticed it first one morning when I came downstairs for breakfast to find him towering over my mother with an iron skillet in his hand, ready to strike her. She was backed into a corner, trying to talk to him, to reach him, but not having any luck. Pop was insisting on making breakfast, something he was no longer able to do. We couldn't let him near the stove. I came up from behind him and grabbed his arm, preventing him from hitting my mom, but he wrestled with me, angrily fighting back.

He wasn't very hard for me to handle, the disease had taken a toll on his body and he was much lighter and smaller now, but it broke my heart to have to manhandle him. I got him into a kitchen chair and held
~~~

him there while my mother got up from the corner, wiped away the tears of her fear and sadness and poured him a glass of orange juice. She placed it in front of him and he immediately stopped struggling, focusing instead on the juice. It was not unlike the reaction one would see in an infant. He took a drink, then asked if I had brought in the newspaper yet. I shook my head "no." He couldn't remember that he hadn't been able to read in more than a year.

Mom made him his breakfast, but he didn't eat. All he wanted was to sit on the back step with his coffee. I came out to join him a few minutes later and found him crying.

"What's the matter, Pop," I asked him quietly, gently putting my arm around his shoulders.

"I don't understand," he said, wiping his eyes.

"What don't you understand?" I asked.

"Why she hasn't at least called me."

"Who, Pop?"

"What do you mean who?" he snapped at me, throwing the remains of his coffee out into the yard.

"Your god damned grandmother, that's who," he said angrily. "She told me she was going to Paris and would be right back. Hell it's been a week… or… has it been a week, Sean?"

I sucked in a deep breath. It was so hard to answer him in this state. Whatever you said might set him off again or completely calm him down. I played along.

"She'll call," Pop. "Don't worry about it. You know how bad traffic can be in Paris."

He shook his head in understanding. It made sense to him. "That's true," he said. "She's probably stuck on the Champs-Élysées." He glanced at his watch to check the time. No one had had the heart to tell him it had stopped working months ago.

"Rush hour over there now. That's what you get for window shopping," he laughed, his mood a hundred and eighty degrees opposite of what it had been just minutes earlier.

I used the opportunity to change the subject.

"You can't hit my mother, Pop," I told him. "You can't hit Marnie, or Sheila or anyone else, understand?" I told him. "I know you get confused sometimes, but if you want to stay hear near the barn and the car, you have to behave."

He looked up at me, a puzzled look in his eyes.

"Why, I'd never hit anyone… um…"

"Sean, Pop. It's Sean."

"That's what I meant… Sean."

He was quiet after that for a little while.

"Did you find the keys to the Mercedes?" he asked out of the clear blue. It had been some time since he had asked about the keys. Maybe a week. There were days when he asked me a dozen times.

"Not yet , Pop, but I haven't given up."

"Because you know that when your grandmother comes home she's going to expect to take a drive on Sunday."

"I know, Pop." He stiffly got up to walk to the barn, his mood vastly improved. We took up our stools and began our ritual of staring at the old girl, her yellow paint almost completely gone now. The tires were all flat and there was rust everywhere. But he didn't see a thing wrong with the Mercedes. To my grandfather, the car was as beautiful as the day he had permanently parked it after visiting my grandmother's grave.

"She's still a thing of beauty, you know it?" he said, looking her over. "And I've been thinking. If we don't find the keys before grandma comes home, we can just jumpstart her. I just need to pull a couple of ignition wires from under the dash…I know how to do it. Just a temporary way to fix the problem. All we need is to gas her up."

I didn't doubt that he probably could recall how to hot wire the old car, but the engine hadn't been turned over since 1982, fifteen years ago. In the environment it had been parked, the chances were high that the engine was frozen solid. Even if it turned over, the points and plugs would be shot and we'd never get her going. But I wasn't about to tell him that.

I had classes most of the rest of the day, so I didn't catch up with Pop again until almost dinnertime. When I walked into the kitchen, my mother was sitting with him, rubbing his shoulder. He was completely out of it, locked on to some thought that made everything else around him completely invisible. It was an impenetrable place that not even drilling could reach.

Sheila and I ended up helping him to bed a little early that night, hoping a good night's sleep would ease him out of the trance-like state he was in. Afterwards, I hit the books for a while, but when Sheila came in to say good night, I realized how tired I was. The day had started out stressful and hadn't ended on a much better note. I turned in about eleven and was lights out the minute my head hit the pillow.

To this day, I don't know what woke me a couple of hours later. Thinking back, I don't recall a noise of any kind. It was like a flash in my head that simply screamed "get up."

The house was completely quiet. I glanced at my bedside clock and saw that it was almost two in the morning. Then I looked out my window and saw the barn light was on. I didn't even bother to check Pop's bed. Slipping into my sneakers, I ran down the stairs, opened the back door and covered the distance between the house and the barn in seconds flat. As I got closer to the barn I could smell the gasoline.

I threw open the barn door and ran inside. It was freezing cold, but the stench of raw gas fumes was strong enough to warm my blood out of fear. Standing in front of me, his pajamas soaking wet with gasoline, was my grandfather, holding the two leads from an electric battery charger in separate hands. He was standing over the open hood of the Mercedes and was about to clamp the cables over the car's battery posts. Even from where I stood, I could see that battery acid had eaten a hole right through the side of the 12-volt case. The small automotive battery was an explosion waiting to happen. A five-gallon can of gasoline was overturned on some canvas that Pop had pulled off the old car. It was a set up for the perfect firestorm.

"Pop, don't move," I screamed as my eyes followed the charger's power cord and saw that it was plugged into an electrical outlet over a workbench he'd built years ago. Instantly, the coming disaster played out in my head. If he connected the cables to the battery or accidently touched the positive to the negative clamps in his hand, the ensuing spark would cause the battery to explode, his gasoline soaked pajamas to catch fire, or both.

"Well, hell, Sean," my grandfather said innocently, very aggravated by my intrusion. "I know what I'm doing. I've been hot wiring cars for years. Just put some gas in the tank." He looked down at his flannel pajamas. "Spilled a little, but they'll be all right. Ceily knows how to get out stains."

He stepped closer to the car, still holding the cables. Abruptly he stopped. The charger was on the ground and the cables weren't long enough to reach over the fender to the battery.

"Damn," he said and went to put both cables into one hand so he could move the charger. In the next second he would be a human torch.

I froze. I either had to make it to the plug over the workbench or knock the cable out of his hands. There wasn't time for either.

Behind me, I felt rather than heard something move quickly in the vicinity of the workbench. It was my father, holding the plug in his hands. He had killed the power to the charger.

"Sean, quickly, get him away from the battery," he said calmly. "He might still cause that battery to blow from static electricity if he connects those cables."

I nodded. "Pop," I yelled to him again. "Stay where you are, I'll come and help you." He turned and faced me, the cables stacked together in his hand. A second's delay by my father in cutting the power to the charger and Pop would have already been engulfed in flames.

I ran to him and grabbed the cables from his hands, picked up the charger and threw it to the back of the barn. He was literally drenched in gasoline, which was probably burning the hell out of his skin even as we stood there looking at each other.

"Pop, what the hell..." I said, too numb to know where to begin. "We gotta get you out of those clothes and into the shower, quickly." Out of the corner of my eye I saw my father begin walking towards us.

"Hell no, I'm taking the car out for a drive, I want to warm her up before Ceily gets home," Pop said, frustrated and angry that I had disturbed him. "Who the hell do you think you are, anyway… um… you…" He had forgotten my name again.

"Sean, Pop," I said. "C'mon, let's head back to the house."

"No," he hollered and reared back and punched me with all his might in the face. The punch caught me on the side of my cheek and dropped me like a rock. As I lay on the dirt floor, trying to regain my senses, he began kicking me in the head as hard as he could. He was enraged, out of control. My father emerged from the shadows of the barn and literally tackled him to the ground to make him stop. Still, Pop continued to struggle.

"Sean," my father said breathlessly, his arms locked around Pop's neck, "call 911 and have them send an ambulance," he said. "This is more than we can handle. He's got to be sedated." I rose, shaken, from the floor.

"No, Dad. We can't do that. They'll take him away."

"Sean, listen to me," my father said, still trying to hold his father down. "We're going to hurt him trying to get him to calm down. Do as I say, please, this is the best way."

I didn't argue anymore but ran into the house and called the Willington police who dispatched a cruiser and an ambulance. Pop was still fighting mad when the police arrived but was losing his strength. My father was all but done in himself from the struggle.

Sheila and my mother, awoken by the commotion, were holding each other, both crying as a couple of burly medics finally showed up and strapped Pop down on a gurney. They injected him with some kind of sedative. He screamed like a wild animal from the injustice he imagined, then passed out as the drug hit.

My father told the cop who had been dispatched that we would come to the hospital as soon as we got dressed. Then he walked over to me, slowly and cautiously, not sure of what to expect from me, and gently wrapped his arms around my shoulders. It was the first time my father had held me in his arms since his mother had died. I began to cry.

"It's all right, Sean, it's all right," he said. "You did good, you saved him. Calling the medics was the right thing to do. He would have had another heart attack by the time we could have calmed him down.

"You did good son," he said again, as he hugged me.

I didn't want him to let go.

Forty-Four

St. Pierre's prognosis was not unexpected.

"A long time ago, I told you that there would come a time when it would be incumbent upon you to place John Evans in a safe environment," he said to us in his office at Hartford Hospital. It looked out over the front portico of the main entrance and there was a nice view of a landscaped green. The setting was peaceful. Even the lobby was inviting. It wasn't until you took the elevators to the uppers floors that you could smell the pain and suffering, the sadness and hopelessness that is such a depressing part of the ambience of any hospital. The smell even crept into Dr. St. Pierre's office, despite his attempts to make it as cheery an environment as possible.

Pop was currently a patient in the eighteen-bed Geriatric Services unit of the Hospital's psychiatric wing, the Institute of the Living. Dr. St. Pierre had moved mountains to make room for him after the incident in the barn. He was a kind, compassionate man under his white lab coat that had taken a particular interest in my grandfather. Pop was safe there, but it was only a temporary arrangement. It was time to find him a place with round the clock eyes that could protect him from himself.

It was a shattering moment in our lives, but one which Sheila and I knew was ultimately unavoidable. Pop had come within mere seconds of immolating himself, driven by hallucinations and a desperate attempt to resurrect the past. His broken heart was as much to blame as the disease that was slowly taking him from us.

My father and mother, Sheila and I all attended the meeting with Dr. St. Pierre. It was if each of us had to hear it from a man we trusted before finally letting go. For my father, the news was not nearly as disconcerting, but it was important for him to hear it – to be sure we understood the decision was not his, nor was he lobbying for it. Over the last several years my dad had successfully managed his feelings for his father by approaching the situation as pragmatically as he conducted his daily professional life. Whatever emotions he now felt for the old man he kept carefully hidden, but I didn't fool myself into thinking they had changed much.

"Clearly, if John Evans were of sound mind, he would choose to age in place, meaning he would desire to live out his last years in the comfort of his own home surrounded by those he loves," St. Pierre said with resignation. "Unfortunately, we have reached a stage where that is no longer an option if we consider his safety, well-being and the constant care he will need in the months ahead. That means he needs to be in a nursing home environment – where he is attended to on a twenty-four hours per day basis, rather than in a retirement or assisted living facility."

He looked at each of us, slowly, giving us time to ask questions or challenge his conclusions. I wanted to tell him that he was wrong, that there was no reason Pop couldn't just come home with us right now and live out his days in the comfort of our care. I knew Sheila felt the same. But the time had come for us to face reality, too. There was no way we could save Pop from himself.

"I don't think any of us can argue with your conclusions, Doctor, as much as we'd like to believe you are wrong," I said. "My grandfather has become a danger to himself, and to some degree, his family. I know he would never want that," I said.

"But I know you will recall the terrible experience he had in the facility he lived in for some weeks after his heart attack several years ago. It was an awful, demeaning and heartless place. The people who ran it were soulless, and most of the patients were walking dead. We can't have that again," I pleaded.

"He deserves better, Doctor. They treated him like an animal," Sheila added, tears welling in her eyes.

St. Pierre leaned back in his chair and shook his head, sighing. "I remember the situation well," he said. "That particular facility is an embarrassment to the entire medical community. But there is some good news in terms of the type of care available now for your grandfather, specifically as it relates to his struggles with Alzheimer's.

"Traditionally, institutional care for Alzheimer's patients, and for the majority of patients in nursing homes, consists of very regimented organization, administration and scheduling. It's typically not unlike a military barracks. For example, all patients are roused at the same time every morning, say six o'clock, and are served breakfast at the same time as well, sometimes an hour or two later after sitting around with nothing to do while the staff does its work. It is an agonizing and somewhat humiliating way to start the day for those patients who feel demeaned to be treated in such a manner.

"It usually gets worse as the day progresses. Everything is organized into a 'one size fits all' schedule, lunch and dinner are served at exactly the same hour for all patients and consists of the same menu, and lights out is at the same time, each night, for all patients. You can imagine that some patients, particularly those not suffering from dementia object to such a lifestyle, and live the last years of their life in misery and often, depression caused by the sheer repetition, inactivity and boredom associated with such a lifestyle. For some victims of Alzheimer's whose symptoms of dementia fluctuate, the same effect can be seen."

"I believe that your grandfather's first experience with institutional care was very much like this model," he concluded. "Some, including your father at that point in his life, would have likened this approach to living in a detention center."

"Exactly. It was horrible," I said.

"And he was so neglected," Sheila added.

"So what is the alternative, Doctor?" my mother asked.

"Nursing homes are rapidly changing their operating culture to what they term 'person-centered' care. In this type of environment, the goal of the nursing home is to provide the patient more of a home setting, in that staff are encouraged to develop one on one relationships with their patients and in turn, to encourage their charges to exercise more autonomy."

"I'm not sure I understand," Sam Evans said. "There are days when my father can barely remember how to tie his shoes..."

"But there are others when he behaves at much greater functional and emotional levels, isn't that true?" St. Pierre replied.

My father nodded.

"Of course, it is the nature of Alzheimer's. The point is a person centered care provider will always be there for your father when he is incapacitated to any degree. But when he is not, this environment allows him greater flexibility of lifestyle in which he can become much more comfortable. For example, he would be encouraged to choose what time he rises in the morning and goes to bed at night. He would have the flexibility of choosing when he eats and selecting his own menu. He can choose hobbies that interest him or other activities that will engage him.

"Compare the difference. In his last experience, he spent most of his day sitting in a wheelchair, parked in a hallway with dozens of other patients with nothing to do and was terribly neglected. I'd say what I just described to you is a major culture change in nursing care and an environment that your father will have a much easier time adjusting to as he makes this difficult transition. If you can find a nursing home that has embraced person-centered care, then I believe you will have given him the gift of living out his life as close to a home-like environment as is possible."

My father looked at the three of us and smiled, rolling his eyes simultaneously. Whether he agreed or not, there was no point in discussing it. St. Pierre had told his wife and children what they needed to hear.

"I suppose this will cost a small fortune," he said resigned to the decision.

"Nursing care in this state costs in excess of $10,000 per month, Mr. Evans. The environment I described will undoubtedly carry a premium," St. Pierre replied.

"Holy shit," my father said, stunned by the number. But I'll be damned. Sam Evans didn't even blink an eye. He turned to us.

"If that's what it takes, thats what it takes."

My mom and Sheila both jumped from their seats and hugged him. I stayed out but smiled at him. He smiled back. That's the way it was between us now. But it was an improvement.

Finding this "Shangri-La" as my dad likened it without really intending to be sarcastic was going to be another magic trick in itself. My mom and sister went to work on visiting the myriad of nursing homes within reasonable driving distances to make sure we'd be able to visit with him at least several times a week. My father let it be, allowing nature to take its course. In the meantime, I spent as much time with Pop as I could, both to safeguard him but also to take advantage of the time we had together that I knew was fast running out.

He was no longer allowed into the barn alone, for obvious reasons, and was very unhappy about it. Consequently, he waited for me to come home from school every day so we could take up our stools and gaze at the old girl. I'd often pull into the backyard and find him pacing in anticipation. As usual, we'd sit inside on our stools either deep in silence or animated conversation. I never knew what to expect. Today he was about as quiet and melancholy as I'd ever seen him.

"I don't think she's coming back, Sean," he said after nearly a half hour of dead silence. "It's been several weeks since she left and I haven't heard a word from her. Traffic in Paris can't be that bad."

It was another example of how his mind was deteriorating. If you put an idea into his head and he bought it, there was no getting it out.

"Pop," I said, putting my arm around him, "just be a little more patient. You know how much grandma loves you. She wouldn't just up and leave you alone. She's probably having such a good time, she's lost track of it." It broke my heart to lie to him, but I had long ago dismissed any notion of resurrecting the truth. Buried deep within him was the knowledge that she was dead. For whatever reason, the truth had disappeared and had been replaced by a fantasy that was far more acceptable to him. If I told him the truth, it would be as if he had heard it for the first time, and the pain it would cause him would be unbearable. He was hurting enough even in his fantasy world.

"But I've got good news, Pop," I said, trying to change the subject.

"What?" he looked at me, puzzled.

I made a big show of standing up and walking over to the car and leaning up against the front fender, where I dug into my pocket. I pulled out a balled fist, then slowly opened my fingers to reveal the keys to the Mercedes.

"Look what I found…" I said, grinning.

"The keys," he yelled in joy, jumping up from his stool. "By God, you found the keys to the car. Ceily will be so happy we can go on our Sunday drive!" He completely forgot about her absence.

"Where in the name of the Lord did you find them?" he said, his eyes glistening wet.

"You're not going to believe it," I replied.

"Where, tell me…"

"In the ignition."

"What?" he roared. "Well I'll be a son of a gun. That's the only place I never looked. What the hell would they be doing there?" he asked, without the slightest hint of embarrassment or the idiocy of his question.

The truth is, I had come upon them the night he almost set himself on fire. Wiping up the residue of gasoline that was all over the car, I had leaned in through the driver's side window and saw the original Mercedes Benz keys sticking out of the ignition. They'd probably been there since he parked the car fifteen years before. I wasn't afraid to hand them over because there wasn't a chance in hell he could start the car now. My father and I had removed the leaking battery and distributor and we'd changed over any gasoline stored inside to the kind of cans with locking caps. The only way the Mercedes could run would be in his dreams

You would have thought he was just a little kid and I was Santa Clause when I handed him the keys. I had to choke back a tear when I saw him hold them up to the waning afternoon light streaming through a hole in the roof to see how they still shone after thousands of turns in the ignition. He wouldn't have traded those keys for the biggest gem in the world, the famous, forty-five karat "Hope" diamond.

Because for my grandfather, the keys represented real hope – and that, you couldn't put a price on.

Forty-Five

~~~

December 25, 1997

The day after Christmas my grandfather moved to the Lakeview Nursing Home in Coventry, Connecticut, about a twenty-minute ride from our home in Willington. It felt like he was moving to Australia.

The facility was literally what the doctor ordered – Dr. St. Pierre, in this case – with a strong culture of person centered care that we were all convinced would suit Pop. Or, at the least, make the transition a little easier for him.

Ironically, the house was quiet for days before we took him to Lakeview, a lovely nursing facility situated on the spring fed Wangumbaug Lake just outside of the center of Coventry. It was a very rural setting, close to Mansfield where I went to school, and from his bedroom, Pop would be able to look out not only at the lake, but at cornfields and several old barns. We were all praying that being out in the country would help him acclimate and that being so close we could stop by every day if necessary.

The hardest part of all was breaking the news to him.

In hindsight, it was probably good that it was one of his better days, that he was relatively lucid when we told him and that he fully understood what was happening. But at the moment the words had to be said, I would have given anything for his mind to be
~~~

mired in that other disconnected world where all he could see and hear was his Ceily and his old Mercedes.

Christmas morning, he came downstairs to the breakfast table with a smile on his face from ear to ear, wearing his red and green tartan holiday vest just as he always had in better times. My father looked up from his newspaper and his jaw dropped. He looked like he had seen a ghost. In a way he had. This was just how Pop had dressed for Christmas a few days before my grandmother was killed in January.

I looked at my mother, who was holding her breath waiting for my father's reaction.

Amazingly, he hid whatever he was thinking.

"Good morning, Dad, Merry Christmas," my father said, then hid his face behind the newspaper again. Pop grinned.

My mom cooked a grand Christmas feast with a huge turkey and all the trimmings and Pop was in the same upbeat mood most of the day, even reminiscing about how grandma would decorate their old farmstead in Maine for the holidays. He told us how the two of them would walk miles into the woods every year to find the right Christmas fir, he pulling Sam on a little red sled and my grandmother lugging a heavy axe. Once they found it, my grandfather would chop it down with a practiced hand and lug it all the way back to the Mercedes, the thick trunk of the tree up on his shoulder. The old roadster wasn't exactly built for pickup truck like duties, but he and grandma would strap the tree across the top and slowly ferry it home. We laughed when he explained how they used to make buckets full of popcorn and thread string through the popped kernels to wrap as decorations around the tree and grandma would add hand-crocheted ornaments to add some color. They only thing they would splurge on would be some flashy tinsel, and by the light of the constantly blazing fireplace in their living room, Pop said their Christmas tree was always a thing of wonder to him.

"How your grandma could make something so beautiful from practically nothing always amazed me," he said, his eyes sparkling with the memory. "I couldn't wait for my work day to end during Christmas season just to come home and sit by the fire and stare at the tree with her by my side and Sam on my lap. Those were wonderful holidays, weren't they Sam?" he asked.

My father surprised us all by playing along.

"Yah, Dad, they were," he replied, smiling at his father. It wasn't often that they communicated in any way. My father must have recognized the importance of the moment to us because he actually continued the conversation.

"The tree was great, but what I remember most was mom making us hot cocoa when you came in for the night," he said. "I don't know whatever happened to her recipe, but we could make a fortune off it today," he added, ever the lawyer looking for a deal.

Then he knocked us all off our pins.

"You know what my favorite Christmas was, Dad?" he asked grandpa. Pop just shook his head. I wondered if he was really absorbing everything my father was telling him.

"It was the year – let's see, I must have been six years old maybe?" he asked himself. "It was the year you made me that huge solid oak rocking horse with the leather saddle and the real horsehair tail. It was huge and looked just like 'Trigger' – Roy Rogers' horse."

"Who?" Sheila and I asked together, laughing.

"He was a famous cowboy, you two, and my hero so don't make fun," he chided us. "Trigger was his brave horse who was always saving him from the bad guys."

We both couldn't help but stifle laughs.

"He was as big a star as Elvis, damn it," he tried again.

"Who?" we laughed again.

"Okay, Michael Jackson."

We stopped laughing.

"That big?"

"Yah," he said, giving us a snide look.

"Anyway, I remember coming downstairs Christmas morning and shrieking with pleasure when I saw it. I was so excited, I'd never seen anything so beautiful. I Think I spent the entire day riding that thing."

My grandfather's face lit up like I hadn't seen in ages. He remembered.

"I carved that rocking horse from a solid oak tree trunk, Sam," he said. "Took me months. Your mom thought I was crazy. You gave me the biggest hug that day. I tried to tell you that it was Santa Clause who'd brought it but you knew better. You were already a lawyer."

The two of them burst out laughing. The sight and sound of the two of them laughing together was truly a Christmas miracle.

Mom's dinner was spectacular and then we all gathered around the Christmas tree in the living room and exchanged gifts. Sheila and I, reading each other's minds, gave each other new cassette tapes. I got Aerosmith, she got Spice Girls. Dad bought Mom a string of natural pearls and she gave him a new cardigan sweater she'd knitted by hand. Pop looked a little confused by now. He was getting tired.

Before he was too tired, we all gathered around him and gave him a gift from all of us — a scale replica of his old Mercedes, painted exactly in the right colors that we had ordered for him specially from the Mercedes Benz factory in Stuttgart, Germany. When he opened the wooden box it came in, he stared at it for the longest time, inspecting it from every angle. Then a big grin came across his face.

"I know where to keep the keys for the old girl in the barn now. They'll go right in the trunk of this one, safe in my room." After he said it, I abruptly felt sick to my stomach, knowing what was coming.

We sat around the fireplace then and my father told him what was going to happen the next morning, that he would be leaving us and moving into a place that could care for him better than we could.

I don't know that I could have done a better job than my father had, he was very gentle in his tone of voice and tried to put as good a spin on it as possible. But Pop's reaction was heartbreaking.

"Why?" he said, in disbelief, the color draining from his face. He was shocked.

"I'm sorry about the gas, I won't do it again, I promise…" he pleaded.

Sheila burst into tears and my mom looked like she was on the verge. The lawyer in my dad and their history together kept my father from getting emotional. I just couldn't speak.

"Dad," my father said, "it's not about the gas or that you've done anything wrong. You just need some help now that we can't give you. It's not fair to you."

My father couldn't bring himself to say, "I love you", or anything that would help to ease Pop's pain. Those words just would not pass his lips. It was left to me.

"Pop..." I began, trying not to choke up, "you have to understand how much we all love you, and how sad it would make us if something happened to you because we weren't there to help you. We don't want this either, but you need to have people help you all the time now, especially with your medications, and we're not able to do it."

He didn't hear a word I said.

"I'll be good, I promise," he pleaded again.

I got down on my knees in front of him and took his hands.

"Pop, you haven't been bad. You haven't done anything wrong. This is no different than after you were wounded in Korea. The doctors and nurses needed to take care of you."

Sheila wrapped her arms around him in a hug. She was crying, tears rolling down her pretty cheeks.

"We'll come everyday to see you and take you out for walks around the Lake. You'll really like it there, you'll see."

He got that far away look in his eyes back again and stared into the roaring fire.

"Ceily," he suddenly blurted out.

"How will she find me?"

My father got up and made himself a tall scotch. I hadn't seen him do that in ages.

"When grandma comes home, I'll drive her there myself, OK Pop?" I promised him.

"Can I take the car with me? Somebody has to look after her so Ceily and I can go for our Sunday rides."

He stared into my eyes. It came to me how a loyal old dog must look at its master at the moment it's about to be put down. A combination of love and betrayal shone in his eyes.

"I'll take care of the car, Pop, she needs to stay here where she'll be safe in the barn. I'll do it myself, " I promised. "Nothing will happen to her and she'll be ready to roll when grandma comes home."

"Please, Sean, don't do this to me."

I would have given my soul if, at that exact moment, he wasn't able to remember my name.

But he did.

He knew exactly who I was and that I alone could save him. But the grandson who loved the old man more than life itself, did what he knew he had to do.

"No, Pop, we have to take better care of you and that's what we're going to do."

"Ceily…?"

"She would want this too, Pop. She would want you to be taken care of."

"When she comes…?"

"I'll bring her to you myself, in the old yellow car."

He stared into the fire for a long time. My dad finished his drink. Given the circumstances he was a square peg in a round hole again. My mother and Sheila sat on the couch and wept. I stared at my grandfather until his mind came back to me.

"I'm proud of you, Sean," he said, and reached for my hand. He used my arm to pull himself up from the chair. I almost lost it.

"Let's go sit on our stools for awhile, okay?" he said. "I need to say goodbye to the old girl, maybe check the oil."

"How about a cup of coffee for out there, boys?" My mom asked. "It's kinda nippy out tonight."

"That would be nice... um... that..."

My mother dabbed at her eyes. "Marnie, it's Marnie, Pop. That's okay." She came over and kissed him on the cheek then went into the kitchen to make a pot of coffee.

Pop and I went out to the back step and sat, staring at the barn. Mom brought the coffee a few minutes later.

"We've been sitting here a long time, grandson," he said."

"Yah, Pop, a long time." I thought about the day when I might sit out here with my own son or grandson.

We sipped our coffee for a while, then wordlessly he stood up and began making his way to the barn. I followed. Half way there, he stopped and waited until I caught up.

Then he wrapped his arm around my neck and hugged me as we walked to the barn for the last time.

Forty-Six

In his last night in the oversized bed in which he had slept fitfully alone for the past nearly sixteen years, she came to him in his dreams.

Before closing his eyes to sleep, he had knelt over the side that had been empty for so long and prayed to God to let him go to her this very night. After all the trials – the agony of Korea, causing the death of his beloved wife, being exiled from the life of his cherished son – this last blow was finally too much to bear. He could not go on.

"Lord, I beg you to take me, let me be with my Ceily. You cannot exact any price higher than that which I have already paid. Punish me more if you must, but please let me die before the sun rises again. Place me in the arms of the woman who saved me so long ago and taught me the meaning of peace and happiness. I beg of you…"

Later, in the shadow of the moon and in the stillness of the black night, he imagined the warmth of her breath on his cheek and smelled her sweet scent. Chanel No. 9. He always said he could tell when she entered a room just by the loveliness of her perfume. Her long, luxurious red hair brushed the side of his face as her lips found his and the soft kiss awoke him.

He looked into her ocean green eyes and felt the heat of joy course through his veins.

"Ceily, my love, you are here for me? At last?" he whispered, barely able to contain himself.

"John, there is one more battle to be won," she said. "Those who love you here still need you."

"No, Ceily, I am done. I am no longer needed. They are sending me away."

"Only to protect you my darling. Not to punish you. You have done nothing wrong. Don't you believe that?" she said.

"I let you die, I could have saved you…"

"John, think… could either of us have lived with the knowledge that you didn't try to save that poor young mother and her child? The answer is no… you did what had to be done. There were other plans for me."

"But…"

"Shh," she whispered. "There are no 'buts' John… the mother and child are here with me and they are happy and together – as we will be, very soon. You made the right choice, my love. There is no forgiveness to seek."

"Sam, my son… he despises me, Ceily…"

"The pain is real for him, too, John, but he is one of the reasons you must stay. Just for a while longer. You cannot give up now, my love. You must help them all heal…"

"Ceily, I can't do this..."

"You must, John. You have always been my hero. I need you now to be brave, just a little longer. And when it is over, and you have healed their wounds, every day will be Sunday for you and me.

"Do you understand?"

He held her in his arms, for the moment living the dream he had each night.

"I will try, Ceily. For you."

"I knew you would," she whispered, kissing him again and gently caressing his face with her fingertips.

"But only if you promise you will come for me… will you?"

"When I come for you it will be for all eternity. Remember what I said: every day will be Sunday."

He thought for a moment about the joy of such a thing. The two of them on another great adventure, holding hands, driving through the streets of Sainte-Mère-Église in the north of France, the humid air warming them in the open roadster, stopping to watch the sun set while sipping an absurdly expensive glass of Romanée-Conti burgundy at a streetside café. Oh, dear God, let it be true…

Just as fast, his tortured mind remembered.

"Ceily… we found the keys."

"I know, my love, I know.

"Now sleep and be brave."

"Soon, Ceily, soon?" he begged again.

"Yes, my husband. When the wounds are healed."

"I love you…" he whispered through tears as her apparition faded.

"Mrs. Evans."

Forty-Seven

~~~

January 1998

The Evans family celebrated the New Year at the Lakeview Nursing Home with my grandfather, where he had moved just a week before. He was quiet and not at all aware of what all the noise and celebration was about at dinner, which was surprisingly well done for its patrons. But he never made it to midnight. About eight o'clock, Pop motioned to me with a nod of his head that he'd like to go to his room. Sheila and I helped him get ready for bed and kissed him goodnight. There would be no champagne on this night.

My sister and I were on Christmas break so we were able to spend a lot of time with him that first awful week. We helped Pop get oriented as best as possible, working up a schedule, meal selections and activities. Sometimes he was engaged and even pleasant. But there were other times he dove into a black hole and just hid from us, refusing to talk. We didn't know if he was just out of it or throwing a tantrum. I thought it was some of both.

At any rate, my grandfather was very unhappy.

A nurse, a woman named Molly, met him at the door on the very first day he arrived and introduced herself as his special assistant. She was early thirties, married with a couple of small children. You could tell just from the sound of her voice that she was sincere and wanted to be Pop's friend, but as you can imagine,
~~~

he treated her like an alien. I couldn't tell what was going on in his mind because he was clearly still in shock from was happening.

Molly was attractive in her own way, a few pounds overweight, but had lovely brunette hair and the most endearing and constant smile. But the thing I believe finally got my grandfather to pay attention to her were her eyes. Not only were they filled with kindness, they were a deep shade of green like my grandmother's. They weren't as radiant as grandma's – her eyes were truly remarkably beautiful. Even I remember looking into them when I was four years old and wondering how they could be so green and bright and happy.

But once Pop noticed Molly's eyes, he began to warm up to her a bit, slowly, little by little. I knew it would take time. Other than my mom and Sheila, he hadn't had any kind of relationship with a woman since grandma had died.

A couple of days after New Years, I came by when he wasn't expecting me and caught the two of them alone in his room. He was sitting comfortably in a large, oversized easy chair, his feet propped up on a hassock that Molly had obviously positioned for him, and she was reading to him. Not just droning on in in a monotone that suggested 'please, just let me get this over so he'll take a nap,' but with real feeling. I listened for a couple of minutes and recognized Herman Melville's "Moby Dick," one of his favorite classics. Pop had a contented look on his face. It made my heart sing.

Looking around his small, but cozy private room, it was obvious that Molly had improved on the personal touches we had tried to add for him. A large photo of the family sat framed on his dresser and the model of the Mercedes we had given him for Christmas was placed on a nightstand next to his bed. But now the trunk of the replica car was open and inside, readily seen, were the keys to the real one still parked back home in the barn.

Here and there were other little touches to make him feel comfortable. There were flowers on his desk and a plant on his windowsill. Several books were stacked by the window and a thick grey cardigan, his favorite that my mom had knitted for him years ago with leather buttons was laid out on the bed. Molly was working hard to earn his trust and his friendship. We couldn't ask for more.

I left without disturbing them, figuring I might stop by later in the day. But when I walked outside, what had been a rather pleasant winter afternoon had turned dark and ominous, the sky filling rapidly with snow-laden clouds. There were a few snowflakes coming down as I left the nursing home. By the time I pulled out on to the main highway to head home, it was coming down heavy.

As I pulled in to the backyard, the snow was coming down so heavy I could barely see the driveway. The barn was only a few yards away but almost invisible from the white curtain that was dropping on us at an alarming rate.

I went inside and asked my mom if she'd heard any weather forecasts but she hadn't had the television on all day. I hit the local stations and the airwaves were full of detailed reports of a full-blown Nor'easter' unexpectedly descending on Connecticut. The news was full of dire predictions of up to two feet of snow and gale force winds. My first reaction was to worry about not being able to get out to see Pop. The last thing he needed was to feel abandoned.

By nightfall, we already had a foot of snow on the ground and it was still coming down thick and heavy. It wasn't just snow now, but a mixture of snow and freezing rain. It made for a lot of weight on the roof, I thought.

Then it hit me.

I threw on a coat and some boots and ran outside. The precipitation was so thick I couldn't see the barn but I knew it was there. Just as I stepped into the yard to check it out, headlights swung slowly into the driveway. It was my father. He skidded to a stop, his car buried up above the door sills.

"Unbelievable," he said as he forced opened the door of the Jaguar sedan—certainly not the optimum ride for driving in a blizzard. "It took me three hours from Hartford, but I'm lucky I left when I did. I just heard on the radio that the highway is completely blocked just outside of the city and the State has shut down I-84." Then he noticed me dressed in coat and boots.

"Where are you going, Sean. Not much of a night for a walk," he jested. "You're going to freeze out here."

"I'm going to check the barn, Dad. This is heavy stuff and that old building is already leaning."

"Oh, geez," he said. To my surprise, he followed me.

It was slow going and freezing cold and we looked like a couple of snowmen by the time we got to the barn. I tried to open the door, but it was slightly stuck. I gave it a good pull and it opened.

"That's not a good sign, " my father said. "She's already leaning more if the door is sticking." We walked inside and flipped on the lights and you could just barely make out the collar ties bowing from the roof load. There were pockets of snow inside, too, from all the holes in the planks.

"How much more of this crap are we going to get?" he asked.

"Two feet or more, a lot of it slushy and then it's all going to freeze over into ice, " I replied.

"Jesus. I don't know it this old thing will hold that kind of load," he said. "Let's get inside and check it again in about a half hour."

We made our way back to the house and my father rigged up a floodlight to shine on the barn from the back porch. It lit up the old building just enough for us to see through the white curtain of snow and note any major shifts of the structure.

Sheila came up behind me and pulled on my shirtsleeve as I stared out at the barn. I turned and found her staring at me, a look of real concern on her face.

"The car, Sean. What about the car? The barn doesn't matter," she said. "That old thing can be rebuilt. But the car… Pop's car…"

Her words hit me like a slap in the face. I actually had forgotten about the Mercedes, worrying instead about the place where Pop and I had spent so many hours. It was like my second home and carried a lot of memories.

I went right to my father, sitting in the living room with my mother. He was still dressed in his business suit.

"Dad… the car."

"Huh?" he said looking up from the television. "I wonder if we'll lose power," he said absentmindedly.

"The car, Dad," I said more loudly to get his attention. "We're going to lose Pop's car if the barn goes."

He continued staring at the television. He wasn't ignoring me, he was thinking.

"What…"

"We can't let it happen, Dad. It means to much to him."

Sheila came into the room and sat next to my mother. We were all staring at him. He was not unaware that the ball had suddenly ended up in his lap.

"Oh, man…it hasn't been moved in more than fifteen years," he said. "We'll never get it out of there without a truck or something… I…"

"We have to try, Dad. Another hour and it may be too late."

My mother was wringing her hands.

"Sam…"

He put his hands to his face, covering his eyes and sighed. We were asking him for more than he thought he could give. We were asking him to care.

Minutes passed. I didn't know if he was working a plan or mulling over the consequences if nature took its course.

Finally, he spoke.

"The damn thing will be crushed," he said.

He looked up at me, and then the girls. I thought he had just announced the car's death sentence. I was wrong.

"Well, hell, we ain't making any progress sitting here," he said and jumped up out of his chair.

He began to bark orders.

"Everybody dress warm and grab gloves. There's only one way to do this. Marnie and Sheila, you're going to have to shovel out a space in front of the garage doors while Sean and I put our backs into pushing that German heap outside. It's the only way. None of our cars will be able to pull it out. We need a tow truck and I'll never get one here in time. We're somehow going to have to do this ourselves."

We looked at him like he was crazy.

"What?" he said sarcastically. "You guys got a better idea? Let's go! Chop chop!" he commanded herding us onto the back porch. The spotlight on the barn revealed that it was snowing even harder now – and that the barn had visibly begun to move.

Fifteen minutes later we were all standing inside the old barn, which as I had feared was now leaning dangerously. It wasn't going to take much more weight for the whole thing to collapse – right on top of Pop's cherished Mercedes. It was no longer a matter of "if" the barn was going to collapse – it was "when."

"Marnie, Shelia, grab a couple of shovels. Sean, help me open these doors," he ordered us. At least we had a little bit of luck on our side. The great entry doors were on tracks and just had to be pushed to slide to either side, just enough to make space to get the car out into the yard. But in front of the door was more than twenty inches of snow that was still piling up.

"Girls, go to work. We need a space at least twenty-five feet deep by fifteen wide. With luck, when she goes, the barn will collapse to the side leaving the car untouched if we can get it out into the yard.

"If…" he repeated, his voice full of doubt.

My Mom and Sheila dug right in, but the going was slow. On top of the bottom foot of wet snow was another eight inches of wet slushy stuff. Each shovel full was like lifting a cinder block. I didn't know if the girls had it in them.

My father and I turned our attention to the car.

"Sean, clear off the tarps and check the trunk and interior," he said. "See if there's anything heavy inside that we can get rid of. I've got to rustle up a hydraulic jack so we can get these tires out of the ruts they've dug in the ground and then get some boards under the wheels. Then, find the air compressor as fast as you can. No telling how long before we lose power. We need to get air in the tires or we'll never be able to get the old clunker rolling."

I'd never seen my father so in charge. If this was how he behaved in a mini-emergency, I couldn't image what working for him in the office must have been like.

I flipped off the tarps and tossed out a couple of old batteries and tires from the trunk. That would save some weight, but not much. The Mercedes was small, but it was a heavy car for a roadster of its era weighing almost as much as a full size Chevy.

My father already had found a jack and had managed to slide it under the differential housing of the rear axle, effectively raising the entire back end of the car and yanking both wheels out of the holes that had sunk into the soft earth. While I searched for the compressor, he slid planks over the ruts and under the tires.

"Found it," I yelled from the workbench. I strung an extension cord to the car and wheeled the tank of the air compressor over to the car.

"Let's hope these old tires will hold air," my father said. "These are tube jobs. If there's holes or cracks in the tubes we won't be able to inflate them."

"Then what?" I asked in a panic.

"Plan B," he said.

"What's Plan B?" I asked.

"I don't a have a clue," he said, never breaking his stride.

I turned on the compressor and it roared into life. Air began flowing into the left rear tire. It held.

"I don't know how long it will last, but let's not waste anytime thinking about it. Do the same to the other tire and I'll get ready to pull the jack. Then we'll do the same thing up front."

Just as the last words came out of his mouth, the barn shifted several feet to the right. It was beginning to come down.

"Sean, we're running out of time. I won't have you killed for this hunk of junk."

"I'm not leaving without it, Dad, so let's keep going."

He sighed, worry lining his face. "Are you ever his grandson," he said, shaking his head in resignation.

"Something tells me I have more of you in me than grandpa," I said, not realizing how profound the words were for us both. He looked me in the eye. It was a moment neither of us would ever forget.

"Well then, lets go," he bellowed.

The back tire held air and he cranked the jack down with the speed of a guy from Dale Earnhardt's pit crew and yanked it out from beneath the axle. Without hesitating, he wheeled it around to the front of the car and stuck it under the oil pan. He began cranking it up, ignoring the old cars rusting groans and protests.

"This is going to raise hell with the drive train and the motor mounts but we don't have time to be dainty," he said. "Get some boards ready to slide under these wheels. And check on Marnie and Sheila."

I ran to the front of the barn. My Mom and sister had a space cleared only half as big as we needed.

"C'mon you guys. It's about to come down," I screamed. They never even looked up, just lifted another shovel full. My mother looked like she was going to expire.

As my father raised the front end, I slid the planks in place and then rolled the compressor around.

"Hold your breath," he said as he began pushing air into the right front tire. It too held although we could hear a hissing sound. He overfilled the tire then swung the hose to the other side.

"Be ready to yank the jack out when I tell you, Sean. Then we're going to have to push this thing with everything we've got."

Seconds ticked by as air filled the left front tire. Air was escaping from the right.

"Now," he yelled and I lowered the car as fast as I could and yanked it out from under the carcass. The old Mercedes sat on four planks now with four round, air-filled tires, giving us a shot at rolling it out into the yard.

"Get behind and push, Sean, I'll pull from the drivers door. Ready…" We both dug our heels into the earthen floor. "Now."

I put everything I had into that heave, imagining in my head it was a tackling sled I'd pushed around the football field in my high school years. I could hear my father groaning from the strain.

"Damn it," he screamed in frustration. "The brakes are frozen…"

"Or it's in gear," I yelled.

My father looked at me, not comprehending immediately, then leaned into the drivers window and mashed the gear lever into neutral, completely bypassing the clutch. The transmission had been in first gear, holding the car in place.

"Hurry," he said, just as the sound of the barn shifting again echoed around us, even catching the attention of Marnie and Sheila who screamed in fright.

"Sam, get out of there… it's no use," Marnie cried.

"No way, sweetheart," he said, never willing to admit defeat. "C'mon, Sean, let's give it another go."

We set up again and gave it a mighty heave. Slowly, the old girl moved an inch, then two, then suddenly broke free from the earthen prison in which she'd been held seemingly forever. The nose cleared the doors and we kept pushing. I thought my heart would burst. My father was screaming from the pain of using muscles he'd forgotten he had. Then it stopped. The front end was right up against a snow bank. Three feet of the back end of the car were still inside the barn.

Breathlessly, my father grabbed Marnie's snow shovel from her and motioned for me to take Sheila's. The girls collapsed into the snow. The freezing rain was coming down like hail it was so heavy and the wind was howling around us so loud you could barely hear. It was a good thing. The barn was crying as it tore itself apart from the weight and moved another foot closer to destruction.

"Dig out just enough for the front end Sean, hurry," he said, throwing shovels full over his shoulder like a madman. I was doing the same. I was getting lightheaded and could only imagine what my father was feeling.

"This might do it," he said, finally throwing the shovel down. "Everybody, get a grip and push as hard as you can."

All four of us ran to a corner and gave a massive shove. The old car inched closer to salvation.

"Just another foot," my father yelled pushing still. Behind us, the barn was coming down. With one last thrust, the car cleared the barn, just as the crack of wood snapping shot through the air in a deafening roar of debris collapsing all around us.

"Dive everyone, jump out of the way!" my Dad screamed to us. No one hesitated.

For long moments, the barn continued to settle down, huge timbers from the post and beam construction snapping like kindling from the massive weight it had held just long enough. Then there was silence.

"Dad, Mom… Sheila," I hollered, jumping over large planks and beams that littered the yard. "Are you okay?"

From the silence that followed, finally, I heard the most satisfying words I'd ever hear come off my father's lips.

"What the hell," he yelled, looking around at the devastation. "Lord Almighty…we did it!" He leapt up and grabbed Marnie and Sheila and wrapped his arms around them in a huge hug. I jumped on the pile and we all fell down in the snow laughing hysterically, soaking wet, covered with snow and screaming with excitement.

When we'd exhausted our relief, we all sat up and looked in the direction of the car.

In the glow of the spotlight my father had rigged up on the front porch, there sat the magnificent, rusted out hulk of a 1955 Mercedes Benz 190sl, proud and completely intact. Her tires were slowly deflating as she settled down into the yard, but she was still in one piece. The wreckage of the barn behind her was a fitting backdrop.

Pop was safe. The car was safe. We were safe.

And the Evans' were, at last, a family.

Forty-Eight

It was a full two days before we could dig out and get a car on the road to visit Pop. Power was still out in many areas of the state, including Willington, but my father's cell phone was working and he was able to get through to the nursing home. Lakeview had their emergency generator running around the clock to keep the power on, and we were assured that Pop was warm, comfortable and well fed. Physically he was fine. His emotional state was another story.

My mother spoke to Molly directly.

"It's just too soon for this to happen, Marnie," the nurse said. "Between the personal care he was getting here and your daily visits he was making progress. But your absence has made him feel abandoned. And we all know that was his biggest nightmare coming here. It's unfortunate and there's nothing you could have done, but the sooner you and the kids get here, the better."

We all shoveled non-stop during the daylight hours to clear the cars out, but the main road was another story entirely. The Governor had ordered the roads cleared of all but essential emergency vehicles, and forbid regular vehicular traffic. It didn't much matter. Once we got the cars clear to move from the driveway we had nowhere to go. The roads were completely blocked.

Finally, after two days, the driving ban was lifted and several hours later, a State plow cleared the highway in front of our house. We piled into the Jaguar mid-morning and headed for Coventry. What should have been a twenty-minute drive took more than ninety minutes, but we made it.

It was lunchtime and we immediately went to the dining room expecting to find him. He wasn't there. Sheila ran ahead to his room while we followed. What we found quickly erased the exuberance we'd felt after saving the car and surviving the barn disaster and the last forty-eight hours without a warm bed or a hot meal.

Pop was curled up in his bed in a fetal position with Molly sitting next to him. She was stroking his head and talking gently to him trying to coax him into getting up and getting back into the world. Shelia stood in the doorway crying.

Molly shook her head.

"This is not an atypical reaction," she said. "Not seeing you and having no understanding of why you haven't come makes him believe he's done something wrong. On top of the guilt that already haunts him, the effect is almost paralyzing. He's in another world right now, poor thing. He hasn't slept a wink in the last two days."

We gathered around Pop's bed and everyone, except my father began talking to him all at once. The sudden noise startled him and he looked up. It was coincidence that the first person he laid eyes on was Sheila, still weeping and holding his hand.

We were shocked to see a smile slowly emerge over his face.

"Ceily!" he whispered. "I'm so glad you came. After we talked I didn't think I'd see you for awhile." He squeezed Sheila's hand and raised it to his lips.

Sheila's mouth dropped and her head snapped back. Pop thought she was his wife again, just as he had on the night he escaped from the rehab center several years before.

She began to correct him. "No, Pop, it's …"

My mother stepped forward and put her hand gently on Sheila's shoulder, stopping her in mid sentence. Marnie understood what was happening. Sheila, now seventeen years old, had become a mirror image of my grandmother. Her hair was the same color and just as long and luxurious and her eyes were the same, breathtakingly beautiful shade of green. In his confused state, Pop once again thought she was his Ceily.

"Grandpa, Ceily is tired after her long trip," Marnie said to him. She needs to rest, too. Close your eyes and get some sleep while she takes a nap, OK? Then you can have dinner together later."

Sheila was wiping tears from her eyes as fast as they were flowing, trying to hide them from her grandpa. She was so confused and horrified that it had happened again, but followed Marnie's touch as her mother helped her away from the bed.

"Why that sounds delightful, Ceily," Pop said, still elated to have seen his wife. "Have a nice sleep before dinner. Maybe we can go for a ride afterward. Would you like that?" Sheila nodded.

Pop closed his eyes.

"What a wonderful surprise," he said, softly. "Isn't your mother beautiful, Sam?" he asked my father, who up to now had remained silent.

"She sure is, Dad. Now get some rest." It was too much for him. He turned and wrapped his arm around Sheila, helping her from the room. The poor kid was an emotional mess.

As my mother and I sat by Pop who immediately fell asleep, overcome by fatigue and emotion, I saw the future. It would not be easy.

The question was for whom would it be more difficult?

Pop – or my father?

Forty-Nine

~~~

April 1998

When Pop awoke later that day, he had no memory of mistaking Sheila for my grandmother and was far more lucid after several hours of sleep. This behavior continued off and on over the next few months, and poor Sheila never knew what role she'd be playing when she went to see him. I felt sorry for her, but she learned to accept whatever his mind wanted to believe at that moment, as weird as it was for her.

My grandfather gradually became more comfortable at Lakeview, largely because of Molly's unending care. We took it one day at a time, dealing with the good ones and the bad ones. Physically, he was well cared for, but he seemed to be shrinking right before our eyes.

At home, life was peaceful and admittedly less stressful without the constant worry over Pop's safety. But at least three of us missed him terribly. I wondered often how the fourth felt about his absence.

A guy from upstate New York that actually restored old barns had carted the shattered debris from ours away some weeks before. There were enough useable planks, each more than a hundred years old that he agreed to clean up the mess in exchange for the lumber. There was also some insurance money paid as well, so my father came out all right on the deal.
~~~

But I hated looking out from my bedroom window and seeing an empty space where the barn once stood. The decrepit old shed was a place where I had gotten to know my grandfather so well, and where he had nurtured me in the lonely years I was essentially orphaned. I missed sitting on our old stools with him, staring at the old car in complete silence or talking about the many adventures of his life with and without grandma.

I did manage to find both of the old stools buried under the debris, and one afternoon when I visited him at Lakeview I brought them to him. He was often expressionless now, so it was hard to tell sometimes if something made him happy or sad. When I presented the stools to him, he didn't say anything but grabbed his and carried it to a place in front of the window in his room. I did the same with mine. Now, when I visited, we always took to our stools and continued on with our tradition.

I missed the barn, but it was even worse to see the shape of the old Mercedes, a car that had meant so much in his lifetime and represented so many happy times, under a canvas tarp, rotting away again.

I didn't know what the future held for the old Mercedes, but I knew I had to do something to at least save the wreck. That meant a new barn. I had no way of fixing the situation myself with a full load of college courses, a part time job and a visit to Pop to squeeze in every day. There was only one way.

Lying awake at night, I wondered how to get my father's support. I burned through a hundred different scenarios, all aimed at disguising my real desire to save the car, but I knew my father was no fool. There was no way he wasn't going to see right through my reasoning. I had only one option. To ask him for help.

I thought about that a lot. There had been times in recent years when I had brazenly given him ultimatums, and surprisingly, he had responded to me even though there was nothing he hated more in life than to be boxed into a corner.

Yes, I had demanded certain things, mostly for the benefit of Pop and my sister. But I had never, in my life, ever asked him for help. Maybe it was my trump card. But I hated to play it.

He was in the middle of a trial that April, a difficult case that was eating up his days and nights. He left the house early in the morning and usually didn't get home much before ten the same night. Often, after making a point of spending at least a few minutes with my mother and Sheila and I, he would retire to his study to prepare for the next day's courtroom battle.

On one of those nights, I waited up for him, sitting alone in his great study, a place that reeked of hard earned success, rehearsing my speech about how we needed to replace the barn and I would gladly be the project manager. I knew he would probably be exhausted and this would be the last thing on his mind, but I was determined to make something happen before much more time passed. Every day the car was exposed to the elements was one day less it had a chance to survive.

I heard the Jag pull into the back yard that night and my father open the back door to the house. He met my mother with as pleasant a greeting as a guy who'd just worked sixteen hours could muster and I knew he was giving her a hug. She handed him a cup of coffee.

"Where's the kids?" he asked.

"Sheila's upstairs waiting to kiss you goodnight and Sean is… he's around here somewhere," she said, aware of my plan and not wanting to give me away.

I heard him climb the stairs, his pace giving away his weariness, and greet my sister. They talked for a few minutes then he bid her goodnight and came down to get to work in his study. As he walked in the double doors, I was sitting in one of the guest chairs in front of his desk.

"Oh, shit," was all he said.

"Hey to you too," I answered, trying to grin. I was nervous.

"Did you flunk out of school or are you getting married?" he asked, trying to release some of the tension he smelled from experience. He threw his briefcase on a couch along the wall.

"I'll graduate Magna cum Laude in engineering in about six weeks and no, there isn't a girl that would have me," I laughed. Hell, I wished I had time for a girlfriend.

"Okay, champ, then let's have it," he said. "What's on your mind? Is it Pop? Something I've done…?"

"No, Dad, nothing like that."

"Then what?" he said, surprisingly patient.

I hesitated. He looked puzzled.

"I need your help."

He looked at me wide-eyed, unable to hide the shock of hearing the words come out of my mouth.

He didn't respond right away, but seemed to be savoring what I had said.

"You know, I don't think I've ever heard you say that," he replied. "I actually rather like the ring of it." He was serious.

"It's about the barn…"

He dropped his head at the words, then leaned back in his chair and looked up at the vaulted, twenty-foot high ceiling of his study.

And then he began to speak in a way that suggested he had been thinking a lot about a lot of things.

"You know, not too long ago, I felt like a pretty important guy sitting in this room. Powerful. Tough. Arrogant, I guess, that I could rule my universe from this room and this desk. I could bark orders into this telephone and people would jump. I could call a judge in the middle of the night and he'd take my call. I negotiated more than one multi-million dollar deal right from here while everyone else in the house was asleep."

He looked down and leveled his gaze at me.

"But you know what? Never have I felt more powerful or satisfied in this room than at this very moment."

I had no idea where The Judge was going, but I expected the worst. Payback maybe, or even ridicule.

I wasn't even close.

He opened the top drawer of his desk and reached inside, retrieving a business card. He glanced at it quickly, then handed it over to me.

"Here," he said. "Call this guy tomorrow. He's a good man. Expecting to hear from you. I told him you were graduating from college after doing a hell of a job in the worst of circumstances – and this was your graduation gift."

I looked down at the business card. It read, "Connecticut Custom Barns, Anthony Prococinni, President." My jaw must have dropped because he laughed out loud.

"You're in charge. I told him to listen to you but to make sure that we build what we need... so we can save that old car."

I was dumbfounded.

"Shouldn't take more than a few months to get a new building up according to Tony. Then we can talk about the rest of it," he said.

"The rest of it?" I stammered.

Suddenly, I felt my mother's presence behind me. She put her hands on my shoulders and kissed the top of my head. She'd been in on it the whole time.

"Yah. We just can't have that thing rust away. I was thinking maybe it's time to restore it, bring it back to life – like he did when I was a kid." He paused to let his words sink in.

"And maybe we could give it to him for his Seventieth birthday. It's not that far away.

"What do you think?" he asked me.

My eyes welled up. Who was this guy? I just shook my head, unable to speak.

I was so shocked I could only manage to get out one word.

"Why...?"

He smiled in satisfaction.

"Why?" he repeated, a grin coming to his face.

"Well, I've also got a couple of selfish reasons to do this.

"One is I've had this vision for a while of driving that old jalopy around with your mother in our old age – we could use some adventure, couldn't we honey?" he said sweetly to her. She giggled like a schoolgirl.

"And maybe someday, I'll get a chance to take my own grandson for a ride and we can sit and get to know each other in the barn." He smiled at me. "Make sure

Tony throws in some three legged milking stools, those are essential.

"But the most important reason is that finally I get to be really powerful."

I managed to say something.

"What do you mean?" I asked.

"For once in my life, I get to do something for my son — because he needs — and wants — my help."

He looked down at his desk and pushed a stack of notes and briefs aside as if they no longer mattered.

"Trust me son, that makes me feel like the most powerful man on the earth."

I looked down at the business card again, shaking my head. This must be a dream, I thought.

I stood up, walked around his desk and stood before him. He got up from his chair and stared into my eyes. He wasn't a particularly tall man, but at that moment I thought he was a giant.

He made the first move, extending his arms and wrapping them around me and pulled me close. I hugged him back.

"Thank you, Dad."

It wasn't enough.

"I... I love you."

I heard and felt him catch his breath.

"Never thought I'd hear that again, Sean, let alone feel it."

I pulled back from his embrace.

"I've got a surprise for you, Dad."

"What's that?" he said, a single tear escaping his eye.

I fell back into his embrace.

"You don't know how good it feels to say it."

Fifty

~~~

August 1998

My father was right about Tony Prococinni. The guy was not only an excellent carpenter and tradesman, he was also about the best untrained engineer I would ever meet. The two of us designed a thirty-foot by fifty-foot traditional Gable barn with massive sliding doors and twelve inch wide, rough sawn siding straddled by one by three inch battens. It had a metal roof that was engineered to take a twenty-five pound per square foot load and withstand ninety mile per hour winds. The whole thing was built on six by six inch posts sunk eight feet into the ground and sat on an eighteen-inch concrete slab. It was a thing of beauty. My father laughed that if we got hit by a hurricane, we'd be safer in the barn than in the house.

The inside was just as amazing. Tony lined one wall with a twenty–foot long workbench and installed a hydraulic lift to raise the car and an engine hoist. We buried a thousand gallon propane tank in the backyard to power up a fifteen thousand kilowatt back up generator that supplied power to both the barn and the house in case of another electrical outage like we experienced in the storm. It also had it's own propane fired furnace for heat in the winter and there was enough overhead fluorescent lights to equip a hospital operating room. Flip a switch and it was almost daylight inside. The barn was so complete I could have run a business out of it. The Judge spared no expense
~~~

and never once complained about the cost. The only thing he bitched about was all the dust from the construction, which tended to collect on his prized Jaguar. His final contribution was to have Tony install a floor drain in the barn so we could wash our cars indoors, year round.

One of the happiest days of my life was hooking up a chain from Tony's Ford F350 pickup to the old Mercedes and slowly towing her from the graveyard where she had spent the better part of spring and summer to her new home. She was safe. My father watched the proceedings but said nothing.

I would have done anything to have Pop see all that we had accomplished, but he knew nothing about the near disaster and how we saved the car. We had a family meeting to discuss whether or not to share it with him and had agreed there was no point to it. In his confused state, we had no idea how he would react. Molly was working wonders with making him comfortable and there was no sense in risking all her hard work to tell him something he might not understand anyway.

That night we all had dinner together for a change. My father was between trials and was trying to take it easy for a few months. I think he enjoyed watching me work with Tony and seeing the new barn come to life.

In the middle of a mouthful of my mother's outstanding lasagna, I nearly choked when he dropped another bomb.

"Hey, Sean, I've got a guy stopping buy to inspect the car tomorrow. He's an expert in old classic Mercedes'. Comes out of Topsfield, Massachusetts."

"What's he going to do?" I asked calmly, a tad alarmed by this news.

"Well, give me a price on doing a complete restoration of the car, I presume," he replied, somewhat surprised by my reaction. "Remember we talked about restoring it and giving it to Pop for his Seventieth birthday? That's less than two years away, you know. I'm told these projects can take far longer to complete."

I didn't say anything.

"Something wrong, Sean?"

I hesitated a minute. "Well… yah."

He raised his eyes in surprise.

"I thought you'd be delighted. Let's hear it, son."

I still hadn't gotten used to this new father of mine. A guy who actually listened to what I had to say. He'd been working hard at it since my mother came home four years before, but he still surprised me.

"The thing is, Dad… well… we have to do it ourselves or it won't be the same."

Sheila was sitting next to me. "He's right, Dad. The present has to be from us."

"We need to do the work," I said.

He leaned back in his chair and sort of chuckled. He stopped quickly when he saw the serious looks on everyone else's face, including my mother.

"They're right, Sam," she piped in.

He looked at us as if we'd all lost the plot.

"Maybe I better think about getting you guys a room next to Pop's," he said, trying to make a joke. No one laughed.

"You all understand this is an extremely complicated car for its time and the people who restore them are highly trained and experienced, don't you?" he asked.

"Yah," I replied quietly. "But we can learn."

"Learn?" he said.

"Sean, that's like saying you're going to take a couple of courses and become a surgeon. It takes years to learn the trade of restoring a classic car."

No one said anything.

He shook his head.

"You mean you seriously want to take on this project yourselves?" he asked, incredulous.

"No, Dad," I said.

"We want all of us to do it," Sheila finished.

His eyes were bulging with surprise.

"Need I remind you guys that I'm not sure of which end of a screwdriver to use?"

I went for the kill.

"If I remember correctly, you did pretty good the night the old barn came down. Figured out how to use a jack, a compressor and get the transmission out of gear in a matter of minutes."

"C'mon, Daddy. There isn't anything you can't learn to do," Sheila said. "You're way too stubborn to admit you can't do something." She smiled and batted her lovely eyelashes at him.

"Marnie... will you talk some sense into these kids?" he begged his wife.

"Sorry, Sam," she said. "Makes perfect sense to me."

He leaned back in his chair and dropped his arms loosely by his side, defeated.

"So we're going to 'learn' how to restore a forty-three year old classic Mercedes Benz? As a family?" he said in disbelief.

"Sounds like a plan, Dad."

"I hope it's better than the last one," he answered.

"Which one was that?" Sheila asked.

"The one in which a barn nearly fell on us all," he said, only half joking.

In the end he agreed that we would give it a shot, but convinced us that we were going to have to depend on some outside resources for a lot of the work. He suggested that I put looking for a full time job on hold and take on the role of project manager again to get the car done. That way, I could manage the myriad welders, bodymen and mechanics that we'd need to at least show us how to do some of the work.

Sheila and I began work the next morning, starting with stripping down the interior of the car until it was nearly a bare shell. We bagged every nut and bolt and labeled every part to be sure we'd know what went where and how. But it was clear as we began that a lot of new parts were going to be needed. The interior was completely shot, needing to be reupholstered, new rugs and a thousand chrome doodads either replaced or replated.

We even took the speedometer, tachometer, water temperature, oil pressure, volt meter and clock out of the dash, a job that took hours alone. Each of the delicate instruments, made by VDO and supplied to Mercedes was going to have to be shipped out for a complete mechanical and aesthetic refurbishment. I had no idea where to turn for help.

The Mercedes expert that my father had hired showed up on schedule and took a long look at the car. We put it up on the lift so he could take a look at the undercarriage. It was the first time I'd seen the underside of the old car. My heart sank at the condition.

He was a pleasant enough guy by the name of Ted, and maybe he was just looking to sell us on a professional restoration by his shop, but he was anything but optimistic.

"There isn't a square inch of this car that doesn't need work," Ted said. "There are large areas of rust in the floor and in the rear quarters, and both headlight buckets are completely gone. Those headlights are held in place only by a couple of screws. Almost the entire nose needs to be replaced. The interior is a complete redo, but you already know that. The suspension and brakes need complete rebuilding. She's sagging real low, maybe two inches, I'd guess.

"As to the engine and drive train, it's anybody's guess." He had put a large metric socket wrench on the crankshaft and pulled with all his might to turn the engine. It wouldn't budge.

"It's frozen solid, I suspect the pistons are rusted in place, so at a minimum we're talking about rebuilding a short block – disassembly, boiling it out, knocking out the pistons, machine work to rehone the cylinders and shave the head, new camshaft, crankshaft, pistons, rings, bearings… kids, I could spend an hour just detailing the engine parts that will be needed. And that's just the beginning. You'll need new carbs for sure, these original Solex's were a bear to tune even when they were new. Distributor, whole new ignition set up, new wire harness…"

"OK, stop," I said getting pissed off. "We get the picture."

"Sorry kid, just trying to tell you what you're in for. This is a minimum hundred thousand dollar restoration if we do it. But I can tell you, this car will only appreciate in value, even with that kind of investment," he added.

"You're kidding," I said, having no idea that the car was the least bit valuable.

"Well, you see the 190sl is the 'baby Benz' roadster of the Fifties and early Sixties. It's big brother was the 300sl – a car that is a legend in the automotive world because of all it's innovations. You'd know the car if I showed you a picture. It has these big gull wing doors?"

"Oh, yah," said my sister, "it's kind of cute."

Ted laughed.

"Cute isn't quite the word I'd pick, honey. At one time the 300sl was the world's fastest production car and the most expensive in the world. You could buy a half dozen new Chevy's for the price of a 1954 Gullwing at the time. The 190sl was designed for a market that was only willing to spend about half as much, say the price of three new Chevy's. Your granddad's car cost at least $4,500 in 1955. That was a lot of money back in those days. You could buy a house for less.

"Problem is, the 300sl today is worth millions – way out of the affordability of common folk. So the 190sl has gained a lot in popularity. But even a rough one like this is worth thousands of dollars. I could probably get you $15,000 cash for this wreck," he said.

"It's not a wreck," my sister said, taking offense.

"Well, it sure ain't a show car neither," he replied. "This is something I'd buy for a parts car, but we'd be willing to do a complete restoration given that it has so much family history. Like I said though, you're talking thousands of hours of work and a budget that will probably exceed a hundred grand."

I wasn't going to lead the guy on. "That isn't going to happen. The only way we're going to be able to get this car on the road again is if we do a lot of the work ourselves."

He laughed out loud, then apologized.

"I'm sorry son, but you have no idea what you're getting into. This is one complicated car even for someone who's been working on them his whole life. If you gave me a blank check right now, I'd say come and pick up the car in about four years."

"We've got eighteen months."

Ted looked at me like I'd just said the earth was flat.

"Can't be done."

I wasn't about to argue with him but neither was I about to admit defeat.

"Look. Here's my card. Give me a call if you rethink things. Even if you don't go for the full restoration, maybe I can help you with some of the component work or give you leads on parts and people who can do work for you. Okay?"

"Appreciate the offer, Ted. Let me talk it over with my dad and I'll ring you up."

We shook hands and he left without wasting any more time. Sheila and I watched his pickup truck pull out of the yard crestfallen. The only good news was that the car was worth something. Other than that, everything he told us was bad news.

I looked at Sheila and shrugged my shoulders.

"I'm going in the house," she said, wiping grease off her hands.

"You're just going to give up? Just like that?" She really surprised me.

"Hell no," she replied. "I'm going to get on my computer and start making up a list of suppliers for parts and places that will do work on Mercedes. Got to find a shop manual, too, if that's possible. There's a

Mercedes Benz dealer in Hartford who might be able to help us."

I smiled at my beautiful sister. There was more Evans in her than I thought.

"I've got another idea, too." She looked at me and struck a fetching, Madonna-like pose.

"There's this boy at school who I know likes me a lot. He's really into cars and shop at school. He does all kinds of stuff with cars. I know he knows how to weld. You should see the old GTO he restored. Maybe with a date or two, I might get him and his buddies to give us a hand."

"Why you hussy," I accused her, laughing. "You'd use your good looks and…" I hesitated for a second… "and whatever… to make this happen?"

"You bet your sweet ass, college boy," she said winking. I watched her walk across the yard like a runway model, swinging her hips like she was out to seduce a rock star just to emphasize the point. She sure wasn't a little girl anymore.

"Holy shit, Pop, what the hell have we gotten ourselves into?" I said as I went to work removing the tattered remains of the cars black, canvas convertible top.

Fifty-One

By Labor day, I had the car stripped down to nearly a bare shell. I worked at least fifteen-hour days just to get that done and what I had to show for it was worse looking than what I'd started with.

My father came home from work one night and surprised me when he came out to the barn in old jeans and a tee shirt, ready to work. He hadn't even had dinner yet.

"What say you and I try to pull the motor and transmission out of this tonight," he said.

"You kidding?" I said, shocked by his offer.

"Do I look like I'm dressed for a night on the town?" he asked.

I had cleared just about everything out of the engine compartment that would be in the way of us yanking the motor. All we had to do was figure out how to disconnect the drive shaft then unbolt the transmission case from the engine block. For a couple of mechanics, no big deal. For my father and I, the project had ominous potential for disaster.

"If you don't know where to start," my father always told me, "find a book." That's exactly what we did. Within about an hour, with the help of the amazing shop manual that Sheila had found and purchased on the internet, we had the drive shaft out of the car and were ready to drop the transmission."

We had pulled all the bolts and disconnected the shift linkage when it dawned on us that the transmission probably weighed several hundred pounds. We weren't about to just grab a hold and lower it to the ground.

"I got an idea, saw this on TV once," my father said. He rolled over a parts cart that was fairly hefty and positioned it under the transmission. Then he told me to slowly lower the lift that was holding the car up until the transmission was just about touching it. Slowly the hydraulic lift lowered the car, and when it was in the right position, my father and I pulled back on the transmission casing, and with a little elbow grease she popped off the spline and fell the quarter inch or so safely on to the cart. Then we raised the lift again and rolled it out from under the Mercedes.

"Ha!" he laughed. "Told you so. Let's get a beer and then tackle that motor."

We walked up to the house and my mother met us at the back door, two beers in hand.

"I read your minds," she said, beaming at the two of us working together. The thought suddenly occurred to me that this was the first beer I was ever going to share with my dad. Life really was full of surprises.

We went back to the barn and went to work on the motor. With the engine hoist that Tony had installed, all we had to do was unbolt the four engine mounts, wrap the chain harness around the engine block and let the motorized hoist do the rest.

"Here," my father said, handing me the controls to the electric hoist. "You do the honors. To the best of my knowledge, the engine hasn't been out of this car since my dad bought it in 1961."

I pressed the up button and the hoist took up some of the slack. We maneuvered the heavy block slowly out of the engine bay, lifting a little at a time, until it finally cleared the firewall and the windshield and then hung a foot or so over the car. Safely out of the chassis, we rolled the Mercedes back and lowered the engine onto a sturdy engine stand from which I could begin to disassemble it tomorrow.

My dad and I wordlessly exchanged a high five. It was nearly midnight and we both were beat.

"Let's call it a night, son," he said, "I'm done."

We walked out in to the backyard side by side and he suddenly wrapped an arm around my neck in a loose embrace. It reminded me of walking to the barn with Pop on that awful last night he was home when he did the same thing. But the feeling was different. Much, much different.

I had never dreamed that having a father could feel this good. If only I could make Sam Evans realize that.

Fifty-Two

I'd been a bit lax in spending time with Pop lately, focusing all my time on the car. The next morning, I drove to Coventry in time to have breakfast with him. I always held my breath when I walked into his room to greet him. You just never knew what you were going to find. I was in luck. He was already showered and shaved and was having a good day. Other than his physical appearance – he was still shrinking – you would have thought he was just a little old man who moved and talked a bit slowly.

"Hey, Pop, how are ya?" I said giving him a bear hug.

"Well look what the cat dragged in," he laughed, a bit startled to see me.

"'Sean Evans, engineer.' That has a nice ring to it," he said. "Reminds me of someone I once knew who thought he was going to build bridges someday," he chuckled at the memory of himself in college.

"So where the hell have you been, off with some sorority queen, I suppose?"

"No, Pop," I said. "I told you I don't have a girlfriend. If I did, you'd be the first person to meet her."

"Well why the hell don't you have a girlfriend?" he asked, half seriously.

"Look, how many times are we going to go over this. Girls like grandma and my mom and Sheila just don't come along every day. Someday it'll be my turn."

I bit my tongue, wishing I hadn't mentioned grandma, but it didn't seem to phase him.

"You're right about that, grandson. Women like that are very special. Worth waiting for." He paused for a second to make me think he was being serious. "But for heavens sake, how long is an old man supposed to wait for his best grandson to find a woman?" he laughed. "I'm no spring chicken, ya know. I fully intend to be around to see me my first great grandchild. So hurry the hell up!"

"Oh, man," I laughed, faking it. He'd be lucky to live more than a few more years. "What the hell have they done to your med's now, you crazy person. C'mon," I said, desperate to change the subject, "let me buy you breakfast.

We sat in the dining room that overlooked the lake. It was a bright morning, warm and humid, but the view over the water was clear and you could see sailboats already dotting the horizon. Molly came right over and said good morning, bless her. She had not only become his trusted assistant, she was his friend. For the Evans clan, she was extended family.

We had his favorite of pancakes and sausage, cooked just the way he liked, then I took him outside in a wheel chair for a spin around the property. I liked to get him outside in the fresh air as much as possible, and it wouldn't be long before winter would be settling in. More than anything, I wanted to tell him about the barn and the progress we were making on the Mercedes, but didn't dare.

I stayed with him until about noon and just as I was leaving Sheila was arriving.

"Guess who's stopping by to see you — I mean 'us' —this afternoon," she said, batting her eyelashes when I met her on the garden path leading to the parking lot.

"Who?" I asked, puzzled.

"His name is Eddie, and he's the boy I told you about who's so good with cars. I told him about our project and he said he'd be glad to stop by and give her a lookover."

"You're amazing," I said, laughing. "Does this poor love struck nerd know who he's dealing with?"

"He's no 'nerd,' trust me," she said. "He's actually quite handsome and one of the most popular boys in school. And he's hopelessly in love with me, " she added without an ounce of remorse.

"Poor bastard."

"Why, I'm not exactly an old hag, ya know," she said defensively.

"That's not what I meant. But does this guy know he's just being used?"

"Well..." she hesitated. "he's not really being used. I mean..."

"Oh!" I laughed. "The plot thickens. So you're interested in him, too!"

"Yah, but he's not supposed to know that! Don't you dare say anything!" she warned me.

"Yah, yah..." I replied. "I'll play along if it'll get the car done."

"Oh, it will," she said. "Count on it," and walked inside to see Pop. I hoped he remembered she was his granddaughter again today. Lately, he hadn't confused her with Ceily, much to her relief.

Sure enough, when I pulled up to the barn, there was a gorgeous 1965 Pontiac GTO already parked outside. She was a stunning car, all black with a paint job you could swim in. I wondered what was under the hood.

I walked inside and couldn't find anyone.

"Eddie?" I called.

From under the Mercedes, parked on the floor, came a voice.

"Oh, just a minute, I'm sorry, I was just taking a look at the floor pans…"

A minute later and a tall, lanky, skinny kid with long blond hair wearing a 'Metallica Live' tee shirt slid out from under the car. He jumped to his feet and stuck out his hand.

"Mr. Evans," he said, politely. "I'm Eddie Bowens, a friend of your sister."

"So I've heard," I laughed, taking his hand. He blushed.

"Hope you don't mind but I was looking over the old car. Needs a lot of work. But mine was worse."

Worse? I couldn't believe it.

"You mean to tell me that beautiful thing sitting outside was in worse shape than this?"

"That is a 1965 Pontiac GTO with a 389 cubic inch motor with the tri-power option that gives it 360 horsepower," he said as we walked outside to take a closer look. "It was an automatic but I dropped in a Muncie four speed and added 4:11 gears, " he said, his voice dripping with pride. "She'll do zero to sixty in five seconds flat." He paused and turned a little ashen. "Of course I never drive crazy with your sister in the car."

I looked over at him quizzically. I'm sure he was regretting mentioning my sister. But what I was thinking was that I didn't know what the hell he was talking about. What he said next however, blew me away – and gave me hope.

"I bought the wreck for $150 from a junkyard in Hartford – Corona's, you know it?" I shook my head, no.

"It had been in a bad wreck. Some kid rolled it over and it caught fire. She was completely totaled. Most of the roof was laying on the seats when I dragged it home. My dad thought I was nuts."

"I can understand that," I said. He thought I was kidding.

"It took me about nine months, but I got it back into shape and then saved up some money to add some of the options I wanted. Whole thing took me about a year to rebuild and cost under five grand. Did it all myself, too, even the paint. They let me shoot the paint in shop at school."

I was in awe.

""One year? Five thousand dollars?"

"That's all Mr. Evans. She's worth a lot more than that now, but I'd never sell it."

I wrapped an arm around Eddie's shoulder and walked him back into the garage.

"First thing, Eddie, my father is 'Mr. Evans.' I'm Sean."

"Ok, Sean," he laughed.

"Secondly, do you know how hopelessly in love my sister is with you?"

"You're kidding..." he said, looking at me incredulously.

"Yup, she told me that if anyone could fix this car, which means so much to her because it was my grandfather's, it would be you. And she'd love you even more for it."

"Really? You're not..."

"Kidding? Would I kid you about something so important Eddie?"

"Well… I can get going right away, if you want. I got some buddies from shop who are willing to help, too. Sheila said this is for your grandfather's Seventieth birthday? When exactly is that?"

"April, 2000."

I thought he'd cringe or something. Not Eddie.

"Oh shit. That gives us plenty of time," he said. "Sorry, didn't mean to swear, Mr. Evans. And believe me I don't talk like that around your sister."

"Sean, Eddie… it's Sean. And it's great to meet you and I don't care how much you swear," I laughed. Then I looked serious so he'd remember who was in charge. "As long as it's not around my sister. Or my mother."

"Gotcha."

"What do we do first, Eddie?" I asked.

"Why don't you help me take off the hood, the trunk and the doors, and we might as well cut this front end off," he said.

"What?" I said incredulously.

"Yah, we gotta get this body completely stripped. I got a friend who'll do it for just the cost of the walnut shells."

"Walnut shells?" I asked. Walnut shells?

"Yah, they spray walnut shells under high pressure and it strips all the paint and rust off without damaging or warping any of the body good panels. We want to save those. Once we have all the paint and rust off, we can start fixing the body. She needs a lot of welding, some new quarters, rockers, couple of floor pans."

He caught the worried look in my eye.

"No big deal man, no big deal. I got this covered," Eddie said.

"Say, Sean, what time does your sister usually come home?"

Fifty-Three

~~~

April 1999

At just sixty-nine, my grandfather looked far older than his years. Although the physical consequence of Alzheimer's had not yet been completely revealed, he was barely a shadow of his old self. The vibrant young war hero who once had the strength to fight off massive wounds and emotional trauma now looked like he'd have trouble fending off a bad cold.

I was very busy with the car project and managing a small army of teenage, high school gear heads that had taken on the mission of helping my family bring Pop's old car back to life. He knew nothing of the effort, of course.

Pop and I still spent hours on our stools reminiscing about his days with grandma and their many adventures together. Sheila would often accompany me and heard some of them for the first time. His tales were so believable, so full of vivid details that it was hard for either of us to believe that there were just hallucinations – scenes painted in his head by my loving grandmother to help him regain his sanity.

One afternoon, Sheila's "friend" Eddie accompanied my sister and I to visit him at Lakeview. I wanted Eddie to meet the man for whom he was working like a slave, with no reward other than the affections of my darling sister. The young guy was so smitten with her it was painful to watch. He would do just about anything for
~~~

her. I wanted him to know that what he was doing perhaps meant more to her than anything else in the world.

We were lucky that afternoon because Pop was in a "social" mood, meaning he could tolerate the company of strangers and even converse with them. We'd experienced situations where former friends or even family had visited and he would refuse to come out of his room or even speak to them. In most cases, he had no recollection of them at all, his mind having erased any memories that might have drawn him to them. Not today. And Eddie, the ultimate car guy, was in for a show.

When I introduced him to Pop, Eddie shook his hand nervously, as if what ailed the old man might be contagious. The kid didn't understand dementia —as if any of us did — and he had never been exposed to it. Pop's odd behavior, even on a good day could be quite unnerving.

He had just finished shaving when we arrived. Neither Pop or Molly could say what possessed him to shave in the middle of the afternoon, but nonetheless, he had taken it upon himself to spruce up. "Why" became clear a little later.

He emerged from his bathroom just as the three of us walked in to find him wiping shaving cream from his face.

"Hey you guys, how are ya?" he said excitedly, a very good sign. I looked at his face. He had only shaved the right side. The left side was untouched. While we watched, he rubbed his hand over his entire face, but didn't detect the stubble on one side.

"Nothing feels better than a good shave," he said.

"You're right about that Pop," I said and winked at Eddie who, as you can imagine was a bit perplexed.

"Pop, this is Eddie. He's a close friend of Sheila's and a really good guy," I told him.

My grandfather reached for his hand immediately, something I hadn't seen him do in quite a while. For some reason, being touched by anyone other than a member of his family or Molly upset him. Even the staff doctors had trouble doing routine exams. For him to invite contact with another human being was really something. It seemed he had taken a liking to Eddie immediately. Maybe he sensed there was more to Sheila's relationship with the boy. To this day, it remains another of those mysteries associated with his illness that I'll never understand and have long since stopped trying.

He motioned me to take my place on the stool next to him. Sheila knew to grab the two guest chairs in his room and bring them closer to the window for she and Eddie. It was then that we learned why he had decided to shave.

"I was talking to Ceily this morning and she said she'd be stopping by this afternoon for a visit," he informed us, delighted and completely serious. "Isn't that wonderful?" Sheila and I simply smiled while Eddie shifted uneasily in his chair.

"I'm so glad you kids are here. Why you haven't seen your grandmother in at least a week... or is it longer? I seem to lose track of time so easily these days. Did you know that I had breakfast with her just the other morning and that she finally got a chance to meet Molly?"

"Why... no... Pop," Sheila said. "But that's great."

"You know, I've talked to her about Molly on a number of occasions and I was worried that she might be a little jealous," he continued. "But they seemed to hit it right off."

He looked out at the Lake. Spring had come and things were starting to bloom all around the nursing home grounds. It was a nice time of year, and the hospital staff worked extra hard to get their patients outside as much as possible when it was warm enough. You could actually see the effect it had on the elderly after being stuck indoors through the long, harsh winter months. But it seemed that the fresh spring air had recharged Pop's illusions.

I looked over at Shiela and she shook her head. There was no sense in telling Pop he was just dreaming, he wouldn't understand and it would just upset him. We had learned to let him have his thoughts and to savor them as long as he wanted. Ultimately, they would fade and he wouldn't remember them at all.

He had some color in his cheeks and I wondered if Molly had gone for a walk with him yet today. Another one couldn't hurt and it would help to distract him from the empty promise of a visit from his long dead wife.

"Pop, it's so nice out, would you like to go for a walk with us, show Eddie around a bit?"

He hesitated. "Maybe later, Sean, I want to make sure I don't miss you're grandmother."

"Ok." It wasn't worth arguing.

"There's something I've been meaning to tell you though, about the Mercedes. There's something I need you to do."

He hadn't mentioned the car in weeks.

"What's that, Pop?"

"The clutch was slipping the last time I had it out and I need you to adjust it. Can you do that for me? Before Sunday when I take grandma out for her ride?"

If he ever knew. I saw Eddie turn his head to avoid looking at the old man.

"Sure, Pop, I'll handle it. When did you notice it was slipping?" I asked, playing the game.

"Well, actually it was when we visited Le Mans last month and drove the course with the old girl."

"Oh, Le Mans, you mean the famous race course in France?"

I looked over at Eddie. His eyes were bugging out of his head. Sheila grabbed his hand and squeezed it. She looked at him and smiled as if to say "Just play along."

"You remember when grandma and I were there, don't you Sean? You know the race isn't held until June but you can actually drive the course during the rest of the year because most of it is actually laid out on the city streets near the village of Le Mans not far from the Normandy coast. So your grandmother and I took advantage of it and put the old girl through a whole lap of the 'Circuit de la Sarthe' — that's the road course they use for the twenty-four hour race. A single lap is a whole 13.65 kilometers, can you believe it? I was exhausted after one lap.

"It was right after coming out of the first chicane in the Mulsanne straight — my God it was breathtaking, I had the old girl flat out — that I downshifted and felt the clutch slip. It's been keeping me awake at night, so you have to get it fixed for me. Ok?"

"Got it, Pop, by Sunday."

"Good." He patted me on the knee, smiling, confident that I would take care of the problem for him.

And then he went back to staring out at the Lake through the window and didn't say another word for the next hour before we kissed him goodbye and left. He didn't even notice.

When we got outside, Eddie was beside himself.

"You mean that old Mercedes has driven Le Mans?" he asked. "Your grandfather has actually been on that course? That's one of my dreams..."

"No, Eddie, his stories are all just hallucinations. He believes them, but they're just his imagination at work. He's never been to Le Mans. It's impossible to explain, just trust me."

"But... if he's never been there or driven there how does he know so many details – the Mulsanne straight, the Circuit de la Sarthe? There aren't many Americans familiar with those things. And how does he know that the clutch on the 190 was shot?"

"I wish I could answer that for you, pal. But I can't."

"This disease is one big mystery, Eddie," Sheila said, pulling him closer as we walked through the garden to the car. "We've learned to accept everything he says as fact. It only hurts him to argue."

Eddie thought about that for a minute and then unintentionally asked a question that really hurt.

"He really loved your grandmother, didn't he?"

We walked a few more feet before answering.

"More than you could know, Ed," I said. Sheila was silent.

"How did she die?"

My sister and I exchanged glances.

"That's hard for us to talk about, Eddie," Sheila said, looking into his eyes and hoping he would understand. "It was in an accident, but it's really complicated."

"Oh, sorry," he said. "I understand."

We were quiet then as we walked.

"Let's take the rest of the day off, hey Eddie?" I said abruptly to break the void. "You and the guys have been working really hard."

"Nah, I want to get back and finish welding those floor pans. Me and the guys got nothing to do tonight, anyway. We're all eager to finish the body so we can shoot some primer and see how she's coming along. That car's got a lot of sweet curves, we want to get it right. The pans are all that's left. Then, after we're satisfied with the body, we can lay some color on her and get going on putting the mechanicals back together."

I punched him on the shoulder, lightly. It was a guy thing to do.

"You're pretty special, Eddie," I said.

"So's your grandfather," he smiled. "Not to mention your sister," he whispered.

When we got back to the house, my dad was home from work early and had the grill going. The backyard was already full of meticulously restored muscle cars. There was a gang of kids inside working on the Mercedes, even with us not around.

"This is amazing, I said. I don't know how I'm ever going to be able to thank you guys."

"Don't worry about that," he said. "We've never had so much fun. Worry about asking your dad for some more money. I need parts and we've got some machining to do on the engine block.

"Oh, shit," I said, hating to be the guy managing the purse strings.

My mom and dad barbecued enough chicken to feed a small army and Sheila cooked corn on the cob and made a mountain of homemade coleslaw. We had a feast that night before the sun went down.

I figured everyone would head out after dinner, but by God, the lights burned on in the barn until midnight, even with school the next day. Even The Judge got into the spirit, joining us for about three hours sanding smooth the thin layer of plastic filler that was being spread all over the roadster's body to make it perfectly smooth before painting. His hands were raw by the end of the night.

"God dammit," he said when we finally called it quits that night. "I've got frigging callouses on my hands.

"I've never had a callous before! People are going to think I work for a living," he said.

The Evans family roared with laughter.

Lying in bed that night, that one moment kept coming back to me, along with a simple thought.

The Evans family house was a happy place.

Fifty-Four

~~~

Christmas Eve, 1999

In his dreams, he remembered the lights, the amazingly bright lights that hung high from the ceiling over his body lying on the gurney. The startling glare stung his eyes, but he hurt in so many other places it didn't matter. He knew they had given him enough morphine to knock out a horse, but it wasn't touching the pain of the burns or bullet wounds and bits of metal that had riddled and torn his legs.

He tried to think of other things before they knocked him out for the surgery, anything to take away the pain. Despite the agony, he thought about his good fortune. He laughed to himself at how lucky he'd been having shot down two jet fighters that were better than his and surviving being wounded, crashing his plane and the inferno that followed that had burned him so terribly. He thought about the guys who pulled him out, how lucky he'd been that they were there for him and were brave. He had least owed them a beer.

But then he centered his thoughts on perhaps the luckiest moment of all during the last few hours. It was meeting that redheaded nurse. "Ceily" she said her name was. Jesus Christ, he thought, if these were his last moments on earth, what a vision to leave with.

It was right then that he decided that he wasn't going anywhere except to a church with that girl to marry her and love her forever. He would fight to heal his shot up, burned up body until it healed, no matter how long it took or how difficult an ordeal it would be.
~~~

She was a girl worth fighting for. And he wasn't about to miss out on the luckiest thing that had ever happened to him.

He had one last thought as the anesthesia finally took hold and knocked him out, while surgeons prepared to peel burnt flesh from his legs and dig deep into his muscles to remove bullets and shards of metal shrapnel.

"Good night," Mrs. Evans.

As he dreamt, out of the darkness, she appeared to him again, her lovely, flowing red hair shining, catching a reflection of the moonlight off the Lake behind his window.

"Merry Christmas, my love," she said and embraced him lying in his bed. Her soft lips brushed his cheeks and she traced the outline of his still handsome face with the tips of her fingertips. He always liked it when she did that.

"There is a Santa Clause," he laughed, reveling in her sudden, silent visit. Visions of their Christmas' past flew through his mind as they embraced. Finding their tree with little Sammy, the decorations, hot chocolate and presents under the tree.

"What was your favorite Christmas, Ceily?" he asked.

"Why, don't you know, John? There can only be one answer."

He thought for a moment, but couldn't decide which one it would be.

"It was our very first Christmas as a family, John. We had not even been married a year, but we were safe and warn in our little farmhouse…"

"And you had just given birth to Sam…" he finished her sentence.

"Yes. Could there ever have been a happier time in our life together?" He grinned at the memory.

"He was the best present you ever gave me, Ceily. My little boy. I remember you holding him in front of the fire and he wrapped his tiny little fist around your finger. I was so

frightened to hold him, but I wanted to so badly, do you know that? God I loved him so. I'm sorry that our love for each other has disappeared. It's my fault, Ceily, because I made such a mistake…such a terrible mistake. I took you from him. He's so angry."

"My love… you only recall our happy moments together. But do you remember how sad and angry you were for so long after Korea? When your mind wasn't right because of all you had suffered?"

Tears rolled down his cheeks as she whispered to him.

"Yes, I do now. You saved me. Made me happy again."

"No, John… it wasn't just me. It was our family that brought you peace and happiness again. It was me… and Sammy."

He thought about that, and knew she was right.

"Your son has endured the same sadness and anger that you did, John, for such a long time. But his family is slowly bringing him peace again.

"And you are part of that family still…you must believe me. His love for you is strong, only buried under pain. But little by little, it is emerging again because of all you have meant to Sheila, Sean and Marnie.

"You were strong when he needed you, John. You cared for those children, kept them spiritually alive. He knows that now. It will just take a little longer for him to truly understand how profound an influence you have been in his life," she said, running her fingertips across his face again.

"How much longer, Ceily, how much longer until I can be with you again?"

"When your work here is done, my love."

"Truly?" he said, desperate to believe.

"Truly, my love. Then every day will be Sunday for us."

"You must come soon, Ceily, I can't last much longer without you."

"Soon, John, it will be soon. You must be my hero just a little longer."

He caressed her hair with his hands and kissed her cheek, reaching up with a fingertip to touch her lips.

"Will you celebrate Christmas tomorrow, Ceily?"

"Oh, yes, my love," she said, a smile filled with joy radiating from her lovely face.

"I will celebrate by looking into the hearts of those I adored when I was among you and seeing their growing love for each other – and for being a family. And I will celebrate by knowing that it was my brave husband who was the power that made them a family once again."

He stared into her amazing green eyes and saw that she believed in him.

"Merry Christmas, Ceily. Please come for me soon so that I can see it too. Please?"

"Soon, John, so soon. Now I must go. Sleep, my love, sleep."

"I will," he said, his heart full of happiness at the thought of their next Sunday together.

"Good night, Mrs. Evans."

Fifty-Five

~~~

March 2000

The freshly painted 1955 Mercedes Benz, wearing a stunning coat of new Glasurit lacquer paint in the original manufacturers color, "Elfenbein DB608" sat in the middle of the barn floor, surrounded by an excited group of high school Seniors. Now a stunning shade of ivory bordering on yellow, the body of the roadster looked just like it had when German craftsman pushed it off the assembly line in Stuttgart in 1955. There wasn't a dimple, wave or chip anywhere in the paint and the body was as straight as an arrow. Even the undercarriage had been shot with the new color, courtesy of the paint booth at the Willington High School. Eddie Bowens himself had sprayed the car, putting seven coats of the finish color and four coats of clear on after four coats of white primer. He had spent eleven hours in the spray booth making the job perfect. Nothing else was acceptable.

The team of boys working on the car, Sam Evans, Marnie, Shiela and I had painstakingly wet sanded the body from top to bottom after each coat, leaving the final job nothing short of magnificent.

Both doors, the trunk and engine bonnet still had to be mounted but they were painted of an equal quality and set aside under tarps for protection as the team began reassembling the old Mercedes. The interior had yet to be touched, and I was in fact nervously waiting for the shipment of new seat covers, door panels, dash
~~~

cover, boot liner and original wool carpeting from a supplier in Ohio.

Pop's birthday was a little more than a month away and they were running out of time. But Eddie, true to his word continued to remind me, "I got this." I had no reason to doubt him. I'd already given my sister a warning that if she did anything to break his heart in the next sixty days, I'd break her face. She laughed and batted her eyes, loving the power she wielded over my master mechanic.

Today was a big day. Only nineteen months after my father and I had somehow pulled the engine and transmission out of the complete wreck without killing ourselves or destroying the car we were set to shoehorn the completely rebuilt and refurbished drive train back into the old car. There was an air of tension and excitement in the barn that only a bunch of totally committed car guys could emanate. After that, and buttoning up the new electrical system, all that remained to be done was to polish out the new paint and remount the newly re-chromed bumpers and the exquisite grill with the three pointed star that made the car recognizable as a Mercedes Benz from a mile away.

My dad came home from work to witness the big moment and Sheila and my mother stood by his side as we took the better part of the next two hours carefully squeezing the big four-cylinder block and transmission back into place. The new Solex carburetors and the huge distinguishing air silencer were already bolted in place and the exhaust manifold hung loosely in the engine bay ready to be attached to the block. Everything we could mount ahead of time to minimize damage to the new paint job was done.

Finally, the transmission and engine motor mounts were bolted down, the distributor was set in place and Eddie placed a new battery into its specially engineered box on the firewall and connected the cables. After installing new Teflon bushings into the shift linkage assembly, it too was reassembled and the car now had a gear shifter. After a thorough final inspection of the fuel and ignition systems, the sump was topped off with oil and coolant added to the new radiator.

The moment of truth was at hand.

Eddie yelled over to my sister.

"Sheila, you get to do the honors," he said, handing her a new set of keys that had been made to fit the original ignition switch. He placed a milk stool behind the dash for her to sit on since the seats had not yet been installed and pulled the choke out. She slowly walked over to the car, stepped over the driver's side rocker panel and sat on the stool. There was no steering wheel in place either, so she looked a little ridiculous. It didn't matter. All she wanted was what the dozen guys and the rest of my family wanted to hear. The sound of that motor roar into life again.

"Ok, Sheila. First, push in the clutch, that's the last pedal on the left. Then put the gear shift into first – that's right, at the top of the "H" pattern on the left side – then turn the key slightly to the right." She followed his instructions exactly.

Immediately, a red light glowed on the dash indicating the ignition was set and a white light followed meaning that the choke had been pulled and the Webers were primed.

"Right," Eddie said. "Now all you have to do is turn the key one more notch to the right and she ought to fire right up." He smiled at her, I could tell he was enjoying this moment maybe as much as she was.

"Fire away."

Sheila turned the key and the engine turned over, coughed a couple of times, then shut down.

"No sweat," Eddie said. He reached into the cockpit and pulled the choke in and out several times. "She needs a little fuel.

"Pump the gas pedal a few times, Sheila, then try it again."

She did. And for the first time in more than eighteen years, the backyard of the Evans family home in Willington was filled with the roar of a running, 1955 Mercedes Benz 190sl. Only this one, at least in the mind of my grandfather, had been around the world with the love of his life sitting beside him. And very often the other love of his life, his son Sam, was strapped into a baby seat in the rear luggage compartment of the car. Cheers erupted in the barn and my father kissed my mother. Sheila jumped out of the car and wrapped her arms around Eddie, giving him a great big smooch on the lips. That really got his crew going. I thought the poor guy was going to pass out.

I couldn't help myself and when Sheila was through I gave Eddie, now officially recognized by my sister as her "boyfriend," a great big bear hug. Man, we had been through some rough nights together, but he never quit. His friends, well they had a different way of celebrating.

Each of them ran out to their beautiful classic rides, each a statement of their own individual personalities, started them up and began revving the engines and honking their horns. You would have thought it was VJ day the way they celebrated.

Oddly, I saw my father quietly leave the barn and go inside the house by himself. He didn't return. About a half hour later, I went in looking for him and found him alone in his study, staring at a family portrait of his mom, dad and him from the early fifties when he was just a little boy. His eyes were wet, and there was a half finished glass of scotch sitting on the desktop.

I startled him when I walked in.

"Oh, sorry Sean, didn't hear you coming."

"What are you doing, Dad?"

"Ah… just remembering some old times. Hearing that old car start up flipped a couple of breakers in my head that I've had shut off for a long time."

"You know what you've just done for Pop, Dad, don't you?"

"It wasn't for Pop, son…" he began.

"Don't tell me that, Dad. I'm grateful that you've made me out to be the hero. But that's not the case. You did this… for your father."

He looked at me a little stunned, perhaps at being found out.

"I can't talk about it right now, Sean, need to sort it through this thick skull of mine."

"I understand, Dad."

""You know how proud I am of you for this?"

"Yah, I think so," I replied.

"Dad?

"Yah?"

"Do you know how proud I am of *you* for this?"

He didn't reply right away and looked away, finding it hard to face me.

"I spent a lot of years hurting a man who was already tortured," he said. "This hardly makes up for it."

Well," I said quietly, "we have different opinions on that, but let's just say this was a hell of a start and it's going to make him very happy."

"Yah…"

I turned to walk out of his study and leave him to think. But I had to say one last thing.

"Dad… you know there's still time to finish the job. It wouldn't only be Pop who would be happy. Think about grandma's feelings."

Then, I said to The Judge what might have been my final summation to the jury.

"And it would make the Evans family whole again."

He looked through me as I said the words and for a long time after, then picked up his childhood family portrait and went back to staring at it, deep in thought.

"I love you, Dad," I said as I walked out of the room.

Fifty-Six

~~~

April 2000

A couple of weeks before Pop's Seventieth birthday, while my mom and Sheila were making plans for an elaborate birthday dinner for him at the house, I sat with Pop at the nursing home on our old stools looking out at the Lake. As we sat in silence on this day, one of his quiet, detached ones, the thought occurred to me that I was going to be twenty-two on my next birthday in June.

By that time, my grandfather had put himself through school, fought and survived a war as a jet fighter jock, been horribly wounded, met the girl of his dreams, married her and became a father.

So far, I had the college thing done, although my father had footed the entire bill. The only other thing I had accomplished was to help rebuild a barn and restore an old car. I had some catching up to do to be the man he was at my age.

He hadn't said a word to me since I arrived and hadn't responded to anything I'd said. He was lost in a world of his own today and there was nothing I could do to drag him back. I reached over and held his hand, hoping he might at least feel my presence. There was a knock on the door and Molly walked in with a younger girl who looked like she might be in training.

"Hi Sean," Molly said, sweet as ever. "Not having a good day today, I know, I'm sorry. I worked with him
~~~

all morning trying to find a spark but it's just not there today."

She turned and introduced me to the girl with her who looked to be about my age. "Sean, I wanted to introduce you to Sarah, she's just joined us here and is going to be working with me with your grandfather. She recently graduated from the UCONN nursing program and has some background that might help us a lot with him. I introduced her to your grandfather yesterday and he seemed to like her." She sighed. "He was an entirely different person yesterday. I actually caught him thumbing through 'Moby Dick.' That's amazing because I have not seen him read a thing since he came here."

"That's more than incredible, Molly. He stopped reading years before he came here." I turned to Sarah.

"It's nice to meet you, Sarah," I said, immediately taken with her. She had eyes like Molly's, just brimming with kindness but much brighter. They made her look full of life. She was very pretty too, about five foot four with a figure that guys my age have been know to stop and take a second look at. Hell, guys at any age.

"Nice to meet you, Sean," she replied. "I've heard so much about your family and your grandfather is just amazing. He's had a very difficult life for a man so young. He's lucky to be surrounded by people who love him."

"He raised my sister and I for a bunch of years when we were very young," I said. "Even after he lost my grandmother he found the strength to care for us. We owe him a lot."

She nodded, genuinely taken with his story. "I hear you've got quite a party planned for him – and a surprise, too, " Molly said devilishly.

"Yah, we've spent nearly twenty months restoring his old car – it's identical to that model on his dresser – and I have to admit, it is stunning. I can't wait to show it to him. You and Sarah will come, of course?" I said.

"Wouldn't miss it, Sean, and it's probably a good idea to keep a bridge between this home and his old one," Molly replied.

"Thank you, Sean, I wouldn't miss it, either."

"Say," Molly piped in. "I've got another patient to see. How about if you and Sarah take your grandfather outside for a cruise in the fresh air. It might do him some good."

"Great idea," Sarah said and went to get a wheelchair before I could respond.

When she was out of sight, Molly winked at me.

"Pretty cute, huh Sean?"

"Molly!"

"Molly, nothing," she said. "It's time you started enjoying life a little, Sean, it goes by fast. Get to know her, she's a lovely girl. Maybe even take her out, hey sport?" she said, elbowing me in the side.

"I'm kind of old to be set up on a date, Molly," I protested.

"Well, then do it yourself and save me the trouble," she smiled.

Sarah was back in a second and together we helped Pop into the chair. He had no idea what was happening.

"I hate seeing him like this," I said to her.

"I know, Sean, I saw my own grandfather go through this. That's why I decided to work in this field. It's really a heartbreaker to see someone you love just slowly fade away, but if you put the effort into it, like you and your family have, their last days can be so much more comfortable."

We rolled him outside together, me doing the pushing. Sarah asked me a lot of questions about myself, school, the car, my family. I told her how my dad and I nearly got killed saving the car and she couldn't believe the story.

"Wow, that's one your grandfather would have appreciated hearing," she said. "What a story. What a father and son team."

"Actually, that experience sort of jumpstarted our relationship," I said. "My father and I had really drifted apart, for a lot of reasons."

We parked Pop in a nice spot under a tree in front of the Lake and sat on a bench.

"Does it hurt to talk about them?" she asked.

"Sometimes."

"I'm all ears anytime if you'd like to talk," she said.

Believe it or not, I was so comfortable with her that I somehow spent the rest of the afternoon telling her the entire story of Pop, grandma, my family and how we'd come together.

"You're some kind of son and grandson, Sean Evans," she said, when I finished. Then she leaned over and kissed me. My heart rate doubled on the spot.

And that's how I ended up with a girlfriend.

Driving home I thought again about all that Pop had accomplished in his first twenty-two years. I smiled to myself and turned up the radio.

I was catching up.

Fifty-Seven

~~~

April 22, 2000

As my father and I watched the Mercedes drive out of sight with Sheila at the wheel and Pop at her side, he shook his head in utter frustration.

"I wanted it to go better than that, Sean. I let you down."

"No, Dad, you don't understand," I said, trying to assuage his disappointment.

"You haven't spent as much time with him in the last year as we have. You couldn't have known how bad he would be. Actually, he did remarkably well for a man who's brain is completely scrambled. Life is just an illusion for him now. That's not your fault."

"That was John Evans on a good day?" he said incredulously.

"Yup."

He was silent for a few minutes, pacing the sidewalk, thinking.

"To be honest, I had hoped to talk with him today. To settle... to fix... aw, Christ, Sean, to tell him that I've been a fool, that I forgive him. And to beg him to forgive me.

"I'm too late...once more, I wasted precious time."

I can't ever say that I had felt sorry for my dad, until that moment. But he was too close for me to let him give up. And selfishly, I had a lot riding on this too. My entire family did.
~~~

"I wouldn't say that, Dad. There'll always be a time to tell him. You may find him a completely different person when he comes back. You may not. But what's important is that you tell him," I said. "You will know, and that's really important. And something tells me that somehow, someway, the message will get through to him… and grandma."

He put his arm around me right there on the nursing home garden path and kissed me on the side of the head. He didn't give a shit if anyone was watching.

"I'd like to say I raised a wise son," he whispered in my ear, his voice cracking. "Unfortunately, I didn't have much of a hand in your raising. Nevertheless, you are a wise man who I am so proud of."

My father was getting into the habit of leaving me speechless.

We drove home together, the windows and the sunroof of the Jag wide open, enjoying the warm spring weather and anticipating the celebration with Pop at the house. My dad was no longer nervous about confronting his own father with a long overdue message of love and forgiveness. Could the day get any better? Yes. Sarah was going to be there for dinner.

As we pulled into the backyard, I expected to see Pop and Sheila having returned from their ride. I still hadn't figured out how to explain the new barn to him, but there was a chance he might not even notice. Surprisingly, there was no sign of either of them or the car.

My father laughed out loud.

"Pop's probably having the time of his life," he said. "He thinks he's with my mom, the car is brand new – I wonder, could dementia actually be enjoyable?"

"Dad!" I said, horrified.

"Yah, really bad joke," he smirked. Only my father.

Thirty minutes passed and my mother came out wondering what to do about dinner. Molly and Sarah were already here and I was showing them the barn to pass time. An hour passed. Still no sign of them. It wasn't like Shiela to dawdle knowing that everyone would be waiting. I was getting worried.

"Dad, something's wrong, I can feel it. Maybe the car crapped out," I said to him.

"No, Sheila has her cell phone, she would have called."

"Cell phone, I didn't think of that." I dialed Sheila and got her voice mail. He looked at me, anxious too.

"Voice mail."

'Damn," he said. "I'm going to call Pat Knapp."

"The police chief Knapp?"

"Yah.

"Hurry up," I said.

"I'm going into my study. I don't want to get everybody else worried. You keep things calm out here."

Molly and Sarah saw right through me.

"What's wrong? Where's your grandfather?" Molly asked. Sarah grabbed my hand.

"Don't know. We're calling the police right now."

"Maybe they went back to Lakeview," Molly offered. "I'll check," she said, pulling out her cell phone.

"I doubt it but give it a shot."

A couple of minutes later, she came back. "No luck."

"OK." My mind was racing. I couldn't just hang around waiting any longer.

I jumped in my car and tore up Route 74, not having a clue where they might have gone on their ride. I decided to retrace the route back to Lakeview. I pulled into the parking lot. No luck. I hit the road again, driving aimlessly.

My cell phone suddenly rang. It was Sheila. She was crying.

"Sheila – where are you? What's happening?" I said, not able to hide the fear in my voice.

"Sean," she sobbed, "come quickly, please."

"What's wrong? Where are you?"

"Wilderness Lake, at the boat launch." She could barely choke out the words. "Bring Daddy." The phone went silent.

I turned onto Route 44 and sped toward Wildnerness Lake in Willington, a small scenic park where Pop and Ceily liked to picnic sometimes years ago. I got my Dad on the phone and told him.

"What's wrong," he said. "Are they OK?"

"I don't know, Dad, Sheila was too upset to talk."

I made the Lake in ten minutes and pulled into the parking lot. There were several police cruisers already there surrounding the Mercedes.

And an ambulance.

I screeched to a stop and jumped out of the car. Sheila ran up to me, crying hysterically and could only point to the ambulance. I let her go and slowly walked to the medics who were bent over a body lying on a portable gurney. Out of the corner of my eye I saw my father's car come racing into the parking lot behind me.

I pushed my way through a couple of cops and medics and saw the top of my grandfather's head sticking out from a heavy white blanket that covered the rest of his body. I ripped down the blanket and saw his face, already turning grey and his lips a strange hue of blue.

His shirt was ripped open and electrodes were stuck to his frail, bare chest, scar tissue from his Korean adventure still evident. A defibrillator was on the gurney at his side, and there was still gel on his chest from where the medics had used metal paddles in a useless attempt to keep him from going into cardiac arrest. One of his arms hung lifelessly from the gurney, an IV already stuck into a vein. It was obvious they had tried everything to save him. But my grandfather was dead from a heart attack.

Mercifully, someone had already closed his eyes and there was a look of peace on his face. I stared at him. You would have thought he died in agony. But of all the thoughts screaming through my head at that moment, I locked onto the one that said this poor old man had spent the last eighteen years in hell. How could anything hurt more than that, I thought. Now he was with his Ceily. And that's why I was convinced that the corners of his mouth were slowly, almost imperceptibly, curling into a smile even as I watched. He was sending me a message.

"It's OK, Sean. I'm with your grandma now. Don't cry," he was telling me.

I didn't. Instead I picked up his arm hanging off the gurney and gently placed it on his chest. Then I pulled the blanket over him to keep him warm. I was always worried about him being warm enough in the old barn. Why should that change now?

My father was holding Sheila in his arms, and tears were streaming from his eyes. He had never had the chance to say what he so desperately needed to tell his father.

"Dad," I said, reaching over and grabbing him by the arm and pulling him toward Pop's body. "Tell him now, tell him… he's with grandma, I know it... tell him, Dad, or you'll regret it for the rest of your life."

He stepped forward towards his father, the toughest jury he would ever face. He took a long, deep breath and let it out, fighting to keep his composure. Taking my grandfather's cold hand into his own, he pulled his fingers to his lips and kissed them.

"Dad…" he began. He looked up at me and I nodded. Do it. The crowd of cops and medics instinctively stepped back to give him some privacy. Sheila and I moved to either side, holding him.

"Dad… you had no right to go this way… do you hear me?" he began. I looked at him, wondering where he was going. "You were supposed to give me just one last chance to say I love you…"

He paused, still holding my Pop's hand, but reached for mine as well.

"But I'm going to tell you anyway, you hear? So please, Dad, listen to what I have to say. Lord knows I should have said it long ago…

"I never told you this, Dad," he said, choking back tears, "but when I was a little boy and you didn't talk with me much… I thought, he will someday, because my dad is a hero who hurts inside. And that day came, and you did learn to talk with me. And you were my hero."

He leaned back and let out a guttural cry of pain into the air before going on. He went on with urgency, knowing his time was short.

"Do you know how sorry I am that I never told you that? Or that you are still my hero? For keeping my family together when I wasn't man enough to do it myself?"

I squeezed Sheila's hand. From behind, my mother, Molly and Sarah wrapped their arms around us.

"I forgive you for what happened with my mother, I should never have judged you. I always knew how much you loved her. I just hurt so much losing her that I needed to punish you.

"Now, I beg of you, forgive me for being such a fool, such a coward…for wasting our time together. For you will always be my hero and I will always love you."

He took another breath.

"Rest now, please, with Mom… our precious Ceily."

He looked down at his father and then turned his eyes to the heavens.

"It's Sunday, Dad! God dammit, it's your favorite day! Now every day will be Sunday for you both…"

Exhausted, he leaned down over his father's body and kissed him gently on the lips. Then he turned and walked slowly to the Mercedes and hunched over it, sobbing. He touched the driver's seat, caressing the place where his father had lived out dreams that had brought back his sanity a long time ago and earned him the love of his son.

The State Police arrived shortly after with a coroner who pronounced him dead. There was no reason to bring him to the hospital. I called a funeral parlor in Willington and told them to expect Pop's body. Taking charge helped me to hold it together.

We each had a chance to kiss him goodbye before the medics loaded his body into the back of the ambulance and drove away. Sheila wrapped her arms around his neck and didn't want to let go. I comforted her as best I could, trying to convince her of how much happier he was now and that his suffering was finally over. She reluctantly let go, and found Eddie patiently waiting to hug her. Someone had called him and he came running. He was some kid.

The police temporarily impounded the Mercedes and had it hauled away on a flatbed truck. Police Chief Pat Knapp, an old friend of my dad's said he would stop by later that night to take Sheila's statement.

"It's best that we give her a few hours to calm down, Sam."

"Yah, I know, but I'd sure like to know what happened."

"Soon enough, Sam, soon enough," he said. "For what it's worth the medics told me that he was gone before they even pulled him out of the car. They tried everything to revive him, but he died in that old car he loved so much.

"There are worse things to happen to a man than to die surrounded by the people and things you love," he offered.

We were all in shock but poor Sheila was still almost hysterical. I drove her home and brought her to her room and made her lay down for a while. Molly gave her a sedative she always carried in case Pop got out of hand, and that helped my sister to sleep.

Pat Knapp came at 7:30 that night and met with all of us. Molly and Sarah had stayed to help out as best they could, but we were all just numb.

My mother and I brought Sheila downstairs and sat her in one of the easy chairs by the fireplace. She was still very shaky. Eddie sat on the floor next to her, just to be there for her.

The Police Chief was a good guy, I'd known him for a bunch of years myself. He always played the tough cop to keep us in line when we were in high school, but he was usually more show than hard ass. Most of the time we'd get a lecture from him for whatever we'd done and a stiff tongue-lashing and that would be it. He had a pretty good feel for kids and the difference between having a good time and a dangerous situation.

"Folks, let me begin by telling you how sorry I am for the loss of Pop," he began. "He was a good man, had some tough breaks in his life. But I admired him a lot."

He turned to my sister,

"Sheila," he said, "I know how hard this is for you and all of your family, but I need to ask you some questions to get an understanding of what happened to your grandfather."

My mom brought her a cup of tea and she took a sip before starting.

"I don't know if my dad told you, but Pop was having a good, but very confused day," she said, calmly. "From time to time over the last few years he has mistaken me for my grandmother, I guess because I look so much like her, and it would get him really mixed up. Today he thought I was his wife, Ceily."

She sighed and closed her eyes.

"When we brought him the car all fixed up this afternoon, he hardly even noticed how beautiful it looked. I don't think he had any idea that it was brand new. He just saw me and thought about nothing other than he was going for a Sunday ride with his wife, a tradition the two of them had always cherished. Being in the car was exciting and the prospect of going for a ride made him happy, but it was the illusion of my grandmother's presence that excited him the most."

She paused for a moment, thinking back.

"But it was odd. He began talking strangely almost the minute I pulled away from the curb. If was if he had been keeping a secret from all of us, and now that he had left my father and Sean behind, he could talk about it openly with Ceily. Believe it or not, it was if he thought she had come for him – to finally take him away with her.

"As we were driving, he continued to talk to me as if I was my grandmother. He told me that he just couldn't have waited any longer and he was so happy I was finally there to take him. I remember that he said, 'You kept your promise, Ceily, and I tried to keep mine. Everyone seems so happy. Are you coming to the party today? You'll see for yourself that the Evans family is very happy. Sean? He's a man now and so strong, I'm so proud of him. Sheila? She could be your daughter, Ceily, and she's the sweetest little girl. You would just love her personality – just full of mischief.

'I'm glad we're going to the old house. It will give me a chance to say goodbye to my grandchildren and Marnie, she's regained her strength too...and especially, Sam.'"

Sheila couldn't hold her composure anymore and began to cry. She looked over at my father, who was hanging his head and wringing his hands in anguish.

"I never knew he was watching us so closely," she said. "When we thought he was confused, I think he was paying more attention to what was happening between us then we gave him credit for. That's why I remember his words so clearly. I was shocked."

She stared at my father, who was leaning forward in his chair, overwhelmed by sorrow, staring at the floor.

"Daddy," she said. "Look at me."

My dad slowly raised his head and looked into her eyes. "Yes, sweetie?"

"I think it's important that you hear what he said next. I remember every word, because I was so happy to hear them."

She took a deep breath and let it out, then wiped the tears from her eyes. I don't know how she was doing this. My own heart was breaking and I hadn't even been there.

"He said: "'And I want you to know that once and for all, I'm going to set things straight with Sam before I leave, Ceily. I still love my boy, I've been a fool for so long. I should have told him how sorry I was that I let him down by losing you and owned up to my mistake. I was just so defensive... it was so hard to admit that it was my fault you died. Sam loved you so, Ceily... he loved you so. You made up for what I couldn't give him for so long.'"

Sheila let my father absorb the words before continuing. He was in agony. There was a long silence as we all took in the meaning of Pop's words. Finally, there was closure between father and son, and buried beneath immense sorrow, love that could not remain buried.

She finally continued.

"Then I tried to change the subject... you know Sean," she said, turning towards me. "How we used to get him to think about something else? I suggested we take the car down to Wilderness Lake where he and grandma used to picnic so often. He was delighted at the idea. He said, 'Haven't been there in years, Ceily, guess we can go any time we want now. Isn't that wonderful? Everyday will be like Sunday!'"

I thought back to all his stories of the adventures he and grandma had shared driving through the winding, narrow roads of small European villages. They had always been on Sundays.

"I pulled the car into the parking lot and turned the motor off. We sat in silence for the longest time. I think he was heading off into one of his other worlds. But then he turned to me and kissed me on the cheek.

"'Ceily, this is now officially the happiest moment of my life,' he laughed. 'Thank you for coming to get me. From now on, I'll do the driving and we can find new adventures. Sound good, sweetheart?'"

"I told him it sounded wonderful. And then he yawned and said he was very tired from the warm sun and asked if I'd mind if he just closed his eyes for a minute."

She burst into tears again and my mother wrapped her arms around her. All of a sudden she was my little sister again.

"Take your time, honey," Chief Knapp said. "I know this is hard."

She managed to compose herself again, but choked on the words, "I told him I didn't mind. If only I hadn't let him go to sleep, maybe he wouldn't have..."

"No, Sheila, no," I said to her firmly, stopping her thoughts dead in their evil tracks. "There's been enough guilt in this family. You had nothing to do with Pop dying. Without you, without your love, he might have died a long time ago. No more guilt, sis."

She smiled at me. We had grown so close over the last few years, always there for each other. I wouldn't watch her torture herself like Pop and my father had.

She continued, each sentence getting harder to speak.

"He just sort of slouched down in the seat and closed his eyes.

"And then he said, 'Good night Mrs. Evans.'"

My father broke down at the sound of the words of endearment he had heard his parents exchange countless times in their thirty years of marriage.

"I sat next to him in the car, enjoying it, the beautiful weather and having Pop so close and so happy. I figured I'd let him sleep for a few minutes, just a quick catnap, and then we'd drive back to the house for the party.

"When he didn't wake up after a while, I touched his arm and shook it, trying to rouse him. He didn't move. I called his name, quietly at first so as not to frighten him, then more and more loudly as I began to panic. I shook him, hard this time but I couldn't wake him up.

"I dialed 911 on my cell phone and told the dispatcher that something was wrong, that I couldn't wake my grandfather from his nap and I thought something was horribly wrong. I begged the person on the phone to please hurry. It was a woman. She told me to listen to his heart. I did, but couldn't hear it beating. She said to check his pulse but there was none. She told me to lay him down flat, so I jumped out of the car and tried to drag him out of the passenger seat, but I couldn't, he was too heavy. Then a policeman showed up and pulled him out and laid him down in the parking lot. He ripped open Pop's shirt and listened for a heart beat then took his fist and pounded him as hard as he could in the chest. He began doing CPR and mouth to mouth, he was trying so hard… and then the medics came and they used that machine with the electric paddles to try and shock his heart to get it going, but they couldn't.

"They couldn't," she repeated, her eyes wandering off towards the window as she recalled the horrifying scene.

"They tried for so long. They kept calling his name and shocking him. It was useless. He just died. Taking a nap.

"After all he'd been through, he died taking a nap.

"But he was so happy.

"He knew.

"Grandma had come for him."

Fifty-Eight

We buried Pop in a plot next to my grandmothers a couple of days later. They really were finally together again, side by side.

It was a simple affair. He had lived a relatively obscure life in Willington, living only for Ceily when she was alive, and his family. After her death, he had faded into obscurity. There weren't many people who really knew him. I think he liked it that way. Molly and Sarah were there and a few other folks from the nursing home, some distant family and a few neighbors. The local VFW offered to arrange for a military 21 Gun salute, but we declined. None of us thought Pop would have wanted that. He'd had enough of guns in his lifetime.

But the biggest surprise of all was that Eddie's entire high school crew of gear heads, the young guys who had done such a miraculous job on the old Mercedes, came as a group. Not a one of them with the exception of Eddie had ever met my grandfather, but they admired the guy because they loved his car. The motorcade to the cemetery more resembled a cruise night then a funeral procession. Sheila and I led the parade following the hearse with the gleaming yellow car. We figured Pop would have liked that. Yah, the whole thing was a little comical, even odd, but so was Pop and most of his life. I think he would have been happy at the unusual show of affection.

A couple of days after his funeral, I sat in the barn where I had parked the Mercedes. Alone, the only noise

I could hear was the occasional whistle of a car going by on the road in front of our house. My mom and dad were inside, asleep, both exhausted from the last couple of days of dealing with the funeral. Sheila had gone for a quiet walk with Eddie.

I had retrieved our stools from the nursing home the day before and Pop's stood empty next to mine. At times I could feel him next to me, a presence strong enough to make me turn and look. But the stool remained empty, as I knew it would, forever.

The car was draped in canvas now, but not to protect it. I couldn't bear to look at it. Not yet.

When I went to bed that night, I couldn't sleep. Something was nagging at me. I tossed and turned for hours but finally gave up about three in the morning and walked over to my window. I looked out at the new barn, a beautiful place Pop would have enjoyed if he had been healthier longer. The only thing inside of importance was the car.

Then it hit me. I suddenly knew what was bothering me.

I put on a sweatshirt and my sneakers and snuck out of the house quietly. I slowly made my way to the barn, remembering all the times when he and I had made the same walk. The first time, I had barely reached his belt buckle. The last time, I was a foot taller than him.

I turned on the lights in the silence of the barn and there, under the bright glare was the car. Covered up and hidden from view.

That's what was wrong.

All those years Pop had suffered in silence and grieved for his beloved wife, the only thing that kept him breathing and remotely sane were the memories that car kept alive. By staring at it, he could recollect their love for each other and their amazing adventures together – from the moment he caught his first glimpse of Ceily's beautiful face, to dragging my father on a little sled through the woods to chop down the perfect Christmas tree, to their incredible journeys in the old Mercedes. He relived his whole life staring at that car. I had made a mistake by covering it.

I sucked in a deep breath, then carefully pulled the canvas tarpaulin off it. The overhead lights brought out the glorious sparkle of its new paint, and I could smell the freshly tanned leather hides covering its seats even from a few feet away.

I sat on my stool and stared at the car for the next several hours in complete silence, just as Pop and I had done countless times over the years. When I closed my eyes, the old Mercedes began to talk to me.

It dragged out my memories of sneaking around up in the rafters as a young boy, secretly watching Pop and wondering why he was so sad and quiet. It retold me the story of my grandfather's fierce battle against three Korean MiG's and how he had survived a fiery crash even all shot and burnt to hell. It painted the picture of him instantly falling in love with the redheaded Irish girl named Ceily, even though he was near death, and it exulted in sharing with me again the many joys in their lives together.

I could almost hear the crunching of snow from his boots as the car brought back the story of how he pulled the sled with his little son behind him at Christmas and how he and my father had become more than father and son, but best pals. And sadly, it reminded me of how alone and desperately alone he was after the tragedy of my grandmother's death and the day he had parked the car forever.

The conversation between the car and I might have gone on forever, except that suddenly a real voice interrupted.

"Sean?"

I turned to see my father at the door. He was carrying two cups of coffee.

"Hey, Dad, I said, just realizing how much time had passed since I had come out to uncover the car. It was morning. The sun was up. It was going to be a warm day.

"Are you all right?" he said walking towards me. He handed me a cup.

"Yah. I'm fine. Couldn't sleep."

He pulled up one of the stools Tony Prococinni had made and went to sit to the left of me. I stopped him.

"No, Dad. Sit here on Pop's stool, please. He would have liked that."

I saw him swallow hard, but he took the cherished throne without argument. He put his arm around me.

"Time heals the pain... somewhat," he said. "Sometimes it never goes away. It's like that for me with my mother... with grandma. But you live with it. You must."

"I know, Dad. I just miss him, terribly. I loved him very much."

"So did I, Sean, so did I. I'm only sorry that it took me so long to remember it. I hope he knows," my father said, almost in a whisper, taking a sip of his coffee to hide the tears welling up in his eyes.

We were quiet for a while, just staring at the magnificent car.

"She's worth a lot of money now," he said.

I turned to him, alarmed.

"You wouldn't..."

"Never crossed my mind, son. Never will. But there is something we need to talk about."

"What's that," I asked, somewhat perplexed.

"Well, you remember when I naively gave you what amounted to a blank check to restore this car, that I said your mom and I might use it in our old age?"

I laughed at his veiled sarcasm about the blank check. He had never once complained about the cost.

"Yup, I think it's a great idea, Dad. You'll love driving it," I said.

"You say that, but... well the truth is I'm more of a realist than your grandfather was. I never had the imagination he did, unfortunately. He got such a charge out of this car that I never will be able to."

"So what are you saying?" I was still afraid he wanted to sell it.

"What I'm stumbling around trying to tell you is that I've decided to retire early. As soon as I can, in fact. Maybe another year or two. The law has been good to me... but my family, especially Marnie has paid a price for it. I'm tired of not being here for her."

"That's fantastic, Dad. I'm so happy for you. You've earned every day of freedom you have left."

"Maybe. Maybe I'm just trying to make up for all the years I made your mom a prisoner," he said, shaking his head. "I've really cornered the market on being a fool in my life."

I smiled.

"All is forgiven, Dad."

He pulled me closer to him.

"So, what I'm getting to is that I don't want the car for Mom and I. We're not going to drive the

Connecticut shoreline imagining that we're touring Europe.

"No, instead, we are going to spend our 'mellow' years really exploring Europe – I mean actually doing it. And the rest of the world, if we're lucky enough to have time."

"Wow. What a dream," I said.

"No dream, son. That's what your mom and I are going to do. She's so excited. I'm not ever going to let her down again."

"So about the car..."

He abruptly stood and reached into his pants pocket, pulling out a new set of keys to the Mercedes. They were hanging from a small, sterling silver medallion key chain.

"What...?"

"Read it," he said, pointing to the medallion. "Read the inscription."

I did.

And I cried.

My father pulled me close again and read the inscribed words aloud.

To my beloved grandson, Sean:
Thank you for finding
the keys to my car
– and our family.
Love you forever,
Pop

I was completely overcome and all the emotions of the last week came pouring out of me. My father let me have a good, long cry.

Finally, I composed myself enough to thank him.

"Don't thank me, Sean. Without you, there would be no Evans family. You brought this family together son, when I didn't have the strength or courage to do it. You cared for my father when I couldn't, you protected your sister when I didn't. And you made me realize that I had driven away the only woman in the world I had ever loved and deprived her of her children.

"But most of all, you made me see my father for what he was. A loving man who never really wanted anything more out of life than peace and the treasure of family. But he was cursed. The truth is, what peace he enjoyed for the last eighteen years of his life came from your love and the knowledge that you would not stop fighting to make the Evans' a family again.

"He loved you for that, Sean.

"And so do I."

I held the keys in my hand, then clutched them to my heart. There were no words to explain to my father what I felt.

"Listen," he said, draining the last of his coffee. "I have to go back into the kitchen and see what your mother is doing. She was going to call a travel agent as soon as they opened. I want to make sure she hasn't booked us on a cruise to a Communist country." He laughed. "We're going to have so much fun together. About time, huh?" He was grinning from ear to ear. He got up to leave then turned to add something.

"Two things I forgot. First, next week a very good friend of mine who owns one of the largest engineering construction firms in Connecticut wants to have lunch with you to explore some opportunities. It's time you start thinking about yourself now, Sean. I think you'll like him.

"Secondly, that cute girl that was helping Molly care for Pop – Sarah was it? I was wondering if perhaps she might help you exercise the old car here sometime. Maybe you should give her a call. Sure is pretty and sharp from what I saw of her. Real kind, you can tell, reminds me of your grandmother and mom. Just a thought," he said, winking at me as he walked out the door.

I smiled at the idea of taking dating advice from my father, of all people. He was hardly an icon of romance. But the more I thought about it, I realized he was right.

I climbed off my stool and walked over to the Mercedes, dragging my fingertips across her nose and front fender. The driver's seat looked inviting. I opened the door and climbed in, imagining myself driving the narrow roads of Europe in this magnificent car. But at the moment, even a day trip to Essex along the Connecticut River seemed pretty exciting – with the right company.

That night, I nervously dialed Sarah's number on my cell phone. She answered right away.

"Hey Sean, how are you feeling," she said, genuinely concerned.

"I'm doing great, actually, Sarah, we're all doing well."

"I'm so glad to hear that," she said. She really was sweet.

An awkward moment of silence passed. My father was right. It was time. It was my turn.

"Listen, Sarah… uh… tomorrow is Sunday. It's my favorite day of the week. I was wondering…"

"Yes?" she said coyly.

"I have this beautiful old sports car that I just inherited. It's really a magnificent car."

"Inherited? Wow... but how deserving. Yes, I've seen it, Sean, it is magnificent. It was once owned by a very wonderful, loving old man. I've been told that he used to take his wife for long rides in it. Is that true?"

"They were 'magical' rides," I said to Sarah. "And they always happened on Sunday. Would you like to take a ride with me in the old girl tomorrow? On Sunday?"

She didn't hesitate a second. "There is nothing else I would rather do, Sean. I think it would be a perfectly splendid way to spend a Sunday... with someone I really care about."

Whoa. I hadn't expected that. Catching up, Pop, I thought. I imagined him slapping me on the back.

Before going to bed that night I went out to the barn and polished my grandfathers prized old car from bumper to bumper. And I adjusted the clutch, just in case.

Early the next day, on one of those late spring mornings when the air is so clear and warm and glorious that it almost tastes like summer, I put the top down on the 1955 Mercedes Benz 190sl and drove through Willington to Mansfield, where Sarah had rented a small apartment since beginning work at Lakeview. I parked the car and walked to her door and rang the bell.

She opened it almost immediately, as if she'd been waiting anxiously right behind the door, then swung it open and greeted me with a hug and a kiss on the cheek. I handed her a bouquet of white lilies that I had surreptitiously borrowed the evening before from her employer's garden.

"Oh, Sean," she said, bringing them to her nose and breathing in the exquisite fragrance. "How sweet. I remember a little old gentlemen who liked lilies, too."

"Yah, we share a lot of the same qualities," I said, smiling, but proud to know it was true. "For one, he also loved beauty."

"Ah..." she sighed, not missing the compliment. "I see you've inherited quite a few of the old gentlemen's most charming qualities."

"I can only hope, Sarah," I said, embarrassed.

"Are you ready?" I asked, changing the subject.

She did a quick pirouette to show off her outfit and asked if I approved. What was there to argue with a sleeveless tank top, a summer skirt and sandals on the most stunning girl I'd ever dated? She was beyond fetching.

"It seems like I'll be in the company of the most beautiful girl in the world today," I flattered her, holding nothing back.

"My, you do have a command of the right things to say to a girl, young man," she said, a bit of color coming to her cheeks.

I hesitated a moment before responding. I knew she was just playfully flirting, but her words struck a chord within me.

"Actually," I said, grinning, "All I know about how to treat a lady came from a couple of guys I know who learned the hard way, but got pretty good at it. They both were blessed with big hearts, but could be a little rough around the edges."

She smiled. "A big heart can make up for a lot of sins, Sean."

"Well, it's the secret of my family's success!" I laughed. "C'mon, this day is begging for us to enjoy it."

I walked Sarah out to the car and opened the door for her, demonstrating the proper way to buckle up the new seat belts my father and I had installed together.

Then I took my place behind the wheel, and for a second, felt the surge of excitement that I imagined my grandfather must have felt every time he slipped into the driver's seat of his lovely chariot, with the girl of his dreams beside him.

"Where shall we go, 'Mr. Evans?'" she asked.

I didn't answer her immediately, instead imagining my grandfather gripping the steering wheel of his prized car at the three and nine o'clock positions, ready for a magical race through the Alps with my grandmother joyously hanging on for dear life. The car had already captured my own imagination.

I turned to Sarah, my heart filled with elation at suddenly knowing just how they had felt.

"Well, 'Sweetheart,'" I said, giving it my best Humphrey Bogart imitation, "I've thought about it and I was wondering."

"Yes?" she answered, laughing.

"Have you ever been to Paris?"

# #

The Author's self-restored, prize winning
1957 Mercedes Benz 190sl, star of *The Barn Find*

Acknowledgements

From start to finish, *The Barn Find* owes many thanks to many people. First and foremost, to my wife, Bobbie, my perpetual love and the inspiration of my life and work; to my friend Lisa Orchen, whose remarkable insights and sensitivities make her the consummate editor and author's friend; to Joyce Rossignol, my very first editor who taught me to love the art of writing; and to my very special friends Genevieve Allen Hall, Bob King and his daughter Cathy whose praise and support are boundless. To my loving family, Jack, Jay and Andrea, for seeing more in me than I deserve; and to Charlie, my Grandson, who one day will find Grandpa's books in the Library, a thought that fills me with joy. And finally, to my beloved Grandfather, William J. McGrath, a man who epitomized love and humility, who taught me so much, filled my imagination and was there for me when I was alone.

About The Author

F. Mark Granato's long career as a writer, journalist, novelist and communications executive in a US based, multi-national Fortune 50 company has provided him with extensive international experience on nearly every continent. Today he is finally fulfilling a lifetime desire to write and especially to explore the "What if?" questions of history. In addition to *The Barn Find,* he has published the acclaimed novel, *Finding David,* a love story chronicling the anguish of Vietnam PTSD victims and their families, *Of Winds and Rage,* a suspense novel based on the 1938 Great New England Hurricane, *Beneath His Wings: The Plot to Murder Lindbergh,* and *Titanic: The Final Voyage.* He writes from Wethersfield, Connecticut under the watchful eye of his faithful German Shepherd named "Groban." Readers are encouraged to visit with Mark on his Facebook page at "Author F. Mark Granato."

Made in the USA
Middletown, DE
01 November 2015